My Phillipe

Barbara Miller

SONNET BOOKS

New York London Toronto Sydney Singapore

An *Original* Publication of POCKET BOOKS

 A Sonnet Book published by
POCKET BOOKS, a division of Simon & Schuster, Inc.
1230 Avenue of the Americas, New York, NY 10020

Copyright © 2000 by Barbara Miller

ISBN: 0-671-77453-0

First Sonnet Books printing October 2000

10 9 8 7 6 5 4 3 2 1

SONNET BOOKS and colophon are trademarks of Simon & Schuster, Inc.

Cover art by Gregg Gulbronson

Printed in the U.S.A.

"I TOLD YOU ONCE THAT I WANTED TO MARRY YOU," PHILLIPE SAID.

"It was after that night we spent in the village by the Coa River. You seemed almost disappointed that the French pulled out, that we did not get blown to bits."

Phillipe moved uneasily to a chair opposite her, watching her. "As long as we were going to die anyway, what I did seemed justified. When the siege ended so tamely, I thought I had let my lust for you trick me into taking advantage of you."

"You have a rather poor memory of the night. I was the one who wanted you. I thought you merely agreed to make love to please me, that it would never have occurred to you on your own."

Phillipe rolled his eyes and Bella laughed at his grimace.

"At any rate, I thought it was gallant of you to offer me the protection of your name when you did not even like me."

"I loved you!" he said so urgently he felt surprised himself.

She stared at him, her ripe lips parted, her eyes strange swirls of amazement and regret. "How could I not have realized that?"

He could see that her lips trembled slightly. "Perhaps because I neglected to mention it," he said regretfully. "I had already asked your father for permission to pay my addresses to you, but he refused. He was right, of course. I had nothing to offer you."

PRAISE FOR BARBARA MILLER

DEAREST MAX

"A dab of Amanda Quick, a dollop of Joan Wolfe, and a drizzle of Andrea Kane, and you have Barbara Miller's delectable romantic mystery. Thus begins a game of mutual seduction that smolders, sizzles, and blazes into a passionate affair."

—*Romantic Times*

"Miller includes just enough detailed hints about what's going on between the bedsheets to intrigue romance readers who want more than a standard Regency tale."

—*Publishers Weekly*

"The characters are a delightful mix. A good time is guaranteed for the reader."

—*Rendezvous*

"Ms. Miller captures the atmosphere of the era with a cast of interesting characters who will fascinate and beguile the reader as the mystery does."

—*Romantic Times*

AND THE CRITICS ADORE THE ROMANCES OF BARBARA MILLER WRITING AS LAUREL AMES . . .

"[In *Infamous*] Laurel Ames spices the light flavor of her innovative Regency hybrid with scandal, stirring in prose that finely echoes the barbed undertones of nineteenth-century high-society discourse."

—*Romantic Times*

"*Nancy Whiskey* is a spirited, moving story written with style and wit. Richly textured with strong, heartwarming characters and a riveting plot that will keep readers on the edge of their seats. A spellbinding romance guarenteed to quicken hearts everywhere."

—*Rendezvous*

"Once again, Laurel Ames creates a delightful tale that is fun and romantic! This time around, she throws in a dash of mystery for good measure. Her writing evolves with each book. . . . Regency fans will be thrilled with *Tempted!* A rollicking romp filled with romance and mystery! . . . If you love Regencies, you will love Laurel Ames! Her writing is fast-paced and fresh!"

—*Literary Times*

"*Tempted* is an exciting, unusual, and delightfully quirky Regency romance that stars two very unique individuals who immediately capture reader attention. Laurel Ames is an excitingly original author whose star is definitely on the rise. Readers will indubitably want more tales . . . from the luminous Laurel Ames."

—Harriet Klausner, *Affaire de Coeur*

Also by Barbara Miller
Dearest Max

Available from SONNET BOOKS

For
all of my Moms and Dads

MY
PHILLIPE

❧ Prologue ❧

Spain,
September 1811

Phillipe lay flat along the mare's neck as he galloped it up the narrow trail to the ruined village. God grant that there were no French dragoons waiting there to capture him. A rifle shot clipped his sleeve, leaving his flesh untouched, and he urged the mare on. Glancing over his shoulder, he could see the French patrol cantering full tilt at him. Even as he watched, a shot tipped one dragoon off his horse. That had come from the village. A nest of partisans. What a stroke of luck.

He jumped his horse over the tongue of a wagon blocking the narrow single street and threw himself off, dragging the mare behind the cover of some buildings as a spatter of shots erupted from the house and smacked against the boulders where the French were sheltering. He secured the mare in a shed with an exhausted army team and dashed into the two-story ruin.

He checked himself on the doorsill in surprise. Almost everyone here was wounded, some severely. One rifleman, still able to raise himself to fire, took a rifle from the Portuguese lad, Carlos Quesada. Arabella Mc-Farlane was also there loading rifles for them.

He strode to the single window and almost got shot in the head when he took an incautious look outside.

Bella gasped, then sent him a condemning look from those brilliant blue eyes of hers. Her eyes also held fear, though she resumed reloading rifles with apparent calm, her elegant hands blackened with powder and her dark curls dusted with straw and mud fragments from the deteriorating walls. She reloaded automatically as though from long habit, and he wondered how often she had been pressed into service in this way. Why had her father even brought her into the war?

"Where is your father, Colonel McFarlane?" Phillipe demanded.

"Harrying the French along the river," Bella shouted. "We were bringing away some wounded, but we lost our direction."

The sergeant who was firing shifted his heavily bandaged leg and turned to Phillipe. "We thought to tuck in here for the night. Get our bearings in the mornin'. Surprise to find the enemy this far behind the lines."

"That may be my fault," Phillipe admitted.

"This is Captain Phillipe Armitage," Bella said flatly without looking up from her work. "Wellington's map-maker."

"Ah, an observing officer," the sergeant acknowledged. "So they be after you."

"Had I known this place was so ill-protected, I would have chosen another rabbit hole."

"We gave you cover," Carlos said belligerently, handing the sergeant another rifle.

"And you did it so well that both I and the French patrol were convinced there must be a few dozen partisans defending this rubble." Phillipe risked a shot with his pistol and frightened one of the dragoons' horses off. "Do you want me to lead them away again?"

The sergeant thought for a moment. "Best not. They'd only get you and come back for us. Doubt they will show any mercy just because we are not what we appear. And there is Bella to think of. If you could get her away on your horse—"

"Stop right there," Bella said. "I am not running and leaving all of you here. We have food and ammunition."

"Bella is right," Carlos said. "We can wait them out."

"I think I will seek a higher vantage point, while there is still light to get off a few shots." Phillipe grabbed two rifles and a satchel of ammunition. He climbed the narrow steps in the corner of the room into what once must have been a bedchamber. After dragging the straw tick mattress under the window, he knelt on it and looked cautiously over the sill.

He could see the backs of several blue jackets and loaded both rifles slowly. He did not want to make a mull of it and get a ball stuck in the barrel. He fired both rifles then in rapid succession and heard a yelp with the second shot. He jumped at a noise from the corner, but it was Bella, coming with a canteen.

"It might be safer downstairs," he warned, taking the canteen and downing one swallow only to wet his mouth.

"The sergeant is too tired to fire anymore. He sent me to load for you."

"I do not approve of women in the field," Phillipe said, realizing after the words left his mouth how pompous he sounded.

"I think that you do not approve of women at all," Bella said as she knelt on the mattress and laid out the ammunition.

"That is not true."

"Well, you are always scowling at me."

"It would not be so bad if you stayed in Lisbon with the others."

"And what would be the point of being here if I am not of some use?"

A spate of bullets from a rock outcropping gave Phillipe the new location of the dragoons, and he replied with two rapid shots. Phillipe picked his shots after that, firing only when he could see the flash of powder from one of the French soldiers. After another ten minutes of sporadically trading fire as Bella loaded for him, he stopped and shushed her, then leaned his ear against the wall.

"What is it?" she whispered.

"A gun carriage. I would swear to it. I would send you back down, but I have no idea which place is more dangerous."

They waited in the lengthening silence. A sudden low roar was followed by the whistling passage of a cannonball. Phillipe threw himself on top of Bella as part of the roof came down on them. He coughed as he raised himself slightly to look at her. "Are you all right?" he asked as he watched with fascination the rise and fall of her breasts.

"Yes, and you?" Her eyes searched his face, and she

reached up to brush a splinter of wood out of his hair.

"So far. I want you to take my horse and see if you can find a way out of here. You can bring back help."

"No, I cannot leave."

"You can ride. I have seen you manage the most contrary army brute."

"I will not leave Carlos and the others. I said I would get them back, and I will."

"Bella, can you not see the hopelessness of our situation? They have a gun, and we have . . . pea-shooters. And . . ."

"And what?" she demanded.

It was almost dark now, and not being able to see her enhanced his awareness of the feel of her under him, the sound of her voice.

"And I cannot answer for their conduct with you when they take this position."

"It depends on whether there is an officer among them with the will to stop them raping me."

She said it with such resignation Phillipe was shocked.

"So much for trying to explain our dilemma delicately." He raised himself enough to peek over the windowsill, but he could see nothing now.

"I had rather be here when they break in and are amazed that we are so few."

"A grand gesture, but it will not save you." He lay back down, half covering her body.

"No, only you can do that, save me from their assault."

"What do you mean?" he asked.

"Love me now," she whispered.

He gaped at her in the darkness until her meaning

came home to him. "Do you mean to tell me that you want me to make love to you now?" he demanded.

"Of course," she said with a shuddering sigh that made him suspect she might be crying.

"Dammit, Bella. We are about to be blown to bits."

He could feel her hand on his shoulder, pulling him toward her.

"Then it does not matter. Phillipe, you would not hurt me as much as they would, and if we die, at least I will have known what it is like."

"You are insane, but I already surmised that."

Another roar, and she grasped him to her as the shot carried away more of the roof and knocked down half the outside wall.

Phillipe slowly rose from his crouch over Bella and shook off the dust and splinters of roof timbers.

Bella pulled him back down. He opened his mouth to protest but found her mouth, eager and insistent. Thinking to frighten her, he thrust his tongue between her ripe lips and explored her mouth so boldly he expected her to slap him or shoot him. Instead, she dueled him with her tongue and ran her hands under his uniform jacket to rub his back and caress his ribs.

Against his will, against all common sense, Phillipe could feel his groin tighten. This was insane, stupid, impossible. He had wanted Bella from the moment he had first seen her, but not like this.

He broke the kiss with a gasp as he knelt over her. "We are both going to die."

"I do not care. Let them find us here. If we must die,

I had rather we were making love than aimlessly shooting at shadows."

"They have stopped," Phillipe said. "Just a taste of what we will get tomorrow when they can see to aim that thing."

"Then we are safe for the moment?"

"Yes. Take my horse."

"No, there is no way out," she said with finality. "I already looked."

Faint moonlight through the shattered roof drew his gaze to her bosom. He pulled the string that closed her peasant blouse. Her breasts were small and tight, the nipples erect with excitement, whether from him or the French bombardment he did not know. He suckled one as she pulled at his shirt, her gasps of pleasure taunting him to a madness he never would have expected. He teased her other breast with his tongue as her hands crept up his back to comb his hair with eagerness.

He could not see her eyes, but her hands were warm and caressing in the midst of this cold, insane war. They were going to die, and he could not see beyond that, could not even dare to look as far as the morning. Suddenly the night opened up. His whole life dwindled to an ineffectual nothing, and he realized all he was would exist only in the next few hours and be gone like a snuffed candle. She wanted him to love her for the experience of being loved, and he wanted . . . what? Only this, whatever love he could find in her arms, even if it were only once.

Her hands moved to the buttons of his riding breeches and undid them one by one, then untied his small clothes and unleashed his engorged manhood.

She cupped it reverently in her small hand. He slid his hand along her thigh and pushed up her rough skirt and petticoat to untie the string that held her drawers closed. She wriggled out of them as he crouched over her, feeling dizzy with confusion, feeling regret and some strange sense of inevitability. This was all he had wanted since he had first met her. She had never before given him any hint that she had wanted this, too.

"This is madness," he mumbled as he poised himself at her moist entrance, trying to grasp his last thread of sanity.

"My Phillipe," she said. "We do not have all night."

He laughed bitterly and thrust into her, meeting resistance. He hesitated and nudged at her maidenhead so slowly and skillfully that its parting caused her no more than a gasp of surprise. He could hear her low moan of pleasure and stopped it with a kiss that mimicked the slow advance and retreat of his manhood.

His exhaustion, pain, and frustration all slipped away as though he had suddenly been healed of some grievous and long-standing wound. Her small gasps and sighs of excitement smoothed his abraded soul, and when she realized her first wave of euphoria, he paused to let her savor it to the full.

"Mi Phillipe, mi corazón."

He pushed himself to the pinnacle of restraint as she experienced wave after wave of pleasure from him. Who would have thought he would be able to satisfy such a woman? If only this night could go on forever.

❧1❧

*London,
July 1815*

Arabella looked up at the horse dangling helplessly in the sling as the boom swung the gray mare over the side of the ship toward the London dock. Sebastian, her father's great white war horse, nickered reassuringly from the quay where Carlos held him. Maria had taken Jamie, Bella's young son, to sit safely on their baggage wagon with his mongrel dog. Bella's grooms, Rourke and Greenley, held the other two mares. She smiled at Greenley, her late husband's only servant. The others had, one by one, returned to England, unable to stand the privations of the war in Spain. Greenley grinned back at her. He had been a boy when the war started seven years ago. Now he was a man, and she was . . . a widow. She thought of Edwin, her husband, who had gotten to be duke for only a little while. She thought of him with his blond hair tousled by the wind and that apologetic smile of his, not how she had last seen him when she had helped to bury him after Waterloo. Already Edwin's features were beginning to blur in her mind, or was it tears come to betray her regrets?

Bella ran the back of her hand across her eyes and turned her attention back to the Andalusian, hoping that it would not panic this first time it was being unloaded in this manner. The ropes squeaked through the chocks as the mare was lowered. The graceful horse started writhing in the sling, and Bella spoke soothing words of comfort to it. Above the noise of the docks and creaking of the ship's gear, Bella heard a carriage arrive, with a tramp of hooves and a squeak of harness, but could spare no attention for the passengers except to hope that they did not further frighten the animal.

"Phillipe! Phillipe!" Jamie called.

In her concentration on the horse, Bella did not stop to wonder why Jamie would be calling for his dead father's cousin, whom they had not seen in nearly a year.

As she stared upward, a rope parted, the frayed ends singing through the pulleys as the mare and sling slithered down toward her. With no purchase, the animal instinctively tried to jump. A strong arm closed around Bella's waist and scooped her out of the way as the mare landed with a grunt on the wooden quay. Its shod feet sent splinters flying, and in its struggle to get to Sebastian, the creature knocked both Bella and her savior onto a pile of baggage.

"What were you going to do?" Captain Phillipe Armitage demanded gruffly. "Catch her?"

"Phillipe! You are all right." Bella flashed him her most brilliant smile as she leaped to her feet and watched him struggle up, the stiff leg still giving him some trouble. She knew better than to inquire about his leg. She had suffered nightmares about that wound leaving him lame forever. And here he was walking, indeed, whisking her out of harm's way just as he did during the war. Her impulse was to hug him to her, and she only remembered they were on a public quay in time to stop herself.

In spite of his having been in England this past year, his blond hair still bore the burnish of the Spanish sun, and his bronzed countenance was more handsome than ever. He looked so much like Edwin it was uncanny. But his voice was not silken and pleading. Phillipe's voice frequently held the hard edge of anger, even when it need not.

"And you are your usual careless self," he said coldly as he cast her a dark look with his brooding brown eyes and brushed the dust off his black coat. "What if that horse had fallen on you? What would have become of your son?"

Her smile melted away as it always did when he criticized her. "But nothing did happen."

"But you might have been killed," he insisted gloomily. "You always take too many chances."

"And you always seem to be there to save me." She wanted him to remember what they had been through together during the war and have that count for something, rather than have him angry with her.

"I know," Phillipe said, looking her up and down, his brown eyes, so unusual for a blond man, skipping critically over her person. "Your father should never have taken you with him into that war."

Bella became conscious of the dust on her serviceable black riding habit and gave the skirt an ineffectual swipe. "Many other officers took their wives and their families as well. At least I was of some use."

"Tending the wounded," he said bitterly with a glance at his stiff leg. "That was no fit work for you."

"I could say haring all over Spain by yourself drawing maps for Wellington was not fit work for you." Bella rested her hands on her hips, ignoring Rourke's throat clearing and Greenley's stifled laugh.

Phillipe gritted his teeth. "That was different. I am a man."

"Are we going to argue immediately?" she asked, trying to joke him out of his foul mood.

Phillipe shook his blond hair out of his eyes, turned, and walked slowly to the mare, displaying only a slight limp. As Bella followed him, she thought that, considering how badly his leg had been shot up the previous year, it was surprising he moved as well as he did. She had fought the surgeon to get Phillipe under her care, and she had managed to convince the doctor that she could save Phillipe's leg without endangering his life. She did not expect Phillipe to be grateful for that, but she wished he would not scowl at her so. She remembered the recent feel of his arm about her waist and wished it had been there for some other reason than saving her life.

He talked soothingly to the mare, and the creature stopped trembling and sweating. Bella could remember how soothing he could be when he chose, and she felt a pang of envy. The mare nuzzled his ear and hair. Bella remembered the feel of his hair, running through her fingers, pressed against her cheek, moving across her skin. She blinked and brought herself back to attention.

"You always did have a way with women," she said, giving flattery a try.

"Some women." Phillipe's lips curled at the corners. He was not in a good mood, but the encounter might yet be salvaged.

"But how did you know we were coming?" she asked, watching his hands stroking the mare.

"Rourke wrote to me. I had expected to hear from you."

"I did not know how you would feel about my return." She was hoping for some hint of tenderness from him.

"Impatient. You dawdled in Belgium long enough."

"Dawdled? I was busy," she protested.

"Tending the wounded again. Yes, I know."

Phillipe was always like this. She could not understand for the life of her why she loved him so much. "Would you like to ride that mare to our hotel?" Bella asked. She had half a mind to give the horse to him since it liked him so well.

"You are not going to a hotel," Phillipe stated flatly. "Which horse were you planning to ride?"

"Sebastian." She nodded toward the pawing war horse. "You know what havoc he can cause in a city. Just like a conquering army, he can never behave himself."

"I shall ride Sebastian. The mare will be quiet by the time they are saddled."

Bella bit her lip rather than argue the point with him. His leg might be healed well enough to cope with a restive stallion. She did not think false pride was one of Phillipe's besetting sins, so she passed over the matter of the horses to light on his other statement. "We can hardly ride straight to Father's farm in what's left of today." To demonstrate, she drew a map out of the pocket of her short jacket. "It must be seventy miles, and I have no idea what the roads are like."

"This is England, not the outback of Portugal," he said, grabbing the much-creased map and flipping it around to look at the line she had drawn. "I merely meant that there is no need for you to stay in a hotel when the Duke of Dorney"—Phillipe nodded toward her young son—"has a perfectly comfortable town house at his disposal in London."

"Has he?" Bella teased. "I keep forgetting my son is a duke."

"I do not forget it," said the young man who had driven up with Phillipe. "That small scapegrace has done me out of a fortune. I am your brother-in-law, Hallowell Armitage. Call me Hal."

Bella looked skeptically at the slight, brown-haired youth, but the mocking tone seemed in good humor. "I am Bella," she said bluntly, reaching out her hand, meaning to shake his. "Edwin spoke of his brother, but I had thought you much younger."

"Your grace," the youth said, taking her hand and kissing it as he bowed. "I am nearly twenty."

"You do that very well," she returned. "You put me in mind of Edwin."

"I always put people in mind of my brother. I wondered if they would keep saying it now that he is dead."

Bella dipped her head to shadow her face with her flat black Spanish hat. When she had schooled herself not to react to this heartless statement, she looked Hal in the eye. "I am sorry for your brother's death."

"It can scarcely be considered your fault, your grace," he returned with a shrug.

Bella winced. Did that mean he really did not blame her or that he did not care about Edwin's death? And how would he regard Jamie? At a motion from Carlos, Bella remembered her manners. "Allow me to introduce Edwin's aide, Lieutenant Carlos Quesada."

"Rather young to be a lieutenant," Hal remarked as he shook hands with Carlos.

"Carlos is Maria's son," Phillipe added with a nod to the gaunt woman who held Jamie, "and the son of Captain Quesada, who was attached to Bella's father's brigade in Portugal."

"It pleases me to meet you, Hal," Carlos said with his dazzling smile and the slightest of accents. When he bowed, his black hair, parted in the middle, licked his forehead.

"If I may inquire," Hal said, regarding the buttons on Carlos's red coat, "since you are Portuguese, how did you come by that British uniform?"

"His grace the duke arranged it," Carlos said formally.

"I take it mighty hard that he granted your wish and refused mine," Hal said with mock affront. "I do not think my brother cared for me at all."

"Perhaps he cared enough *not* to buy you a commission," Carlos suggested, raising one black eyebrow.

Hal shrugged and turned to Phillipe. "I perceive you are going to ride, Phillipe. That means I shall have to drive your team."

"You mean the young duke's team, so mind you do

not gallop them and overturn the curricle. In fact, I think you should take Jamie and Maria up with you so they do not have to go in the baggage wagon."

A petulant look passed over Hal's face but was replaced almost immediately by a smirk. He wandered off to make the duke's acquaintance, cozening Maria, who served as Jamie's nurse, while carefully making friends with Jamie's mongrel dog, Lobo, before shaking Jamie's hand. After all this, he spared a moment to wink at Bella.

"Playful boy," Bella said as Phillipe helped her to mount the gray mare. His hands on her waist were strong and possessive, or was that just her hopeful imagination? Seeing him again was a surprise. Actually to be staying in the same house with him overjoyed her. Since it was his left leg that was stiff, Bella wondered how Phillipe would get on Sebastian, but he merely mounted from the right. The horse turned to stare over its shoulder at Phillipe but stood patiently, except to throw its head up and sniff the air, curling its upper lip in an effort to catch the scent of any mare in heat.

Greenley now had charge of the mares, Rourke looked determined to ride the baggage wagon, and Carlos seemed inclined to follow along beside the curricle and talk to Hal. It looked as though she could have a private word with Phillipe, but when their strange train started through the London streets, Bella found she did not know what to say to him after this year apart.

Phillipe had every right to be angry with her. When she had thought he was dead, she had married his cousin Edwin, only to have Phillipe return from a

French prison and break her heart with those sad eyes of his. He had kept his emotional distance in Spain, and she had tried to do the same no matter how much she wanted to throw herself into his arms. His wound near the end of the Peninsular campaign had terrified her but had seemed to come as a relief to him, since it got him shipped back to England. Bella had endured the triumphal entry of the army into Paris without joy, had tried to appear gay during the protracted peace negotiations, and had prepared for battle when Napoleon had escaped his Elba prison to ravage Europe again. Edwin's death had set the cap on the brutal Belgium campaign and finally made it a necessity for her to return to England.

"It was kind of you to come to meet us," she said.

"And why would I not be here? I am responsible for your household now that Edwin is dead. At least until your child comes of age."

"What do you mean?" Bella asked. "Why am I not Jamie's guardian?"

"If he were an ordinary little boy, perhaps you would be. But Edwin was a duke when he died, and this is how he left things."

"He trusted you," Bella said, glancing at him under the low brim of her hat. "He said I could trust you as well."

"When was this?"

"The last time I talked to Edwin. It was almost as though he knew he would not come back."

"But you let him go," Phillipe said.

"How could I stop him from going into battle? I could never stop you."

"If only I had not been captured," he growled desperately, then looked away as though he had not meant to voice the thought. "You would not have married Edwin."

Bella was silent for a moment as the horses' shod hooves rang smartly on the cobbles. "The men said you were dead. Every one of the soldiers who saw those French lancers drag you away swore you were dead. And I did talk to every one of them, looking for some thread of hope." She was trying to keep the tears out of her voice. Phillipe hated weepy women.

"And Edwin, whom I trusted. I should have known he would be as eager to marry you as any of the others. A beautiful young English girl was a rare commodity in the Peninsula."

Bella ignored his reference to commodity. "I waited three weeks, but I was so worn down, losing both you and Father in the space of days, I did not particularly care what happened to me." She turned toward him. "Phillipe, after my father died, I had to marry someone. You always knew that. Why do you bring it up now?"

"How could I speak about it, sitting at table with you and Edwin?" he almost whispered.

"You sound so bitter over something that happened almost four years ago."

"You never told Edwin about our . . . engagement. How could I?"

"But I did tell him." Bella stared distractedly about her. The streets were no longer full of carts and workmen but were lined with shops and businesses. She began looking for an inn or hotel. Now she thought that anything would be better than staying under the same roof as Phillipe.

"Before or after I was captured?" Phillipe persisted.

Bella stared at him in confusion. "Before, but I do not see what difference it makes. When you returned, I was overjoyed that you were alive. Then it hit me what I had done by marrying Edwin. You looked as though I had wounded you myself. Then you drew away as though you were a stranger and there had never been anything between us."

"I used to care about my cousin."

"Meaning I did not care about him?" Bella demanded, rising slightly in her saddle.

"I did not say that."

It was only then that she realized how neatly she had trapped herself. How could she say she had not loved Edwin when he had done everything in his power to make her happy and provide for Jamie? But if she did claim Edwin's love, that meant she forever denied her yearning for Phillipe. She expelled an impatient breath. "If the truth be known, I did not love him, but I did care."

"I do not think you are capable of love, your grace," Phillipe snapped, "only agility. I had Edwin's promise he would look after you while I was away. I imagine it took little skill to turn that into a betrothal."

The arrow went home. So nothing was changed at all, not even by Edwin's death, Bella thought. Phillipe still resented her marriage to his cousin. The love she had always felt for Phillipe had still to be tamped down and kept secret, just as she had hidden her feelings during the war, during her four years of marriage to Edwin. That Phillipe only wanted her, that he did not love her, mattered not at all. In spite of all his flaws, he was the best man she had ever known, and she both admired and loved him. It was a secret treasure she kept to herself, even from Phillipe.

They had ridden in silence for almost an hour when they came to the broad squares and tall houses of Mayfair. Phillipe breathed a sigh of relief as they neared their journey's end. He thought there was no more infuriating woman in the world than Bella. He bit his lip and glanced sideways at her and was surprised to observe still that look of hurt as she faced straight ahead. She had said nothing more, in that way she had of ending conversations that were beneath her. Damn her. He had never won an argument with her in the six years he had known her. If he said something truly devastating, her generous mouth pulled down at the corners and she stopped talking. Those blue eyes iced over, that aristocratic chin came up, and he saw only her profile revealed by the nearly black hair pulled back into a braid.

She had cut her hair short at Vitoria because of the heat, and the men had competed for locks of it. Now it was long again as he remembered. If it were undone, it would ripple over her shoulders far enough to cover her breasts. He looked away, trying to dismiss the image of Bella from his memories, but if he had not been able to do so in all these months away from her, what chance had he with the woman herself only an arm's length away?

He had wounded her, that he knew, but it was not what he had set out to do. There was so much he wanted to tell her, how he had loved her, loved her still. But her independence brought out the worst in him, and he could never understand why. Riding through the streets of London somehow did not seem like the proper time to trot out the words *I love you*. And he never could seem to find the proper time to tell Bella how he really felt.

He realized she was watching his hands, perhaps worried, he thought, that he would mistreat her dead father's prize horse. Sebastian picked that moment to scent a mare and neigh a greeting. The creature answered, and the great horse turned to look at Phillipe. "Walk on!" he heard himself say so harshly that even the war horse snapped back to the matter at hand and forgot the mare.

Was that how he sounded to Bella? Always harsh and commanding? Suddenly, it occurred to him that she watched his hands to see which way he meant to turn. She had no idea where he was taking her. This gave him a slight feeling of control, but he knew it was an illusion. No one could control Bella or make her do anything she did not wish. He would have to remember that. No matter how much the law was on his side, he could not control her except by force, and he did not want to use that.

When they reached the house in Portman Place, he had the satisfaction of seeing her gape at the four-story town house of rose-colored brick.

"This is Edwin's house?"

"Yours now, your grace. Or, rather, your son's."

"Stop calling me that," she ordered, giving him a sharp glance.

"It is one of the penalties for marrying a duke. Get used to it."

"Edwin was not a duke when I married him. He was a major."

"His father had been in ill health for years," Phillipe reminded her. "Waiting at his deathbed kept me in England when I should have rejoined the army in Brussels. It was only a matter of time until the old duke died. You must have known that."

She did not wait for him to dismount but threw her leg over the pommels of her sidesaddle and slid off the mare herself, reluctantly turning the reins over to a liveried groom. Phillipe dismounted stiffly and watched Bella stand uncertainly on the steps. She had pulled off her black leather riding gloves and was drawing them through one hand, over and over, an old habit that spoke of her nervousness.

"Surely Edwin told you what to expect," Phillipe said with satisfaction as she scanned the facade of the large house in agitation.

"We never spoke of England at all. He did not want to come back."

"He might have sent you home after he knew you were with child."

"Never!" Bella picked up the tail of her riding dress. "Why not?"

"He . . . he had his reasons. Besides, I could not bear to leave him, just as I could never leave Papa. And I was right. Had I come back to England . . ."

"Edwin might have sold out of the army," Phillipe said bleakly.

"Never," she said as she watched Carlos carry the sleeping child out of the carriage. "He meant never to return but always to reside abroad," she whispered.

"And leave his estates for me to manage?" Phillipe asked as he watched Jamie's tousled blond head. The blond hair was something he and Edwin had in common from the Armitage line.

The great doors were flung open, and a small army of liveried footmen issued forth.

"The servants will take care of your baggage," Phillipe said more gently. "Come inside and meet the dowager, Lady Edith."

"I had rather wait until I have bathed," Bella said as she followed Carlos and Maria, who were being directed up a great set of spiral stairs by the housekeeper.

"She does not like to be kept waiting," Phillipe remarked, halting Bella in the foyer.

Bella stared at him, making him writhe uncomfortably in his tight riding coat.

"Jamie is covered with ship dirt. You do want him to make a good first impression?"

"I was not considering. By all means, take as long as you like. Hoskins, where is her grace?"

"Her grace has not descended yet," the butler said stiffly.

"You make her sound like a hot air balloon," Bella remarked, startling a smirk from Hoskins. "When does she usually *descend* for the day?"

Hoskins turned a wary eye on Phillipe before answering Bella. "Not before noon, your grace."

"See, Phillipe? There is plenty of time for me to bathe. I rather think I shall like being called *your grace* the way Hoskins says it, so genteelly. Thank you, Hoskins."

"My very great pleasure, your grace." The servant bowed deeply. "I shall have hot water carried to your chamber immediately." So saying, he clapped his gloved hands and sent three footmen scurrying to do his bidding. "Allow me to escort you."

"Thank you, but I wish first to see where they have taken my son."

"I shall show you the nursery first, your grace. By then, your trunks will be unpacked and your bath drawn."

"You run an efficient household, Mr. Hoskins," Bella said as she marched up the stairs beside a servant who had become almost instantly her devoted slave.

Phillipe stared after them in so much awe he did not hear Hal approach until his cousin cleared his throat.

"I say, Hoskins is behaving a bit oddly. He is usually pretty stiff-rumped with guests."

"Bella has a way with servants and a nose for a powerful ally." Phillipe smiled when he recalled all the times in Spain that had gotten them better provisions than Wellington had seen on his table. As Edwin's cousin, Phillipe had been considered part of their household when in winter quarters in Lisbon. As much as it hurt him to sit at table with her and Edwin, then go alone to his solitary cot, it would have looked odd had he and Edwin become publicly estranged. Besides, he would not have given up seeing Bella for the world. Even though she was out of his reach, her courage sustained him without her knowing how essential she was to him.

The faint smile faded when he recalled all those empty nights of coveting Bella. He had thought he was over her, that he had cured himself of that painful infatuation. But she no more walked back into his life than he began fantasizing about her undressing, bathing, going to bed under the same roof again.

He had seen her bathing in a stream once, and the vision was forever engraved on his mind like an icon of ideal feminine beauty. Her stomach was flat, her limbs firm, and her hair—God, that dark mass of ropy coils could ensnarl a man forever. Wet, it had reached nearly to those perfectly rounded buttocks of hers. No, he would never get over Bella.

❧2❧

"*I* need a drink," Phillipe rasped.

"Now you are talking," Hal replied. "Let us go wait in the red salon. There is always brandy in there." So saying, Hal led the way into the large room, poured the amber liquid, and handed one glass to Phillipe, who leaned against the mantel as a more comfortable alternative than sitting on one of the stiff Adam chairs. Hal lounged on the matching sofa.

"That Carlos seems like a nice enough chap. Bit irregular, though, him being her nursemaid's son and still accompanying Bella."

Phillipe glanced at his cousin, who had never worried about propriety in his life before now. "Maria and Carlos are of a noble family. Bella and her father were billeted at their house in Lisbon, and they have been with Bella ever since. Edwin took them into his household after Bella's father was killed."

"That's all very well, but to be traveling together . . .

I tell you, Phillipe, it does not look right. If Mama asks about him, say he came on another ship or something. Say he is going back to the army."

"I am sure he will, once he sees Bella and Jamie safely settled."

"Well, they are safely settled. I tell you, if Quesada hangs about, half the women in London will fall in love with those black eyes and that white smile. A mortal man has no right to be so handsome."

Phillipe smiled. So Hal was not worried about propriety; he was simply jealous of Carlos. "After what he has been through, do not begrudge Carlos a few months of pleasure."

"Gadding about in a cavalry uniform, and moreover one that should have been mine."

"You have some strange ideas about army life. The first time I encountered Carlos and Bella, they were helping to tend the wounded sent back after the Battle of Talavera. Her skirts were wet with blood where she had knelt in it."

"What?" Hal sloshed his brandy on his riding breeches and swore as he searched for a handkerchief.

"They faced some horrendous wounds and knew that most of those they helped would die anyway. I asked her why they bothered. She said simply, so that the soldiers would know someone cared."

Hal left off his blotting and turned a shocked face toward Phillipe. "I . . . I had no idea."

Phillipe tried to close the door on that look into the past. He had shocked Hal, and he had meant to. He and Bella had shared something Hal knew nothing about, and that should make them allies.

Phillipe and Hal both looked up as a strident, whining voice boomed down the great stairway. Phillipe decided that Hoskins's term *descended* accurately described the approach of the dowager Lady Edith. And because of Bella, his aunt would forever put him in mind of a hot air balloon. He smiled in spite of the uncomfortable predicament in which he now found himself.

"She *what?*" echoed from the hall, followed by the door being thrown open and the entrance of a large, billowing pillar of black silk, wielding a dangerous-looking cane. "Where is she?" the dowager demanded, stamping across the room, stabbing at the tile floor with her stick.

Phillipe swallowed a mouthful of brandy before answering. "Freshening up, your grace."

"I told you both expressly that I wanted to see the child and his mother directly they arrived in Portland Place."

"Uhm . . . uhm . . . the little blighter went off to sleep," Hal said valiantly. "Thought we would not disturb you until he woke."

"Do not think, Hallowell. In your case, it is a mistake."

"Now, see here—"

"Go fetch them," Lady Edith commanded, jabbing at the floor tiles until Phillipe expected them to crack.

Seeing a chance of escape, Hal set down his glass and exited. Phillipe sent him a wistful look.

"Well, *Phillipe?*" the dowager demanded, plumping down on the sofa Hal had vacated. "I cringe every time

I have to say your damned French-sounding name. Whyever did your mother do it?"

"Perhaps because she was French?"

"She did it to spite me," Lady Edith said, her hand raised for emphasis.

"What do you want me to say, your grace? I have brought them, as you asked. A few moments more can make no difference."

"The child is three years old," she snapped. "If he is the Duke of Dorney, he should have spent those years here with me."

"What do you mean, *if?*" Phillipe set down his glass and came to attention.

"I only mean that the woman may be a fortune hunter. We have no assurance at all that this child is Edwin's."

Phillipe stared at her in shock and wondered what she knew. The dowager's usually stiff countenance looked more implacable than ever. "What reason have you to doubt it, *madam?*" he asked coldly.

She darted a knifelike look at him, the wattles of her double chin jiggling.

Phillipe knew she hated to be called *madam*. It was his way of letting her know that he was angry.

"Why did Edwin never send them to me before, unless he was ashamed of them?"

"Because he could not bear to be parted from them," Phillipe said automatically, having asked himself this question before and already prepared an answer, the answer he would have given in Edwin's place.

"He told you this?"

"I knew it without being told," Phillipe said gruffly.

"You had only to see the look in his eyes when Bella and Jamie were by him." Edwin had looked happy, happy but guilty. Edwin had known Phillipe had wanted Bella, and he never stopped visually apologizing to Phillipe for stealing her.

"And that outlandish name—*James*. A Scottish name. Why was the child not named Edwin or—"

"He was named for his grandfather, Colonel James McFarlane."

"I never heard of such a thing."

As usual, when she had spent her initial fury, the woman launched into a disconnected complaint that encompassed every wrong Edwin had ever committed, not the least of which was dying in such an outlandish place as Waterloo.

When they had got word of it, Phillipe would have gone to Brussels, though it would have been too late for anything like a funeral, but the dowager would hear none of it. Phillipe had missed the entire Belgium engagement, that bloody epilogue to the action in the Peninsula. He had been strangely disappointed, especially so since Bella had been there, no doubt nursing the wounded as she always had done. He had always looked out for her, even after she was married to Edwin, and he had resented not being able to do so.

But Lady Edith had commanded Phillipe's presence in England to handle the many affairs of the dukedom. She disowned Edwin, Phillipe thought, to expunge her grief for him. She never really had grieved, and he thought she should. But it was not a thing one could tell his aunt. There was, in fact, very little one could tell Lady Edith, even if one had been given the opportunity. He only hoped that by the time Bella put in an appearance, the old woman would have worn herself out with complaining.

After what seemed an eternity, the door boomed open again and two figures in black stood on the threshold, one slender, the other so short he could scarcely reach Bella's hand. Phillipe knew an impulse to walk down the long room and whisk Jamie up as he had done many a time, but that would spoil Bella's entrance.

Jamie twisted his neck uncomfortably, his blond hair haloing around his head as he tried to see all the paintings, walking hand in hand with Bella toward the dowager. Phillipe thought Bella looked no more than a waif in the filmy black muslin she wore. Her hair had been severely braided and coiled around her head like a Madonna's halo. Her creamy neck was unadorned. She was not sunburnt but had the dusky look of a Spanish maiden. If ever a woman looked the part of a grieving widow, it was Bella. No wonder she had insisted on the bath and change of garb. She had not wasted her time in Paris with the army of occupation between the wars, having shopped at the finest modistes. And the black made her look not nearly old enough to be the child's mother.

"Dowager Lady Edith, allow me to present the Duchess of Dorney." Phillipe felt his lips curl at the shudder this sent through the dowager.

"Your grace," Bella said sweetly as she curtsied.

Lady Edith merely stared at her. "You kept me waiting."

Bella's chin came up. "Did I?"

"Come here, boy," the old woman commanded.

Jamie glanced at his mother before taking the two steps that put him within the dowager's reach. She grasped his chin. "You do not look like Edwin."

The boy wrenched away from her and stepped back, never taking his large brown eyes off her.

"Speak up. What have you to say for yourself?"

Jamie turned to his mother and in perfect Spanish inquired, "*Es diabla?*"

Bella gasped and cast an accusing look at Phillipe, who was ineffectually covering a guffaw with a coughing fit.

"No, Jamie. Where did you hear that?" Bella asked.

"Carlos," the boy said, not at all intimidated by his grandmother.

"Do not listen to Carlos," Bella warned as she forced a smile to her lips.

"What did the child say, and who is this Carlos?" the dowager demanded.

"Maria Quesada's son. Maria is my companion, but born of a noble Portuguese family. My parents and I were billeted in their house in Lisbon because Captain Quesada led the troop of Portuguese who were put under Father's command."

When Lady Edith stared at her as though she did not believe a word of this explanation, Bella continued. "Wellington integrated the Portuguese soldiers into the army to get them under our commanders. And it was an effective—"

"Enough," the dowager gasped. "Do you imagine I care what Wellington did?"

Heels clicked together in the doorway as Carlos

came to attention and strode up to the dowager's chair. "Your servant, your grace," he said, taking her hand and raising it to his lips.

Lady Edith ran critical eyes over the tight white pantaloons and scarlet uniform coat. "How do you come to be traveling with . . . them?"

"Your son was kind enough to buy me a commission and offer me a post as his aide-de-camp. Could I do any less than become Bella and Jamie's devoted servant . . . and now yours, your grace?"

Lady Edith narrowed her gaze but did not protest when Carlos seated himself beside her.

Jamie looked at Carlos in surprise. "*Es diabla?*" he repeated, causing Bella to snatch him up.

"No," Carlos said, and spoke several sentences in rapid Spanish to Jamie, who nodded sagely.

The dowager gasped. "Do you mean to tell me the child speaks nothing but Spanish?" The inquiry was thrust at Bella, but Carlos answered it.

"No, how could you think we would be so careless with the child's education? He speaks Portuguese and French as well."

Phillipe actually cracked into laughter at this, then tried to cover his gaffe with a cough.

"Carlos, do not tease her grace," Bella said impatiently. "Of course Jamie speaks English."

"I hear little evidence of it," the dowager complained.

"But he is only three," Bella protested. "He does not know many words yet. It just happens that they are not all English."

Once more the ponderous doors were thrown open

with a crash. "Dinner is served," Hoskins announced. Hal was cowering behind the butler.

Bella meant to carry Jamie upstairs, but Maria was waiting in the hallway to take him from her arms and went off cooing foreign endearments to him, causing Lady Edith to spike the marble floor loudly with her cane as Hal led her into the dining room. The warmth of Jamie had no more left her arms feeling empty than Phillipe took Bella's arm and guided her in the dowager's wake, saving her from feeling quite so lost. She sneaked a peek at his face. Was he smiling ever so slightly? If so, it was for the first time today. And she had actually heard him laugh. That was almost a miracle. She had thought Phillipe unchanged, but she saw now he was not so thin as before. When he did smile, he looked happy, not just desperate. Perhaps her imprudent actions on the dock had put him in a passion, and now he was over it.

They were seated around the end of a table long enough to hold Wellington's general staff and all of the Spanish and Portuguese officers of importance. The courses, all three of them, consisting of twelve dishes each, were commanded, inspected, then either dismissed or devoured as fitted the dowager's pleasure. Bella thought it was a terrible waste of food, but she supposed the servants would eat well. She was feeling too uncomfortable to enjoy even a mouthful of what she ate. Phillipe and Hal seemed not to mind the dowager's rude ways. It was all very well to assert one's authority when it was necessary, but to berate a helpless footman for the quality of the lobster when he could have had nothing to do with it was supercilious and lent Lady Edith no credit in Bella's eyes.

Bella sent the footmen all sad, understanding smiles which they seemed to notice. One did not win loyalty and devotion by being a beast. Bella decided that for every ill thing the dowager did she would counter with a kindness. The contrast alone might kill the woman.

"I still do not see why Edwin had to go to Spain," Lady Edith said as she thumped the table.

Phillipe sighed and put down his wineglass. "Yes, the campaign was a mistake, all things considered. Perhaps it would have been better to let Napoleon have Europe."

"Do not be facetious," the dowager said. "Of course, we could not let the tyrant win."

Carlos intervened with a calming gesture. "I think her grace is merely wondering why her son had to go into the army."

Phillipe went silent, but Edwin had told Bella why he had left England. Just because he had never taken a wife or mistress, there had been rumors that his passion was for boys. Now that he had died a hero, no one could ever speak ill of him again.

"Edwin never confided his reason to me," Phillipe answered, not looking at anyone but staring into his wineglass.

"If Edwin had stayed here, where he belonged, he would be alive today and with a nursery full of likely heirs." The dowager sent a menacing look toward Bella.

Bella could not have missed the snub even without the stare. She took a sip of wine while assessing the dowager with a measuring look, not trusting herself to speak without returning the insult. She continued to stare at the woman until the dowager found an excuse to turn her eyes away.

Hal motioned to the footman for more wine. "Now, Mother, you have been over this ground a thousand times. If I had been older, I would have gone in his stead. We cannot change what has happened."

"Fortunate for you I cannot change history," the dowager countered.

Bella saw Hal shrug off the veiled insult as though he were used to it. For him also she had a sympathetic smile. Considering his mother's temperament, it was remarkable that Hal had turned out as well as he had. She credited Phillipe and Edwin with any good that was in Hal. Phillipe especially was a paragon—always courageous and dutiful, though he tended to be hard on anyone else who did not measure up to his standards. Time and again, he had given his last ounce of strength in pursuit of information for Wellington. Then he always came back to check on her and Jamie, no matter if they were encamped at the very end of the army train. He always found them.

Lady Edith was a formidable opponent, moreover one who was aching for a fight. Bella knew enough about war to know that you chose your own ground and your own time for battle if you could. She must take Wellington as an example and not let herself be pushed into argument unless there was something to be gained by it. In a day or two she would take her entourage to her father's farm in Suffolk and, at the worst, would have to see the dowager once a year during the holidays. No, there was nothing to be gained by coming to words with this bitter old woman.

"The ladies will rise now," Lady Edith said abruptly.

Suddenly it occurred to Bella that she would be alone with the old woman until the gentlemen had killed a bottle of port. She followed the dowager back across the hall into yet another overheated room and took the chair opposite her. But instead of the cool blues, whites, and silvers of the dining room, she was being subjected to a blaze of red and gold that in the effulgent light of far too many candles made her head throb dully even without the grating voice of Lady Edith.

"Do you play backgammon?" the woman demanded querulously.

"Yes, I do," Bella replied.

"Hoskins! Where the devil is that man?"

"Shall I find him for you?" Bella offered, starting to rise in the hope of escaping into the cool hall if only for a few minutes.

"The Duchess of Dorney does not go in search of servants. You do not know the first thing about being a duchess."

"In the army, we never stood upon ceremony."

"Well, you are not in the army now—oh, Hoskins, there you are. Set up the backgammon table. We must find some way to spend the evening. I suppose the gentlemen will drink their time away."

Bella thought she detected a warning glance in Hoskins's look as he turned to do the dowager's bidding. Had he been telling her that Lady Edith did not like to lose? She had already surmised that for herself.

As they played, Bella pretended to lend a sympathetic ear to the dowager's monologue about the inconveniences of her situation, from the insubordination of her servants in the London house to the high cost of nearly everything. They were hot into the game when the gentlemen entered the room, still discussing the war. Bella would have loved to join in their reminiscences, but she was far too engrossed in a neck-and-neck race with Lady Edith to get her pieces all safe. Bella had nearly made the fatal mistake of underestimating her opponent. She had always intended to throw the game. Now she found herself hard-pressed to make any sort of decent showing. It was only by executing her utmost concentration that she even made it a close match.

"Aha, got you," Lady Edith said triumphantly when it was over.

"A tolerably good game, your grace," Bella replied. "Do you care for another?"

"Another? I think you need to study the rules before you match yourself against me again."

Lady Edith gloated about her win all through the pouring and drinking of the tea, nearly spoiling Bella's enjoyment of a treat they had not always had in Spain or France. Not with cream and sugar, at any rate. Was the woman so dense she did not realize how others regarded her preening and self-congratulation? It was only a game, and not even a complex one. It was pathetic that this was all the woman had left and did not even realize it.

Then Bella felt a bothersome tug at her heart. Oh, no. She was feeling sorry for this woman whom she had such vast reason to hate. This could not be happening. Lady Edith deserved no pity after the scathing letters she had sent Edwin, upbraiding him for marrying out of his class. Yet there it was, niggling away at Bella like an unquiet conscience. People got old and perhaps acted badly because of that. One had to make allowances for age and pain. One had to put the past away and salvage what was left. Jamie should know his grandmother, and if Bella could promote that relationship, it was worth any pain the dowager might cause her.

Bella rose when Lady Edith did, thinking to walk upstairs with her and begin her campaign of acquaintance.

"Phillipe will see me to my room," the dowager said with a rebuff so blatant even Hal cocked an eyebrow at his mother.

Bella waited until the tap of the cane had died on the stairs before she left Hal and Carlos, discussing the rival merits of Madeira and burgundy, to make her way to her bedchamber. The room assigned to her was not the duchess's apartment. The dowager still occupied that, but Bella looked forward to spending the night in such a chamber as she now had. The bed was large enough to sleep four and with the most beautiful flowered hangings in greens and browns. There was a writing desk and shelves of books to peruse.

If only Jamie were not an entire floor above her. But Maria had promised to sleep in the nursery. And what had she to fear for Jamie here in England? There would be no attack in the middle of the night, no need to throw on your clothes and begin a forced march, nothing to fear at all except the vagaries of an old woman.

She took up a candle and made her way up the grand stairs, the dim light flickering on portrait after portrait, people she should have known had she lived here. There was one at the head of the stairs that stopped her cold. It was the old duke staring a challenge at her, and Lady Edith looking lovingly down at a small boy. It must have been before Hal's arrival and, judging by Edwin's age, had been painted twenty years before. The arresting face was Lady Edith's. Freed of excess flesh and lines of frustration, she was beautiful. And the doting expression with which she regarded Edwin was no pose; it was mother love.

The one irrefutable argument in favor of Lady Edith was that she had loved her son, no matter how brutally she had treated him because of his unwise marriage. That love may have been perverted into a selfish idolatry of her dead son, but she had loved him. So she did know regret. And if that were possible, perhaps other human emotions lurked beneath the formidable exterior of her grace. Subtly Bella's plans for conquest turned into a campaign of reform.

She tiptoed when she started down the long hallway, but there was no need. Voices were still being raised in the duchess's apartment so loudly that no one could possibly have heard her approach.

"I tell you the girl is impossible, Phillipe. I would not pass her off as the Duchess of Dorney even if I could."

"She is Edwin's widow," Phillipe said quietly. "You cannot change that."

"We shall see. If I can prove that Spanish-speaking whelp is another man's child, you should be able to get some kind of bill passed to get rid of her."

"Divorce her from Edwin after his death?" Phillipe gasped. "Impossible!"

"It will be enough if we can get the child declared illegitimate."

"You would do that?" Phillipe shouted. "Destroy Bella's reputation and cast them off without a penny? I knew you were heartless, but I had no idea your selfishness ran this far."

"Do you think I care about the money?" she shrieked.

"I think you care about little else, madam."

"Do not dare ever call me that again."

Bella could hear anger bulge in the dowager's voice.

"I will call you witch, or anything I damn well please, madam, if you plan to pursue this course."

"Are you forgetting that both you and your sister were raised in my household as my own? I can turn you out without a penny."

"I think you are forgetting that I am very well able to take care of both myself and my sister, not to mention Bella and the young duke. Remember, I am his guardian now."

"He is not the duke!" she shouted.

"Is that it?" Phillipe's voice dripped scorn. "It rankles that Edwin has been superseded?"

There was a dead silent pause for a moment, and Bella thought perhaps Phillipe was leaving.

"Children are not supposed to die before their parents," the old voice growled as it descended into tears.

"That is not the way it is supposed to happen," she sobbed.

Silence again. Bella stood suspended in the hall, her lips parted in rapt attention. She swallowed finally, feeling both hot and chilled at the same time. Hot with anger at the brazen cruelty of the woman and chilled at the remorse that lay behind the dowager's plotting. She wandered to her room, feeling oddly comforted. Throughout the whole nightmarish conversation, Phillipe had defended her hotly. Perhaps he was only being gallant, but still, it felt good that he was willing to stand by her no matter how much he personally disapproved of her taking part in the war.

All things considered, she was glad she had eavesdropped. Spying was not all that honorable, of course, but no one need ever know, and this made it all so easy. They were not wanted, so no one would object to them leaving.

When she got to her room and set the candle down, she found that her hand was trembling. It finally occurred to her what the dowager was implying, that she had foisted another man's child on Edwin without him knowing it. She was trying very hard to turn that hurt into anger, but she was too tired. She had felt much pain these last six years, most of it physical, but she had never taken a blow like this. And she could never tell anyone what had really happened.

As always, she drove off despair with action. The maid who came in to assist her was told to pack her trunks. They would be leaving immediately.

Maria did not like this house. Bella had sensed that. It was too big. Maria would willingly pick up the sleeping Jamie and hold him the night through till they reached their destination. Rourke would do as Maria said. He would grumble about it, but he would do it. Rourke and Maria had been married in France, and Bella had not even had time to tell Phillipe that.

It had been a long time since she had been to the farm, but if she could wind her way through the tangled lines of Torres Vedra in Portugal, she felt it would be no great trick to find the place, even in the dark. Why had she listened to Phillipe? she thought as she stripped off her evening gown and got out her oldest riding habit. Because she had wanted to be close to him, to hear his voice and look at him again, even if he knew nothing of what she was feeling. But Phillipe had not known how Edwin's mother felt about her. The dowager had previously written Edwin of her contempt for Bella, so her reception had been no surprise, except to Phillipe.

Bella finished changing into her riding outfit and went to wake Maria and then find Carlos. She felt it again, the old excitement, an urgency and purpose she thought she had left behind a continent away. It was a familiar feeling, starting an expedition, and she felt very like a military commander, making a hundred small decisions in her mind and translating them into orders for Maria, Rourke, Carlos, the servants and grooms. She doubted she would meet with any resistance except from Phillipe.

Phillipe had always opposed her involvement in matters military, though by now she was more expert at giving orders for transporting and treating wounded than many a green surgeon. She had seen horrendous wounds and never lost sight of what men needed most, to feel like men, even if they were dying.

Why could Phillipe not understand that inaction would have driven her mad? He had always hated for her to nurse him when he was wounded, as though he did not want to owe her anything. He was a complex man. It was her misfortune that she could love only this one man whom she could not understand, when all the rest of them were so simple.

⊸3⊷

"What do you mean, she is gone?" the dowager shouted as this news was delivered to her in her bedchamber with her morning chocolate. "Where is the child?" she asked from her throne of pillows.

"The duchess's entire household left last night," Hoskins said with a veiled accusation. "She did not want me to disturb your rest to say her good-byes but bid me deliver them this morning."

Phillipe had been leaning on the windowsill, and he pushed himself to his feet. "Hoskins, please have my horse saddled for me."

"Very good," the man said as he bowed himself out.

"How could you let this happen, Phillipe?"

"Perhaps I could have prevented her had I not gone off with Hal to his club. They must have been gone by the time we came home."

"But where has she gone? Where has she to go to? She cannot possibly know anyone in England."

"I think I know. Her father left her a little farm in Suffolk County. Fortunately, I had a look at her map," Phillipe said as he resumed his position on the windowsill.

"But why leave? I had not even . . ."

"Had not even done anything to her yet?" Phillipe asked. "You did plenty. I know of no other woman in the world who would have managed to tolerate your snubs and boorish behavior so well as Bella. Also, I suspect she overheard that extremely indiscreet conversation we had last night."

"You shouted at me." The dowager fortified herself with a sip of chocolate.

"You had it coming and more," Phillipe replied.

"Well, what are you going to do about it?"

"I am going to find Bella and escort her safely to her farm, then make sure she has enough servants to raise her son. Beyond that, nothing for the moment."

"You must bring them back!" She clapped her cup into the saucer.

"So you can have another go at her? No, madam, not likely."

"But he may be my grandson," the dowager said tearfully.

"Last night you said he was not. Make up your mind."

"I want you to bring them back."

"Will you give up this nonsense about having the child declared illegitimate?" Phillipe folded his arms and waited.

The dowager pursed her lips and straightened her lace wrapper. "I want proof that he is Edwin's son."

Phillipe hesitated. Now that the question had been

raised, he would be interested in knowing the answer to that himself, but he did not say so. Jamie had been born eight months after Bella's marriage and nine months after she and Phillipe had spent one extraordinary night in a ruined village along the River Coa. There was every possibility that the dowager was right, that Jamie was illegitimate. "Bella's word should be enough," Phillipe said firmly. "The entire British army would back her on that."

"That is hardly a recommendation I wish to hear."

"Are you going to be nicer to her next time?"

"I will . . . try."

"Bella will not tolerate your bullying."

"I said nothing wrong," Lady Edith protested.

"It is fortunate for you that you never listen to yourself." Phillipe stood up and went to kick at the logs in the fireplace with one booted foot as he waited for her to capitulate.

"Is this the thanks I get after all I have done for you? That commission did not come cheaply." Lady Edith jerked her shawl more tightly about her.

"Pardon, madam. I never thanked you or my uncle for six freezing winters, seven blistering summers, and four wounds."

"You mean you did not want the commission?" Her nervous hands were arrested as she stared at him.

"It was my duty. The duke thought that if I went, Edwin would not feel compelled to do so." He could feel those alert eyes drilling into him. "I did not think it would serve," he said as he paced stiffly from window to door and back again.

"Well, it is over now, and I want my grandson."

"Then may I suggest a remove to Dorney Park? That will cloak the scandal of this rift with something like normalcy. Bella can be thought to be checking on her father's property on the way to Dorney Park, though it is a rather circuitous route. But if I contrive to have her meet you there, no one need ever know that you drove her and her son out of their own home."

The dowager looked mutinous. "I want her brought here to me," she enunciated, poking the tray with her stubby finger.

Phillipe walked toward the door. "You are not queen or anything close to it. If I can persuade Bella to visit Dorney Park, I will. But I will never bring her to you again. If you wish, you may visit her at Dorney. It is, after all, her home now, not yours."

"How dare you!"

He glanced over his shoulder. "Shall I have the dower house put in repair when I get there, madam?" Phillipe closed the door behind him just before the cup of hot chocolate crashed into it.

He left the house, chuckling to himself. How like Bella to mount an expedition in the middle of the night without causing the slightest stir. This was like old times, him riding off at a moment's notice with a mission to accomplish and with the image of a defiant Bella in his mind. He did not care if she was the most provoking woman on earth. He must have Bella or he would never know any peace.

Even knowing Bella's endurance and persistence, he was surprised not to overtake them on the road. He found the farm without the slightest difficulty. The main house was a two-story timber and stucco affair that looked to have been standing for hundreds of years. But the stucco was freshly painted, the slate roof was in good repair, and an assortment of flowers edged the building. McFarlane had clearly left someone competent in charge. The courtyard was also surrounded by a smaller but just as ancient cottage, a long row of stables, outbuildings, and storage sheds.

It was not to the house that he went but to the stable, and not just to deliver his horse. He had heard the rap of a hammer and concluded there was farrier work going on. Sure enough, he found Carlos standing at Sebastian's head, talking to the horse, while a thin figure bent over the nigh back hoof rapping a shoe into place.

"That should hold him a good month on these roads," Bella said, straightening up and pushing a lock of hair out of her eyes.

Phillipe scowled. "I had forgotten you knew how to do that."

"Armitage," Carlos said. "Ride into the village with me. I am being sent to reconnoiter for provisions."

"Phillipe may be tired," Bella said, showing no surprise at his appearance. "Perhaps he will have dinner with us and rest a bit before he goes back to London."

Carlos laughed. "Those sound like marching orders to me. Much as I will hate to miss the delightful meal, I am off. And, yes, I will remember your marketing, Bella." So saying, Carlos led Sebastian out and mounted. The beast snorted its impatience and launched from the yard at a full gallop.

Phillipe shook his head as he looked after Carlos. "How old is he?"

"Sebastian or Carlos?" she asked as she untied the strings of the leather apron and pulled it off, revealing a much-worn blouse and her tired buff work skirt.

"I was inquiring about the boy." Phillipe watched Bella wash her hands in a bucket of water, then open a stall door as if to lead his horse in. "I shall take care of him," he said.

"He is not a boy any longer. He is nearly twenty-one. It seems like only yesterday he was begging to go off to war."

Phillipe unsaddled his horse, then went to take the bucket of fresh water Bella was drawing from the well. "Have you no help here?"

"The Deans, who care for the place, have two fine sons, but they are all out haying. Rourke took Jamie to watch, but I expect them home soon. You will stay, of course."

"I suppose I should be glad you are not out there in the hot sun as well."

"They insisted they did not need my help, but I am not sure I believe them. What business is it of yours, anyway, what work I choose to do?"

"You are a duchess now, and some things should be beneath you."

"No task is beneath me, and I am grateful I learned how to do so many. It will stand me in good stead now that I am taking care of Jamie myself." She tilted her chin up in challenge.

Phillipe bit back the reply he was going to make and rubbed his forehead. "I did not ride all this way *expressly* to argue with you."

"That does seem to be what we do the most," Bella

agreed, picking up a pitchfork with the intention of getting his mount some hay. "But you always start it."

Phillipe sighed tiredly and placed his hand over hers on the handle. She looked up at him with those challenging blue eyes. "Let me help," he said simply, meaning *with everything*. She relinquished the tool to him, and he forked some hay off a clean pile into the rack as she poured a ration of grain into the manger. He took off his coat and was aware of her regarding him as he curried his tired beast. He wondered, not for the first time, what Bella really thought of him. That he was churlish and temperamental, a thorn in her side compared with the jovial Edwin? He must not let his fatigue prompt him to argue with her again if he were going to get her compliance.

After five hours of sleep, he had set out at ten and been in the saddle for six hours, less a brief stop at an inn. Not good for his leg, but he felt no more than a tired ache from that quarter. If Bella had left at midnight, they could not have arrived before dawn, especially if Sebastian had thrown a shoe. She had not slept all night, but she did not seem to feel the loss of it. She merely looked subdued, not tired.

He finished grooming the horse, and when he had exited the stall, Bella brushed the hair from his shirt for him, sending a thrill up his arms wherever her competent hands touched him. She had no shyness around men, having nursed hundreds of them. She treated them all like little boys, and they liked it, all except him. He did not want to be regarded as just another wayward boy, not when he desired her so much. Their gazes met, and whatever she saw in his eyes made her look down with a troubled frown.

"Let me show you the house," she offered. "It is almost as I remember it."

Phillipe slipped on his coat as they walked together toward the picturesque lodge, and he knew an impulse to duck as he passed through the low doorway directly into a large sitting room. Inside was more whitewashing and a passionate neatness. The furniture was old and homemade. The more rustic pieces reminded him of Spain, but in those days they would have been delighted to stay in so fine a place as this.

"Have you ever been here before?" Bella asked. "I cannot remember."

"No, never. But I know there is a huge kitchen behind the dining room and sitting room."

Bella sent him a puzzled look as she led him through another low door into the kitchen. "How goes our dinner, Maria?"

A flood of Portuguese detailed all the delights Maria had planned for them. Her flushed face beamed at Phillipe, and he found he had to smile at her and compliment her in her own tongue, though he was sure she giggled at his accent. Bella picked up a bottle of wine and two glasses and led him back into the sitting room.

"How did you know the layout of the house?" she asked with a puzzled frown.

"You used to talk about this place all the time. Do you remember how angry you got when I said I did not believe you really had a farm?"

"Yes," she said with a sad smile as she seated herself. He would have uncorked the bottle for her, but she opened it without difficulty and poured him a much larger amount than she took. "It was as though you had snatched it away from me by disbelieving in it. And there were times when I thought never to see it again." She handed him a glass and looked toward the other end of the wooden settee where she sat, but he chose to stand by the mantel.

"Do you regret leaving here to follow your father off to war?"

"Mother could not bear to be parted from either of us. They are both buried in Portugal now, but I do not think she regretted her decision, so I must not either. I had more years with them than I would have if they had found a place to leave me in England, and . . . it is rather hard to explain."

"What?" he asked, wanting to know every thought that entered her head, no matter how dangerous it would be to do so.

"I would have been disappointed in myself if I had not gone."

"No one would have expected you to do half the things you accomplished, nursing the soldiers . . ." He hesitated as she glanced at his leg.

"I have never paid much attention to what other people expect of me," Bella said, her blue eyes looking at him with a frankness that was rare in a woman. "I think that is always why you disapproved of me so severely. I only cared what I thought of myself."

"I never disapproved of you," Phillipe said earnestly. "Not until—never mind. Why did you think I disapproved?"

"Then why did you always scowl at me so in Portugal? And do not bother to deny it. If you were laughing when I entered a room, you were sure to clam up and look daggers at me as soon as you realized I was there."

Phillipe flicked his mind back over the war years and discovered to his surprise that she was right. "I was—I was concerned about you."

"You did not think I belonged there."

"No, I did not." Phillipe stared into the ruddy liquid in his wineglass. "I would have wanted something better for you," he said passionately.

He risked a glance at her and found that he had puzzled her. It was not an expression she often wore. "I told you once that I wanted to marry you." There, he had said it. Now she would crown his frankness with insult by laughing at him.

"I remember." She stared at the empty fireplace. "It was after that night we spent in the village by the Coa River. You seemed almost disappointed when the French pulled out, that we did not get blown to bits."

Phillipe moved uneasily to a chair opposite her, watching her. "As long as we were going to die anyway, what I did seemed justified. When the siege ended so tamely, I thought I had let my lust for you trick me into taking advantage of you."

Bella smiled, her blue eyes glittering merrily. "You have a rather poor memory of that night. I was the one who wanted you. I thought you merely agreed to make love to please me, that it would never have occurred to you on your own."

Phillipe rolled his eyes, and Bella laughed at his grimace.

"At any rate, I thought it was gallant of you to offer

me the protection of your name when you did not even like me."

"I loved you!" he said so urgently he felt surprised himself. He slid back into his chair to await her derision.

She stared at him, her ripe lips parted, her eyes strange swirls of amazement and regret. She blinked to banish any possibility of tears and said, "How could I not have realized that?"

He could see that her lips trembled slightly. "Perhaps because I neglected to mention it," he said regretfully. "I had already asked your father for permission to pay my addresses to you, but he refused. He was right, of course. I had nothing to offer you."

"I had no idea," she said in shock, shaking her head slightly. "When was this?"

"In October of 1810. He said he could not possibly do without you."

"So that is why you never danced with me at all of the balls in Lisbon. He had already turned you down, and I did not even know it."

"Which makes what I did that much worse. Your father was my commanding officer. He would have thought—"

"You loved me? Truly?" She stared at him intently, as though replaying some memory in her mind, then turned her vivid blue gaze away from him. "But past tense. I am sure I managed to kill your love when I married Edwin."

"He was like a brother to me. I should never have confided to him my passion for you. But I never expected him to compete with me for your affections. How could he not get your father's approval? He was a duke's son."

"I knew it!" she said, her eyes alight with pleasure. "All those times you sat and watched us, it was not disapproval . . ."

"It was jealousy," he said, and thumped his glass down on the table. He moved restlessly in his chair, then rubbed the tiredness from his face before he said, "I am sorry now that I kept such a distance between us, but I was afraid the temptation . . . And as for what may happen between us in the future, there would be a better chance of us reaching some kind of understanding if we were not half a day apart. I have come to ask you to come home."

Bella looked longingly at him. "But I am home," she said, staring around the small, neat room.

"I mean to Dorney Park. It is Jamie's future home. He should know something of it now while he is young."

"Will *she* be there?"

"I told Lady Edith she had better meet us there, if she wants to see her grandson."

"Her grandson? She wants no such thing."

"Did you overhear us?" Phillipe accused.

Bella ignored the question and stood abruptly. "Did Edwin never tell you about the letters she sent him?"

"No, Edwin and I ceased to be close after . . . your marriage."

Bella cast her eyes down, then said, "Stay here. I will fetch them from my trunk."

While she was gone, Phillipe poured himself another glass of wine. It was not going well. No matter how calm he tried to remain in her presence, he could not help thinking of her as the woman he loved. That she cared nothing at all for him seemed to make not the slightest difference to his contrary heart. It was beyond all reason that he should still covet her so. And he could not control what he said when he was with her. Yes, she did make him angry. Her very indifference fanned his desires.

She had been far from indifferent that night they had made love. He remembered how they had lain together in the protection of the mud hut wall, thinking they were trapped and both going to die along with young Carlos and the soldiers downstairs. He had held her in his arms to still her fears. That had been a mistake. His face had been too close to her lips. The kiss, when it came, surprised him, yet she did not pull back and slowly let him in, opening her mouth to duel with him, surpassing him with the urgency of her need.

She had still trembled, but with excitement, not the chill of the mountain air. He had loosened the drawstring of her peasant blouse and suckled at those tight young breasts like a babe. Her response had been immediate and volatile. She had writhed under his touch and arched her back. He had found his way into her clothes, and she had let him, nay, invited him, removing any barrier that was in his way. And when his questing manhood reached her opening, it had been hot with inviting wetness. She had clung to him as he thrust into her, panting little endearments in Spanish. The words still spilled around in his mind during his hottest dreams of her—*my Phillipe, mi amor, mi corazón.* He remembered wondering at the time with some fragment of his mind if it were the wisest thing to be making love not five hours from your own death, but part of his mind knew it was the only thing that mattered. That they should have each other finally when they were about to die did make sense to him at the time.

He did not remember their lovemaking ending. All he remembered were her hands stroking his back and shoulders, her whispered words of love, and the hot needfulness of the coupling. He closed his eyes, trying to go back to that night, when his heart had opened and his life had seemed to begin.

~ 4 ~

*B*ella came back into the room, and he jerked back to reality, sloshing wine on his hand. He pulled out a handkerchief and mopped up the mess as she ignored him to unfold a much creased piece of parchment.

"This is what she sent on hearing of our marriage."

Phillipe saw her pulling a second missive through her fingers as he scanned the diatribe. "Yes, this is just what I would have expected from my aunt, but anyone who knows her would realize she does not mean half the things she says. It is a letter designed to bring the culprit craving her forgiveness."

"But it did not work." Bella handed him the second paper. "She sent this when Edwin wrote of Jamie's birth."

Bella waited as Phillipe took a long draught of wine before perusing the worn letter. The date was August 10, 1812, and Jamie had been born in June. But the words dripped with the hot anger of the dowager's initial wrath, so Edwin must have delayed writing so as to put the birth in the best light. Whereas the first letter had ended with a promise of aid if Edwin chose to divorce Bella, the second held only scorn for him and the army slut he had seen fit to ally himself with. He was forbidden to return home with her or the bastard whelp she was forcing on the house of Dorney. Phillipe would give much to know who was the father of her child, himself or Edwin, but he had already decided that it did not matter, that the only face they could put on things was that the boy was his cousin's.

Phillipe looked up finally, trying to keep the shock from his face. The words sounded bad enough to someone who knew the dowager. He could guess what they must have cost Bella, coming as they did from a stranger. "But I do not see why Edwin gave these to you. He knew what she was. He should have tossed them in the fire where they belonged."

"He did not give them to me." Bella seated herself and stared gloomily into the empty grate.

"Careless of Edwin to have left them about," Phillipe said as he tossed off the rest of the wine, thinking of his cousin, who looked enough like him to be his brother but who never thought or acted like him.

"I am glad he saved them. They were in his papers." Bella wrung her empty hands. "Do you see, Phillipe? She would never have accepted me even if Edwin had lived."

"I think you may be wrong there. Lady Edith frequently says things in the heat of the moment that she later regrets. For instance, she now wants to see her *grandson.*" He made as if to toss the papers into the empty grate.

"Do not," Bella said as she came to take them.

"Why keep them, such bitter memories?"

"Do you wish to erase a scar just because the wound has healed?" she asked as she carefully folded the letters and put them back into a leather case. Her phrasing of the question had seemed so very Spanish at that point. He wondered if she would ever lose the flavor of that country, would ever forget all that had happened to her there.

"But these pieces of paper wound over and over again," he insisted. "What is the point?"

"The point is never to forget who your enemies are," she said coldly. "You may have to sit at table with them and be polite, but you must always be on guard."

"This is not war, Bella," Phillipe pleaded, seeing his task of bringing her to Dorney growing more impossible by the minute.

"Everything is war, Phillipe," she snapped with finality as she sat down.

The door burst open. "*Madre. Un tortuga,*" Jamie said as he displayed a fist-sized turtle. When he laid the offering in Bella's lap, Lobo, hot on his heels, tried to grab it with what purpose Phillipe could guess.

"I think Lobo is jealous of the tortoise," Bella said, standing to hold the creature out of reach of the dog's leaps. Lobo licked his chops and whined. "Remember to answer in English, now, Jamie. You need the practice."

Jamie pressed his lips together in concentration. "Yes, Mother. Put back?"

"I suppose you may keep it for a few days. But I have no idea what to feed it. Phillipe?"

"I think *Señor* Turtle will survive quite well in the fenced kitchen garden where Lobo cannot go. If your mother keeps Lobo here for a few minutes, Jamie, you and I can find a nice cabbage for your turtle to live under."

Jamie nodded vigorously and rescued the turtle as Bella grabbed Lobo's collar.

"Phillipe, what is cabbage?" the child asked, mouthing the word on the way out the door.

"*Un col.* I shall show you."

"Mind you wash your hands before dinner," Bella called after them. "Both of you."

Bella helped Maria bring in the trays of flat corn cakes and chicken, the fried beans and spicy sauces. She was proud that Maria had managed such a splendid feast here their first day at the farm, especially since Phillipe had come. When she insisted that Maria, Rourke, and Greenley eat with them, she looked a challenge at Phillipe to see if he would disapprove of this arrangement, but he was too busy discussing the rival merits of the claret he had just sampled and a dusty bottle of burgundy Rourke had fetched from the basement. Both tasters pronounced the burgundy superlative, Phillipe blessed the meal, and they all set to eat in deadly earnest, including Jamie, who had rolled his shirtsleeves up to the elbow so as to do himself the least damage.

Talk flew back and forth, along with the platters of food, comparing the meal with many they had shared in Spain and making Bella feel quite at home now. Phillipe could be gay if he made an effort, and Jamie seemed to lighten his mood. She began to hope that Phillipe might forgive her for marrying his cousin. She would have preferred to marry Phillipe over any other man just because she loved him so much. But she had been told by two dozen witnesses, including Edwin, that Phillipe was dead. And besides that, she had never thought that love was mutual, not even along the Coa River. She had only thought he was gallantly offering marriage because they had made love and he was embarrassed by his lack of will.

She swallowed hard as she thought of that night, and a pulse started throbbing in her stomach. She had known they were going to die, and she had been frightened enough to want to take that one and only chance to love him. If she was thinking of love and he was thinking only of need, that had not mattered to her. In her own mind, it had been perfect. But to discover after all these years that he had loved her . . . Bella played out the scene in her mind again as she had so many times over the years. The throbbing moved lower now, and the pounding of her blood made her rock slightly in her chair. He had been so hungry for her, and she had gloried in that. She had wanted him on any terms, and she had never regretted that night, nor any of the hardships that had led them there.

Yet when she had awakened him and told him the French had pulled out, he had said they must be married when they got back to camp, as though it were his duty, not something he really wished. She had nodded her agreement to the order. She could hardly have called it a proposal. But she would have taken him on any terms and tried to make it right later. Best not to think of it. She had never known Phillipe's true feelings, and then he had been sent on a mission from which he did not return. He had almost made it, had, in fact, been within sight of the British lines when he was shot from his horse. One of the French had dismounted under British fire to bind a sash around Phillipe's wrist and drag him out of sight as though his body were some prize. Edwin's humble proposal, coming hard on the heels of Phillipe's death, then her father's, made it possible for her to shift some of her burden onto someone else's shoulders.

The subsequent years of close contact with Phillipe when he had returned, sullen and uncommunicative, had been both agony and joy at the same time. If she had hurt him in the past, she was sorry, but she had never intended to do so. Was it possible that they could mend what had been broken by what he must have considered a betrayal on her part? She had married another, not just any man, but his beloved cousin.

She looked up at Phillipe, trying to see into the future for them, but he sensed nothing of her confusion and hope. He only smiled in that heart-stopping way, with his blond hair hanging over his brow as he laughed at one of Carlos's jokes. Bella so wanted to brush that unruly hair back, to touch him in any way that would show how much she cared. Words of love did not come easily to her after all she had been through.

The one thing she had to keep remembering was that the war was over. There was no need to feel as though she were in a state of siege. But, at the same time, she resented the lack of necessity for it. She had been important, had played a part. Now she had no idea what her role was beyond mothering Jamie. She should be glad they were safe in England, but she felt strangely out of place and unnecessary.

Toward the end of the meal, Rourke was looking very sleepy, and Bella heard Phillipe say, "You amaze me, Rourke. An ocean voyage, then a forced night march with Bella cracking the whip over you, and a full day of haying. You are getting a bit old for this sort of thing."

Rourke laughed. "I did manage to keep up with the young lads, but 'tis sure I shall seek my bed soon. Maria, is there any hot water for washing?"

"Sí, Rourke, I will fetch it as soon as I clear the table."

"I will help," Bella said. "Jamie, you could show Phillipe the pigs until we are finished. Then we will all walk up to the woods and show him the whole farm."

Bella noted with satisfaction the soft smile that spread across Phillipe's face as Jamie tugged him toward the door. Phillipe was a man meant to be a father. Perhaps he had also been meant to be her husband. Why did every comforting thought have such a sad counterpart? She shrugged. One could control so little in life. And the past was totally beyond reach.

Only the future held any promise, and Bella thought she could live quite comfortably here on her father's pension. She did not look for anything from the dowager, who so obviously did not approve of her, but if Phillipe was in charge as he said, she did hold out some hope he might pay for Jamie's schooling. Really, things had turned out much better than she had ever expected. And Phillipe was whole again and seemed to be healing both outside and inside.

After Maria had shooed her from the kitchen, Bella found Jamie and Phillipe admiring a litter of thirteen piglets. Because of their number, they had to struggle constantly for a nipple in a surging contest of poking, snorting, suckling, and squealing that made their human observers all laugh. The smallest of the litter was thrust away again by the legs of its brothers but plowed back in to steal a drink by climbing to the top of the pile and stepping on someone's head.

" 'Once more into the breach again, dear friends,' " Phillipe quoted. "That looks like us at Badajoz." He turned his laughing countenance to Bella's incredulous one. "Sorry, it was not an apt comparison," he said as the smile slowly faded from his lips, leaving him looking more melancholy than when his mouth was compressed in anger.

"We were cut to ribbons," Bella whispered. "Wellington should have waited for the artillery to do their work." Her blue eyes looked angry.

"You always did identify with the soldiers. Why is that, when you did not approve of the war?"

"I realize the necessity of a lot of things I do not like," Bella said. "The trick is to keep your wits about you. Listen to counsel, but make sure your decisions are your own."

Phillipe nodded and took Jamie's hand as they walked a path up a low hill. "As I recall, you followed orders when they were given to you."

"In the heat of battle, it is the only thing to do," she argued.

"And what about now?" Phillipe asked.

"No one can order me to do anything now," she replied. "I plan to live here."

Phillipe was looking down at Jamie when she said this, but he glanced up at her in that speculative way of his, with his blond hair raking his brow, and she knew he could persuade her to do unwise things with a mere suggestion. It was fortunate he did not realize how heart-stopping those brown eyes of his were.

"You were a child when you left here, Bella. You have known nothing but hardship ever since. In a year, civilian life will seem normal to you."

"That is what I hope," she replied. "That I will not feel always as though I should be somewhere else, on higher ground or something."

"Living at Dorney Park could seem normal to you if you would give it a try."

Jamie sighed heavily, his signal that he was tired, and Bella picked him up automatically, carrying him on her hip. "Do you mean to try to dislodge me from the farm?"

She tossed the question at him like a gauntlet, Phillipe thought, and he spent a moment studying her, knowing that he had to play the diplomat here. In point of fact, removing her from the farm was his intention, but he did not think a frontal attack would work in this case. "I know better than to try." He walked in silence, his good leg taking a longer stride than the other. "Do you want me to carry him?"

"He is not heavy," Bella replied.

"You always used to say that, but he was lighter when he was a baby."

"And you used to carry him for me." She turned her head to smile at him. "Even though the other soldiers laughed at you for it. I do remember some good things. Was that because he was Edwin's son?"

"No, it was because he was yours." Phillipe took Jamie into his arms. The child was half asleep already and rested his head trustingly on Phillipe's shoulder as he had so often in the past. Why was that? Phillipe wondered. Had Edwin not paid any attention to Jamie, that the boy would put such faith in a man he saw only a few times a month? Or perhaps the child sensed something from Bella. Phillipe wished he could ask the boy why, but he would rather Bella told him when she was ready.

Bella turned and pointed out the hay field where they had cut today, the horse pasture where the mares grazed, and the small knot of gray sheep that called the farm home. "It is less than eighty acres but enough to sustain us."

"What would you have done last night if your father had not left you this farm?" Phillipe asked.

"I would have thought of something," Bella said with false bravado.

"What of Jamie's inheritance?" Phillipe glanced at the sleeping child.

She stared at him, and he thought she realized he still meant to persuade her to do something she did not wish.

"You will take care of that until he comes of age," she said. "Then he will decide if he wants it. I trust you."

He leveled his gaze at her. "You trust me with his fortune but not with his future."

Bella stood thinking for a moment as though she were going to throw him some kind of crumb.

"You have always stood our fast friend. And you have always given me good counsel. What would you have me do?"

Phillipe chuckled. "Now that you have asked my advice, however reluctantly, live at Dorney Park so that the boy does not come to it a stranger when he should be growing up there."

"But I like it here."

"Visit here when you grow homesick for it, but only with a proper escort."

"That is what you want for us?" she asked.

"It is what Edwin would have wanted."

Bella shot him a suspicious look that made him cringe inside.

"That is a low blow, using Edwin's wishes, if those were his wishes, to compel me to do what the dowager wants."

"I am not here on her behalf," Phillipe whispered so as not to wake Jamie.

"You said she wanted to see her grandson."

"I mean not entirely on her behalf. God, Bella, you cannot raise a duke of the realm in a pigsty." Phillipe regretted his rash words as soon as he saw the mulish light come into those blue eyes of hers.

"I see your plan. It is perfectly all right for me to live here, but not Jamie. She does not want me around, just the child."

Phillipe sighed. "She never said that."

"I will not give up my son," Bella said, pulling the ends of her shawl through one hand.

"Then take possession of his home, Bella." Phillipe thought to appeal to the soldier in her. "I have never known you to run from a fight."

"The dowager is right about one thing." Bella kicked a rock out of the path. "I know nothing about being a duchess."

"So, that is the problem. You are afraid."

"I am not," she whispered desperately. "I simply do

not desire all the physical trappings that go with the position." Bella wrested the sleeping child away from Phillipe and started down the hill.

"Well, you are wrong. You know everything about being a duchess," Phillipe called after her, unable to match her rapid walk. "You already have most of the London servants eating out of your hand. It cannot be much harder to charm the ones at Dorney Park. Come with me there and take possession of it before the dowager can stir from London. We shall steal a march on the old battle axe." This last was shouted after her, almost like a battle cry.

Bella paused and turned to stare at him. "You think to awaken in me that old urge to break camp and be off. You want to appeal to my need for excitement. You make Dorney Park sound like some fortification that might have to be taken by storm if ever the enemy gets inside its gates. But the enemy owns it, and I have no desire for it. It is not strategic for my plans, and any commander prideful enough to spend resources taking a position of no tactical value is stupid . . . And why do I always think like a soldier?" She almost shouted this last at him.

She cast an accusing glare at Phillipe, who was toiling toward her. "You try to tempt me into battle when there is no need. I have everything I desire. There is nothing to be gained from confronting her." She carried Jamie back to the house then and left Phillipe standing in the yard, half-minded to saddle his horse and leave.

Carlos rode in then, so drunk Phillipe could not trust him to stable Sebastian safely. So he put the horse away and then half-carried Carlos to his room, follow-

ing Maria along the narrow corridor of the second
floor. The woman also showed him which room was
his, and he took that as tacit permission to stay the
night. Indeed, he felt too weary and defeated to ride
the extra forty miles to Dorney Park. He had failed,
but, then, he had never expected to succeed so easily
where Bella was concerned.

Though how he was going to sleep with her no more
than a plaster wall away from him was a puzzle. No
doubt he would dream of that night along the Coa
River again and try to make it do. He had no choice; it
was all he had of Bella, and all he was likely to get if
she now regarded him as an enemy.

"Ihe what?" Lady Edith demanded, eyeing the soft-boiled egg on her plate with disgust.

Phillipe, too, looked at the item of food with unease, remembering the cup of chocolate. Last night's burgundy plus his restless and unfulfilled dream, not to mention a four-hour ride, had left him with a buzzing head and an unrequited ache in his groin. He was in no mood to humor the dowager duchess today.

When he had been able to stand and dress himself that morning, he had ridden away from the farm at first light with no food. Greenley had accompanied him to Dorney, ostensibly to visit his mother. Phillipe had arrived to find her grace sitting down to a breakfast in the small dining room. Inwardly he owned to some surprise, for he had never known his aunt actually to take his advice until he had been proved right, or to bestir herself from the London house in less than a week.

"She does not wish to leave her farm," Phillipe said.

"She cannot do this to me. You said you would bring her to me here, and you shall." Lady Edith pounded the table in a childish way, and Phillipe leaned on a corner of it in fatigue. "Now sit down and eat something before you fall over. We must plan our next move."

To his own surprise, Phillipe obeyed the command to sit. He stared tiredly at his sister, Ann, who got up from her seat to make up a plate for him. As she set the offering of ham, kippers, and warm bread in front of him, she pressed her other hand lightly on his shoulder, saying more about her sympathy for his position than any words could convey.

Ann was not yet twenty, yet she had taken upon herself the duties of chatelaine at Dorney Park. But not even the severest gowns or most modest caps could hide her blond beauty. Phillipe longed to see her dancing and gay. Perhaps he would take her away from here to London. Then she might find someone, but Lady Edith was right about one thing. He could not dower Ann as she should be. And Lady Edith would never do so for fear of losing someone from her household so essential to her comfort. He suddenly realized how much Bella and Ann had in common in that respect. They both needed employment. If he persuaded Bella to take her rightful place as Duchess of Dorney, would Ann then feel displaced?

He wanted Ann and Bella to know each other and could not think how to contrive it. "Perhaps a visit," he said out loud as he devoured a mouthful of ham and washed it down with the strong coffee Ann had provided.

"A visit?" Lady Edith queried. "You mean lure Bella here on a visit and entice her to stay when she sees all the luxury to be had at a ducal estate? Is that your plan?"

Phillipe stared at the dowager in horror. "No, that is not what I meant."

Lady Edith chewed another bite like a cow masticating its cud. "Surely," she mumbled, not quite clearing the food from her mouth. "Surely, you do not mean that I should visit her?"

Phillipe stared into space, trying to picture the dowager Duchess of Dorney observing Jamie's pigs. He laughed and shook his head. "No, I have a mind to take Ann to see her. Perhaps once Bella realizes this place is not so menacing—"

"Phillipe," Ann protested with a laugh.

"Menacing, am I?" Lady Edith demanded. "I shall give you menacing. I want my grandson!" She thumped her knife handle on the table for emphasis.

"What are you going to do?" Phillipe gibed. "Cut his little heart out?"

"Do not be absurd. I want him with me. Perhaps when I get to know the child . . ."

"There can be no perhaps about it. You have already made him afraid of you. Let me speak plainly, madam. It was your rude treatment that caused Bella to bolt, and I cannot say that I blame her. She does not need Edwin's money."

"But her position in society," the dowager sputtered. "Without my support, she will never be accepted."

"Bella does not care a fig for society. So you have no carrot to hold out to her there. You managed damn badly, trying to lord it over her when you have no real authority."

"But I . . . I am Edwin's mother."

"That might have carried some weight with her if Edwin were still alive."

"But it is her fault he is dead," Lady Edith insisted.

Phillipe stopped chewing to trade puzzled looks with his sister. "How do you arrive at that conclusion?"

"If he had not married her, he would have come home after the army was victorious in Spain. He would not have stayed in France."

"He might have come home with Bella and Jamie if not for your letters. You warned Edwin never to darken your door so long as *that woman* was with him."

"You know about the letters?" the dowager asked timidly, shrinking back into her chair. "Ann, dearest Ann, I fear I shall need my vinaigrette."

"I will fetch it," Ann said with resignation as she got up. "When will you need it? In five minutes or ten?"

"Ann, do not be impertinent. Leave us now."

"Very well, your grace." Ann curtsied pertly. "Phillipe, you do ruin more meals," she mumbled on her way out.

Phillipe cast her a sad smile. "Yes, she kept the letters, and I think I know why."

"They were Edwin's. She has no right to them."

"But if she presented them to our solicitors, she might just be able to wrest custody of Jamie away from me."

"But it would be as good as admitting her infidelity. She would not dare!"

"A woman who has marched with the army in Spain, a woman who has nursed wounds more ghastly than you could ever imagine, moreover a woman who killed her share of French when the need arose, such a woman will dare anything." Phillipe finished this sentence leaning forward over the table, staring intently at his aunt.

The dowager seemed shocked. "I do not know what her life has been like, but that is not my fault."

"But for those letters, I have no doubt Edwin would have sent her home as soon as he knew she was with child. It is very much your fault, *madam*."

The dowager's dark eyes snapped fire at him. "Do not call me that!"

"I call you foolish, old woman, to have shut your heart against Bella and Jamie without ever knowing them. If you get another chance, it will be more than you deserve."

Lady Edith stared at him resentfully, then at the silver epergne which graced even the smallest dining table at Dorney Park. She struck the flat of one plump hand on the polished oak surface. "Call Ann. Tell her to have my traveling carriage brought around. I will go to this farm."

Phillipe leaned back in his chair, satisfied that he had finally brought the dowager to see reason. "Perhaps tomorrow would be a better day."

"I want to see the child now."

"It is noon already. If we leave now, you will be forced to spend the night in the farmhouse or at an inn. If we leave early tomorrow, we can be there by noon and home again by nightfall."

The dowager chewed this over in her mind, relegating her impatience to a secondary position to her comfort. "Very well. We leave at eight o'clock tomorrow, and not a moment later."

"A wise decision, your grace." Phillipe rose, took her

hand up, and saluted it with a brush of his lips, causing a shade of suspicion to cross her face.

"If I ever thought you were conspiring with her against me . . ."

"And Bella accuses me of conspiring with *you* against *her*," Phillipe said, snatching one last scone from the sideboard. "The life of a messenger is not an easy one, but it is a job I am well used to."

"An aide-de-camp to Wellington," she said scornfully.

"Oh, worse than that, his cartographer, attached to the Quartermaster General, of all things." What Phillipe did not say was that the whole army had depended heavily on his maps and the other intelligence he had gained of troop placements. He had spent his share of time briefing Wellington.

"Too bad you did not distinguish yourself in the recent conflict. You might have gotten a title out of it," she growled.

"I had no such ambition. Staying alive was quite enough for me, thank you."

"You knew the job was dangerous when you took it."

"And you said you could dissuade Edwin from joining the army if I—how did you put it? If I sacrificed myself."

"You did it to get a commission."

"I did it because I cared about Edwin. I was perfectly willing to die in his stead. But protect him through a whole war, I could not. Why did you not keep him home?"

"I tried," she said, choking on gusty sobs. "I used every argument I could think of. It was the only time in my life I have failed to get what I wanted."

"Not the only time. I recommend you handle Bella with a gentler touch. She is far more willful than Edwin ever was."

The old woman sighed and straightened her back. "I shall be kindness itself."

"I shall believe *that* when I see it."

Phillipe found Ann in the morning room and, besides warning her of the expedition, asked her to send to the stables for a groom. Phillipe sat immediately at the small writing desk and began to compose a letter, but Greenley was cooling his heels in the hallway long before Phillipe had chosen the words he thought would warn Bella without offending her. The diplomatic corps would have been an easy career by comparison. There you had only to deal with men.

Greenley arrived after dinner that evening, and Bella cracked open and read the letter right there in the courtyard as he stood tiredly by his sweating horse and Carlos played ball with Jamie. She looked up finally and said, "How did you find your mother?"

"Hale as ever, miss—your grace."

"No need to stand upon ceremony after all we have been through together, Greenley. You will have to decide which household you will attach yourself to."

"I wish to stay with you, miss."

"No reply is necessary," she said, folding the letter with finality. "As soon as you have tended to your horse, Maria will give you dinner. We will need your help in the morning to prepare for Lady Edith's visit."

"Yes, miss," Greenley said before leading his horse away.

Carlos looked an inquiry at her. "You are joking, Bella. The old she-devil is never coming here."

"Es *diabla?*" Jamie asked.

"No, she is not a devil, child. She is your grandmother, and you must treat her with respect, no matter how badly Carlos behaves," Bella replied, glancing at Maria's errant son. "Understand?"

"*Sí, madre*—yes, Mother."

"What will you do, Bella, another forced march?" Carlos grinned.

"Let her drive us from our home? Certainly not. We will be disgustingly polite to her."

"She seems to me a determined old she—woman."

"And I am a determined young one. There is nothing she can compel me to do."

"What about Phillipe?" Carlos asked.

"What about him?"

"If he is Jamie's legal guardian, it seems to me he could compel you to do many things, including surrender Jamie to him."

"But Phillipe would not. He is not the enemy."

Carlos made a pantomime of listening for guns, and Jamie laughed at the playacting. "Do you hear any boom-boom, Jamie?"

"Guns," Jamie corrected. "Not boom-boom."

"All right, the both of you," Bella said with a laugh. "So it is not a war. But we must use all of our skills to evade this old—Lady Edith's trap, so I am counting on you both to be on your best behavior."

"Your wish is my command," Carlos said with a sub-servient and exaggerated bow.

"Your wish is my command," Jamie mimicked, his bow sending Bella into gales of laughter.

"Very well. What shall we serve Lady Edith for lunch? Help me think of something," Bella said, thrusting the note into her jacket pocket.

"Roast piglets," Carlos teased as he tickled Jamie.

"No, no," Jamie protested, jumping up and down. "Not my piglets. Let us cook her something that is already dead."

"I can see I will get no sense out of either of you, so I am going to consult with Maria. In the morning, Carlos, you can ride into the village and see what can be had there."

"Foraging," Carlos said. "I am good at that. Want to come, Jamie?"

"*Sí*—yes, please."

"Only if you take the gig rather than Sebastian," Bella stipulated. "I do not want my son tossed on his head, not with his grandmother expecting to see him in one piece."

The dowager's entourage consisted only of Phillipe and Hal on horseback, an elaborate traveling carriage, and a coachman with two grooms riding post. Bella greeted the dowager with cool respect and Ann with unreserved warmth. She found herself plotting how she could get Ann alone for a long talk. Instead, she had to invite Lady Edith and Ann into the sitting room and offer them tea and the gentlemen an aperitif before luncheon. The dowager chose the only upholstered chair, staring about at the bare walls and rustic furniture with piglike alertness.

"And where is James?"

"James? Oh, Jamie. He and Carlos went into the village to see what was to be had in the way of fresh fish."

"And you just let him go off?" Lady Edith asked. "Without a footman or guard or anything?"

"Guard? But there are no French soldiers in England."

"Anything might happen to him," the dowager insisted.

"Carlos will be careful with him," Phillipe said. "He always is."

"Much he would care if something did happen," Lady Edith grumbled. "Another man's son."

"Carlos helped keep us safe through an entire war," Bella replied. "I think he can be trusted to take Jamie to the village and back."

Ann waited patiently for this interchange to reach a pause before she intervened. "Phillipe has told me so much about you, I feel I know you. Now that I recall, he did mention Captain Quesada's son in his letters. Carlos must be very devoted to leave his family and country to escort you to England."

"Maria is Carlos's mother. They were so kind to me and my mother in Portugal that when my father died, Edwin took them into his household. In return, Carlos vowed to Edwin that if anything happened he would see us safely settled in England."

The dowager cast Bella a sharp look. "If the woman really is a captain's wife, why would she be acting as a cook and nursemaid?"

"Maria is my devoted companion now. She does as

she wishes. Besides, she has married Rourke. Perhaps I will check with Maria about our lunch."

"The Duchess of Dorney does not run errands like a servant," the dowager said.

"No," Bella replied. "She does them like a duchess." So saying, she rose and left the room with her head held high.

"Well!" Lady Edith gasped.

"If you are wishing to reconcile," Phillipe warned, "so as to see your grandson, you are going about it the wrong way, *madam*."

"But this is so ramshackle! She has no staff here but this so-called companion of hers, her father's batman, and I do not care if they are married, as though that makes the situation respectable, and this young Spaniard. Whoever heard of such a thing?"

"Portuguese," Phillipe corrected.

"What?"

"Carlos and Maria are Portuguese. I promise you it was quite common in the Peninsula to have a reduced staff," Phillipe retorted. "Especially when they kept deserting and returning to England."

Ann patted the dowager's hand. "We must remember what Bella has been through."

"She has been through nothing like the hell I have suffered." Lady Edith stared out the window, willing the discussion to be at an end.

Hal looked up at this sullen silence on the part of his mother and passed his glass to Phillipe for a refill. "Not according to what Phillipe says. Some of his tales will stand your hair on end."

"Shut up, Hallowell. You know nothing about it."

Phillipe sighed tiredly. "If you ever want Bella to bring Jamie to Dorney Park, you will find an opportunity to apologize. Else she will not take your invitation seriously."

A rattle of wheels on gravel announced the arrival of the truants, and a moment later, Jamie flung open the door and rushed in with a large dead fish clutched under one arm and Lobo in hot pursuit. The dowager squeaked and Ann gasped with delight as Phillipe dove for Lobo's collar. The fish had been inadequately wrapped in butcher paper, but by the dead-eyed head and tail hanging out either end of the package, it was clearly a large pike.

Jamie paused momentarily, startled by so much company, and, seeing the dowager, clutched the fish even tighter and ran through into the kitchen. He was followed by a laughing Carlos, who eyed Ann with a flirtatious glance until Phillipe released Lobo and introduced them. Though Carlos kissed Ann's hand, it was Lady Edith he sat beside, prattling on about the village in a manner that drew her menacing stare upon him. Hal tried to catch Carlos's eye and warn him he was about to be blasted, but the boy rattled on as though the dowager could not kill with a look.

Bella reappeared. "I feel luncheon will be delayed until Maria and Rourke can dismember our prey and cook it. But at least all the guests have arrived. I suggest a stroll through the garden to work up an appetite."

"You have a garden?" the dowager demanded.

"Well, it is a vegetable garden rather than a rose garden, but a garden all the same."

"I do not care to go."

"Well, I want to see it," Ann said, rising and taking Phillipe's arm. "Come, Hal. If there is wine for lunch, you will need to clear your head."

"That is a good idea. I say, Carlos, can you show us the horses again? I barely got to look at them in London."

When the room had cleared, the dowager looked accusingly at Bella, who shrugged and took a seat next to hers.

"Not very subtle, are they?" Bella asked. "I take it we are supposed to make up our differences and be friends. How long will they allow us, do you think?"

"There is not enough time in the whole world," the old woman said bitterly.

"No, I suppose not. You never do forgive a fault. Edwin told me that."

"Do not quote my dead son to me."

"We do have one thing in common," Bella countered.

"And what is that?"

"Jamie," Bella answered with a glance toward the window.

"Do we? Is he really my grandson?"

Bella thought for a moment. "I am not at all sure I want him to be your grandson. And it is my choice, you see. If I once say he is not, you will never see him again."

"You would not dare whistle a fortune down the wind . . ."

Bella smiled at her, finally feeling that she had the upper hand. "What is money to me? I need very little. What is it good for, anyway? You can buy food or clothes with it. But you cannot buy time, loyalty, or love with it. And if you have too much money, someone is always trying to take it away from you."

"You talk like a simpleton. I believe you mean it."

"I mean everything I say." Bella stared into the dowager's eyes until the old woman looked away. "That, too, we have in common."

"I loved my son," she growled. "Do we have that in common?"

"I love my son."

"You evade my question."

Bella sat back in the chair. "I did not love Edwin when I married him. I grew to care for him."

"You married him because he was heir to a dukedom."

"No, I married him because he was the highest-ranking officer who would take me. Rank has privileges, you know. Do you wish to know my fate had I been orphaned with no senior officer about? The captains would have drawn lots for me."

The dowager gaped at her.

"I see I have shocked you, and I did not mean to. I had meant to be good, but I will not put on airs for you. You are determined not to like me, and I do not blame you. I do not curry your favor. But Jamie is without another blood relative in the world besides your family. If something were to happen to me, Carlos would be saddled with a child much too young to carry into the army with him. That is not a good prospect. It would be better if Jamie were to have a family."

"You will give me my grandchild, then?"

"Give him to you?" Bella spit out. "What do you mean by that, your grace?"

"Let him come to live at Dorney Park," Lady Edith corrected.

"Without me? You must be insane."

"I did not say without you." The dowager shot Bella a measuring look.

"But that is what you would prefer—do not bother to deny it. Lies do not become you."

"All because of those stupid letters. If you knew how I regretted them . . ."

"Your regret can scarcely be more than mine. I found them after Edwin's death. Only then did I understand why he was so reluctant to return home."

Lady Edith stared at her, a look of realization creeping over her flushed features. "But he did not . . . surely, he would never have . . ."

"What?" Bella asked impatiently.

"Did I kill my own son with those letters?" she demanded, her jaw trembling.

Bella looked into the desperate brown eyes, puzzling over the strange question, then realized whither the old woman's thoughts drifted. "No, never," she whispered, getting up and embracing Lady Edith as spontaneously as she would have comforted any grieving mother. "Edwin would never have thought of such a thing. And he did love you." Bella stood up then and moved to the window, but her eyes were quite dry.

"Do you forgive me for the letters . . . Bella?"

Bella turned with a tickling suspicion that the dowager was playing on her sympathy. Lady Edith's fear had been real, that she had driven her son to suicide, but with the strength of an assurance to the contrary at her back, had the dowager now gotten under Bella's guard?

"Forgive you?" Bella said lightly. "You had only to ask. Of course, I forgive you." Bella looked across the courtyard at the party now visiting the stables.

"Then you will both come to live at Dorney Park. I will tell Ann to have rooms prepared—"

"No."

"What did you say?"

"Forgiving is not forgetting. Jamie and I will live here. You may see him when you visit."

The dowager stood in stunned silence, her jaw working for all the world like that of a fish out of water.

Phillipe pushed the door open and carried a giggling Jamie in, casting a hopeful look at Bella. There was something so appealing in that look, as though she were determining his fate as well as her own. Perhaps that was why she felt she had to soften the blow to his aunt.

"We will, however, come for a visit to Dorney Park. A week should be enough to get acquainted."

"A week?" the dowager squawked.

"A fortnight," Bella replied.

"That is all settled, then," Phillipe said with genuine relief just as Maria announced lunch.

The party trooped into the small dining room and filled it. Although Maria and Rourke were serving rather than dining with them, and the coachmen and grooms were eating with the caretaker's family, Bella wondered what the dowager thought of their casual country manners. She half expected her to refuse some of the dishes that must be strange to her. But she tried everything, from the poached fish and olive bread to the chili sauce, and, so far as Bella could tell, ate a tolerably good meal.

Jamie made several unsuccessful attempts to convey his portion of fish to his mouth with his fork, and when that failed, he resorted to fingers.

Lady Edith shot Bella a menacing look. "It is not the custom to allow children at table at Dorney Park."

Bella grinned at the way Jamie's feast was arrested by the word *children*. His English was improving. Since Maria had never grasped much English, they were all in the habit of using Portuguese or Spanish in the household. It had never occurred to Bella that this would put Jamie at a disadvantage.

"Since you now have a three-year-old duke as the head of the family, you are going to have to make an exception in Jamie's case."

Jamie turned expectant brown eyes on the dowager to see what she would counter with, but she merely harumphed, so he went back to eating.

"Besides," Phillipe continued, "how will his table manners ever improve if he does not get to watch his elders?"

The dowager glared at Hal, who had just dunked a corn cake in the spicy sauce and was holding his head sideways under it so as not to lose a drop. "You are assuming his elders will be a good influence," she grumbled.

Phillipe chuckled, and Lady Edith turned her attention to Carlos, who ate ravenously and efficiently, using his knife and a piece of olive bread cake more than his fork. Bella wondered what the dowager made of Carlos and wondered why he had not yet provoked her ire. Perhaps because he would have laughed off any attack. And perhaps Lady Edith knew that Carlos taunted her with impunity just as Phillipe did. Bella decided she must master the trick of that.

The ladies rose from the table first, and Bella showed them to the guest bedchamber so that they could rest before their journey back to Dorney Park.

"I shall take a short nap," the dowager stated. "It will give you time to pack."

"Pack?" Bella asked. "We do not journey back with you."

"Why not?"

"I have matters to arrange here. Certainly, if Ann keeps house for you, she will want a day or two to prepare for our arrival."

"I will take the child on ahead with us," Lady Edith stated.

"No, for you would have no idea what to do with him if he woke up crying for Maria or me. You have had children. Surely, you remember how nerve-wracking it is to hear them cry for hours on end, knowing there is nothing you can do to comfort them. No, it would be entirely too hard on you to travel with a baby, let alone keep him in a strange house overnight."

"I suppose there is sense in what you say. Ann, draw those draperies so I can rest my eyes."

Bella left Ann to tend to Lady Edith but could not miss the wink the girl gave her as she closed the door on her. So it was possible to manage the dowager. No doubt Ann and Phillipe had done it all their lives.

~❧ 6 ❧~

$\mathcal{A}$s always at the beginning of a campaign, Bella was impatient for the expedition to start, halting her gray Andalusian mare to look back and make sure the last of the baggage had been tied down and Lobo had been induced to hop into the carriage with Jamie and Maria. Rourke would sit up front with the elderly coachman, while she, Carlos, and Phillipe rode. Greenley would lead the spare horses. Even though she was reluctant to leave her childhood home after struggling so hard to return to it, she had the comfort of knowing what it looked like, that all was well with it.

The coachman gave the order to start, and Bella looked back only once more, mentally promising to return in a few short weeks, long before the harvest. For this was not a military expedition with an unknown outcome. She was not dressed in rough clothes but in a forest green riding habit purchased in Paris. Her hair was caught up in a knot of ringlets under a fetching imitation of a forage cap, rather than trapped in a serviceable braid. It reminded her of the allies' successful march into Paris after Napoleon's first defeat in 1814. They had owned the city, and they had enjoyed it, the shops, the boulevards, the parks and museums. Edwin had a year of back pay to spend, and Phillipe had sent money from his father in England.

Edwin had never been so happy, and Bella had reconciled herself to a quiet and loveless marriage. She had not objected to the idea of taking up residence in Paris, though she had despaired at the thought of never seeing Phillipe again. At least she had expected to avoid the dowager.

Then Napoleon had escaped from his prison on Elba, and they had fled to Brussels as they waited for the armies to reform. She had had a bad feeling about the next battle and had tried to dissuade Edwin from going. But he was still an officer and had no choice. He was, in fact, excited at the prospect of beating Napoleon again.

His death among so many had hardly been noticed except by his own household. She kept wondering, if she had loved him better, would he have taken more care of himself? But he had been in the thick of the fighting. Of his entire brigade, only a handful had survived.

She forcibly shut the door on her past, hoping Phillipe was not aware of where her mind had drifted. She forced herself to smile, and when she looked at Phillipe, the face he turned to her was not full of concern but held a look of amused expectation. Rather than avoid talking to him, Bella felt it might be a pleasant way to pass the hours on the road. "It was considerate of the duchess to dispatch her traveling carriage with a fresh team on her return to Dorney Park." Bella tilted her head, inviting contradiction. "Or was that your work?"

Phillipe shrugged. "I had a word with Ann. Besides, it is your carriage now. If you were so minded, you could force Lady Edith to dwell elsewhere than Dorney Park."

"That would gain me no credit with anyone."

Phillipe's mouth twitched. "On the contrary, the servants might thank you for it."

Bella laughed outright. "And Hal might be allowed to turn into a man once out from under her thumb." She looked ahead at Carlos and Hal talking and laughing as they rode side by side. "Did she sit on Edwin like that and squash his pride?"

"You do not miss much. She tried, and sweet as Edwin was in some ways, he had a stubborn streak."

"Hal needs a grand tour. Perhaps we should send him off with Carlos. But you and Ann do not seem much cowed by her grace."

"She likes people who stand up to her."

Bella looked over at him. "I had surmised that. I think I may come to enjoy these little excursions to Dorney Park. It will seem like old times, us riding in a column. No drums, of course, but one cannot have everything."

Phillipe looked sharply at her, then used his crop to scratch the mane of the easy-stepping chestnut he was riding. "I do not want you to think I conspired to dislodge you."

Bella cast him a derisive look. "You did not influence me in the slightest. It was my decision."

"I was intending only to bring Ann to meet you."

"And Lady Edith rushed into the breach. I understand, and I thank you for your note of warning."

"It was the least I could do."

"I must admit, one of my reasons for coming is to better my acquaintance with your sister. I want to compare notes with her."

"About what?" Phillipe cast her a suspicious look.

"You, of course. I want to know if you have always been as quarrelsome as you have these last years."

Phillipe gaped. "I have not said one disagreeable thing . . ."

"I grant you have been on your best behavior today. Is it a great strain?"

"No!" he shouted. "I mean yes, with you baiting me like this. Have you any idea how difficult it is to hold a family together when a shrewish woman seems to be bent on rendering it asunder?" Phillipe's brown eyes looked earnestly at her.

"That depends on who the shrew is, me or Lady Edith."

"I was speaking of my aunt, of course."

"A moody woman. Impossible to predict what she will want from one moment to the next: to have a grandson or not to have a grandson. I place so little reliance on her good faith that I will never let myself be in her power. She is too capricious."

Phillipe looked thoughtful for a moment. "She is always sorry afterward."

"But too proud to admit her error and astute enough to lay a trap if one is not careful."

"I have seen her shed genuine tears," he assured her.

Bella looked at him. "So have I. That does not mean I trust her."

"What passed between the two of you while we were out walking?"

"Some frank speech. We do not agree on much, but we do agree it is better for Jamie to know his family now than come to them a stranger when he is of age."

"Surely you did not mean to let it go unresolved so long?" Phillipe's frown was genuine.

"What do you mean?"

"There are business matters that need to be settled."

"Who has been taking care of them up until now?" Bella asked.

"I have, and as executor I will continue to do so. I am responsible for Jamie . . . just as you are."

"Is that why you are so adamant about getting him to Dorney Park?" Bella admitted to herself some disappointment that Phillipe's attentions had nothing to do with her.

"The life of a duke is not a private one. There are unscrupulous men who would prey on both you and your son once your whereabouts are known."

"So the dowager was not being overly dramatic when she expressed concern about Jamie going with Carlos to the village?"

"No. When Edwin was twelve, an attempt was made to kidnap him. She has never forgotten."

Bella stared ahead at the road. "I am not sure I want Jamie to be a duke, then."

"That is beyond your control."

"Is it?" She toyed in her own mind with the sentence that would rid them of the troublesome dowager but would mean breaking her promise to Edwin.

"Do not do it, Bella," Phillipe warned with a pained expression on his face, as though he did not expect her to listen to him. "Do not even think of it."

"But to be always under guard. The life you are describing sounds more like that of a prisoner than of a duke."

"You have no right to throw your son's inheritance away. It is not your decision to make. What would Edwin think?"

"I do not know. Was that what his life was like in England? Always hedged about by guards? No wonder he would sooner face the French guns."

"That is not why he joined the army," Phillipe almost shouted, then kneed his horse and rode ahead, effectively ending the conversation.

Bella heard Carlos, who had dropped back to ride next to the carriage, say something in Portuguese to Maria about Bella making Phillipe angry again. Then Carlos laughed as though that were to be expected.

She should have known Phillipe's good humor would not last. But she knew why Edwin had really taken military service, for he had told her. Phillipe could know nothing of that, so why was he angry? Perhaps at her suggestion of removing Jamie from his power and effectively ending Phillipe's control of the Dorney estate. Phillipe's sudden interest in Jamie being the young duke was beginning to make sense to her. So long as Jamie was the heir, Phillipe controlled the family fortunes and would for many years. In those years, he could mold Jamie into the responsible man that Hal clearly was not. Was it all power and money, or did Phillipe's care go deeper? He clearly liked Jamie. And what of his initial accusation that she had married Edwin for his money? If he really believed that, he would not have defended her so hotly to the dowager.

She did not understand him, but she accepted Phillipe's complexity the way she accepted the simplicity of other men. Their motivations were mostly based on instinct, and once you understood that, unless they were in a battle frenzy, you could control them. But Phillipe always surprised her.

The night they had both thought they were going to die and she had reached out to him, asking for the thing she wanted most and was least likely to get in life, she had half expected him to scorn her entreaty. Instead he had fulfilled her desires to a degree that she thought would make all other men pale by comparison. These last two nights she had dreamed of their one encounter in the ruined house, of his hot flesh against hers, of the taste of him, the feel of his hair as she ran her hands through it.

She had hoped all those dark looks he had cast at her in the intervening years had not been resentment. Now she knew the truth. He had said it. He had loved her, coveted his cousin's wife. He had probably suffered because of it. He must have restrained himself just as tightly as she had, so as not to betray Edwin. Now there was nothing but a mourning period to stop him from marrying her. Yet his thoughts seemed to be only of Jamie, and he spoke of their love as some vague future possibility once the important matters of the estate were settled.

Did he realize Jamie was his son? Or did he only know it as a possibility? She could no longer sit on the fence on this issue, could not now retreat to the farm and pretend that it did not matter. It mattered very much to both Phillipe and Jamie, not to mention Lady Edith and Hal. If she kept quiet, she could have everything a woman could desire, but she was not any woman.

Everything that came to her came too late. And yet, when she thought about her life, there was very little she would now change. She had been a comfort to both her parents. There were many soldiers alive today who would not have been except for her nursing. And she had been very much desired by many men. That Phillipe had been one of them was not a new idea, but that she now knew he truly loved her mattered very much.

Yet could she let it affect what she thought was best for her and Jamie? When she had traveled with the army, she had been bound to play by its rules; first following her father's orders, then Wellington's after her father had been killed and the general demanded that she marry. Finally, she had obeyed Edwin when she believed Phillipe was dead. In truth, she had cared very little at that point in her life what happened to her. But now that she finally had control of her life, she must not lose it. And she must remember what she had promised Edwin in exchange for his name.

As their entourage passed under the entranceway into the courtyard, Phillipe looked at the huge pile of granite known as Dorney Park and thought, *Home*. It was built around a courtyard like a castle with the rooms all letting into one another. It was not only pos-

sible to get lost in the place but dead easy to evade
someone. He thought with a chuckle of how often he,
Edwin, Hal, and Ann had escaped Lady Edith within
its confines by merely slipping from room to room
ahead of her and then hiding under the furniture.
They had never had a tutor who could keep up with
them, and Ann's governess had never even tried to
find her.

Since Phillipe and Ann's mother had died young
and their father had been a military man, Dorney had
been the only real home he and Ann had known. And
because they were grateful, they had been much more
attentive to the whimsical duchess than her own children, and perhaps they knew her better. No, they were
not cowed by her—exasperated but not cowed. For she
said much she did not mean, threatened much she
never executed. And in her own fussy way, she loved
them. How he could explain this to Bella without
making it sound as if he was on Lady Edith's side was a
puzzle. Perhaps Ann could manage it.

Bella threw her leg over the pommels of her saddle
and slid off her mare before any of the corps of footmen could arrive to help her. She scanned in bewilder-
ment the huge mass of the house and cast a hopeless
look in Phillipe's direction. But Ann was there on the
doorstep, welcoming Bella with a kiss and a warm hug
to soften the cold and efficient reception of the staff,
Lady Edith's troops. No matter—Bella would win them
over. Philben, the arrogant butler, stiffened at the sight
of Lobo leaping out of the ducal carriage. The man did
not look much better pleased to see Jamie. But Ann
caught the child up and fussed over him, finally skip-

ping into the house with him. Bella looked hesitantly in Phillipe's direction, and he remembered that he had shouted at her for no reason she knew of. He forced a smile to his lips and came to take her arm and escort her into her new home. He suspected the dowager would receive them in state in the first-floor morning room adjacent to the ducal apartment. Hugs and kisses were not in her style. While Ann shepherded the travelers through the black-and-white tiled hallway and up the stairs to their quarters, he went to seek out Lady Edith.

To his surprise, she was not ensconced in her favorite overstuffed chair but standing by the tall windows overlooking the courtyard with a smile of triumph on her face. "You have brought them. I knew you could do it."

"No," Phillipe said patiently, laying his hat and crop on a side table. "Bella has brought Jamie for a visit. I think you might have greeted them."

"That is what I have Ann for. We shall have lunch in the large dining room. I want Bella—what is her given name?"

"Arabella, but I do not think—"

"I want Arabella to see what it means to be a duchess."

"You will not impress her, if that is what you are meaning to do. She has lived in castles before. They may have had half the roof caved in from cannon fire, but she is used to elegance. She simply does not prefer it. She does, however, think that she could come to enjoy an occasional visit to Dorney Park."

"Visit? She had damned well better get used to the idea of James living here."

"But a visit is what was agreed to. You had better remember that."

"Ah, I see your point. But how could she want to leave once she comes to know the place?" Lady Edith scanned the lovely room, and Phillipe found himself agreeing with her, but he knew Bella.

"We shall see. To that end, it would be politic for you to remove from the ducal apartment so that she can take her rightful place." Phillipe had no notion of actually dislodging the dowager but meant to push Bella's claim at every opportunity. By demanding far more than he knew he would get, he thought he could nudge Lady Edith into a grudging admission of Bella's rights.

"That I shall not do, not until I have the proofs I require." She pressed the tip of her walking stick firmly into the rich Turkish carpet.

Phillipe cleared his throat. "I am sure she has the certificates of marriage and birth that the lawyers will wish to see."

"Such proofs can be counterfeited."

"What start is this?" Phillipe demanded. "I thought you wanted your grandson. Or was Bella right? You want the child here but not her?"

"The child is young enough to forget his short past and be brought up to be the man his father should have been. Arabella is too set in her ways. Were she to leave the child here, she might live at her farm with my blessing."

"But that is monstrous!" Phillipe shouted. "You are asking her to abandon her son."

"To a better life, a life of ease and learning, a life—"

"Without her." Phillipe raked his **hands** impatiently

through his hair. "I knew you were selfish, but to plan to come between them to get the child to yourself . . . I will not be a party, madam, to any attempt, no matter how subtle, to part Bella from Jamie."

The dowager looked shocked. "Stop branding me a monster. I do not care if the girl visits. She may live here if she wishes, but she must be governed by me," Lady Edith said, punctuating the pronouncement with three jabs of her cane into the carpet.

"No. She should be mistress of Dorney now. You cannot accept the son and relegate the mother to an attic because she does not jump with your notions of what a duchess should be."

"She is too independent." The dowager shook her cane at Phillipe as if she were wielding a staff of command.

"Like you," he accused.

"I will not be shoved aside like a . . . like an old woman." She cast the walking stick from her angrily, and it clattered when it hit the polished oak floor.

"I am sure Bella has no such intention. But you must relinquish the position to her. The law is on her side . . . and so am I."

"And what are your intentions?" Lady Edith placed her hands on her ample hips as though she were scolding a child. "To step into Edwin's shoes by marrying Arabella and raising his son? If we are speaking of self-interest—"

He stared at her and realized that this was exactly what he planned to do. He turned on his heel and left the room, striding down the stairs and across the courtyard before an ache in his leg reminded him of the imprudence of walking so fast. The fact that he had fully intended to marry Bella someday made the dowager's accusation doubly galling. It was out of the question for a year, of course.

And as the executor of the estate and guardian of both Jamie's and Bella's interests, it would be unconscionable for him to push Bella into marrying him. It would look to the world as though she had been coerced. He walked the rest of the way to the stable more sedately. He could not saddle a horse and go pelting around the countryside to ride off his ill humor as he would like to. For one thing, it would not work. His ill humor seemed to sit on him like a flea on a dog, not to be shaken off for more than a moment. For another, he had to appear at this meal in order to lend some semblance of normalcy to the situation. It would be unfair to leave Ann to carry on alone.

He made the grooms nervous for a full twenty minutes as he inspected the accommodations being made for the new horses. As he had ordered, Sebastian was quartered at one end of the stable block surrounded by the mares. Phillipe conferred with both Greenley and Rourke, then gave the head groom one or two pointers to keep in mind when handling old studs. Rourke and Greenley were listening to Phillipe's remarks about keeping tempting mares away from Sebastian and not tolerating the stallion's pawing or other displays of ill humor. Rourke's smile and knowing look and the punch in the shoulder he gave Greenley sent Phillipe back to the house feeling somewhat abashed and more in control of his temper.

The entry from the courtyard was into the newest

wing of the house, and he found Jamie, quite alone, creeping down the marble steps, slipping his hand speculatively along the satin smoothness of the banister. Phillipe smiled in spite of his depression. "I would not recommend it for a ride," he said kindly to the boy. "I tried it once, and it almost unmanned me. You see, there is a finial on the newel post at the end."

Jamie stared around at the ornament, looked at Phillipe, and nodded his agreement with the advice. "Phillipe?"

"Yes, Jamie." Phillipe took the child's hand and led him toward the large dining room.

"What is a valet?" The little blond head tilted much in Bella's manner as the child looked up at him.

"A personal servant. Since you are a duke, I think you might need one to do your laundry and iron your clothes."

"Oh, like a batman. Like Rourke." Jamie gave a little skip to keep up with him.

"Just like Rourke." Phillipe picked him up when he realized how far it was to the dining room, measured in Jamie's tiny steps.

"What is a duke?" the boy asked, reaching his arms around Phillipe's neck.

Phillipe sought the answer that would lead to the least new questions. "A man with lots of servants."

"Like a general?"

"Yes, but without the shooting."

"Was Father a duke?"

"Yes he was, and you are a duke, too."

"But I want to be a soldier like you."

Phillipe felt Jamie's small hand laid flat against his

cheek, and his heart jerked inside him. "I thank you for the compliment. But you can be both, you know. Wellington is a duke and a soldier."

"No, I want to be like you."

Phillipe hugged him, not trusting himself to say anything more. At the time the war was happening, his chief fear had been for Jamie and Bella's physical safety. He realized now there had been more at stake than that. He carried in his arms a child who took as a matter of course that he might be awakened out of a sound sleep in the middle of the night, with shooting and explosions all around him, bundled into a wagon or taken up onto a horse, and wake up miles away from any place he had ever known.

He was a child without a home in a very real way. At least Bella had her memories of England. Jamie had only the deserts and mountains of Spain and Portugal or the fields of France and Belgium. He knew nothing of England and probably had no expectation that things would be any different, since he had slept in two beds the three nights he had spent here and had indeed spent part of one night on a horse.

There was nothing Phillipe could say to make the boy realize that life could be better. All he could do was show him day after day what it was like to lead a settled existence, to be able to count on something.

Ann grinned at Bella on the stairs as they waited for Phillipe and Jamie to get ahead of them. "After luncheon I will give you a tour of the house so you do not get lost. Your rooms are in the original hall."

"I could tell by the unevenness of the floors and ceilings," Bella confessed, swallowing the sadness of all the days Phillipe had not been with Jamie. "They are charming rooms, and they remind me of the farm."

"I thought they might." Ann smiled at her, and it was then that Bella could see the most resemblance to Phillipe.

"The nursery and schoolroom are directly above," Ann said. "The two ends of the house were added in 1780, and the arches across the courtyard with the stable block and the large drawing room were put up in 1804."

"I can get the whole way to the stable without ever getting wet. That will come in handy if I am poulticing one of the horses."

"Oh, but you would not—" Ann chewed her bottom lip in confusion.

"Would not be poulticing a sprained hock?" Bella asked. "Perhaps not. I have a feeling there are a great many things I should not be doing. I rely on you to set me straight. Are you sure this gray dress is all right?"

"Yes, the black ribbons are enough. You look good in gray and black."

"Fortunate for me, since I spend so much time in those colors."

Ann cast her a worried glance.

"I have mourned—still mourn for every soldier lost in that war. And Edwin, in so many ways, just a large boy, he was the worst of my griefs. But I did save a few lives, and for that I must be grateful."

"Phillipe was one of them?" Ann asked hopefully.

"Yes, but sometimes I do not think he is glad." Bella smiled at the disbelieving look Ann cast at her. "Come, we do not wish to be late."

Jamie was already seated at the head of the table on a large book Phillipe had fetched from the library next door. Bella laughed when she saw her son presiding over such a vast and serious-looking table. Would Jamie grow quite spoiled by all this pomp? she wondered.

To Bella's disgust, the dowager once again made a show of rejecting the soup and the first three dishes that were shown to her. She pasted a resigned smile on her face and waited, but Jamie, though patient enough when he knew there was no food to be had, was patently angry at having so many perfectly good plates of food wafted under his nose and then pulled away again. The adults sat through the dowager's monologue on the inadequacies of the fare in their own fashion, Carlos rolling his eyes occasionally, Phillipe staring at Lady Edith, Ann sending apologetic glances toward Bella, and Hal tapping his fingers in an annoying fashion.

Finally Jamie turned to Carlos and said quite distinctly in perfect English. "She is a she-devil."

Carlos burst out laughing, and Phillipe's eyes glittered merrily. Ann looked on Jamie with amazement as the dowager scowled.

"Just what is that supposed to mean?" the old woman asked.

Bella rose from the table and picked up Jamie. "That you are a cruel person to be making a hungry child wait for his dinner just to puff up your consequence."

"Where do you think you are going?"

"I am taking Jamie to the kitchen, where I am sure we can come by an excellent meal, for you have just sent one back there."

"You would not dare," the dowager warned.

"I would *dare* anything, your grace. Ask Phillipe."

The dowager's beetling gaze fell on her nephew, and Phillipe nodded. "Bella has crossed enemy lines to get food for Jamie. She will certainly invade the kitchen."

The dowager nodded at the next thing presented to her and had a portion put on Jamie's plate.

Bella put her son back in his chair, and a footman pushed Jamie up to the table with a smirk. Bella solemnly sat down and indicated that she wanted some of the fish.

"Are you going to discipline him?" Lady Edith asked.

"The child is little more than three. He says what he is thinking. That is more honest than just thinking it," Bella said.

The rest of the meal passed in relative peace. When Jamie looked to be full and about to fall asleep, Bella excused herself to carry the child to Maria.

"Is she coming back?" the dowager finally asked.

"I have no idea," Phillipe admitted.

"We are having guests to dinner tonight. Mr. George Thackery and his sister Miranda. Their father, Reverend Thackery, is invited as well, but he seldom comes to dine."

"I wonder why," Phillipe said innocently, drawing his aunt's glare.

~❧ 7 ❧~

"**W**here were you?" Phillipe asked a few hours later as he overtook Bella in the home wood. Her cheeks bloomed with color, and her eyes flashed a challenge at him when she looked at him from under her flat black Spanish hat.

"Walking off my anger."

"If you are feeling overheated, we have a substantial lake." Phillipe gestured toward the body of water, visible down the path. "You could always go for a swim."

Bella smiled and took his breath away. "And you would guard my clothes, I suppose. I have already been around the lake."

He opened his mouth and hesitated, wondering for the first time if she had been aware of his stolen glimpse of her bath so long ago. "Only you could take a four-hour ride, sit through a dull lunch, and need a five-mile hike to work off your excess energy."

"I have been reconsidering my position."

She unfurled the fan she carried and plied it, causing the loose tendrils of hair in front of her ears to frolic in the warm breeze. Phillipe blinked to try to clear his head.

"Do not burn any bridges. This is only your first day here."

"Who can guess what other tortures she has in store for Jamie? It is one thing for her to taunt adults, but to be spiting a child . . ."

Phillipe exhaled tiredly. "Do you mean to flee again? For I am getting tired of chasing you."

Her wide, ready smile reappeared. "As it happens, I only mean to change my mind about him eating with us. I have told Maria that she can feed Jamie when it is convenient. I will not see him as much, but there will be fewer altercations with Lady Edith."

They had by now left the naturalized woodland and gained the stone path through the formal gardens. Phillipe hesitated so long that Bella prompted him. "What is the matter?"

"Lady Edith has hinted that it might be better for Jamie to be exposed to English-speaking servants for a time." Phillipe finally dared to glance at her profile. He had seen that look before, when they were besieging the French at Ciudad Rodrigo.

"So, she wants to send Maria and Rourke away," Bella concluded, the corners of her mouth drawn into a thoughtful frown.

"You have to admit there is some justice in what she says," Phillipe countered, breaking a rose from the trellis and offering it to Bella.

She took it by the stem, then cradled the bloom in her other hand. "I will take care of Jamie myself, then."

"Between the nursery maid and his valet, I think they can manage."

She stared at him, her lips compressed in frustration. "Valet? What does a three-year-old need with a valet?"

"Would you have us discharge old Timms, the duke's valet?"

"You mean than ancient scarecrow of a man has been inherited by Jamie? How is he supposed to keep up with a boy? What can they have in common?"

Phillipe became conscious of the sheen of sweat on his brow and finally wiped it with the back of his hand. "I am sure there is much Timms can teach him."

"Jamie is a little young to be learning how to tie neck clothes or dip snuff."

Scrambling from one indefensible position to another, Phillipe said, "Lady Edith also wishes to engage a tutor for Jamie."

"That tears it." Bella smacked the flower against Phillipe's shoulder, and all the petals trickled down his sleeve. "Phillipe, this has ceased to be a pleasure jaunt. She is acting as though we are permanently entrenched. I cannot find space for a valet and a tutor at the farm. As soon as the fortnight is up, we are leaving. And she had better get used to the idea." Bella paced rapidly down the walk toward the back door of the house.

Phillipe strode to keep up with her. "I know that, and by then Rourke will have fortified the farm well enough to make it a safe home for Jamie. Bella, wait." Phillipe reached for her arm, and she turned in his grasp to stare at his hand as though it had committed a mortal sin. When he let go of her, she looked him in the eye.

"Fortified? I feel as if I am still at war. I suppose we must erect another cottage to house all the extra staff, the child's Praetorian guard, no doubt."

"As a matter of fact, I was going to suggest some such thing. The estate will bear the cost of the improvements, of course."

"Did Rourke fall for this ruse?" Bella had her hands on her hips, angry but not yet dangerously so.

"No, he surmised that the old witch wanted rid of him and Maria. I heard him giving Greenley pretty specific instructions on watching out for you." Phillipe smiled nervously.

"So Rourke does not trust you, either?"

"Either? I thought you believed in me. I only want what is best for you and Jamie."

"But do you really know what that is?"

Her gaze bore into him as though she were reading his soul. As much as he wanted to look away, he knew it would be fatal to do so. "I know a great deal more about England and what it means to be a duke than you do."

"I do not want this kind of life for me or my child." Bella spun and started for the house again.

"You must make some concessions for the sake of his safety. And you cannot win against the dowager." Phillipe followed her up the steps haltingly. "You simply have to wait for her to come to the rational point of view and think she got there on her own."

She turned at the top and waited for him, her eyes looking a shade less as if they would slice him in two. "How long does this usually take?"

"Depends on how much she thinks you want something. How important is it for you to win against her on any of these matters?"

Bella tapped her booted foot impatiently. "I see your point. So long as I do not make an issue of something, so long as I do not seem to attach any importance to a position, she has nothing to fight with me about. I will consider my war has been won when my enemy is my ally. But there is far too much in the way for that to happen."

Bella moved to open the door, but a liveried footman obsequiously threw it open for her, and she shook her head impatiently, hurrying toward the bottom of the stairs.

"I am supposed to tell you we are having company for dinner tonight," Phillipe called after her.

"Was she afraid I would turn up in an apron and mob cap?" Bella looked over the banister at him.

"She just wanted me to warn you."

"I am happy to hear we are to have company. Perhaps she will behave."

Phillipe heard Bella's assertive stride in the upstairs hall, then the door to her room open and shut with such force the timbers shook.

Ann peeked into the withdrawing room and, finding only Phillipe there, breathed a visible sigh of relief. "Well, brother, do you think the horrors of the evening will exceed those of the day?"

"I do own to some reluctance to introduce any company to the volatile combination of Aunt Edith in a temper and Bella when she has been backed into a corner. Hence the double brandy before dinner. If I am too numb to notice what happens, give me a full report in the morning."

"Is it you who have Bella in a corner?" Ann arched an eyebrow at him. "The better to steal a kiss?"

"The better to get my face slapped, the mood she is in now."

"But you do love her," Ann stated matter-of-factly as she expertly rearranged the flowers in a vase.

Phillipe stared at his sister so long she shook her head and came to take his hand.

"Am I that obvious?" he asked.

"No, only I who know you well can read the signs. You are off your feed. You would in fact poke and torture any food put on your plate without realizing what it was. You sigh at odd times and stare through walls as though you are in another world."

"I . . . I am sorry."

"I am not," she said, looking up into his face earnestly. "It is time you found someone."

"What about you? Are you coming to London when we go to settle things?"

"What would I do in London? I have enough to occupy me here. Besides, I have nothing to wear."

"It is Thackery and his sister who are coming tonight. Does Thackery still court you?"

"Not in a serious way."

"Given up, has he?"

Ann wrinkled her delicate brow. "No, I think rather that he is so sure of me he feels he does not have to assert himself. I said I had no wish to leave Dorney Park, and he replied that he would not be averse to living here."

"Not averse?" Phillipe blustered. "I should say not. You do not seriously mean to have him, do you?"

"I think after tonight Thackery will be more of a worry to you than to me." Ann tapped Phillipe's chest with her fan as she walked by him.

"What the devil do you mean?"

Bella threw open the door to the room and drifted across to Phillipe, the black satin of her dress gleaming in the candlelight like the silken fur of a lithe cat. A Spanish comb now adorned the topknot of curls, and a silver locket was her single ornament. A lace shawl completed her outfit. She had broken no convention, but she did not look like a woman in mourning.

"What do you think, Phillipe?" Bella asked, spinning in front of him. "Am I fit for company?"

Phillipe swallowed his mouthful of brandy and coughed before he could find his voice. "I think you will surprise the dowager."

Ann laughed. "You will surprise everyone."

"Ann, you are sweet. Phillipe, Ann will not wear the gowns I bought in Paris, and I cannot wear the brighter ones while I am in mourning. They will be out of fashion in another year, never having been worn at all."

Phillipe looked from one to the other of the women. "You are much of a size. This solves the problem of what Ann is to wear in London."

"Then we do have to go back there?" Bella asked.

"Yes, eventually, when it is time to put our affairs in order."

Carlos and Hal came in talking about horses and paying no obvious attention to Bella or Ann. Then the Thackerys arrived. They were both in their twenties, pleasant-faced and brown-haired. The girl, Miranda, sent Bella an appraising look. But George Thackery literally gaped at Bella. He looked like a veal calf that had just been dealt a stunning blow with a hammer.

Bella brushed off his belated stammered greeting and asked him about his studies. Phillipe had seen her do this a thousand times—take a raw recruit who was agape at her poise and beauty and put him at his ease. By the time Lady Edith descended, Thackery no longer gaped but greeted her with his usual flattering drivel.

When Lady Edith approved every dish that was set before her, Phillipe sent Bella a smile, but her rueful look said that the dowager was not being gracious for her benefit but for the Thackerys'.

"I think we have found a position for George," Lady Edith said.

"Indeed, your grace?" the young man asked. "Are you going to give me the curate's living at Whitchurch?"

"We can speak of that another time. What I have in mind is tutoring my grandson, James."

Bella raised an eyebrow at this admission of kinship.

"I would be most honored to instruct him and prepare him for school."

"Let us not push the chick out of the nest too soon," Bella said. "Jamie is only three. I think he is too young to need a tutor."

"Oh, but I could do something with him," Thackery insisted.

"Teach him English, for one thing, and his numbers," the dowager ordered.

"Jamie can count up to fifty," Carlos said.

"Fifty?" Thackery asked.

"That's how many men were in our company," Carlos returned.

Bella laughed in spite of Phillipe biting his lip.

"When can I meet the child prodigy?" Thackery asked.

"Tomorrow we lunch alfresco," the dowager promised. "Do come."

"I shall not know how to talk to a duke so young," Thackery said with a smile. "What if he misbehaves? How does one discipline a duke of the realm?"

"I hardly think an infant is in need of discipline," Bella said at this latest criticism of her child.

Phillipe tried to catch her eye, to warn her not to start an argument over such a trifle.

"When Edwin was the heir, he carried himself like a duke from the day he was put in short coats," Lady Edith said as she dug into a serving of veal and ham pie. "Even when those scoundrels tried to abduct him, he did not cry but shouted for help like an adult."

"Someone tried to kidnap your son?" Miranda asked.

"Years ago. That is why I sent footmen along with him to school. It would have cost us a fortune to ransom him."

Bella finally saw Phillipe's speaking look and hesitated before saying, "How medieval."

Lady Edith stared at her, not knowing how to take the comment. "That is why Jamie needs reliable servants about him," the dowager said.

"And that is what he has always had," Bella stated.

"But someone who has no other job than to watch out for him," the dowager insisted.

Bella had opened her mouth to reply when Phillipe

bumped his wineglass and then caught it with the same hand without spilling a drop. He was not quite sober, but his reactions, even when drunk, were better than those of any sober man. She suddenly came to a realization of the tightrope he had been walking between the two of them. Perhaps his counsel on not arguing with the dowager had been meant well, or perhaps he was only trying to get what he wanted, her capitulation, without creating a scene. She was just going to have to decide in her own mind how far she was going to let things go before she balked. So long as there was no permanent harm, she would let the dowager run her length. But if Thackery ever raised a hand to Jamie, she would shoot the upstart tutor someplace in his anatomy that would serve as a permanent reminder that she was in charge.

Except for watching Phillipe play cards with the other three men, the evening in the drawing room left Bella feeling out of place. Phillipe played well, though he cared little for the game. Hal bet on the most forlorn hope. Thackery really concentrated but could not count the cards. And *he* was supposed to teach Jamie his numbers. Carlos, though half-sprung, played with his usual flair, so he was the winner for the night.

The dowager played one game of backgammon with Miranda, who lost stupidly and ineptly. They were, however, not treated to any crowing on the dowager's part. Apparently she did not value her win over Miranda as much as she had the one over Bella. Ann played the pianoforte, and Bella stood behind her and watched, trying to make sense of the notes on the page. Bella could carry a tune but had never learned to read music and envied Ann that one thing. She had a feeling something so fine as music could not be learned by observation. But perhaps it was not past mending. It would give her employment to see if Ann would teach her.

She realized with a shock that she no longer had an occupation. There were no more wounded to take care of. If she were at the farm, she would at least have the crops and livestock to fuss over. Here her only value was in being Jamie's mother, and considering the number of servants competing to take care of him, she felt even that role growing smaller.

Bella wondered if Phillipe felt this same strange detachment after the war, this lack of purpose. She glanced at him and discovered he had been watching her, not with his usual scowl but with a hungry look that triggered a powder flash of desire for him. The heat of it ran through her like a strong dose of brandy, leaving her feeling warm and comfortable. She felt as though she had completed a long march and taken a fragrant bath and was now waiting in her tent for . . .

Carlos laughed, and she looked away from Phillipe, hoping she was not blushing and that no one had seen her look so needy. But Carlos merely remarked on Phillipe's blunder at cards. Phillipe was smiling sheepishly and sent her a helpless look that coiled the knot of desire even tighter in her stomach.

When Ann was clearly finished with music for the night, Bella left the drawing room with the excuse of saying good night to Jamie. The stairs in the old part of the house groaned pitiably as she made her way to the nursery. Janet, the young maid given nursery duty, was reading to Jamie but went to her adjoining bedroom to give Bella a moment alone with her son.

Jamie was not asleep but not full of questions either. She held him quietly, and he went to sleep in her arms. She had been separated from him and Maria once for two days, and now he could not go to sleep unless he had seen her. The world had broken faith with him in so many ways, and he no longer trusted that she would come but had to wait for her. And she knew from her own experiences what terrors filled those waiting hours.

She had wanted always security for her son, but now that it was within reach, she wondered if she had miscalculated. It was her Jamie needed, and a father, not a house and a corps of servants. Of course, if she told the truth, that would mean uprooting him once again. But if she were going to do it, she had better act soon, before he got used to Dorney Park.

She heard the stairs creak ominously and waited expectantly until the door cracked open. Phillipe appeared and smiled at her, trying to tiptoe across the room.

"With the state of the floors, this house keeps few secrets," Bella said.

"I cannot move about as silently in it as I did as a boy. I have not the patience."

"Phillipe, are you sure this is what is best for Jamie? I have nothing to compare it with."

He sat on the bed and regarded the sleeping child. "He will never know want. Men will look up to him. He will have the best education . . ."

"But is that enough?"

"He will have you and me . . . and if we ever get

around to thinking of ourselves, we might be able to provide him with a brother or sister."

"Something is missing, but I do not know what. I try to picture a family, a happy family, but I have the most profound dread that it is not to be, that something stands in our way."

"The war is over," Phillipe said with a tired sigh. "What could possibly happen to us now?"

"I do not know. I have no experience of peace, you see, so that I am more suspicious of it than war."

He reached across the sleeping child to lay a gentle hand on her shoulder. "Perhaps I can contrive to improve your expectations. New experiences are not always unpleasant."

"No, but the anticipation of them is," Bella said. "I should be looking forward to tomorrow. Instead I look back to what we have passed through. That is all we hold for certain."

"You will feel differently after a year, believe me."

"I trust you, Phillipe, but, forgive me, I cannot quite believe you yet, that everything will be all right."

"Do you want to go for a walk?"

"Yes, but I need to stay with Jamie this time. I never had to choose between you before. It will take me some time to make space for you in my life. Forgive me."

"I understand." He left the room as silently as he could.

He left her wanting him, uncertain of herself, and not knowing what to do about it. But he did not laugh at her or chide her for her foolishness. So he had been through this himself.

* * *

" 'Do come,' " Bella quoted Lady Edith to her horse as she saddled the stallion for a dawn ride. She was wearing her scarlet riding habit because it reminded her of a time when she had felt competent and in control. Never mind that she had been in danger. She almost missed Spain. She could have done without France and Belgium, but Spain and Portugal she had genuinely liked.

"The Thackerys are coming for a picnic," she told Sebastian. "What a high treat. I wish I had been less kind to Mr. Thackery. I think he will hang about the place like an ivy vine, hardly to be got rid of except with an ax."

Greenley's tousled head appeared from the loft, and he hastened to button his coat when he saw Bella standing on tiptoe to put a bridle on Sebastian. The horse dipped his head, as eager for a gallop as she was.

Greenley was wearing his batman's uniform rather than the blue livery of the household. "Miss? You should have said you wanted a horse saddled. But Sebastian? I mean, I know you can ride him, but I must come along."

"Well, if you mean to come, saddle Altamira. She needs exercise, too."

Bella accepted a leg up from Greenley and managed to keep Sebastian in check until Greenley had gotten the mare out of her stall. Then the war horse started pawing the plank floor and carving up splinters with every stroke.

"I am going to start. I mean to follow the trail around the lake. I must take the edge off him before he tears the stable block down."

"But, miss . . ." Greenley argued feebly as he bitted the mare, then ran for the saddle.

At night, a wooden gate closed off the entrance to the courtyard. Rather than dismount to move the heavy thing, Bella put Sebastian at it and jumped it, launching into the gold-green world of late summer as though this were the last day left to her before she was to be locked away in prison. Out of the corner of her eye she caught a flash of blue at the window of the morning room. Had one of the servants been watching her? Ah, well, too late to worry over that now. Best not to think beyond the joy of the moment. She was more used to doing this with an occasional glance over her shoulder to make sure there were no French after her. She had been captured by the French once herself, but the memory was not a bitter one. She smiled as she thought back on her escape and eased the reins to let Sebastian have his head a little

Typically wagons and carts of wounded were let go unhindered by either side unless a town had been stormed. But the French officer who had detained her had other things on his mind than prisoners. He had, in fact, let the cart of wounded go on its way with the Portuguese cart boy to guide it and had taken her onto his saddle before him. "*Interroger*," he had said. Questioning. Even then, Bella had been sure he had something other than questions to put to her, but she had had the foresight to feign ignorance of French.

She had observed as much as she could on the way to the French encampment. He had thrust her into his tent and placed a guard. She had searched his belongings and found a heavy pistol, which she hid under the mattress, but no ammunition. He had, in fact, questioned her later in his painfully broken English, which was so much worse than her French that she was almost prompted to confess that she did know his tongue. Then he kissed her, and she had feigned confusion, fear, shy interest, then flirtation. She had run the gamut, and it was not even hard to convince him of her sincerity, of her attraction to him. Still, she hoped to throw him off his guard.

The memory of her desperate deceit made her glance over her shoulder, but the figure that pursued her on horseback was a man in a blue coat, not a red one. So it was not Greenley. Without thinking she pressed her left knee into Sebastian, and he shot forward, gleefully stretching every muscle in his powerful body. At full gallop she took the trail about the lake, breathing fast as the horse kicked up clods of mud and joyfully leaped a log in the way. The thunder of hooves from behind was gaining, and she took another brief look. He was mounted on her mare. It was the blue coat that had made her think *French*, but it was Phillipe. She could tell because of the long stirrups.

She laughed and set Sebastian at a rock outcropping, which he jumped with ease. Where the woods opened up, she abandoned the lake and rode full tilt onto completely unknown ground. It might as well have been Spain for all she cared. After another half mile, Sebastian's measured breathing reined in her rampant spirits, and she guided him into the denser growth, bringing him to a circumspect trot.

Phillipe cantered past, and she chuckled, then gave chase until he turned his head. A grin split his face. She laughed, for he might have been angry, but he was not. She turned Sebastian and walked him back the way they had come.

"You are the maddest girl. I nearly overshot you." Phillipe brought the mare to a walk, and Bella was glad to see that she was still spirited and not sweating much at all.

"She carries you well. Would you like to keep her?" Bella asked.

"Do you mean it?" Phillipe looked amazed.

"Of course, I mean it. She has been bred to Sebastian, you know. The foal will come in the spring."

"A double gift." Phillipe patted her neck. "But why? I thought you were angry with me."

"I bought her for you. When you were shipped—left for England last year, you were in no position to do anything about horses." Bella almost dreaded bringing up his last wound, but no thundercloud darkened his brow.

"No, flat on my back in a ship's cabin. What is her name again?"

"Altamira."

"Strange and foreign and wonderfully exotic." He tilted his head. "Like you."

"I do feel more Spanish than English. Perhaps I cannot really rest in any one place again. I have been too long a vagabond soldier."

"Life needs to be a mixture of journeys and homecomings to be able to appreciate both." She saw Phillipe sigh and look around him at the woods. He liked it here, and for that she envied him.

"I felt at home in the army, wherever our camp was, the same friendly faces."

"Except the morning they almost shot you," Phillipe reminded her.

"I was just thinking about my narrow escape from

the French camp. Lucky you came upon me and helped me discard that French uniform."

"Luck had nothing to do with it. I had been looking for you all night."

Bella halted Sebastian and stared at him. "Really? Did my father ask you to help?"

"No, he had already turned down my offer for your hand. He would hardly have turned to me when you came missing, even though he was my commander."

Bella let the stallion walk on and touch noses with Alta. "Father did not always make the best decisions."

"He thought he was looking out for your best interests. He warned me away from you in the most explicit way. Of course, with a duke's son as competition . . ."

"I do not think that was it. He just did not want to be alone. Selfish, I suppose. I do wish I had known you wanted me back then. I always felt you were beyond my reach."

"Why?" Phillipe asked.

"Because you were not a foolish boy, like so many of them—like Edwin. You were a man, and you took the war seriously."

"So, if I had said anything at all to you . . . Why did I let him drive me away?"

"Because you are a man of honor. What else could you do?"

Phillipe shrugged. "I heard later you left the French captain tied naked to his bed. You never said if that was true."

"Well, he was unconscious and tied, but not to his bed. The rest of it is true." Bella gave one of her quick flashing smiles and urged Sebastian into a discreet parade trot.

Phillipe laughed as he kneed Alta into a trot. For the first time in many months, his leg felt fine, and so did he. He had brought her home to Dorney Park. Now he just had to keep her here.

Phillipe followed as Bella let Sebastian choose a path through the woods. They came out in a clearing, a small meadow rife with daisies. She halted the horse but did not dismount, waiting expectantly for him to lift her down. He slid off Alta and performed this service for Bella, not letting go of her once he had set her on the ground.

She felt warm and vital in his arms, and he bent to kiss her, tentatively at first, in case she might have second thoughts. But she tipped her head back and was as bold, as hungry about exploring his mouth as he was hers. Her hands also were not shy, stealing inside his coat to run over the muscles of his back as though trying to make sure he was real. When she paused for breath, he kept her captive in a crushing embrace.

"My Phillipe," she whispered. "I have dreamed of this, but I never hoped . . ."

"I am sorry Edwin is dead," he said, apologizing for being happy.

"Do not think about it," she warned. "Do not even speak."

He kissed her savagely and picked her up, looking about for the best place to lie with her. But Sebastian's head came up, and so did Alta's. When he heard the hoofbeats, he let Bella slide from his arms to stand on her own feet. She gave an impatient sigh of disappointment.

"It must be Greenley," she said. "God save us from faithful servants." She picked a few daisies as he watched her. If only his need could be put aside as easily as hers.

After Greenley's apologetic entrance, Phillipe helped Bella back onto the horse, and the abashed groom kept a respectful distance behind.

When the lake came into sight again, Phillipe watched Bella halt the horse and look out over the mist-shrouded water. A gray heron was fishing the shallows, and the night sounds of frog and cricket were still echoing about them like a comfortable blanket. How could Bella not love it here? He halted the mare beside the war horse. Bella was normally shorter than he, but the extra inches of Sebastian put her at eye level with Phillipe. "It is beautiful, admit it," he said.

"I could like the grounds, and the lake, of course. But will I be able to come and go as I please, like this morning?"

Phillipe grinned. "Not without Greenley losing a lot of sleep."

"Phillipe, what is to become of me? I need work, and they will not even let me open a door for myself or saddle my own horse. If they catch me sewing on so much as a bead, I get reprimanded. I cannot live like this."

"I know. Perhaps in time you will become gruff enough to keep the servants at bay."

"Like Lady Edith? God forbid. I am used to being friends with the people who work for me."

"We will find a way. Just as you need both journeys and homecomings, you need a middle ground between adventure and safety. Trust me."

Bella inhaled, and Phillipe was keenly aware of the

damp scents of water plants and the lap of water against the shore.

Bella turned her smiling face to him. "You love this place. I can see it in your face. But Jamie and I do not."

"You could learn to feel at home at Dorney Park, learn to love it for my sake."

Across the mist-shrouded water, above the quack of duck and peep of frog, carried the shrill scream of Dowager Lady Edith upbraiding a servant.

Bella cast a speculative look at Phillipe. "I doubt it."

Bella and Phillipe came into the breakfast parlor laughing and surprised Ann over her morning tea. "You two are up early."

"Not really," Bella said. "If this were a marching day, we would have been two hours on the road by now."

"Can I hope that Aunt is breakfasting in her room?" Phillipe asked.

"Yes, but she wants to see you," Ann warned, looking over her teacup at him.

"Damn. Well I will not face the Gorgon on an empty stomach." Phillipe loaded a plate and sat next to his sister. "How do you bear with her?"

"She never shouts at me," Ann said. "I am her only ally."

"But why shout at anyone?" Bella asked as she buttered a muffin.

"I think she would be unhappy if everything went well," Ann said.

"That is absurd," Phillipe replied with his mouth full.

"No, I believe it," Bella agreed. "Some people enjoy

conflict. I used to think that was a male trait, but I am revising my opinion."

Other than casting her a suspicious look, Phillipe said nothing and kept on eating.

Ann nodded in agreement.

"What does she want to see me about?" Phillipe asked, trying to redirect the conversation. "I am sure you know, and if you have an ounce of compassion, you will tell me rather than sending me to her unprepared."

"She wants to know if you have persuaded Bella to overstay the fortnight."

"Indeed?" Bella raised an eyebrow. "I have been meaning to speak to you about a permanent schedule for our visits."

"Schedule?" he asked, his teacup arrested halfway to his mouth.

"Yes, like an agreement. Here, I have written them down. We will come for the holidays, of course, and one month in the summer."

"Two months altogether?" Phillipe asked. "Is that all?"

"We could come sometime in the fall," Bella conceded.

Ann looked at the list. "Aunt goes to London from February to May and then to Brighton in August and September."

"Then we could come in October," Bella offered.

Phillipe's brow was furrowed in thought. "This is so . . . almost like a treaty."

"Yes, that is it," Bella said. "I wish to make a treaty, and you will negotiate it for me. I knew I could count on you."

"But what about her plan to have Thackery tutor Jamie?" Ann asked.

Bella pressed her lips together. "I am trying to nip that in the bud. The man is a boor. I do not see how he can teach a small child."

A footman burst into the room and was about to apologize for interrupting Phillipe's breakfast when Phillipe replied, "I am coming now." He rose and kissed Ann's cheek, then Bella's, before making his escape.

Anne raised her eyebrows. "My brother is in a good mood. Let us hope Aunt does not change that."

"What shall I wear to this alfresco luncheon? If I go in black, I shall perish in the sun."

"Let us go to your room, and I will advise you."

"Here, this lavender dress will do if you have some black ribbons," Ann said, pulling a filmy garment out of the wardrobe.

Bella was stepping out of her riding skirt and took the dress as offered. "Good. I shall put this one with those I can wear. Help me separate them."

Bella pulled out all the gowns and dresses that would not do and threw them on the bed.

"Shall I get a trunk and some paper?" Ann asked.

"No, I really want you to take them. The deep blue and green look well enough on you. The amber we shall soften with some lace or a scarf. Really, you would look better in pastels, but more vivid colors are suited to a lady . . . a young lady . . ."

"A lady not in the first blush of youth?" Ann began waltzing around the room with the emerald green gown to see how the silk moved.

"Stop, Ann, you are making me laugh. You know you are the most beautiful and angelic-looking woman."

"I owe you some merriment," Ann replied. "Do you realize how long it has been since Phillipe smiled?"

"Yes, I do, for I was with him much of that time." Bella slowly threaded a piece of black ribbon through the openwork at the neckline of the dress.

"How long have you been in love with him?" Ann asked without skipping a beat in her mock waltz.

Bella hesitated, surprised at her perception. "Since Talavera," she said, thinking of the night Phillipe had carried in a wounded companion and demanded a surgeon. He had been aghast that Bella and Carlos were the only help the surgeon had and had hovered over them as they worked to clean the wound.

"Bella," Ann said, standing in front of her to get her attention.

"Sorry, that was the first time I saw him and the first time he scowled at me. All the other men smiled at me. Phillipe has a . . . presence."

"Not all of us tell time by battles. When did you first meet him?"

"July of 1809. My parents and I had arrived in April. We were billeted in Lisbon at the house of Captain Quesada."

"Carlos's father?"

"Yes. Wellington wanted to integrate the Portuguese units into our own army, and it was effective. I would hate to think what—oh, you are not interested in the war, just Phillipe."

"And I thought I had schooled my features into a mask of absorption." Ann laid the dress down and sat on the bed.

"Phillipe and Edwin came in July. Talavera was their first engagement. Phillipe thought tending the wounded was no fit task for me."

"And he probably reminded you of that at every meeting."

"During the rest of the summer and fall, he was kept busy as an observing officer for Wellington. He was much in demand because he had some skill in mapmaking."

"When Phillipe wrote, he always made it sound as though he were in no danger, yet he was wounded four times."

"But that is because—you do not know what an observing officer is."

"Someone who watches the enemy?"

"Someone who rides into enemy-held territory to report on troop strengths and movements."

"Behind enemy lines? Phillipe, a spy?"

"A spy after the British fashion. He rode out wearing a red coat and relied on the swiftness of his horse and his luck to bring him home again."

"Why did he not disguise himself?"

"Then he could have been shot."

"But he was shot, repeatedly," Ann insisted.

"I mean, if he had been discovered out of uniform, he would have been executed. Whereas being captured in the line of duty merely meant imprisonment." Bella thought how bland these rules of war seemed now that they no longer had to play by them.

"Oh, well, that is so much better than being shot.

Did you and Phillipe never do anything that was fun?" Ann asked.

"We wintered in Lisbon, and there were balls and parties. Phillipe always seemed to be around when not on a mission, but he never approached me. I was attracted to him because he seemed so serious, and . . . I did not think he approved of me."

"That sounds like Phillipe. Did he try to tell you what to do?"

"After my mother died that winter, he made a point of asking if I was going back to England. Since I knew no one in England, I had no such intention. During the summer campaigns of 1810, Maria, Carlos, and I were in the field with my father's brigade."

"And what happened that winter? Were there more balls?"

"Yes, and I hoped that Phillipe might declare himself. Certainly all the other men were doing so."

"But you refused them all," Ann guessed.

"I did not know it at the time, but Phillipe went to my father and was refused permission to court me."

"And being a man of honor . . ."

Bella looked up from her work into Ann's sympathetic eyes. "If only I had known."

"I bet that made him scowl."

"Yes, he was always watching me like an overprotective hound, but I did not know it was because he had been forbidden to speak to me. In the spring of 1811 we were with the army again, but Captain Quesada was killed at Fuentes de Orono in May."

"That must have been hard on Carlos."

"He was only seventeen then and would have

joined the Portuguese unit if his mother had let him."

"What happened then?"

"Badajoz was sieged unsuccessfully, and we won at Albuerra. Then there were some minor engagements along the Caia River and the Coa," Bella mumbled.

"That was the fall Edwin wrote that Phillipe was dead."

"Oh, I had not even realized how much pain that would cause you. We had agreed to be married, and he was captured within a few days. Then my father was killed."

"So you had agreed to marry in spite of your father. I find that very romantic."

Bella wondered if Ann would have thought their hot coupling under enemy fire as romantic. Perhaps.

Ann leaned over to embrace her. "Now I realize why you married Edwin."

"Phillipe returned a few weeks after our marriage. It was very difficult facing him, for I felt I had betrayed him."

"But you are together now, or will be. That is all that matters. You and Phillipe can build a new life together. At least I think that was what he was hoping . . . until you excluded him from your life with that treaty of yours."

"What?" Bella drew back to look at her.

"Phillipe has so many responsibilities here and in London, he would scarcely get to see you if you withdrew to your farm for three-quarters of the year."

Bella bit her lip. "I had assumed—hoped—that he could spend some time there."

"If he marries you, he might, but you can hardly live apart most of the year."

"I should not marry for a year anyway, but how we are to get through this year I do not know." Bella looked helplessly at Ann.

"Why must you wait? Who will know or care?"

Bella sat on the bed and readjusted her vision of the world. Could Jamie be happy here, and could she learn to tolerate it for Phillipe's sake? A sudden sad thought struck her: that the only objectionable part of Dorney Park was the dowager and that she would not live forever. How terrible. She had never bartered for her own happiness with that of another, not even when she had been married to Edwin, and she would not consider it now. She must find a way to make that irascible old lady more agreeable.

～❈8❈～

$\mathcal{T}$he breeze was blowing toward them off the lake, so the air was pleasantly cool as Phillipe helped Ann supervise the placing of the table and chairs for the outdoor feast. The dowager would arrive by carriage, and Hal and Carlos were still off riding. Bella had gone to the nursery to get Jamie, and he could hear the boy's excited voice as they walked out from the house

"Will I see a turtle?" Jamie asked, looking up at Bella as he swung on her hand.

"Perhaps, maybe even a frog," Bella promised.

She and Jamie had liberated Lobo from the stable, and the dog was cavorting about them in gratitude.

"What do you think?" Ann asked her.

Bella scrutinized the table with its white cloth. "They forgot the epergne."

"The epergne?" Ann gaped at her. "What do we want with an epergne?"

"What do we want with a table, for that matter?" Bella asked.

Phillipe howled with laughter.

"What is so funny?" Ann asked.

"Nothing," Bella said. "I just expect to see them hanging paintings from the trees."

Phillipe tossed a stick for Lobo to keep him away from the table. "If you think this is absurd, you should try it on a rainy day or when she has a notion to move furniture."

"Compared to this, your time in Spain must have seemed like a holiday," Bella quipped.

"Oh, I still had her grace's wonderful letters to cheer me up," Phillipe said as he curled his lip.

Jamie tugged on Bella's hand, begging to go see the ducks that had come across the lake to check out the prospect of bread crumbs. Phillipe walked to the dock with them. There were two rowboats tied up there, and Lobo leaped into one of them to get a better view of the waterfowl.

"How deep is it?" Bella asked.

"Shallow along the edge, as you can see by the amount of weed, but twenty feet toward the center. At least that is what we measured when we were boys. We fought out the Battle of Trafalgar on this lake."

"Ah, so you had aspirations to command a ship?"

"Right now I would settle for commanding a household. If Lady Edith is late and the food is cold . . ."

"We will eat anyway. I will overrule her."

"And draw her fire upon you?" Phillipe asked.

"I doubt she will ever like me, so I may as well make her respect me."

"Why do you even care?" Phillipe leaped to grab Jamie, who was in danger of tipping into the lake.

"Because you seem to." She knelt to wring out the wet cuff of the boy's coat sleeve. "Ann says I seemed to be excluding you from my life with that treaty I gave you. I had not meant to, but I simply had not realized how much your work ties you to this place and London."

Phillipe kept his hand on Jamie's shoulder but stared into Bella's eyes. "That is a relief. I know that nothing can—nothing should—happen between us for a year, but after that . . ."

"Yes?"

"After that, please consider my suit rather than accepting the first high-ranking officer to beg for your hand."

Bella laughed and leaned into him, almost, he thought, as though she would like to kiss him. "I will never let someone make my decisions for me again. Maria and Rourke can have the farm, and we will only retreat there when we need to get away from everyone."

Phillipe stood so close he could see her pulse beating in her neck. He had a flash of the intensity he had felt that night in the ruined house along the Coa River, and a persistent stirring in his groin. How in God's name was he going to wait most of a year?

Jamie escaped his grasp to walk out on the dock and lie full-length, peeking through the boards at the ducks. He had picked a handful of grass and dropped it to them blade by blade. Lobo barked at the activity, but the ducks ignored him.

The sound of a gig announced the approach of the Thackerys, and Phillipe took a step back from Bella. A shout from the other side of the lake came from Carlos and Hal. Phillipe grinned as they began to race their horses along the edge, thinking again of his morning ride with Bella and what might have happened. He really owed Greenley a debt of gratitude for frustrating their amorous impulse.

When he looked toward the house, he saw to his relief the lumbering carriage that was conveying the dowager and food to their party. Perhaps it would not be a disaster after all.

After brief greetings, everyone had been seated and the wine approved and served. Then the dowager kept them in suspense as she scrutinized the first dish. Phillipe saw Bella inhale, and he sent his aunt a speaking look, but she motioned to her plate, and a universal sigh of relief went up. The talk flowed amicably enough, though Carlos and Hal kept to themselves and Phillipe caught stray words that told him they were speaking of the war. Thackery spent all his efforts flattering Lady Edith and Bella, though his comments were wasted on Bella at least.

Miranda kept trying to draw Phillipe out about the estate. For the first time Phillipe looked at Miranda and tried to form a reply to her query on the crops. "I have no idea. We have an estate manager to take care of that."

Bella sent him a bored look. He wanted nothing better than to take her hand and run off with her. Jamie finished eating first and asked to be excused. Bella warned him to stay in sight.

Since Carlos had won the horse race, Hal now challenged him to a row across the lake, so the party had some entertainment to see them through the creams and aspics. Stripped of their coats, Hal built up a good lead until Carlos got used to the oars and boat. Carlos's broad shoulders and muscular arms might be more than a match against Hal's expertise. The sounds of the oars in the locks and the boats surging through the water brought back Phillipe's youth, and he thought perhaps he would offer to row Bella and Jamie out later. If Jamie was intent on capturing a frog, he knew where there were many.

Carlos was just past halfway across when Hal touched the other shore and pushed off again to turn his boat and start back. Carlos collided with him at the three-quarter mark to the uproarious laughter of the onlookers. Undaunted, Carlos reached the other shore, touched it with an oar, spun the boat, and started back. Hal's progress was somewhat impeded by a splintered oar. He had to keep righting himself so as not to miss the landing. Carlos had the hang of it now and pulled for all he was worth. Bella saw Jamie perched on the edge of the dock, so she got up and ran to him to help cheer Carlos on. Phillipe went to them and was glad his aunt presided over the contest from the table, since many of the encouragements were in Portuguese or Spanish.

But Carlos missed the water on his last stroke, and Hal touched shore a moment before him. Phillipe smiled to himself. That had been on purpose. Ann carried a glass of champagne to Hal for his victory, and Miranda made much of him. Hal then commandeered one of Carlos's oars to take Miranda for a row. As they passed the dock, Jamie said, "Me too, me too," so Hal feathered the boat to drift it to the wooden pilings.

"Are you sure, Hal?" Bella asked. "He is a handful."

"He is just a little boy," Hal said, still flush with victory. "How much trouble can he be?"

Jamie was installed beside Miranda as Phillipe said, "Keep close to shore, Hal."

Bella sat on the end of the dock, looking more relaxed than Phillipe had seen her. "May I get you some lemonade?" he asked.

"No, sit with me. There is nothing I need."

Awkwardly, Phillipe sat and took her hand and watched her watching her son, a small blond dot receding down the shoreline. Once again he wondered if Jamie was really Edwin's son or his. It was not a question one asked lightly of a woman. And perhaps she did not know. That thought rather comforted him, for he had already decided it did not matter to him. He would play father to Jamie no matter who his real father was. Of course, that cut out Hal. He could imagine the speculation in London right now. Hal was not a mean prospect by any means. The second son of a duke would be well provided for, but there would not be the title, and that mattered very much to some women and not at all to others. Phillipe glanced at Bella, who was smiling as her fingers curled and intertwined with his.

He could hear Jamie and Hal's voices and the word *frog* as the rowboat made its way along the shore back toward them. Suddenly it occurred to Phillipe that he would not be able to row as he used to. His knee would not bend that way. He would have to contrive a way in private just as he had found a way to lengthen his stirrups for riding. He felt as secure on his horse as he ever had.

A large splash snapped his head toward the boat.

"Jamie!" Hal yelled.

Miranda screamed, but Bella did not. She got up and ran down the dock and along the shore to where she could see the boat better. Everyone was running in that direction but the dowager. Lobo barked and plunged into the lake.

Phillipe stripped off his coat and boots and dived into the water. It was faster for him than running. Indeed, he had got much of his flexibility back by swimming the lake. When he surfaced, he could see Jamie's head bobbing and calculated three more strokes would take him to the boy. He surfaced again, and Jamie was gone, but Hal was in the water diving for him.

Bella was waving from the shore, and he stopped to listen. "Phillipe, Jamie swims!" she shouted.

Just then Jamie popped up again, took a breath, and dived. Phillipe shook his head and dived as well. Leave it to Bella to teach her baby to swim. She never left anything to chance.

Phillipe followed Jamie to the surface and grabbed the culprit by the coat collar.

"Got him," Jamie said of the frog in his hand.

"Well, put him in your pocket and hang on to my shirt," Phillipe said as he treaded water awkwardly. "We have drifted too far from shore."

After depositing the frog, Jamie grasped Phillipe's shirt collar with one small hand and giggled as Phillipe did the breast stroke into the shallows. When Phillipe could stand, he looked back to see Hal in the boat again, very wet and cross. He chuckled, picked up Jamie, and carried him to shore.

"Jamie, you little wretch," Bella said as she wrapped

a shawl about her dripping son. "You have worried everyone."

The Dowager Lady Edith was standing there, not even leaning on her cane, the tears streaming down her face. Phillipe went to her. "It is all right. He is just a boy. He did not mean to worry you."

"I cannot do this, Phillipe," Lady Edith protested. "I cannot go through this again. Every one of you almost died on this lake. I will not have it."

Bella led Jamie to the dowager, but before he could make his apology, Hal was upon them.

"Bella, why the devil did you not tell me the boy could swim? I thought I had killed him."

"Hal, do you really think I would let him go out in a boat without me if he could not swim?" Bella asked reasonably.

"So, you do not trust me?" Hal demanded.

"No, I do not trust Jamie, not with his penchant for slimy animals. What do you have to say for yourself, Jamie? You worried your grandmother."

Jamie hung his head. "I'm sorry."

"And to Hal and Phillipe. You know they might have died, diving to look for you."

"Sorry." Jamie looked utterly dejected. Phillipe thought he was very good at it.

"Oh well, no harm done," Hal said generously.

"The day is warm, but the lake water is cold," Bella said. "I had better take you to the house and get you dry clothes."

"I will take him, since I have to change anyway." Phillipe took the boots Ann was carrying and Jamie's hand, walking toward the house in his wet socks.

Bella thought it was a very fatherly thing to do, but when she saw Jamie's small hand steal toward his coat pocket and pat it, she had no doubt that they were engaged in a conspiracy to smuggle some creature into the nursery. She shivered, hoping it was not anything too disgusting and that Jamie would remember to take it out of his pocket.

"That is what comes of lax discipline," Thackery said. "When I have the boy in my charge . . ."

"Thackery," Bella said in a voice so military it got the attention of everyone. "When we were hiding from a French patrol and I asked Jamie to be quiet as a mouse, he obeyed me then because he knew our lives depended on it. When he was not yet two, he had more sense than you, so do not be trying to inflict your discipline on my son. I will not have it."

The dowager looked shocked, but Thackery and his sister seemed merely affronted. Ann smiled at Bella and handed her Phillipe's coat.

Bella thought she should pen up the dripping Lobo before the dog caused more havoc, and Ann volunteered to walk with her to the stables. On the way, Ann paused at a sunny bench in the small garden outside the library and invited Bella to sit. Lobo rolled himself in the flower bed, then dropped into a happy sleep.

"I was thinking about your marriage to Edwin," Ann said. "It must have been difficult for you, in love with Phillipe, to accept another man, even one who looked so much like him."

Bella sat and folded the coat in her lap, stroking it as though that would bring her closer to its owner. "I was trapped. I could not go home, so I had to marry someone. It was a kindness for Edwin to offer. I think Phillipe had charged him with watching over me in his absence, so perhaps Edwin thought it was his duty." Bella hesitated to call up such bitter memories, but she felt she owed Ann some explanation. And she could never confide such things to Lady Edith. Perhaps if Ann knew how it had been, she could comfort Lady Edith about her son. "Edwin was the one who told me about Phillipe. I have seen grown men cry and for good reason, but I have never seen a man so bereft in my life. I felt utterly hollow and destroyed myself, yet I did not think I felt it as Edwin did." Bella sniffed, determined not to cry.

"Then to lose your father."

"Edwin was such a rock through that whole week, taking me, Maria, and Carlos into his household. When he asked me to marry him, it seemed the simplest solution, and there was no point in waiting."

"When Phillipe returned . . ."

"He walked more than a hundred miles to get to me, arriving one freezing night when we were making merry. Rourke took care of his frozen fingers, but Phillipe would not let him tell us he was back. I found out from Maria the next morning." When Bella squeezed her eyes shut, she realized the tears were there against her will. "I did not know how to face him. I was both happy and devastated at the same time."

"At least Phillipe was alive."

"He did not appear so to me. He looked like a lantern with the light blown out. I tried to put up a brave front. After a while, Phillipe also was able to pretend there had never been anything between us." She looked away toward the placid lake.

"How awful for you."

"The worst of it was that Edwin knew we were in love. We were all trapped. But . . . we did not know when one or all of us might be killed. As it happens, it was Edwin we lost."

"Perhaps you and Phillipe were meant to be together," Ann said, putting an arm around Bella.

"At Edwin's expense?"

"Edwin had you for four wonderful years, and you gave him a son. There are men who get less from a marriage than that."

Bella stared at her and brushed the tears from her cheeks, biting her lip with the remembered pain of losing a man she had not loved. It had been almost as bad as losing Phillipe. She gave the coat another squeeze and got resolutely to her feet.

"It just seems so unfair to Edwin."

"As Lady Edith says, 'Life is unfair. Get used to it.' "

Bella laughed. "I cannot argue with her there."

Bella had some reservations about even going down to dinner that evening, but the dowager's tears had been genuine, so Bella owed her something. Thackery and his sister were not present, and her grace refused the first three dishes with a challenging look at Bella.

Bella finally said, "I shall have some of that fish, Hanson. I like it well done."

"So do I," Phillipe said, and the spell was broken.

Lady Edith looked aghast at them but accepted the

fricassee of duck that came next, and the meal proceeded in peace for a time.

"I have looked at your list of dates, Arabella, and it will not do," the dowager said.

"Oh, we would be taking too much of your time," Bella concluded. "I know how tiresome Jamie can be when you are not used to children's antics. We can shorten those visits."

"I mean that Dorney Park is to be James's principal residence, not that pathetic farm of yours."

Bella took two more bites of the meal as she thought over her reply, and she could feel all eyes upon her. "I suppose we could stay here while you are in London or Brighton, but what would be the point?"

"No, Jamie will go to London and Brighton with me."

"What has that to do with Dorney being his residence, then?" Bella asked. "He may as well be in Suffolk as London or Brighton."

"I want the boy with me. He took a year off my life today with that scare at the lake. I want that year back again."

"Scared me half to death too," Hal said. "I thought Miranda had hold of him."

"Hal, do be quiet," his mother said.

Bella stared at Phillipe, who was studying his plate and not eating a thing. "Very well, we will spend this first year with you to get acquainted and only visit the farm. After that, we will decide what to do."

Phillipe looked at her, no longer troubled but smiling with approval. By capitulating, or seeming to, Bella had made his life so much easier, and she was glad for that, but would she be able to hold out for a year? It was a great deal like being in the army, this not having control of your life.

"And Thackery will tutor him."

"What are his qualifications?" Bella asked.

"He took a first at Oxford in mathematics."

"You would think he could do better at the gaming tables, then," Hal observed. "Every time he goes to Brooks, he gets plucked featherless."

"Hal, I take it very badly that you introduced Thackery to a gaming club," his mother said.

"Me? It was you who said, 'Take him to your club, Hal.'"

"I did not know Thackery had a house in London," Bella said.

"He does not," Phillipe said. "He is usually the dowager's guest."

"The boy needs the libraries there to further his studies. It would be ungracious to refuse to put him up."

"Does Miranda come, too?" Bella asked.

"What of it?" the dowager demanded. "Thackery will travel with us in his post as Jamie's tutor. That way the boy's lessons will not be interrupted. And London can be very educational."

"Not for a three-year-old. Jamie needs some time to play in the dirt and catch frogs." She sent Phillipe a look that told him she knew about Jamie's new pet.

"A duke does not grovel in the dirt and muck. I do not know what you were used to in Spain, and I do not care to know, but things will be different here. For one thing, he will go to church. I do not even know what religion you have brought him up in."

"Religion?" Bella asked. "Survival was our religion,

your grace. And I imagine I prayed more than you, with soldiers dying all around me and the mortar shells dropping like kites from the sky. I prayed without benefit of clergy because most of them, theological students like Thackery, were too squeamish to go into the army. Wellington did not want them. They made the men uncomfortable. Religion has nothing to do with God. Religion is a luxury you can afford, not me."

"Well! I can see you are no fit guardian for my grandson. I think I shall speak to the lawyers about removing him from your custody."

Phillipe stood up. "That you shall not. Bella is Jamie's mother, and you will not come between them." He said this with such finality that Lady Edith pouted.

"But you heard what she said. You could take him from her, Phillipe. You are his guardian."

"On paper," Phillipe conceded. "Jamie and Bella will stay together, and wherever Bella chooses to live, I will try to make that place safe for her."

"Perhaps we can hire a troop of riflemen," Bella suggested with a resigned smile. "They have little enough to do after the war."

"There is an idea," Phillipe said, resuming his seat and draining his wineglass.

"Well, I never thought to see the day when my own nephew would turn against me." The dowager got up with the assistance of a footman and limped out of the room.

"Sorry, Phillipe," Bella said.

Ann got up. "I will go to her. She will need a shoulder to cry upon. I personally applaud you, Bella. Lady

Edith has been spoiled her whole life. It is time some-one stood up to her . . . besides Phillipe."

Ann left, and Bella turned to Phillipe. "I suspect I will pay dearly for my resistance, and you will, too, for defending me." Bella stood.

"I do not doubt it," Phillipe said as he rose to help her with her chair. "Where are you going?"

"To read to Jamie. That will give Carlos and Hal a chance to beat each other senseless at cards."

Carlos laughed at this and motioned to a footman to refill his wineglass.

"May I come?" Phillipe asked.

"Of course. You are, after all, his guardian." Bella led the way up the stairs to the nursery. When Phillipe set foot inside, a wave of memories swept over him. The boys had been barracked here to share their childhood diseases while Ann had slept in the dowager's maid's room. It had always been control with Lady Edith, how to control the children and her husband. When com-mand did not work, tears usually did. And Edwin had always been the one to lead revolts against her, with Phillipe as the voice of reason, but Hal following blindly in whatever mad scrape Edwin thought of. That worked when the penalties where not so severe, a missed meal. But Edwin had grown up to lead a fatally foolish charge and had paid along with several score of others. Survival had not been Edwin's religion, but victory at any cost.

Phillipe stared at the blond child sitting in bed so angelically and listening to Bella's expurgated retelling of the King Arthur story. Phillipe sat on the other side of the bed and tried to see Edwin in the boy, but any resemblance could have been only a family one. Edwin would never have apologized to the dowager and Hal. Edwin had been much like his mother in that respect. Edwin never admitted a wrong, he merely changed his tack and went on. Not one word of apology had he offered to Phillipe for marrying Bella in his stead. He had just looked sadly at Phillipe and gathered him into his family of intimates as though nothing untoward had happened.

When Bella had finished her tale, Jamie hopped up out of bed to check the glass bowl of water where his frog now resided with a rock and a handful of grass. The boy extracted a promise from Phillipe to help him catch crickets to feed it on the morrow.

"Do you feel like a walk?" Phillipe asked Bella on the way downstairs.

"Yes, let me get a shawl."

It was just dark when they let themselves out the back door. "Do frogs eat crickets?" Bella asked as they turned their steps toward the gardens.

"I have no idea, but if you hear any, help me catch them and I will keep them in my pocket until tomorrow."

Bella laughed and grabbed Phillipe's arm. "But you did not admit you did not know, and now you will have to read up on it tonight."

"When I should be going over the estate books." He put his arm around Bella's waist. "But first things first." He guided her toward one of the more secluded paths.

"Jamie does come first with you, as he does with me," Bella said.

"You are both my chief concern, as inseparable in my mind as you will be in fact."

"I do trust you, Phillipe. I suppose a year is not such a long time to humor Lady Edith."

Phillipe was silent, and Bella stopped to look up at his face. "I suppose I should be glad for a year of luxury. We do not have to forage for food, it is brought to us. And if we are allowed to eat it . . ."

Phillipe laughed. "I fancy you have spiked her guns there. She will not risk you overruling her again. Do try to enjoy this year. And remember, she may seem petty and controlling, but she does care."

"I saw her tears today and had vowed to be good at dinner, but when attacked I tend to defend."

"I know." He pulled her to him and held her for a moment, feeling her hair feathering against his chin, feeling the warmth of her vibrant young body through their clothes. "God, a year will be such a long time for us."

"Must we wait?" she asked.

He could also feel her hands, hot and compelling, massaging the muscles of his back. He groaned with pleasure. "It will not look well if we break convention too soon. At least we must get the legalities out of the way. Then, when we are back here . . ." His mouth sought hers, and she kissed him as though she had been wanting him for a long time. Her hand crept up to stroke his hair and neck. Some memory drifted back to him from France. That last time he had been wounded in the leg and had lain in a fever, she had whispered to him and stroked his hair and washed him. She had loved him then, and he had been too bitter to realize it. Everything she did for him when he lay wounded had been an act of love. But he had resented being powerless then just as she resented being powerless now.

She broke the kiss to rest her head on his chest and breathe, "My *Phillipe*. I should have trusted you more. I should have stayed your secret widow and not married Edwin."

"Do not think about it." He lifted her face to his and kissed her again. Her body bent seductively in his arms as he kissed her neck and the tops of her breasts. He wondered how far she would let him go in a garden when he heard Ann's joyful laugh on the other side of the hedge and froze.

Bella hesitated, too, though she kept her hands against his chest as she listened. It was Carlos teaching Ann some words of Portuguese. They passed on along the path, but Phillipe released Bella. "You would think that in six hundred acres, we could have a little privacy," he growled.

"Someday we will have all we desire. Do I look decent?"

"You look . . . beautiful, tempting, I run out of adjectives." He drew her hand through the crook of his arm and proceeded back along a path toward the house and away from Carlos and Ann.

"You left here a boy. So I suppose you never bothered to discover any very secluded places."

Phillipe laughed. "I will think of something."

"Perhaps one of the rowboats . . ."

"Ah, you are thinking the middle of the lake might be more private, but I must warn you all boats leak, and there would be nothing comfortable about a gunwale poking you in the back. No, leave the hiding places to me."

He was about to draw her into an arbor when a footman popped into view and nervously cleared his throat. "Her grace would like to see you."

"I am coming. Tell my aunt I will be with her in a few minutes."

When the man did not salute and turn on his heel, Phillipe said, "Well, do not just stand there."

The man in blue livery bustled off.

"You should not take your impatience out on Jenks," Bella said.

"Damn, but we are crawling with footmen. And how did you know his name?"

"I make it my business to learn as much about the enemy as I can, his movements, his strengths, his weaknesses. These poor beggars are so starved for a kind word, they might come over to my side if I but asked them."

He put his arm around her waist again. "This should not seem like war to you."

"I know no other metaphor that fits. My damnable soldier's language permeates everything I say. I need as much training as Jamie. What trial do we face on the morrow?" she asked as they approached the steps of the house.

"A tour of the estate, including the cattle farm."

"Does her grace come with us?" Bella asked.

"I fear so. We lunch at Scorton Farm."

"What is that?"

"One of Jamie's lesser estates," Phillipe said. "It might have passed to Hal, but not the way things were left by Edwin."

"Poor Hal."

"He has made his life, as we all have," Phillipe said at the bottom of the inside staircase. "Do you go up now? I dare not keep her waiting too long, or she will come looking for me herself."

"Yes, I must pick out something suitable to wear for cows."

∞ 9 ∞

*B*ella had told Jamie the day before that Rourke and Maria would be going to work on the farm to make it ready for his next visit, and he had accepted that, but when he saw Rourke loading Lobo into the gig, he protested most violently. The dog broke his leash and leaped out to grovel at Jamie's feet.

"The beast must go," the dowager decreed. "He is always muddy, rolls the carpets in a ball, and growls at Thackery. It is only a matter of time before he bites someone and has to be shot."

Phillipe knelt beside Jamie, mentally cursing his stiff knee. "Lobo will be safer with Rourke and Maria, and he will have the whole farm to run over. Here he has to be locked up all the time."

Jamie bent to pet the shaggy animal, then stood tearless and pointed to the light carriage. "Lobo, get up."

Maria got a good hold on the dog's collar this time, and the gig left.

Bella had worried that it would be a tearful parting from Maria, but the emergency over the dog had forestalled that. The problem would come tonight, if at all, when Jamie had to go to sleep without Maria's rocking or singing.

The big traveling carriage pulled up at the door to take them to the cattle farms, and Jamie was content to look out the window for a time. Phillipe, Carlos, and Hal rode, but Ann had made some excuse not to come. Bella thought perhaps it was because Thackery and Miranda were to accompany them.

Thackery was a strapping man who might have looked well in a uniform or on a great war stallion, assuming he could have handled such a beast. But he moved more with the gait of a wrestler than a horseman, and when he got into the carriage it swayed precariously.

"This will be an educational expedition for the boy," Thackery informed Bella, perhaps to excuse his presence or to approve the dowager's decision to make the expedition in the morning which was supposed to be given over for study. "Jamie should learn something of his possessions."

"You do not think Spain and Portugal were educational?" Bella asked.

"But this is Jamie's own estate," Thackery said. "It will mean more to him."

When the child looked puzzled, the dowager said, "This will all be yours someday, James."

"I would rather have Lobo," Jamie said, his brown eyes looking sad and brooding just as Phillipe's often looked.

"You will have a pack of hunting hounds when you are older," Miranda said. "You will like that."

Jamie sighed and ignored the promised treat. Lady Edith was regarding Miranda's frivolous frock and parasol and comparing it with Bella's worn buff walking suit and boots. "That is hardly proper attire for a widow. What will people think?"

"I did not think you regarded what your cowmen thought," Bella replied glibly, having prepared the answer in advance.

"Of course not," the dowager returned. "But you do not do honor to George and Miranda."

"A cow farm is hardly the place to be flaunting Paris fashions. Ten to one, we will come away covered with manure."

"I hardly think you have to worry about that," Lady Edith said.

Their way led between squares of pasture where the bulls were kept to a large calving barn, with fields full of cows and calves at a distance and downwind of the bulls. Jamie sat up to look at the calves, but since none of these looked cuddly, subsided onto the seat, gently patting his coat pocket. Bella took it from this action that he had secreted his frog and vowed to remember to search his pockets tonight. Perhaps she could find him another pet that could not be objected to as either muddy or slimy.

After they alighted in the barnyard, Phillipe introduced Winslow, the head cowman, who was put in charge of the tour of the barns. Bella had to admit to some surprise at how clean everything was. Hal and Carlos were going off to have a look at the bulls, and

Jamie begged to go along. Bella bit her lip, wondering if this would be a good idea. But since Miranda was going with them, arm in arm with Carlos, she did not think they would get near any really dangerous animals.

"I will go along and look out for him," Thackery said.

"He can be gone in a second," Bella warned.

"How much trouble can he be?" Thackery asked, smiling as he shepherded Jamie after the rest of the party.

Bella tried to be an attentive student of cow husbandry, but it was so easy for her mind to wander with Phillipe right there.

"When we are moving a bull, we always have a man standing by with a rifle in case the beast should try to savage someone. They are unpredictable animals. Mind, we had a man killed just last year by a bull he had handled since it was a calf."

"Why so many bulls?" Bella asked.

"We sell them," Phillipe supplied.

"It is a popular bloodline," Lady Edith added.

"But is it worth keeping so many of these bulls if they are that dangerous?" Bella persisted.

"There is always a risk," Winslow conceded.

"But it is a preventable one," Bella said. "This business, no matter what income it brings, is not worth even one man's life." Bella could see Phillipe smiling at her interference, but he kept quiet, perhaps to see how Winslow would handle an outspoken woman.

"It is kind of you to say so, your grace, but this is the way of it. We make far more money on the breeding stock than the meat calves. If we see a likely calf, 'twould be a shame to castrate it."

"Bella," the dowager said, "I am quite sure Winslow knows his business."

Bella looked up when she saw Carlos wave from the top of a fence. They were several fields away on the road, and Hal was jogging along looking into the fields as though he had lost something. A tightening of her scalp caused her to take a few steps in their direction, completely ignoring Winslow, Phillipe, and the dowager. What could they have lost but Jamie?

She strode to the edge of the first paddock and scanned the rail fences and green pastures until her eyes watered from the sun. Miranda stood unhelpfully by the fence talking to her brother. They did not seem to be aware of anything wrong. Winslow came toward her, still carrying the rifle and cartridge pack, and asked what was wrong.

"I had better go," Bella said. "I think Jamie has wandered off. Is there a stream or spring close by where a boy might go to water a frog?"

"A what?" Winslow asked.

Phillipe climbed up three rails to sit on the top of the fence. "There is a stream that runs through all the pastures, but I do not see him anywhere along it."

Bella grabbed a pitchfork from a passing cowman and started off purposefully down the line of paddocks to where she could get a better view of the stream.

"Bella, wait," Phillipe said. He turned to follow her but came back to grab the gun and cartridges from Winslow. You never knew. He ran and limped after her, scanning the pastures and every furrow in the ground for a small blond head.

Bella halted abruptly and stood stock-still, staring at

a large black bull that was looking attentively toward the stream. "Jamie!" she called. "Be still. Do not move."

Phillipe could see the bull scenting the air. It was big enough and had enough growth of horn to be dangerous and was so young it had never been bred. Bulls of its age did not yet know exactly what they wanted, but they knew they did not have it. The animal froze when it saw the child by the stream. Jamie moved a little, probably making his frog safe. Phillipe slid through the rails and began working his way around the pasture, trying to move fast enough to draw the beast's attention to him rather than Jamie. But, perversely, the animal pawed the ground and made a short charge in the child's direction.

A flash of red from the other side of the pasture caught the bull's eye as Carlos waved his coat and also worked along that side of the fence, flapping the jacket enough to get the creature to change its stance a little and point in his direction.

When Jamie saw the bull move, he got up and started to run toward Bella, who had come at the beast in a straight line so as to put herself between it and Jamie. She froze as the bull spun toward her and her child.

Carlos ran straight into the field then with no weapon at all, throwing Portuguese taunts at the beast. It swung its head in his direction and spent a moment regarding that tempting red coat, then turned its attention back to Jamie. Phillipe clenched his teeth as he checked the priming of the rifle and advanced into the field.

Jamie was almost to Bella when the animal bellowed, pawed the earth, and began its charge.

"Run to Grandmother!" Bella shouted at Jamie.

Phillipe glanced at his aunt and noticed that Thackery was standing safely on the other side of the fence with her and Miranda. Damn him.

"Pick up Jamie and run, Bella!" Phillipe shouted as the beast thundered forward. He could feel the very ground shake, and he was afraid it might spoil his aim.

"Run to Grandmother, Jamie, fast as you can," Bella repeated as the boy passed her. She took a stand, planted the handle of the pitchfork in the ground like a lance, and put her foot on the butt of it, directing the tines at the beast's chest, as though that would stop him. Phillipe knew he could never get to her in time, could never save her if he did. He had only one chance, and he had to take it. He raised the gun and, without ever having fired it before, trusted that it would carry true. A head shot would be too risky. He must try for the heart. The report echoed off the hills and trees, and for a moment he thought he had missed, but the bull checked its stride, its momentum carrying it forward with a blind stagger till it hit the pitchfork. The slender handle of the tool snapped like a matchstick, and the creature crashed down. Phillipe began to run, wondering if he would find Bella crushed to death or gored by the animal's death throes.

But she was dragging herself away, finally getting up and running toward Jamie. For the animal was on its knees again, the tines of the pitchfork still embedded. Phillipe stopped and reloaded as calmly as he could while the bull staggered to its feet. Carlos continued trying to distract the thing, and it did make one faltering charge at him, but it fastened its persistent attention on Phillipe this time.

Riflemen could get off three shots a minute. In that ruined hut, with Bella loading for him, he had managed a shot a minute. One minute, he thought as the animal pawed the ground and oriented itself. Its charge was slower this time, but Phillipe was ramming the ball home by then. It did not matter what happened now. Jamie and Bella were safe, but they might need him later. He waited until the shot was a sure thing, then fired and halted the animal. Blinded in one eye and confused at the creeping death overtaking it, the beast went to its knees, then its side, a crumpled ton of murderous flesh. Phillipe reloaded as smoothly as if this were a battle. He felt strangely calm. He had certainly faced much worse than this, but never with so much at stake.

Carlos was at his shoulder then. "*Madre de Dios!* What a monster! Do you want me to make sure he is dead?"

"If you do not mind," Phillipe said as he handed the rifle to Carlos.

Phillipe strode toward Bella and Jamie, relief washing through him as he listened with half his mind to Thackery's rambling excuses and Miranda's unhelpful interjections about Jamie not listening to them.

"Is this what you call watching him?" Bella demanded savagely in a voice that would have shaken the resolve of a general.

"But he is not hurt," Thackery insisted. "And this will be a lesson to him."

"A very costly lesson, Mr. Thackery," Phillipe said.

"Bella!" The dowager was pointing down. "There is blood on your skirt."

"There usually is," Bella agreed. "But do not worry. It is the bull's. Had anything happened to Jamie, it would have been Thackery's."

"You cannot mean that," Thackery said, taking a shocked step backward.

"Oh, she most certainly does," Phillipe said. "She was willing to face down a charging bull. Would she stick at putting you out of your misery? Though she would have to stand in line."

Carlos came back, his coat thrown over his shoulder. "Well done, Bella. Your second shot killed him, Phillipe."

"Carlos, will you oblige me by lending me your horse for the return trip?" Bella asked.

"Certainly. I take it this is to keep you from murdering this ninny?"

"Now, see here," Thackery blustered.

Hal came up, shaking his head. "I say, Bella, this will give the cowmen something to talk about for years."

"It would be better if this tale did not make the rounds," Phillipe said.

"Of course not," Hal said. "I am the soul of discretion. Just glad I was not the one who promised to watch the boy."

"So am I," said Bella with finality as she picked up Jamie and carried him toward the horses.

"Savage woman," Hal commented. "It fair stopped my heart when she faced down that bull."

"Mine, too," the dowager said, regarding Bella's retreating back.

"Mother?" Jamie said as he crawled into bed. "I want Maria."

"I want her, too." Bella sat on the bed and hugged him, then tucked him in. The oak-paneled room no longer looked cozy with just Janet there hanging up Jamie's clothes. It looked cold and lonely.

There was a hesitant tap at the door, and Bella said, "Come," in that military way of hers.

Phillipe stepped inside. "How did your frog survive the trip?"

"He is feeling dry," Jamie reported.

"Perhaps we should return him to the lake tomorrow, you and I. I do not think he is getting enough to eat."

"I will turn him loose." Jamie rolled on his side and curled up as Phillipe had seen him do a hundred times, in a wagon, on a blanket, or on a crude bed.

"You know how to get to my room if you need me," Bella said as she left him.

"Good night, Mama, Phillipe."

Bella drew the curtains aside to let the moonlight illuminate the nursery. Then she left with Phillipe.

"Have you sacked Thackery?" she asked on the way down the stairs.

"I certainly tried. But her grace has promised him this post instead of the living at Whitchurch."

"Is that how it works?" Bella asked. "She bestows the guardianship of a church as a favor rather than by merit?"

"Actually, she has no say in it. I suppose the decision

is mine. Do you want me to give him the job and get him out of our hair?"

"Inflict him on a hundred innocent peasants? I think not. I will manage Thackery."

"Walk with me," Phillipe invited.

"A welcome alternative to sitting in the drawing room, fuming at the dowager," Bella agreed. She got her cloak and followed him down the final flight of stairs. "I intend to spend the mornings in the schoolroom with Jamie and go with him and Thackery on any of these *educational* jaunts."

"That will be boring for you." Phillipe took her arm and guided her away from the gardens and toward the lake.

"It serves a need," she replied, taking his offered arm. "Keeping me occupied and away from the dowager. And I can read for those three hours in the schoolroom. Tomorrow we are to go to see some abbey ruins."

"I would go with you, but I have received a letter from the solicitors. Have you your marriage license handy?"

"Yes, I will get it for you. Do you want the record of Jamie's baptism, too?"

He hesitated. "That will help," Phillipe said as he stared out over the lake, shimmering in the moonlight, wishing he did not have to talk business on such a night. She would not offer the baptismal certificate if the dates were wrong. Perhaps Jamie was not his after all. But it did not matter. He loved the boy for himself.

Bella stopped and turned to him. "Why do I feel I am giving you the edicts that will imprison us here?" she asked.

"Because you have not made it your home yet. You

will come to love it just as I do. Look at the lake and the moon. Is such a prison not worth your freedom?"

"I have come to respect it." Bella leaned against him as though she were suddenly tired, and spoke in that small intimate voice she used only with him. "I thought Spain was dangerous. Now I see the truth of it. Death can seek you out anywhere."

She heard the breath hiss through Phillipe's teeth and knew why he embraced her even as she buried her face against his shoulder, even as she clung to him, never wanting to let go.

"You almost died today," he whispered savagely.

"Almost does not count," she said in a voice wet with tears. "You could have died today, too."

He ran his hand up into her loose hair and cupped the back of her head. "I would not have wanted to live without you."

"Me, either," she whispered as her lips sought his. She drank of his breath, tinged with sweet brandy, sought his tongue in an intimate duel, wishing desperately for more, for some private place where they could be themselves.

Ann's distinct musical laugh and Carlos's chuckle drew a savage and exasperated "Damn!" from Phillipe, though the sounds of the pair only made Bella laugh.

"Phillipe, what if Ann falls in love with Carlos?" she asked, still clutching his arms.

"What if she does?" Phillipe ran his hands down Bella's back to rest them possessively on her hips. "He can sell out of the army and live here. There is work aplenty for an ambitious boy." He bent to kiss her again, bruising her eager lips and leaving her breathless.

"What will her grace say?" Bella asked as she rested against his chest, feeling his chin touching the top of her head.

"She will make no objection so long as he does not plan to take Ann away." Phillipe pulled her mane of hair aside to kiss her ear, her neck.

"Ann needs someone," Bella mused, then moaned a little as the kisses descended to her neck and finally the tops of her breasts.

"Ann who?" Phillipe asked distractedly.

"Your sister, silly." Bella gasped again as Phillipe's talented tongue brushed the satin of her dress and brought one nipple to full arousal. "But she should have a choice. I think I have convinced her to come to London when we have to go."

"London? Yes, of course." Phillipe busied himself with the other nipple and had to hold Bella when she arched against him.

"Will she be able to get about . . . meet some people?"

"Yes, I will arrange it." He stopped as though remembering something. "Speaking of London, I must go there tomorrow."

"Phillipe, no." Bella curled her arms up around his neck, reaching for his hair.

"I will be back the next day." He cradled her waist in his hands. "What can happen in a day?"

"Kingdoms have been lost in a day," Bella warned, running her hands through his blond hair, touched with gold by the moonlight.

"Do not burn any bridges while I am gone, Bella." He held her protectively against him.

"What about an incompetent schoolmaster?"

"Have your way with Thackery. Just do not argue with the dowager while I am away. I do not want to have to start from scratch when I return."

"A shame you must leave now."

"Not until morning. Shall I show you the private place I have reconnoitered?"

"By all means."

Phillipe took her hand and pulled her across the lawn to the closest grove of trees. There was a huge willow there with a divided trunk, and something like a shooting blind had been built where the tree forked.

"It is our old tree house," he said proudly, showing her the ladder nailed to the trunk.

"But Phillipe, to get up there I would have to hike my dress up above my knees."

"I know. You go first."

Bella laughed and climbed up slowly, allowing Phillipe's hand to caress her leg in passing. She boosted herself up through the hatchway, and when he managed to get his shoulders through the opening and climb up after her, he flipped down the trapdoor.

"Ah, I perceive it is fortifiable," Bella said as she made herself at home on the nest of pillows someone had thoughtfully provided.

Phillipe threw himself down beside her to resume his seduction. His broad hand, callused from so much riding, sent shivers up her spine as it crept tenderly along her leg. She wished he would take his coat off so that she could feel the heat of him. He must know seduction worked both ways.

He untied the ribbons at her bodice and fumbled with the tiny buttons. She laughed and undid them for him. His tongue aroused her breasts and caused the arching that was so instinctive. She had known she needed him, but she'd had no idea how much. His thigh lay between her legs, causing her to rear against him. If only there were grapeshot falling on them to hurry him along a little.

Finally, Phillipe pushed himself up to remove his coat. Bella took that moment to kneel, the better to disrobe, when she heard Ann giggle.

Phillipe groaned as Carlos's distinct voice crept across the lawn through the velvety darkness. "Are you sure about this place?"

"No one has used it for years," Ann said. "It was our old tree house."

"Phillipe," Bella whispered. "Do something."

"Halt!" Phillipe challenged. "Who goes there?"

"Phillipe," Ann complained. "How did you know?"

"It is my business to know everything. Lieutenant Quesada, you do not seem to remember the watchword."

"I suppose it might be *caution*," Carlos replied. Bella could almost see his smirk.

"Try *patience*," Phillipe recommended. "Now, get back in the barracks, you young scoundrel, or I will have you court-martialed."

When Phillipe turned back to her, after watching Ann and Carlos depart, Bella was resolutely buttoning her dress again.

"Why go now, Bella? Rank should have some privileges. Besides, we took the tree house first."

Bella picked up his coat and handed it to him. "Because unless they are both great fools, they know I am up here, too. It is not fair, Phillipe, besides setting a very bad example for your sister. It is one thing for us to be pulling such tricks, but Ann is an innocent young girl."

"I was not thinking," Phillipe said as he rubbed his forehead.

"I know. Our morals have been ruined by the war. And probably Carlos is not to be trusted with her, even though he is among the best of men." Bella straightened her dress.

"But I think they are in love," Phillipe protested. "Am I to play the beast and keep them apart?"

"No, we must make a way for them to marry."

"But I want to get married first," he said so much like a little boy that she laughed at him.

"We may be able to manage that, but we cannot let our affair distract you from your responsibility for your sister."

"Very well, but I wish your reason did not prevail quite so often." He opened the trapdoor, looking down through the small opening. "When I get back from London, at least, I will be able to tell you how things stand. Perhaps we can get married without it appearing that I have trapped you into it."

She followed him down the ladder, somewhat disappointed herself that she had come to her senses. But if it turned out that they could not marry for a while, another baby would be hard to explain.

"Who would care what we do?"

He took her hand and laced his fingers through hers. "If you were still Bella McFarlane, you could do as you please, but as the Duchess of Dorney you are under the public eye."

"Are there any advantages to being a duchess? For I tell you, Phillipe, I have yet to discover one."

"You can consign me to the devil any time you please."

"I shall keep that in mind."

Their first day in the schoolroom with Thackery proved as boring as Phillipe had predicted, but Bella read half of a history of the 1745 rebellion as she listened to Jamie recite. The trip to the abbey ruins was more interesting since Ann and the dowager came along as well as Miranda and Carlos. Hal had attached himself to Phillipe for the London expedition and planned to stay in town until the family removed to the city.

Bella thought about Edwin and Hal on the drive to the ruins. When Bella had confided to Edwin that she was carrying Phillipe's child, he had said that was all the more reason she should accept him as a husband, that if the child were a boy, he would prefer to have Phillipe's son inherit the dukedom rather than the irresponsible Hal.

But now that she was on the brink of cheating Hal out of his fortune, now that she knew him, she was sorely tempted to follow her original inclination and remove Jamie from the dowager's influence before the old woman became too attached to him. All she had to do was break her promise to a dead man. She thought about Edwin, so like Phillipe in all ways but one: he had no interest in women. But so long as the world thought he had been happily married and had fathered a child, there would be no more gossip. And if Bella declared Jamie to be illegitimate, there would be plenty.

No matter how much she thought about it, and turned the alternatives over in her mind, no solution to her dilemma occurred to her. After exploring the ruins to her satisfaction and after reflecting on what sort of bombardment it would have taken to bring down the structure, Bella sat on a warm rock and watched Miranda in her merciless pursuit of Carlos, who adamantly preferred the company of Ann. Bella glanced at the dowager once or twice, wondering what she thought of all this, but the old woman seemed oblivious to Miranda's simpering. Once Jamie escaped Thackery's dull lecture, he took to playing hide-and-seek among the rocks. Carlos and Ann joined in the game, Miranda as well, until she turned her ankle.

Bella was sure she was faking. That is why she suggested the fomentation and described the hot comfrey plaster process in enough gruesome detail to get Miranda back on her feet. While the others rested from their exertions, Thackery drew Bella aside to expound on his teaching methods. But she insisted they walk while he talked, and she set a pace that was more like a forced march than a stroll.

"But Mr. Thackery, Jamie is little more than three. Beyond learning his numbers and more English, I do not want him taught anything."

"I meant in future years. I think your concern for him admirable."

"He is my son. Of course I am concerned."

"Beauty and devotion sit on your head like a double crown," Thackery intoned.

"What on earth is that supposed to mean?"

"Why, it is poetry," he gasped as he tried to catch up to her.

"I got that, but it is incredibly bad. Who wrote it?"

Thackery flushed. "Why, I—I cannot think of the author's name at the moment."

"No poetry for Jamie."

"But I thought he might memorize a bit of *Childe Harold*."

"What a depressing thought. I assure you he would much rather have some lessons on plants and animals."

"But I do not know anything about flora and fauna."

"Well, you have the whole library at Dorney to assist you. How difficult could it be to stay ahead of a three-year-old?"

"Are you always going to interfere in the curriculum?"

"Yes, of course. As you said, it is part of my devotion to him. Tomorrow we will do a tour around the lake."

Thackery was sputtering, and she was not sure if he was angry or simply out of breath.

"Step lively, Mr. Thackery. Were we in Spain, the French snipers would have gotten you by now."

Phillipe had not returned that day, and Bella walked on eggs during and after dinner in her attempt to stay out of trouble. The second morning, she was rather proud of her efforts as she curled up in an overstuffed chair in the schoolroom enjoying a novel. She actually might have found a benefit to being a duchess: time to read. She was half listening to Jamie correcting Thackery on certain elements of Spain's geography when a rap at the door announced the arrival of the maid with tea. Bella opened the door, and Lobo scooted in, leaping for joy at finally discovering Jamie.

"Out!" Thackery commanded, making the poor dog cringe.

Two shamefaced footmen appeared with a drapery cord, but Bella dismissed them.

"Lobo has run forty miles to get to Jamie and probably has not eaten in two days. You will not banish him to the stable."

"The schoolroom is no place for a mongrel dog."

"But this mongrel dog has kept Jamie warm in the coldest weather, besides watching him for me."

"But why would you choose such a disgusting creature?"

"Lobo's flock of sheep were bought by the army. He followed the train until the last of the flock had been consumed, then fastened his care on Jamie."

"That is disgusting."

"He must guard something," Bella said. "Jamie is much safer with Lobo about. If Lobo had been with us at the cattle farm, he would not have hesitated to place himself between Jamie and a bull."

"I could not get there in time," Thackery said lamely.

Jamie was delighted to have Lobo back since the frog had been returned to the lake. He fed him all his bread and butter, and when he looked wistfully at Bella's, she gave it to him for Lobo as well.

After Jamie's nap with Lobo curled at his feet, Bella held to her plan for a walk around the lake with a field guide as a useful way to spend the afternoon. When the party set out, it was in full sun, and Lobo, in spite of his recent trip, was capering ahead and hiding, to leap out at Jamie when they approached.

"That dog is filthy," Thackery complained.

"I feel sure he will fall into the lake at least once before we get back, so there is no need to worry."

"You should keep a nice lap dog. That would be more fitting for a duchess."

"I like Lobo. He suits me." She was trying to look a tree up in the book she had taken from the library but was not having much luck with Thackery interrupting her.

"And to see you riding that stallion gives me chills. You should not."

"The number of things you think I should not do would keep me paralyzed if I had any regard for your opinion."

"Your unconventional marriage and travels certainly have drawn far too much attention." Thackery strode pompously along with his hands clasped behind his back. "You should plan to marry and live quietly in the country."

Bella stared at his pious mouth and frowned at him. "What concern is it of yours how I live?"

"Because it may be hard for you to find yourself a respectable husband after riding with the army."

"Oh, really?" Bella almost shouted. "I have had dozens of offers from soldiers."

"I said respectable."

"Those men are heroes. You say one more thing against them, and I shall dismiss you, dowager or no."

"I only thought to warn you how you might be regarded in London. If you want a husband . . ."

"And what if I do not want a husband?"

"Of course you do."

"Do not tell me what I want, Thackery. It is very ill-bred of you."

"Every woman wants respectability. Even Ann, if she would admit it. Instead she spends all her time with the Spaniard."

"Portuguese," Bella corrected, closing the book with a snap and tucking it under her arm.

"What?" Thackery asked densely.

"Carlos is Portuguese," she said slowly, as though talking to an imbecile.

"Oh, what is the difference?"

"Other than language, culture, geography, and political alignment, why, nothing at all," Bella quipped, but Thackery was too dense to be insulted. "And before you say any more about Carlos, need I remind you his family provided a home for me in Lisbon? He is like a brother to me."

"That is not what people will think." Thackery held his index finger up as she had seen him do when making a point with Jamie, and it infuriated her.

"Just what is that supposed to mean?" Bella demanded, hefting the book as a possible weapon since there were no rocks lying handy.

"You arrive here accompanied by three men, not to mention Captain Armitage, and with no chaperone other than that Spanish woman who was nursing James."

"Portuguese."

"What?"

"Maria is Portuguese!" Bella shouted. "She is also Carlos's mother, so if you cast any aspersions on her character, he will be forced to call you out. As a mat-

ter of fact, I have a good mind to call you out myself."

"Women do not fight duels." Thackery looked dis-
dainfully down on her.

"Women generally do not shoot rifles or throw
knives, but I have had an exceptional upbringing."

"I caution you not to talk like this in front of any of
Lady Edith's London acquaintances. You will cause a
scandal."

"What is it to you what impression I make in London?"

"It is my duty to accompany James and continue his
lessons."

"Not if I have anything to say about it. You are
barely to be tolerated in the country, let alone have all
my acquaintances laughing at you in London."

"You know no one in London."

"Do not be such an idiot, Thackery. The army is
back. I know everyone in London, and you are not to
accompany us."

"If Lady Edith—"

A sudden splash and the squawking of more than
one duck alerted Bella to Lobo's location, and she
made her way through the weeds to discover both boy
and dog soaking wet and causing havoc among the
flock of ducks. When they seemed inclined to dog pad-
dle after the retreating birds, Bella asserted herself.
"Back to shore, both of you."

"You see what I mean about him needing a mentor?"
Thackery said, but not lifting a finger to aid Bella in
getting Jamie ashore.

"As I recall, you were not much use at the cattle

farm." She removed the boy's wet shoes and stockings to send him happily running ahead of them barefoot and playing chase with Lobo. They had nearly rounded the lake and were approaching the gardens which led toward the stables.

"That was the most undignified romp," he said, pursing his lips.

"Thackery, are you really dense or just pretentious? It was a life-and-death situation."

"You should not have gone into that field."

"And you should have, instead of cowering on the sidelines," Bella challenged.

"I can see there is no reasoning with you today. I am going home."

"You coward."

"What did you call me?"

"A coward. And I am not used to cowards. You were afraid to help Jamie at the lake and at the farm. Any time you are losing an argument, you retreat, saying that there is no reasoning with me."

"I do not have to take these insults."

"No, you can leave," Bella said as she turned her back on Thackery and marched toward the house. She peeked over her shoulder and was satisfied to see him heading toward the stable.

Jamie ran back to her. "Mother, may Lobo sleep with me tonight?"

"Yes, of course, but just for tonight."

"Why can't Lobo stay?" Jamie bent to let the worshipful dog wash his face.

"We really should take him back to the farm before he gets into trouble here."

"Can we?" Jamie begged. "Can we go to the farm? I want to see my piglets."

"Hmm, I suppose returning Lobo would be a good excuse for a lightning visit back. We shall start early tomorrow."

"Can I ride Sebastian?"

"I should like to take him, but I think we had better bow to convention and use the carriage."

~❧10❧~

*B*ella mentioned her planned expedition at breakfast the next morning to ascertain that no one else needed the carriage. Lady Edith argued so much against the trip that she completely forgot to reject any of the food, and Bella made an excellent meal. She also went to the kitchen to order a picnic lunch and waited while they prepared it. She rather wished that Phillipe had returned, for he would have liked to go with them. But perhaps he did not have time for them as he did in Spain.

When she and Jamie went to the stables to have the carriage put to, the stable boys were all standing about looking sullen, including Greenley. Philben, the butler, was there looking out of place in his bag wig and breeches. And the head lad was red in the face as though he had just been arguing with him.

"Hanley, where is the carriage I asked for?"

"Lady Edith does not think it wise for you to take the carriage out today," Philben answered for him.

"Why? Does she need it? Then a whiskey or curricle will do. Actually, I should like that better. I can drive myself. Why are you all just standing there? Harness me a team, someone."

"But, your grace," the head groom said, "you simply cannot go driving off alone."

"That is why I asked for the carriage, so that I could take a driver and footmen. But Philben seems to think it will not do. However, I see plenty of horses and my pick of equipages, but no one with the expertise to harness a team. Do you imagine I cannot do that for myself if I have to?" Bella threatened so forcefully the head groom cringed like a raw recruit suffering the saber tongue of Lord Wellington.

"But, your grace," Philben said, "Lady Edith gave express orders—"

"Lady Edith is not the Duchess of Dorney. She does not pay your considerable salary. If you feel disinclined to take orders from me, then get out of my way."

"You cannot harness a team yourself." Hanley blocked her path, and she handed the picnic basket to Jamie as she prepared to blast the man.

Lady Edith could be seen making her way from the house, and Bella waited to have it out with her.

"Captain Armitage is in charge here after Lady Edith," Philben blustered. "If they do not think it wise for you to leave unescorted . . ."

"I am taking my groom with me, of course," Bella replied, keeping a tight rein on her anger.

The dowager arrived and planted her cane between two cobbles. "You are unused to the customs that obtain at the park."

"I am unused to being disobeyed," Bella snarled. "Were Philben a sergeant in Edwin's brigade, he would have been broken to private within the first three days. And what you are proposing to do today, virtually hold me captive, that would be a court-martial offense."

"This is not the army!" Lady Edith shouted.

"When I am in command, it will be run a little more like an army," Bella said.

"You will never command here." The dowager swung the heavy stick in her general direction. Jamie sniffed and Lobo growled protectively, taking up a stand between Lady Edith and the boy.

"I want to see my piglets and Maria!" Jamie cried.

"I know, dear," Bella soothed.

The dowager glowered at her. "You will not take James away."

"He is *my* son. I will take him where I please."

"He is the duke."

"That has not been determined yet." Bella shot her a look that told the dowager she could easily change Jamie's status. "Is there no one here competent to harness even a whiskey for me?"

The grooms studied their boots, except young Greenley, who looked inclined to speak. He even stepped forward but was restrained by a firm grip on his arm from the head groom.

Bella could see Jamie fidgeting and looking a little afraid. She would have to end this confrontation and quickly if the child was not to be frightened to death of Lady Edith. Bella stared at each face in turn, committing them to her infallible mental slate. "This will be remembered," she said ominously, laying a medieval emphasis to the word. She then turned on the duchess, who was looking smug in spite of her red face. "Is it only Jamie who is a prisoner, or am I to be detained as well?"

"I do not give a tinker's damn what you do," the dowager spit at her.

"Then is there anyone willing to saddle me a horse while I say good-bye to my son?" Bella could see Jamie's lip quiver and pulled him to her with a whispered "Don't worry."

Greenley pulled away from the head groom and strode forward. "I will do it, miss," he said with his usual willingness.

"You are fired, then!" the dowager shouted.

"You cannot fire Greenley," Bella said. "He has worked for me since Edwin's death. Saddle Sebastian for me and Rufus for yourself, Greenley."

So saying, she knelt by Jamie and said, "I need you to be brave and go back to the house now." The rest of her instructions were in a mixture of Spanish and Portuguese that brought a devious look to Jamie's face and made Greenley smirk. She kissed Jamie and hugged him when she had finished and waited to see her son walk calmly back to the house, carrying the picnic basket, and enter the door as she held Lobo's collar. She stepped up onto the mounting block and hopped on Sebastian's back, causing Philben and the dowager to stagger back as the stallion gave his usual impatient plunge. Once Greenley had mounted, Bella said, "I will be back tomorrow, and so will Phillipe. I wonder how you are going to explain this to him."

"I have nothing to explain," Lady Edith maintained. "I am merely doing my duty."

"This is only one battle, *madam*," Bella taunted, having picked the slur up from Phillipe. "Not the whole war."

"How dare you?"

"I told you before, I will dare anything where my son is concerned."

She came as close as she dared to overriding Philben as she launched Sebastian from the yard in a clatter of hooves, scanning the house as they rounded the drive toward the front. By luck, no servant had seemed inclined to halt Jamie's progress since he seemed to be going in the direction they wanted. If only he was not detained in the house. If he was, Bella thought, she would merely take a short ride and return. But if ever she got her son away from here, she would not walk into the enemy camp under a flag of truce again, unless she had a whole brigade to back her up.

She could hear Greenley close behind her, but neither looked back nor halted until they were down the drive and out of sight of the house. Then she pulled Sebastian to a stop and Lobo halted ahead of her. "This lane runs behind the formal side gardens?"

"Yes, your grace." Greenley's face split into a grin.

"Come, then. Let us see if Jamie has made good his escape."

They trotted down the lane, scanning about to make sure they were not seen. The gate in the farthest garden wall was standing open, and when they approached, a small head peeked around the corner of the stone wall.

"Excellent, my imp," Bella said. "You have done well. And you have even managed to save our lunch."

Greenley laughed and got down to lift Jamie to sit in front of his mother, as Lobo leaped for joy. Greenley shifted the provisions to his saddle pack and tossed the basket into the stream.

"Let us be off," she said as she turned Sebastian and struck out across the fields toward the main road.

"They have grown, Mother," Jamie said as he gazed at the thirteen piglets.

"Do they remember you, imp?"

"Yes, this is my favorite." Jamie picked up the runt and hugged it. "Can he sleep with me?"

"You do not think Lobo might make a meal of him in the night?"

"Lobo likes him, too," Jamie said, stroking the chosen pig as they walked back toward the house.

"But as what, a snack? We must remember Lobo's upbringing. He was a sheep dog and only protects sheep by instinct. Any other creature is fair game to him."

"May I play with him in the kitchen, then?" Jamie begged.

"Just for a few hours. Then he goes back with the other pigs to sleep."

After dinner Maria and Rourke sat contentedly in the kitchen as Bella and Jamie lounged on the hearth rug and told them about the bull adventure. Jamie amused himself by watching Lobo and the piglet compete for hazelnuts on the stone kitchen floor. A galloping horse arrived in the courtyard in a spurt of gravel.

"That will be Phillipe," Bella said calmly.

"How do you know?" Rourke asked, making his way to the door.

"I know Phillipe. You might go and walk his horse for him."

Rourke laughed and went to the front room. A moment later Phillipe strode in, a look of intense concern on his face, melting into relief at the sight of Jamie. Bella felt almost jealous of that look. "I suppose the dowager lied to you about what happened today," Bella said calmly.

"I am quite sure she did," Phillipe said, sitting down tiredly and resting his head in his hands. "It is very nearly her only skill—prevarication." He was still breathing hard, and Bella rose to get him something to drink.

Maria rolled up her sewing and went upstairs with a knowing smile.

"Phillipe, I cannot live my life as a prisoner. Neither can Jamie. I am going to say he is not Edwin's son. I see no other way out."

Phillipe stared at her for a moment, then leaned back. "When I was a very green young officer, a surprisingly young girl told me something quite profound."

"What did I say?" she asked, handing him the glass.

"Do not burn any bridges you might need later."

"Hah! I did say that, as I recall."

"It is still good advice."

"One thing is a certainty. We cannot go on as we are. If I allow Jamie to be the Duke of Dorney, it will have to be on my own terms."

Phillipe reached for her hand and gave it a quick squeeze. "You know that it does not matter to me. I will agree to anything so long as it allows me to protect Jamie," he said desperately.

"Would I do anything to endanger my own son?"

"Not knowingly." Phillipe took a sip from the glass and coughed when strong brandy burned its way down his throat instead of wine. "But you and Greenley would have been no match for a highwayman or any other ruffian with a pistol."

"I had planned on bringing the carriage and half a dozen servants, but the dowager would not allow the trip at all."

Jamie picked up the piglet and carried it to Phillipe. "See my pig?"

"And a fine one he is," Phillipe said, scratching the animal between the ears. "We shall have to tell the Deans this one is a pet."

Jamie kissed the creature on the head with a resounding smack.

"That, for example, would send her grace into a fit of the vapors," Bella said with a laugh.

"Not after having the lake and the stream dragged all afternoon."

Bella stared at him. "What are you talking about?"

"They missed Jamie after you fled and assumed, once they had searched the entire house and all outbuildings, that he had drowned in the lake."

"Why in God's name would they think that?" Bella demanded.

"They found the picnic basket floating ominously on the water."

Bella hesitated, thinking back. "Greenley ditched it in the stream. I guess it floated down to the lake. Oh, dear."

"It was Thackery actually who ordered them to drag the lake," Phillipe said.

"Officious busybody. What was he doing there, anyway? I fired him."

"I don't know," Phillipe said tiredly.

"I suppose I will have to send Greenley back with word that Jamie is safe. What a bother."

"Is it true that all the servants defied you except Greenley?" Phillipe followed her with his gaze as she tidied the already neat room and stirred the fire.

"Yes, though many of them did so reluctantly. Any of the grooms, including the head lad, would have done my bidding had they not been expressly ordered otherwise by Philben and the dowager. She would have fired on the spot any of them willing to defy her."

"Do you want the man turned off?"

Bella cast Phillipe a sideways look. "Do you really mean that?"

"It would make an example of him," Phillipe said, taking another drink of brandy and closing his eyes as he swallowed.

Bella sent him a measuring look. "When was the last time you ate?"

"I . . . I do not remember. I am used to riding all day and half the night in a desperate attempt to keep the war on an even keel. Nothing has changed so very much."

Bella noted that Jamie had fallen asleep on the hearth rug with his pig on one side and Lobo on the other.

"Eggs and ham?"

"Only if Jamie's pet does not object."

Bella cooked for him and watched him eat, then poured him a second mug of tea when he finally pushed his plate away. "What is it to be, Bella? Sack the lot of them?"

"That would hardly demonstrate my fair-handedness. But someone must be punished as an example."

"That is what Wellington would have done. Shall I move Lady Edith to the dower house?"

"You are assuming I am going back to Dorney Park."

Phillipe hesitated. "That is up to you, but if you mean to let Jamie be duke, I think you have to go back, or you will never have any influence there. And if all those servants did indeed defy you, I think I shall let them search for Jamie through the night. Greenley can ride over in the morning with a note."

"Philben must go," Bella said flatly.

"Will sacking him suffice or shall I have him drawn and quartered?" Phillipe asked with a grin.

"Do not sack him. Send him to London. I would prefer to have Hoskins as a butler."

"I wonder if Hoskins will prefer Dorney Park?" Phillipe mused.

"Hoskins will butler wherever I am expected next. So long as I never encounter Philben again, I do not care that he has a job."

"But he will have no real authority in either place."

"I know. That is the beauty of it," Bella said. "The other servants will see his punishment day after day."

"You are vindictive enough to be a general."

"Thank you."

"I shall carry Jamie up for you. But I will leave the disposition of the piglet to you."

Phillipe laid the boy tenderly on the bed. Lobo hopped up and made a nest in the blankets at the foot. Phillipe straightened up, groaning a little as he put his full weight on his bad leg and his boot rubbed the blister on his ankle.

"What is it?" Bella asked.

"Do you have any of that salve you used to give me when I had rubbed my ankle raw from riding so much?"

"Phillipe, I am sorry. Yes, it is in the stable."

She went to her room and got a cloak.

"If you tell me where it is, I can find it," he offered from the narrow hall.

"I want to check the horses anyway, and I may as well return the pig."

"That is Rourke's job," he said as he followed her downstairs again.

"He is not a young man. Besides, I heard him go up to bed with Maria." Bella gathered up the dozing pig, and Phillipe came to take him from her.

She tossed her cloak about her shoulders and made her way through the darkened downstairs rooms and out through the kitchen, grabbing up some carrots along the way. She went to the stable, and Phillipe followed her, closing the door behind them and returning the piglet to its pen. Bella made her rounds, talking sweet cozening words to each of the beasts, just as she had to him that night along the Coa River.

Phillipe came to hug her from behind. "What have you decided?" he asked softly. "I will support you no matter what you want to do."

She was not startled but turned in his arms and hugged him about the waist. "No matter what I promised Edwin, I must tell you the truth."

"You promised to be faithful to him and you were,"

he protested, reaching up to caress her dark, shimmering mane of hair.

Her crystal eyes searched his face for understanding, and he managed to smile through his pain to reassure her.

"Edwin guessed about us, that we had loved each other," she whispered. "And when he thought you were dead . . . he begged me to marry him anyway."

"Along with half the army," Phillipe joked. "All things considered, I am glad you chose Edwin." He ran the backs of his knuckles along her soft cheek, and she dipped her head to kiss his fingers.

"But it was not a real marriage," Bella said, laying her hands on either side of Phillipe's face. "He wanted to keep me safe, so that no one else would have me."

"What are you saying?" Phillipe shook his head, trying to banish the image of Bella and Edwin lying together. "You were married to Edwin. You must have gone to bed with him."

"No, Edwin never made love to me, not even on our wedding night."

Phillipe held her at arm's length, watching the slow tears drip down her cheeks. He was amazed and suddenly joyful beyond all measure. "Then Jamie *is* my son!" He hugged her to him as though some barrier had been removed from between them.

"Yes, I refused Edwin when I realized I was pregnant, but he convinced me it was the best thing for the child. I had just buried my father. I did not know what to do."

"What a position for you to be in. If only I had not

been captured." Still, he could see in his mind's eye Edwin pointing that pistol at him. He shut his eyes tight and blinked away the hideous thought. At least let Bella preserve the illusion that Edwin was noble.

"I could not remain a single woman with the army. I would have had to marry someone, and I could not bear the thought of it being anyone but you. Binding myself to Edwin meant I could be your widow, would never have to have another man than you." She had her hands on his shoulders, regarding his face as though she were memorizing it.

"You loved me that much?" Phillipe asked huskily.

"And my punishment was to see you come back and not have you." Bella sniffed back her tears.

"I had always thought you courageous, too strong to feel anything. Now I see you were stronger than that. You were strong enough not to show what you were feeling."

She began trembling in his arms as she had that night on the Coa, and he knew she remembered that time as well. He kissed her, his hands locked around her waist. She opened for him as she had then, desperately, as though he possessed some life force that could save her, unaware that he had been as hopeless as she had.

When he broke the kiss, he nuzzled her hair as she spoke her Spanish love words into his ear. "My Phillipe. Mi amor. I was terrified that night, but I wanted to do one thing while I still lived. I wanted to see you smile, and I did manage that."

"Yes, you did that and much more. Is that how you thought of me?" he asked as he used one hand to massage a breast, drawing a gasp from her. "A challenge?"

"I thought of you as a great mystery, the only man beyond the reach of my jokes and smiles, perhaps beyond the reach of my love."

He could feel the nub of her aroused nipple through her shirt and unbuttoned it to give him access. "Why did you do it?" he asked, then fell to suckling her other breast, feasting his mind on the sighs of pleasure he was producing from those seductive lips.

"Because I wanted you and we had nothing to lose, or so I thought."

"Yes, we were going to die, as I recall."

She arched her back and swayed in his arms. He felt powerful, in control for once.

"We are still going to die," she said, sliding one hand down his chest to his enlarged manhood. "We simply do not know when."

Phillipe groaned and picked her up, carrying her to the mound of fresh hay that had been brought in for the horses. She squirmed under him as she had that night, not in protest but in passion. Her hands ran over the muscles of his back, and he remembered how those hands had made him tremble when she tended his wounds. His restraint had been enormous then, and she was even more desirable now. He wanted her out of all reason. He had been cheated out of his life with her, cheated out of his children and out of his happiness. To hell with restraint. He would never let life cheat him again.

She stopped his hands, but only to take off her clothes. As she disrobed, he chuckled at her lithe, unabashed nakedness.

"This must seem tame to you without the French

shooting at us," he said as he helped her out of her garments and carefully hung them on one of the stall partitions. She had a scar under her right breast that she had not had then. It looked as if the tip of a saber had caught her. He held her and ran his fingers reverently over the mark. "God, how close you have come to dying a thousand times."

He coveted her as she reclined on the pile of hay and looked up at him, her hair loose about her shoulders. Even if she had been another man's wife at that moment, it would not have stopped him from wanting her as she coyly watched him strip off his clothes.

Bella watched Phillipe appreciatively. She had seen his body before, but aside from that one night, only when she was dressing his wounds. No matter how tenderly she tried to help him, she always ended up hurting him. She must never hurt him again. She held her breath as he revealed the slash on his left forearm, the bullet mark on his shoulder, the scarred rib cage, and, finally, the leg wound that had nearly done for him. But the scars no longer held her attention, for his enlarged manhood, even in the dim light of the lantern, pulled her gaze away from the past to the present. She could feel a hot wetness between her legs and knew she had been waiting for this moment, hoping for it from the time she had seen him on the docks in London.

He knelt beside her and dipped his head to kiss the scar under her breast. "I did not know you were wounded," he said as he kissed her breast.

"It was just a scratch," she replied, caressing his face with her hands.

"I can scarcely believe it," Phillipe said. "We are together finally against all odds. Let us never be parted again," he said as he knelt astride her, and his manhood pressed urgently against her. She wrapped her legs about his waist, and he entered her with reticence, trying to stretch out the experience for her. She closed her eyes to savor the touch of him, the give and take of him. Lovemaking was a metaphor for life. You felt always that tug of war between self and beloved, wanting him to stay but letting him go. Each foray into her was more desperate, more urgent, and accelerated his breathing until Phillipe was like a lathered horse, rocking her with every plunge until she could no longer suppress her small screams of ecstasy.

She lost herself then, could no longer control the words of love, both Spanish and English, that rushed from her lips. His restraint broke, and he surged within her, moaning softly as he settled down to rest on top of her. She ran her hands over his back, grasping him to her as though she could keep their love safe forever.

❧11❧

When Phillipe awoke, he knew a terrifying moment when he thought he was alone again. But it was not so. Bella lay warm in his arms with her cloak covering them. He felt a bandage on his ankle. She must have gotten up in the middle of the night and taken care of him. That was her way. She snuggled against him and he held her tighter, wanting to deny the dawn, wanting the night never to end.

Whatever pain their separation had cost him, it had hurt her more, for she had borne the guilt of it with every condemning glance he had sent her. And she had not been guilty, had in fact been trapped by his cunning cousin Edwin. So Edwin had known she was pregnant and married her anyway. It was perfect for Edwin's purpose. He had joined the army to put to rest the rumors about his sexual preferences. Returning to England with a wife and son . . .

Phillipe froze as the suspicion washed over him

again. He saw it all in his mind. Edwin stood in the vanguard of the British lines as Phillipe rode like a madman just a few dozen yards ahead of a troop of French lancers. The British riflemen attached to Edwin's brigade all raised their rifles just as Edwin raised his pistol. A volley of shots obscured the vision in his mind with powder smoke. And a searing pain shot through him and crashed him to the earth.

Family honor was important to Edwin, but was it important enough to sacrifice his cousin so he could have the wife and child he needed?

Phillipe shivered, and this woke Bella.

"What is the matter? Are you cold?"

"No, just a bad dream." He kissed her, and his hunger for her returned. Not just for her body. He wanted to be with her, beside her all the time. He groaned. "We are never going to be able to wait a year."

Bella pushed herself up and looked at him, then stroked his hair back. "I want to tell Lady Edith the truth as soon as we return to Dorney. I cannot bear the thought of cheating Hal."

"People will only think my aunt rejected you and you could not prove your claim. Some will always believe Jamie is the duke."

"Let there be a great mystery about him then. When he grows up, all the ladies will fall in love with him."

"They will, but not because of any mystery, because he is your son and you will raise him sweetly."

"And yours. You have much time to make up for."

"I have always hoped he was mine, treated him as though he was. I am glad now."

"We should get back to the house," she said.

"Let me hold you another moment. We will dress and pretend we have been out checking the horses."

"We have been. We checked them all night."

They rode side by side with Jamie up on Phillipe's saddle this time and Phillipe riding Sebastian. They had sent Greenley off early in the morning with the news of Jamie's survival. Bella rode with Lobo draped across her lap part of the way to save his worn paws. This was what it could have been like if they had married, Bella thought, if Phillipe had not been captured. Perhaps there would have been another child by now. She had lost four precious years, but at least she had finally told Phillipe the truth. And now they could be free of Dorney Park and all the trappings of the dukedom.

They were almost to the gates when Phillipe turned to her and smiled. "I could tell the dowager myself," Phillipe said with a lift to his eyebrow.

"It would be cowardly of me to let you. There will be a scandal."

"Inevitable," he said with a devilish grin.

"Do you care?"

"Not a fig."

"This changes everything, does it not?" she asked.

"Yes, everything," he whispered.

They could see the lake glittering through the trees now. Bella watched Phillipe tear his gaze away from it.

He loved Dorney Park, but she thought he loved her and Jamie a great deal more.

"We will not be destitute," he said. "Edwin left me a small place in Norfolk with a decent income. You will like it there. It is much like Spain at certain times of the year."

"Excellent. We will have a place to go to when we feel restless. But what about all your friends in London?"

"If they really are friends, my indiscretion will not weigh with them."

Bella stared at his profile, trying to detect any possible regret. "And what about Ann?"

"Perhaps Carlos will solve that for us. Or she can live with us."

"Edwin would have been furious if he had lost his command."

"What are you talking about?" Phillipe asked. "He did lose it. They nearly all died." Phillipe waved to Ann at the window as they rode under the archway.

"He was dead himself by then. I mean he would have resented losing the power you now have over all the estates. You manage everything. But you would not have liked a command in the army."

"No, I would not have liked to send those poor fellows into battle to die. So long as the risk was all my own, I did not worry. Hal will waste everything, of course, just as the old duke surmised. But there is no help for it. Hal is simply not a strong character."

Lobo leaped out of Bella's arms as Greenley came out to take their horses.

"Phillipe, I am sorry," Bella whispered. "Edwin told

me what it would be like." She slid off the mare and took Jamie. They waited for the tired horses to be led away.

"But this is what I had always hoped," Phillipe said. "That Jamie is mine. About the rest of it I do not care." He took the boy from Bella's arms and held him, feeling for the first time that he had a future that mattered.

Carlos emerged from the stable to glance at their wrinkled clothes and dusty boots. "Pleasant campaign?" he asked.

"You heard what happened," Phillipe surmised.

"Yes, I got back very late last night. That will teach me to take a bolt up to town to buy presents. I tried my best to convince her grace that Bella would never leave Jamie, but she persisted in believing the child was at the bottom of the lake and could not understand why I was not out there in the rowboat with the grappling hook trying to find him. I very nearly lost my patience with her."

Jamie had been looking at Carlos. "Grandmother thought I was swimming?" Carlos bit his lip, took Jamie from Phillipe, and set him on his shoulders. "Yes, she thought you had turned into a seahorse and would never come back to her."

Jamie chuckled and grasped his head as Carlos reared and whinnied. "Now she has branded me an uncaring fool for not helping with the search."

"That is absurd," Bella said. "Of course I would never leave him."

By the time they entered the house, Ann must have informed the dowager of their return. Unfortunately, this had given Lady Edith time to stoke the embers of the previous day's anger, and she was standing by the window in the morning room waiting for them.

"How could you?" the dowager asked accusingly. "You secreted James away and left me thinking I had killed him."

"You are the one with a guilty conscience," Bella said. "If you had let him come with me in the carriage with a proper escort of servants, there would have been no danger at all."

Carlos put the boy down and said, "I think I will take Jamie to wash up so you three can talk."

The dowager watched the boy leave hand in hand with Carlos before she said bitterly, "You might never have come back."

"Now, why would I leave?" Bella asked. "Just because I had been insulted, imprisoned, scorned, and chided? Why would I not want to come back to that?"

"Phillipe, you must do something," Lady Edith demanded.

"I warned you not to push Bella, that she would not knuckle under to you the way everyone else does."

"She will obey me if she wishes to be recognized in society as the Duchess of Dorney."

"But I do not," Bella interposed. "Oh, I suppose I am that after all. I did marry Edwin. But Jamie is Phillipe's son."

The dowager stared at her, and Phillipe could almost see the wheels turning as she realized her power over Bella was gone. "You . . . you are lying." The old woman faltered and made her way to a chair.

"Why would I lie about that?" Bella reasoned.

"Phillipe and I were intending to marry but could find no cleric. Then he was killed, or so I thought. Marrying Edwin gave Jamie a name and a father."

"Are you saying you deceived my son, foisted another man's child onto him?" She stared back at Bella like a wounded lioness, curled up in her lair.

"No," Phillipe said. "It was Edwin's idea. He did it out of respect to me, when he thought I was dead. He was generous." It all came out just as he had rehearsed it in his mind, and he did not believe a word of it.

Lady Edith looked as though she were going to say something, then her face went quite tired and she closed her eyes. "Why did you not tell me before?"

"Edwin made me promise," Bella said. "One does not lightly break a promise to a dead man."

"He was a good boy," the dowager said helplessly, the tears real this time.

"He was a hero, a great man in every way," Bella assured her. "But I had no interest in any man except Phillipe."

"And Edwin promised to raise Phillipe's child as his own," the dowager mused. "People would believe that. Phillipe and Edwin looked much alike."

"As soon as I am out of mourning, Phillipe and I plan to marry." Bella raised her chin, waiting for condemnation.

The dowager stared at her for a moment, then nodded. "Yes, that will do. There is no problem there. So why then must you declare Jamie illegitimate? Phillipe can raise him as well as a stepfather as he can a father." Lady Edith looked at Phillipe. "Jamie already looks upon you that way. To do anything else would confuse the child."

Bella thought she must be gaping. Phillipe's brow was furrowed in confusion. "But what—what are you suggesting, your grace?" Bella stammered breathlessly. "That we continue the pretense? That I maintain Jamie is Edwin's child?"

"Yes, of course. What possible difference can it make if you do?"

"A great deal of difference to Hal," Phillipe answered.

"Oh, Hal would only make a muck of things anyway. Besides, Edwin promised he would be well taken care of. No, we must go on as we have. You owe me that much, Bella. You owe Edwin that much. You did promise him." The old woman looked at her as though it were the most reasonable thing in the world to take on a bastard grandchild and cut her own second son out of his fortune.

Bella glanced at Phillipe. His face had taken on that tired, strained look it had often worn in Spain. It was odd. She had felt such a sense of relief at finally telling this old woman the truth and knowing her son could lead a normal life, and the dowager had surprised her again.

"Does anyone else know?" Lady Edith asked as she waggled her finger toward the liquor tray. Phillipe obediently went and poured her a small glass of sherry.

"Carlos may suspect," Phillipe said as he handed the glass to her. "He was with us at the time, in the downstairs room."

"Or Carlos may have guessed," Bella confessed. "But he would always defend my honor."

"You know him better than I," the dowager said. "He has everything to gain by keeping quiet."

"Carlos? But he is not interested in money," Bella said staunchly.

"But he is interested in Ann," the dowager said with a smirk. "Do you think I have not seen them together? He would do anything I asked if I approved their marriage. He is almost family, so I think he is safe."

"But I am tired of being a prisoner at Dorney and I want my son back," Bella protested.

"You are far too careless with him," Lady Edith replied. "Anyone could have snatched him on your way to that farm."

Bella glanced to Phillipe for support, but he was pouring himself a large brandy and wearing a pained look between his eyebrows.

"I think you exaggerate the danger from highwaymen and abductors," Bella said, fiddling with her riding crop, drawing the lash through her fingers as she tried to think of a way out of this mess.

"They almost got Edwin," Lady Edith reminded her.

"But that was years ago," Bella said. "Surely England is not so lawless now."

Phillipe came to sit on the arm of the dowager's chair.

"Perhaps more so," Lady Edith maintained, "with this rabble of soldiers released from the army, unemployed and penniless."

"She may be right, Bella," Phillipe said tiredly as he took a drink. "You know they are not all saints, and the English have ever been wary of a standing army."

"And whose fault is that?" Bella asked. "Nothing has been done for them by Parliament. If Hal were duke, he could take some action within a year. Jamie would not be able to do anything for decades."

The dowager laughed outright, holding her glass with both hands so as not to spill it. Phillipe opened his mouth to say something, but the words did not come.

"Well, Hal might," Bella said hotly. "It is possible." Bella looked from one to the other of them, but Phillipe only shrugged.

"The problem is not Hal," Lady Edith said resolutely. "He will be provided for. There is no point in denying Jamie the dukedom for one very important reason." The old woman took a long drink and sighed, back in control as usual and liking it.

"And what is that?" Bella demanded finally, clenching the crop in both hands.

"The problem is that even if the world knew the child as Phillipe's son, I would still pay an enormous ransom to get him back."

Bella stared at her with her mouth open. "You—you love Jamie too?"

"He is an engaging little chap. Puts me in mind of Phillipe when he was little, ever so quiet and patient, even with me. Not like Edwin at all. Edwin was always fighting, ripping and tearing, never listening to me. He never bore anything quietly, never brought me wildflowers, like Jamie, or any pictures he had drawn. Jamie actually seeks me out, and apparently not at your prompting."

"No, I did not know he visited you," Bella said in surprise.

"It is our little secret."

"Then . . . you already suspected," Phillipe surmised, staring at his aunt with his brows furrowed.

"Do you know he had a pet frog?" the old woman asked.

"Yes, but I did not know that you were aware of it," Bella said.

"Jamie brought him for a visit . . . without being called." The dowager glared at Phillipe. "He came to me of his own accord because he thought I might be bored."

Bella glanced sideways at Phillipe, uncertain whether this was a good turn of events or not.

"Usually I have to command company, even my son or nephew. Ann is the only one who cares a farthing about me."

"So," Bella said, continuing to toy with the riding crop. "We are each other's prisoner."

"Of course, my dear," Lady Edith said smugly. "That is what family is all about."

Phillipe choked on a swallow of brandy and then broke into unexpected laughter.

Bella stared impatiently at him, then turned back to the dowager. "But we cannot be confusing the troops with two of us giving countermanding orders."

"Are you saying you want me to step down as mistress of Dorney Park?"

"No, I am suggesting separate staffs. If Wellington could solve such a problem, surely to God we can come to some accommodation."

"And when we cross?" Lady Edith challenged.

Bella glanced up with a wicked smile. "Phillipe will decide."

Phillipe stood. "Putting me forever on the horns of a dilemma, always moderating between my wife and her mother-in-law."

"But Lady Edith is not your mother."

"She is as close to a mother as I had, so please try to work things out amicably between you two."

"We will try," Bella said. "I am going to read to Jamie. He has had to leave his piglet again and will be feeling sad."

Phillipe stared after her as she left the room, contemplating another moonlight walk after dinner, but that would never be enough for him, and a tryst was much more dangerous here than at the farm. He turned back to his aunt with a strained smile. "Do you realize that if the truth is ever found out, I could go to prison for conspiring to steal Hal's fortune, not to mention his title, and you will be ruined socially?"

"And what of Bella and Jamie?" she asked with a resigned smile.

"Innocent victims of our machinations. They will never be called to account."

Lady Edith finished her sherry and licked her lips with satisfaction. "Ah, well, what is life without a little uncertainty?"

Phillipe laughed. "Too comfortable by far. I am not used to feeling safe." Phillipe leaned on his good leg and thought back over his more dangerous exploits. Usually they had been over in a few weeks, a few months at the most. This would remain dangerous for the rest of his life. He shook his head. It would be like the army forever.

"Your job will be to keep Bella from ever telling people Jamie is your son, no matter how much you want him to be."

Phillipe hesitated with his glass halfway to his mouth as this remark sank in. He slowly turned his gaze toward his aunt. "What do you mean by that?"

"Do you think she is telling the truth?" Lady Edith prodded.

"About what?" Phillipe asked dryly, anger catching in his throat.

"About Jamie being your son. Do you really know?"

Phillipe rubbed his hand over his brow. "Why do you do this to me? She has no reason to lie now."

"She wants Jamie for herself. And she wants you. You are right about her not caring about the money." The dowager heaved herself to her feet and said, "Do not drink yourself into a stupor."

Phillipe stood there for a long time, his heart thudding in his chest as he listened to his aunt's cane tapping across the marble floor. He threw the glass across the room and watched it smash against a marble column. Then he went down the back stairs and out into the gathering gloom, not knowing anymore a safe course for him and Bella.

Just when he thought his aunt was finally becoming human, she did something as vicious as trying to make him doubt Bella. This meant that the dowager had not heard the rumors about Edwin, that she thought Jamie might really be her grandson. The worry was not that Bella might reveal the truth someday but that Lady Edith might do so. She would no doubt keep them all dancing attendance on her with the veiled threat that she might one day expose them all.

It made for a very uncertain future indeed, but he did know the one thing that had always burned inside him like a strong dose of spirits. He knew he loved Bella and wanted her out of all reason, even if it meant becoming his aunt's prisoner, even if his soul be damned for it.

～12～

$\mathcal{B}$ella sat numbly in the breakfast parlor over hot tea laced with cream and sugar. They had never had anything so good during the war. And she resented that she should have so much now when she did not want it, after having so little then when she needed it most. It made no sense to feel this way, to resent wealth and plenty. Did she still want to be hungry? The odd answer was yes. Hunger kept you on your toes, like a hunting wolf. Hunger gave you an edge, meant you could not be surprised. It was not good always to be satisfied, always to have everything you wanted. Such a life could be a complete bore, which probably accounted for Lady Edith's temperament. She could have everything she wanted except her youth or her son back. No wonder she was bitter.

Phillipe came in looking as though he had not slept at all. He went to the sideboard and poured himself tea, fixing it the same way she did, with milk and sugar.

He sat then and looked at her, as uncertain as the first time she had seen him at Talavera, as though she were a mermaid washed up on the beach and he did not know what to do with her.

"Can you go through with this?" he asked finally, stirring his tea.

"You know Hal better than I. Would his lot be better if we were to make him duke?"

Phillipe sighed and thought for a moment, staring out the window. "You ask me to judge the future man on the boy that I have known. I should say we have a better chance of making Jamie into a duke than Hal, but I have only been with Hal, the man, for a year."

"I see two roads for Jamie. One is carefree and full of laughter. He would become a soldier like his father and love the adventure, or pretend to."

"That could be a short road." Phillipe dropped his spoon into the saucer with finality.

"I know it. The other future is of a serious boy, with books more than people, trying to learn as much as possible so that he can do the right thing."

"I think we should do what my aunt wishes, but the choice is yours."

"Would she ever betray us?" Bella asked.

"I do not know. Her trust is hard to gain, but once you have it, it is like having a rock to lean against. In this case, she cannot betray us without hurting her own reputation."

"But what would she demand in return for our pretense? I am considering stepping into this prison, you see, but I should prefer to know all the terms ahead of time."

Carlos came in and put an end to their discussion.

He had no scruples about being well fed and piled his plate high with the appetite of a young man. But before he set to, he looked at them, his dark eyes flashing with sudden awareness. "Is neither of you hungry? Or have I perhaps interrupted something? I can go away again." His teeth flashed into a smile that was both seductive and boyish at the same time.

"Do not be silly, Carlos," Bella said. "Perhaps I will have something to eat, after all. What about you, Phillipe? I will get you something."

He nodded and watched Bella make up a plate of food for him as she had a hundred times before when he had been away on a mission and returned late. She always seemed to have something warm for him. It amazed him how she knew when he was coming. Or perhaps she had always held a little food back and kept it warm just in case. "Thank you," he said as she set the plate before him. He was trying to remember what on earth he had said to her when she was married to Edwin and he was billeted in their house. Had he spoken always in monosyllables and then devoured her hungrily with his eyes?

Had Edwin noticed how much he had coveted his wife? If he had, would he not have been angrier? But he always looked so apologetic about marrying Bella. Or perhaps he had only been sorry about Phillipe coming back.

He took a bite, but he could not taste anything for a moment. Bella had said Edwin had planned to live abroad, never to come back to England. Phillipe could think of several reasons for this, but the one that presented itself as the most likely was to avoid his scowling cousin.

He noticed that Bella was picking at her muffin as though she were expecting to find something disgusting inside it.

Lady Edith came in with Ann and requested an enormous breakfast, signifying her victory over them. Well, the battle was not won yet. Bella might still bolt.

Carlos got up and waited on both Lady Edith and Ann, making a ceremony of delivering their breakfast. Ann blushed becomingly, and Phillipe wondered how long she could keep a man as hot as Carlos to heel, before she either had to marry him or let him go. Whether London would help or hurt their affair was not something he could trouble his mind with right now. He would not feel safe until all the documents were signed, including the one binding Bella to him as his wife.

"I am so glad you are coming with us," Bella said as she pressed a folded gown into a trunk.

"I should not," Ann said. "I should stay and get the household back to normal. But I suppose her grace may need me."

"Carlos may need you."

"He did press on me all the advantages of a bolt to town, not the least of which is saving him from the flock of women who are sure to be after him. Do you think he is exaggerating?"

"Unfortunately, no. You are in love with him yourself, are you not?" Bella asked.

"Am I so transparent?"

"No. All women fall in love with Carlos. It is part of his charm that he can please them all. But until now he has never really loved. It is not good to . . ." Bella paused and stared out the window.

"What is it?" Ann asked.

"It is not good to have so many love you when you cannot return it."

"You are not talking about Carlos anymore."

"I never loved any man but Phillipe, and yet nearly every man I met fell in love with me. That is why I felt so alone."

"But you have Phillipe now. And by next June you and he can get married."

"I wish we were safely married," Bella said. "I have the most awful feeling that something will happen to prevent it."

"What rub could fall in the way?" Ann asked. "Aunt seems almost benign this morning."

"Yes, I suppose you are right. That is the last trunk." Bella slammed the lid decisively. "If you have them take it to the downstairs hall, all will be ready for our departure tomorrow."

"Aunt says we will leave by eight o'clock," Ann reported. "I will be surprised to see it."

"And I will be glad to get the trip over with," Bella said, sitting on the bed. "I dismissed Thackery a week ago, and yet I trip over him in the drawing room every day."

"I know you do not like him, Bella." Ann curled up on the bench at the foot of the high four-poster. "It is wonderful how well you have kept that fact hidden."

"But I have not. We come to verbal blows every time we meet. He is so impervious to snubs that it is hardly worth the effort."

"He is in love with you, or so he says."

"He is in love with my jointure," Bella replied.

"If you must know, you have cut me out with him," Ann teased. "If Thackery were to marry you instead of me, he would not only get to live at Dorney but would have plenty of money for his jaunts to London."

"Thackery? It is hard for me to picture him cutting a figure in London. He looks as if he would be more at home . . . in a factory."

"Hal says he once dropped a quarter's allowance in one game of faro. Hal was sorry he had taken him to that club. Of course, Thackery's quarter's allowance cannot be anywhere near what Hal's is, so perhaps that was not so daring an exploit anyway."

"It does explain why Thackery was so eager to keep Jamie as a pupil. He needed the money. And as for transferring his attention to me, it is the only gracious way he can give you up. No one can hold a candle to Carlos."

"I know," Ann said joyously, her face beaming. "He is the most handsome man in the world. His face is so perfect I sometimes have to touch him to make sure he is real."

"So, what are you two planning?"

"We have not dared to plan. If there is another war, he may be able to get a promotion. I will go with him, of course."

"No!" Bella said desperately. "He must not make the army a career. There is no future in it."

"But I have nothing," Ann protested. "Or very little."

"Phillipe will know what to do. Why, Carlos could

help with the estates. He knows about leading men
and giving orders. Have you spoken to Lady Edith yet?"

"I have been afraid to," Ann said. "She will never
agree."

"Do you want me to speak to her?"

"You?" Ann looked at her aghast. "Bella, oh, no.
When I think of the many times you have come to
cuffs with her, I think it would be far better for me to
break the news."

"Perhaps she will be more receptive than you think,"
Bella hinted.

"Perhaps she will have her long-promised heart
seizure. No, more likely she will tell me to take my un-
grateful self off, and I had rather not hear that until
after I have had my London fling."

"Ah, London, that will be a real test of your love for
each other."

"How so?" Ann asked. "I do not care about these
other women. Carlos will not succumb to them."

"Of course not, but the army is back, and you will be
their darling now. Can you handle being worshiped by
every man you meet and having them all flirt with you?"

Ann held her head high. "I have managed to keep
Thackery at bay."

"Thackery is a fop. I am talking about real men,
handsome men, men with muscles. Men who can fight
all day, day after day, then stand up at a ball and dance
half the night. Men who—"

"Stop, stop," Ann begged, holding her hands over
her ears. "None of them can be an equal to my Carlos."

"I know, but I am warning you what to expect. London will be like Paris was last year."

"And how was that?"

"Gay and sad. Momentous and trivial. Exciting and depressing."

"Bella, I do not know if you are looking forward to this trip or not."

"I do not know either."

Bella laughed as she went up the stairs before lunch to find Jamie in the playroom. She thought that she was going to enjoy London now that she could go there with a clear conscience.

When she entered, she saw Thackery and stopped dead. She hated finding him here in her house when she had not invited him. She gave a start when she realized she had thought of Dorney Park as her house.

Jamie was sitting on the window seat occupied with watercolors and a large sheet of paper. "What are you doing here, Thackery?" Bella asked.

Thackery looked up. "James is making a picture of the lake to take with him."

Bella walked over to look at the work of art. "Will it have any ducks and frogs in it?"

"Yes, Mother, and a turtle," Jamie said.

"Well, Thackery, we are leaving early tomorrow, so I will bid you good-bye today." Bella extended her hand to him, and he took it, grasping it between his own damp palms.

"You will see me again soon. I am going home to get Miranda, and we will be joining you in London."

"What?" Bella jerked her hand away.

"I could not bear to be away from you for so long."

"I told you that you are not going to instruct my son. I cannot be plainer than that." Bella took a step back.

"It is you I would miss. I have spent as much time with you as with your son, enough time to know my own mind. Will you marry me when—"

"No!"

"What? I mean to wait the proper period."

"No, I will not marry you at any time," Bella shouted. "What the devil ever gave you the idea I would be interested?"

"But you need to lead a quiet life with a circumspect husband."

Bella noticed Jamie listening to them and tried to tamp down her hot temper. "Considering that we argue at every meeting, it would hardly be quiet."

"But your presence in the schoolroom. How was I to interpret that but as an indication of your interest in me?"

"As my interest in my child," Bella snapped. "I have no other interest now. Please do not speak of this again."

"You are taken by surprise," Thackery said. "I should not have spoken so abruptly."

"You should not have spoken at all. I gave you no indication of interest. I have, in fact, pointedly and repeatedly told you to mind your own business."

"But our alliance could have so many advantages. It would not take you away from Jamie, for one. If you marry anyone else, you will have to leave the boy here to go live with your husband."

"As though I would leave Jamie. You must be mad." Bella went to stand by her son.

"The reason I was so precipitous is that you are

going to London, where you will be importuned by every fortune hunter in the city. The Duchess of Dorney will have a handsome income settled on her, and you are too young to know how to fend off these fellows."

"I have fended off the French troops often enough." Bella gave him her most arrogant look. "I think I can handle our own."

"Come, we could be married privately and not make the news public until you are out of mourning. I am desperate."

"Are you deaf or stupid? I will not marry you now or in a year. And that is final."

"Mother, it is finished," Jamie said as he stood up.

Bella inspected it carefully. "It is very good, Jamie. I can tell what all the animals are. Carry it downstairs. When it is dry, you can show it to your grandmother."

Jamie opened the door and Lobo rushed in to the boy's squeals of delight.

"Out, you beast!" Thackery picked up a pointer and brought it up to hit the dog, but Bella got in the way and gasped as the rod caught her on the arm.

Lobo leaped at Thackery, nipping his hand and making the man stagger backward into the desk.

"He should be shot," Thackery said, sucking the wound like a large child.

"He should get a medal," Bella said calmly, holding the dog by the collar. "Come, Lobo," Bella called. "Thackery was just leaving."

While Bella was reading to Jamie that night, the dowager came in and sat in the single armchair, waving her walking stick in a wordless command to continue. As soon as Bella had finished and tucked Jamie in for the night, Lobo hopped onto the foot of the bed and made himself a nest in the covers.

"Oh, Bella, has that disreputable dog appeared again? You will have to send him back to the farm."

"Why can Lobo not go with us?" Jamie asked.

"What would a dog, and such a dog, do in London?" his grandmother asked.

"He liked Paris," Jamie said. "He will like London."

"Lobo likes being anywhere Jamie is," Bella said. "To be sure, if we shut him up either here or at the farm, he will track us the whole way to London, and his feet are still sore from his last two trips."

The dowager was silent for a moment, seemingly impervious to the pathetic look Jamie cast at her. But Jamie did not beg.

"We shall see. Have you no kiss for your grandmother?"

Jamie hopped out of bed and kissed his grandmother's cheek when she presented it. Janet, who had been standing all the while, cast Bella a look of surprise, then hastened to open the door as Lady Edith heaved herself up.

"Walk with me," the old woman said.

"Where shall we walk?" Bella asked.

"To my room, you ninny. Do you think I go traipsing out onto the wet lawn at this time of night like Ann and Carlos?"

"Or me and Phillipe. No, I should say you do not." Bella took the dowager's arm as they descended the stairs.

"You are a bold piece. Phillipe may rue the day he marries you."

"I will never betray him again. Why will he ever have cause for regret?"

"Because he loves you far too much to keep his senses. You will ruin him and make him miserable." They had come to the dowager's door, and she thrust it open as though it had committed some crime.

"But he is unhappy without me. How could I hurt him by marrying him?"

"You have given him something to care about, something to lose." Lady Edith sat in her favorite chair by the fire.

"What do you mean? He loves Ann and you, that is obvious. He was devoted to Edwin." Bella took the poker and adjusted the small fire.

"It is not the same. Phillipe was always alone, and his solitude, his oneness, made him a strong man. You will make him weak. You will bring out the worst in him."

Bella propped the poker in its stand and turned to face her. "Then why did you consent to our marriage?"

"Because I cannot prevent it, and it is the best thing for the boy."

"But you do not like me," Bella insisted, her hands on her hips.

"No more than you like me. We were not meant to like each other. So long as you behave circumspectly and cause no scandal, we may deal well together."

"Is that what you fear? Scandal? Is that why you accepted Jamie?"

"Do not put words in my mouth. I have my own reasons, and you could never understand them. Now go

away and let me sleep. I have to rest if we are to leave
for London in the morning."

Bella had turned to go when the dowager shouted
after her, "And see if you can find that lazy dresser of
mine and send her to me."

"I thought you said a duchess does not run errands,"
Bella returned with a smirk.

"That is enough impertinence from you."

Bella found Miss Sells in the dowager's dressing
room distractedly packing all the clothes the dowager
had selected to take. She then went down the hall and
through the passage to the old part of the house, listening to the waxed floorboards creak under her tread. It
was as though the house were trying to comfort her,
like an old coat, so well worn as to take the shape of its
owner. The house was old, and so was the woman. It
seemed only natural that both would have some flaws
and creaks. So what if the dowager cared more about
preventing scandal than about Jamie? It meant that no
matter what passion she might fly into, she would
never divulge the truth.

But Bella sensed Lady Edith played a deeper game
and that she might never figure out what it was. And
that made the woman interesting. She would never be
the comfortable lap Maria was or dote on Jamie like a
grandmother, but Bella believed Phillipe, that once
committed to the lie, the dowager would hold fast to it
in the face of any evidence or testimony. If only they
were not all making a tragic mistake by cutting Hal out
of the title.

~13~

$\mathcal{P}$hillipe dispatched the vanguard of maids and baggage wagons in the early morning along with Greenley and Carlos leading the extra horses. This way the riding horses would be rested by the time they reached London. He meant to ride Sebastian himself, and that would probably not tire the war horse enough.

As extra trunks—mostly the dowager's last-minute requirements—were brought downstairs, he had them loaded into the carriage but would not have the team put to until Ann fluttered a white scarf in front of the bedroom window, indicating Lady Edith was descending.

Bella and Jamie had been walking by the lake and playing in the hedge maze all morning to take up the time until their departure. Another woman might be frustrated, but Bella had always to await the pleasure and caprices of an army train. So she took her amusement where she could find it. Phillipe listened contentedly to the tinkle of her laughter and the light chatter of Jamie, who seldom now slipped into Spanish or Portuguese.

An occasional yip from Lobo reminded Phillipe of the one fly in the ointment. If the dowager refused to let the beast travel in the carriage or go to London at all, Lobo would have to be penned up, and he placed no confidence in any of the staff being able to keep the dog from escaping and following. Ann's signal was finally given, Phillipe called to Bella, and she took Jamie in to wash his face and hands as the team was led around. Bella returned with a scrupulously clean child, and still there was no sign of the dowager.

"How long can you keep these horses standing?" Bella asked as Sebastian was led out, pawing the cobbles and eager to be off.

Phillipe pursed his lips and glanced toward the house again, then looked at the horses. The team of four was restless, but the grooms who were to ride post on the leaders had not mounted yet, so there would be no trouble holding them. Sebastian was another matter and threatened to get away from the two grooms who were tugging on his reins. "If need be, I will take Sebastian for a quick canter."

"He hates a false start," Bella said. "Have a care he does not bite someone."

"He will behave for me," Phillipe said, and knew it to be true, though why Sebastian listened to him he had no notion. Perhaps because he expected him to and conveyed that with every thought. Bella, on the other hand . . .

"Yes, I find that very odd," she said.

Phillipe stared at her, wondering if she could read

his mind. "Oh, you mean . . . yes, he does listen. Did Edwin ride him much?"

"Only into battle. He said there was no horse more to be trusted in heavy fighting."

Phillipe nodded. "Too bad that did not count for more in Belgium. My first report was that Edwin had escaped harm."

Bella looked away, biting her lip. "That was a difficult letter to write. I knew how close you were."

Phillipe cast his mind back to what he was feeling on that particular day. Black despair, less at Edwin's death than at his own lack of grief. Of the two, he had blamed Edwin more than Bella but could not make himself feel sorry for Edwin. "Aunt did not take it well. I thought—here she comes. But what the devil is all that stuff?"

"It appears she was raiding the schoolroom for toys. Is there any more space in the boot of the carriage?"

"A little, a very little," Phillipe warned as he motioned to the footmen to load the booty.

Phillipe handed the dowager, Ann, and Bella in and was surprised that Jamie climbed in and sat beside Lady Edith. "We will be stopping in Hatfield for luncheon," he said as Lobo leaped in and settled himself on the floor. Phillipe slammed the door before her grace could protest and waved at the coachman to whip up the team. Phillipe mounted Sebastian and let the horse have a gallop before he turned him and went back to ride beside the coach. If his aunt had caused any unpleasantness over the dog, it must have been resolved by the time it was too late to go back.

With this late start, it would be well nigh two o'clock before they reached Hatfield. From there it was only two hours to London. But Phillipe doubted if they would actually reach the city until well past dark. The meal would take an hour or more, and then her grace would have to rest. He blew out an impatient breath. His aunt was worse to manage than an army train.

He occupied his mind on the way with all the ramifications of the course they had chosen. It was true that Edwin's interest in the funds amply provided for Hal, and Phillipe had no doubt that when the boy came of age he would succeed in beggaring his share of the estate with wild living. Had Edwin been alive, he might have exerted some small influence over his brother. But that was no excuse for the scandalous ruse they were proposing to commit. He could see no way out for them that did not involve disgrace for everyone, including Edwin, who was beyond caring. Had he really meant to help by taking care of Bella and Jamie, or had he only been looking out for himself? The image of Edwin, pistol pointed in his direction, swam before Phillipe's eyes, but he shook his head to obliterate it. He had not wanted anything that was Edwin's, not even Bella. But now he knew that she had never been Edwin's and that Jamie was his. That was all that mattered.

The dowager's initial response to Lobo's presence, which was to beat the roof with her walking stick, had abated when Jamie hugged the dog and said, "Please, Grandmother."

Lobo had added his mite by licking Lady Edith's shoe, and he was in favor.

"Perhaps it is fortuitous the beast has come," she said. "He can help protect us on the journey. But when we reach London you must promise to keep him out of the state rooms."

"Yes, Grandmother."

The journey, which should have taken no more than four hours, was considerably delayed by the dowager almost turning around at the first village to go back for her ostrich plumes. Ann convinced her she could find plumes just as nice in London and deserved new ones anyway. When they stopped for luncheon at Hatfield, Bella was distressed to see the whole equipage being unhitched. She would have sent Phillipe in for bread and cheese and eaten in the carriage. Instead they had to endure such a lengthy inspection of the fare that Bella could hear Jamie's stomach growl as he crawled onto her lap.

"Hold me, like you did in Spain," he pleaded.

"Are you sleepy?" she asked.

"No, hungry like in Spain. But we had no food, none of us. And you were crying because you could not feed me."

Bella felt her eyes mist up as she hugged her son. "I had hoped you were too little to remember such things." She kissed the top of his head.

The dowager was staring at them. Well, let her stare, the old biddy, claiming attention for herself with this stupid trick. "Do you remember what Phillipe did?" Bella asked to distract Jamie.

"Yes," said Jamie, smiling at Phillipe. "He brought us a goat."

"You had to eat a goat?" Lady Edith demanded.

"No, Grandmother. We did not eat her. Mama milked her, and I had milk to drink. What happened to Nanny?" Jamie twisted in her lap to look up at Bella.

"We left her in Spain before we crossed the mountains. Do you remember the lady with many children?"

Jamie nodded.

"Enough of this maudlin talk," the dowager said. "Feed the boy before he falls asleep."

After Jamie had finished his soup and apple, Phillipe carried the boy to the adjoining bedroom, and Lady Edith said she would lie down for a few minutes as well.

Ann sighed heavily. "I have never seen the outer reaches of London in daylight. It is always almost night or full dark by the time we get there."

"She reminds me of one of the old Spanish generals," Bella said. "We lost a few important battles for lack of ambition."

"You and Phillipe are used to life at a different pace," Ann said. "I feel it has been passing me by."

"No more, Ann," Phillipe said bracingly. "You will be the center of a swirl of gaiety when we get to London. And here is your shopping money."

"Phillipe, so much! I will not be able to spend half of it. And I do not need to since Bella has compelled me to take all her pretty gowns."

Ann volunteered to stay at the inn and wait on Lady Edith and Jamie when they awakened, so Bella and Phillipe occupied themselves with walking Lobo around Hatfield and buying some colored chalks and peppermints for Jamie. It reminded Bella of being on the town in Lisbon or Paris, though she had never had Phillipe for an escort. But everyone assumed they were married, and it was a comfortable feeling. Perhaps the next year would pass so quickly she would not even mind it.

When they resumed their journey, the day was much advanced. Bella was dozing herself when a volley of shots ripped through the darkness. She put Jamie on the floor by instinct and told the dowager and Ann to get down. Her next thought was for Phillipe, but she could not see him from the left window. A groan from the top of the coach alarmed her, especially since the equipage lurched violently as though they had run off the road.

She reached into the pocket of her cloak for Edwin's pistol and was glad she had thought to load it. She could see riders and horses, four at least, herding the lumbering carriage to the side of the road. Were neither of those grooms riding post armed?

When the traces had stopped creaking and repeated shouts from the rude highwaymen brought the footman's rifle crashing to the ground, Bella knew there was something seriously wrong with Phillipe. Men attacking a carriage would first shoot the outrider. He must be lying on the road some distance back, and she could not even know if he were alive or dead.

"Stay inside. I will speak to them," she said as she grabbed her reticule and opened the door, the pistol concealed in the folds of her skirt.

"Here is all the money we have," she said, tossing her reticule to the leader, who had dismounted. "You may as well take it and go. We brought no jewels with us."

"I'll have the rest o' ye out here." The fellow waved a pistol at her.

"There is only an old woman, and she is ill. She cannot get out."

"Trot out the nipper then," the spokesman commanded.

Bella froze, for there should have been no way for them to know there was a child inside if this were a random holdup.

"No, he is asleep. Be on your way."

"That little begger will be worth more to us than a diamond *tiaree*. Fetch him out."

"I said no." Bella barred his access to the coach.

The highwayman aimed his pistol at her, but one of the other riders pushed his horse up and said a muffled "No."

There were four of them, and they probably each had two loaded pistols to start with, but each must have fired once. Four horsemen meant at least four more shots could be fired, besides hers.

Bella retreated to the door of the carriage as the leader approached. He pushed her aside and flung the door open to be greeted by an ominous snarl from within.

"Shoot the dog," the muffled voice said, keeping his distance. He was holding a gun but made no move to extinguish Lobo himself. His hand was indeed bandaged already. The dismounted highwayman grabbed Bella's arm to drag her aside and was bringing the pistol to bear on the dog when a muffled report from the gun Bella had brought to his ribs made him stare at her in the most surprised way. She dropped the spent weapon and grabbed the pistol in his death grip, directing it, as well as she could while he fell, toward the highwayman covering the post boys. When she squeezed the trigger, the weapon went off, knocking that man off his horse. The muffled one swore violently and pointed his pistol at her. "I want the boy."

Jamie popped his head out of the carriage. "Lobo, *matar!* Kill!"

The dog gamely launched himself at the horse's legs, causing the man to have difficulty aiming at the yapping animal. The fourth gunman left off gaping and took aim at Lobo. Bella bent to reach for her boot dirk. In one swift movement it slithered out of her hand and connected with her target. Though she caught him only a glancing blow on the arm, his horse dumped him. Lobo put all the loose horses to rout, and the muffled one finally made his escape, with Lobo in pursuit.

"Jamie, call him back," Bella said as she made her way to the wounded highwayman and kicked his pistol out of his reach. She handed this off to a dismounted groom and told him to guard the man. Then she knelt over the driver, who had fallen by the front wheel. "He's dead," the footman said in some surprise. Bella felt for a pulse, but the man was indeed dead.

Bella turned to the two white-faced women who now stood beside the carriage. "Keep Jamie here. I must find Phillipe. Jamie, you watch out for your grandmother."

"You cannot go alone," Ann said.

"I would prefer to, since you need what men you have to hold the horses."

"I will stay, Mother," Jamie said bravely.

"Good boy, Jamie. I will be right back." Bella grabbed a lantern from one of the grooms, who was finally released from his paralyzed state, and started back the way they had come, half running in her anxiety. Fortunately, Phillipe had been riding Sebastian, and the horse's white shape stood out in the darkness. The animal had stopped and parked himself a few feet from where Phillipe had fallen on his right side. She steeled herself for what she might find but could not keep herself from chanting My Phillipe as she ran to him.

It had been easy enough to keep calm as she had dealt with the highwaymen, but to lose Phillipe now after all they had been through . . .

Bella knelt beside him, biting her lip, almost afraid to touch him, but when she rolled him onto his back, he moaned, and his heart, as she felt his chest, beat as steadily as always. There was blood on his forehead and shoulder. He groaned again and moved his left arm.

She tore the hole in his right sleeve bigger to see the wound, but it looked to be no more than a bloody graze. Phillipe started as he came awake with a gasp.

"Bella? Where are we?" He shielded his eyes from the lantern with his left hand and moved his legs to assure himself that the worst had not happened.

"The London Road," she choked out as though she had been sobbing. "You have been shot."

"Are you sure?" Phillipe reached for his head, and his fingers came away wet.

"Not there," she corrected in a more normal voice. "In the arm." Bella tugged at his coat as she rent the hole in his shirt bigger and produced an "Ouch" from him. Yes, it was beginning to burn now, but if he mistook not, it was no more than a scratch.

"What happened?" Phillipe asked as he struggled to sit up.

"Four highwaymen. Let me get your arm tied up."

Phillipe blinked his eyes and shook his head as she expertly removed the flounce from her petticoat to bind up his sluggishly bleeding shoulder. It had happened again. He was the soldier, and here Bella had saved him.

"I suppose you took care of them," he said grudgingly as he watched her work.

Bella paused, trying to detect criticism, he thought, in his remark. "One got away," she said dryly as she tied the makeshift bandage off tightly.

He gave a bark of pain and laughter. "Getting a little careless, are we?" He must not make her feel bad just because he was disappointed in himself. He had been riding along with the journey complete in his mind, thinking what he had to do on the morrow. He had not been thinking of the matter at hand, and that could have cost them . . . what?

Bella gave a small sigh. "What about you, taken completely unawares? Wait until I tell Wellington," she joked.

"Is everyone all right?" Phillipe asked, staring around at her dressing his shoulder wound.

"The coachman is dead, but everyone else is fine," she said as she helped him to his feet. Phillipe shook his head again, staggered, then realized he was flinging drops of blood on her. He produced his handkerchief, and she helped him tie it around his forehead.

"What a mess," he said as he blinked, trying to clear his vision.

"Do you want to ride?" Bella asked, going to pick up Sebastian's reins.

"Best not until my head clears." He leaned against Sebastian and took hold of the saddle.

"I will lead him and you hold on to him."

"How far?" Phillipe asked as Bella picked up the lantern.

"Just around the bend."

"Bella, I am so sorry."

"You were right. I cannot protect Jamie myself."

"Was he frightened?"

"No, but I was," Bella confessed. "They were not after money," she whispered. "They knew Jamie was in the coach and meant to take him."

He stared at her in the dark. "This is my fault. It makes me have second thoughts about this scheme."

Phillipe walked in silence, willing the dizziness away. His arm just burned now, and except for that ringing in his ears, left over from when his head had hit the road, nothing hurt all that badly. When they walked toward the carriage, he paused to survey the carnage. They had only the footman and two grooms left, besides the wounded highwayman. "Who can drive a team of four?" he asked weakly.

Three shrugs caused him to laugh bitterly and even cast a speculative glance at the highwayman, whose hands had been bound with a leather strap from one of the trunks.

"No one can drive us?" Lady Edith demanded, her hand on Jamie's shoulder as he stood by her side. Lobo had returned and danced around Phillipe's feet as though in apology for not being able to drive the team.

"Well, I could if I could trust my arm, but it is still numb. Bella can, and I suppose that is what we will have to do. Hatch," Phillipe said to the footman, "you stay and guard the wounded highwayman. We will send you some help within the hour. Rawlins, get

Jamie and the ladies back in the carriage, help Bella up, then mount the leader. Simms can lead the team back to the road, then get on the other leader. And mind you do not let them get away from you." Phillipe tied Sebastian to the back of the carriage.

"But what about them?" the dowager asked, staring at the three bodies as Bella checked the harness to make sure none of the horses had stepped over a trace during their abrupt stop.

"They are not going anywhere," Phillipe said harshly.

"What is the matter with you, Phillipe?" his aunt demanded. "You sound so different, almost drunk."

"If only that were so," he grumbled.

Bella fetched her cloak, settled Jamie and Lobo back in the carriage, and appealed to Ann to get the dowager into the coach. She then climbed onto the driver's seat without any assistance and waited for Phillipe to scramble up.

"Are you sure you will not go tumbling off here?" she asked him with a wary eye to his head wound.

"If I do, I hope you will stop for me."

She gave him a quick smile to let him know that she could manage now. It did nothing to bolster his confidence.

Once they were back on the road, Bella told the grooms to release the horses and kept the reins in order so that none of the team was straining. There was a half moon ducking in and out of the clouds, so even on an unfamiliar road Bella should have no difficulty.

"Damn, Bella," Phillipe said. "We almost lost him."

"Do not blame yourself, Phillipe," she said confidently. "We are safe . . . mostly."

"But I am very much to blame. I should have had half a dozen footmen on guard rather than one."

"That might only have meant more men killed," Bella reminded him.

"And old Bailey, the coachman, should have retired and taken that pension I offered him. He could not give up his position of pride, coachman to the Duke of Dorney."

"And it appears he has been reluctant to pass on his skills," Bella observed. "We shall have to do something about that."

"That also is my fault," Phillipe said, forcing himself to stay awake by lashing himself with blame.

"At least I now know how much danger Jamie is in. Personally I plan to make this stay as short as possible. I feel almost as though we are invading enemy territory without a safe conduct and with not nearly enough troops to guard our rear."

Phillipe chuckled at her comparison.

"Sorry, I know how you hate military analogies."

"No, your assessment of the situation is accurate. But we go to a place where we do have allies. I assure you the city proper is not that bad so long as you do not go out at night or stray into some of the poorer districts."

"I give Ann credit for not fainting. And Lady Edith has been a rock."

"Not to mention Jamie. Yes, now that their mettle has been tested, I own to some surprise that Aunt, at least, did not suffer a case of the vapors. Did she realize their purpose was abduction?"

"Perhaps she was too frightened to have reached that conclusion, but it may occur to her eventually. Which means Jamie and I will be even more hedged about."

"It is not too late to change our minds."

"I must think," Bella said, "and I cannot do that until we are safe."

~14~

When they finally pulled into the stable yard, Greenley was just saddling Rufus for Carlos.

"Bella?" Carlos said with a laugh. "What are you doing? I thought you had given up driving."

"Our coachman was shot dead," Phillipe said, jumping down and reaching up with his one good arm to help Bella.

"What of Jamie and Ann?" Carlos demanded. "And her grace?"

Jamie opened the door and tumbled out of the coach, with Lobo barking. "Carlos! Mama shot two *banditos*. You should have seen."

Carlos picked Jamie up and held him as his eyes directed a silent inquiry toward Bella. Phillipe saw Bella nod, meaning she was all right with what had happened.

"Someone has to bring them back," Bella said. "We left a footman guarding a wounded prisoner."

"I will lead a party of grooms out," Carlos said, "and send someone for— Whom should I inform, Phillipe?"

"The local magistrate. I will take care of that. You had better take the landau for the dead men. Bring them back to the stable here."

Bella had taken Jamie from Carlos and was walking toward the back door. Phillipe suddenly noticed his aunt standing silently, and he began to wonder if she were in shock. He took her arm and steered her toward the house, to let Carlos and Ann have a moment alone. When he looked back, they were locked in each other's arms, disregarding the curious grooms and stamping horses.

"Are you all right, Aunt Edith?" he asked as they went in the back door and down the hallway.

"Aunt Edith? You have not called me that since you were a boy."

"A stupid boy is very much what I felt like tonight, letting myself be taken by surprise. It will not happen again, I can tell you."

"Come into the morning room," she commanded. "We must see to your wound."

"I thought you might want your maid," Phillipe said. "You can go to your room. I shall deal with the magistrate."

"Not for the world. This is the most excitement I have had since . . . I guess since Jamie fell into the lake—no, since the bull almost got him. Is life always so exciting around Bella?"

"Yes, always." Phillipe chuckled. In spite of everything that had happened, Bella had sailed through with flying colors. It was as though they had never left the war. He really thought she was a match for anything.

Bella came back downstairs with her sewing kit. "Janet is going to feed Jamie and Lobo and put them to bed. Do you want me to send for a surgeon, Phillipe?"

Phillipe glanced down at his arm, which he had almost forgotten about. "I thought maybe you could stitch it up. You are rather handy at that."

Bella followed Phillipe and the dowager into the morning room. "I thought you did not like it when I treated you."

Ann came in and Lady Edith sent her for bandages and hot water in a subdued voice. Bella undid the makeshift dressing and helped Phillipe out of his coat. She glanced at Lady Edith to see if the bloody shirt would upset her, but other than pursing her lips, the old woman seemed in no danger of fainting.

Hoskins appeared, concern writ large on his face. "Is there anything I can do, your grace?"

When the dowager did not answer, Bella said, "Some tea would be nice."

"Tea?" Lady Edith asked. "Hoskins, bring Phillipe a brandy. Tea, indeed. And some bread and cold meat. Whatever is in the kitchen."

Ann reappeared with the basin and water before Hoskins returned, so Phillipe had to endure having the four-inch gash across his upper arm washed while he was sober. Fortunately Hoskins brought a tray of brandy and tea just as Bella was threading her needle. Bella soaked the needle and thread in hot water as Phillipe sipped the amber liquid with a sigh.

"Ann," Bella asked, "would you mind checking on

Jamie for me? He was still a little excited, so he and Lobo may be more than Janet can handle."

After Ann had left, Lady Edith said, "She did look about to faint."

"It is not so bad watching a stranger being sewed back together. But when it is someone you care about . . ." Bella set the first stitch and Phillipe grunted.

"Then how do you manage it, dear?" Lady Edith came to watch the operation.

"By pretending I do not know Phillipe. It is the only way I can treat him."

"I see," Phillipe said. "I had wondered why you were always so silent."

The magistrate was shown in just as Bella finished the last stitch and was binding up Phillipe's arm under the dowager's supervision.

"What about your head, Phillipe?" his aunt asked.

"I feel fine, now," he vowed.

"Because you are two parts drunk," his aunt judged. "Eat something before you disgrace yourself."

Bella removed the handkerchief and inspected the small wound. "I think it will close on its own, once the bruise goes down."

The magistrate, Mr. Wren, was a small man who had been called away from some entertainment and now looked worriedly from one duchess to the other. He was relieved when Phillipe finally addressed him.

"They are bringing your prisoner here along with the two dead highwaymen and our coachman, whom they killed."

"Very good, my lord. I am glad you have taken no other hurt from the encounter than this."

"Actually, it was her grace who disposed of the high-waymen." Phillipe grinned in Bella's direction, and she sent him a vengeful look.

The man's eyes bulged as he pulled out a small note-book and wrote this down. "They robbed you, your grace?"

"Yes. That is, one of them took my reticule, but he dropped it . . . later."

"Dropped it," the man said as he recorded it.

"After Bella shot him," the dowager supplied helpfully.

"I see. I shall have to question the wounded man."

"One of them got away," Bella said. "He was wearing a muffler, so I could not get a good look at his face or hear his voice at all well."

"Anything you can tell me . . ."

"He was riding a job horse, no distinctive markings. He had a bandage around his right hand."

"Bandage," the little man said as he wrote in his notebook.

Hal opened the door with a scowl on his brow and came in to take a seat. At the sight of the bloody gar-ments, he turned quite pale. As the magistrate was fin-ishing up his questions, Hal poured himself a drink.

"I shall return in the morning with what I have found out," Wren said. "What hour would be convenient?"

"Ten o'clock will do," Phillipe said, then turned to the roast beef and bread, suddenly ravenous.

The magistrate was hardly out the door when Hal demanded, "So it is true what Hoskins has been telling me? You shot two men down on the London road and just left them lying there?"

Bella stared at Hal. "I had no choice," she said,

putting the rest of the bandages and her sewing kit away.

"And you knifed another one," he added.

"He is not dead yet," Bella said in her own defense.

"Oh, not dead yet," Hal repeated. "I am sure we should all be glad that you are not so skilled with a knife as a pistol."

"Hal," Phillipe said with his mouth full. "Let it rest. You know nothing about this. Besides, you are drunk."

"Not too drunk to know that this will be all over town by morning. If we were wishing to avoid scandal, Bella has flown in the face of that."

Lady Edith had poured herself a small glass of sherry and was moving toward a chair by the fire. Phillipe could see that her hand shook a little, and he followed her with his eyes, sending her a speaking look that asked from old familiarity with her infirmities if she were all right. Her hand waved his concern away even as he was rising to help her. A wave of dizziness, either from the brandy or the knock on the head, dissuaded him.

"I am all right," Lady Edith said, "but you should be in bed, Phillipe."

"Bad enough Edwin married you in the first place," Hal continued at Bella, who was calmly making herself a cup of tea. "Did you have to drag the whole family down to your level?"

"So," Bella said, "this is what you are really like. This is what you think of me."

"Yes, this is what I really think. I have tried to make the best of the situation, but how am I to face my friends with this tale, that my sister-in-law has killed in cold blood?"

Bella compressed her lips and held her chin up. "I do not see that it concerns you at all. You were not even there." She stirred sugar into her tea and took a drink.

"No, he was not there, and perhaps he should have been, rather than capering about town," Lady Edith said.

"So it is my fault Bella has made a scandal?" Hal demanded, spinning toward his mother.

"No, it is mine," Phillipe said. "I should have been on the alert and prevented the entire incident."

"You were shot off your horse," Lady Edith complained. "I do not see how you could have predicted or prevented that. It is my fault for delaying our arrival past dark."

Hal rose and slammed his fist on the table. "Do you think I care whose fault it is? I have friends here whom I must face. How am I to explain this?"

"Perhaps my uncontrollable temper," Bella said as she slowly tapped her nails on the small table that still contained the basin of bloody water and the scissors.

"If I know you, you did not fire those shots in the heat of anger but with a cool deliberation that—that . . ." Hal regarded her warily as she picked up the basin.

"If you know what is good for you, Hal, you will take yourself off to bed," Lady Edith said.

"But she has ruined us. I will be a laughingstock because she has killed a man and I never have."

"So that is it?" Bella snapped.

"You should have given them your money," Hal countered.

"I did. It was not enough."

"You should have given them your jewels," Hal insisted.

"I have no jewels," Bella said angrily. She stood as though she were about to throw him out.

"Well," Hal blustered, "you should have . . ."

"Hal!" the dowager said in a voice that jerked all their heads to attention. "They meant to take Jamie from her. Do you really think she would have let them have him while there was still breath in her body?"

The question hung in the air like a challenge. Bella stared at Lady Edith, the hint of tears gathering in her eyes. She licked her dry lips. "I thought . . . I hoped you had not heard them."

"I hear everything. We were wildly wrong in assuming the child was safe with us. From now on he does not leave the house for so much as a walk in the park without half a dozen footmen besides his nurse in attendance."

"I do not believe it," Hal said. "Why would they take him when they could have made off with your jewels?"

"Hal, go to your room now," the dowager said.

"I will not be treated like a child."

"Then stop acting like one."

Hal rose and left, looking back over his shoulder in puzzlement at the sudden turn of affairs. His right hand lingered on the doorknob long enough for Bella to see a bandage on it.

She sat down as a sudden wave of nausea overtook her. Surely Hal's bandage looked cleaner and neater than the one the highwayman had worn.

Bella was still feeling amazed and sent Phillipe a confused look. He shrugged, for he had been taken by surprise by his aunt as well.

Bella finally found her voice. "You supported me, and you do not even like me," Bella said.

"Hal is a fool. The Duchess of Dorney need not care what anyone thinks of her."

Bella was still picturing the bandage and only half heard the dowager. "Are we talking about you or me?"

"We are talking about you. If anyone asks about the incidents of last night, you are to stare them down. You need not answer to anyone for what you did."

"Aunt is right, Bella," Phillipe said. "Just ignore any comment on the incident."

Lady Edith rose. "I assume you can deal with the magistrate tomorrow, Phillipe?"

"Yes, of course."

"I am going to bed then."

Phillipe helped her to the door and rang for Hoskins, who carried a candelabra before her up the broad stairs toward her apartments.

When Phillipe came back in, Bella was shaking her head. "Just when you think you know her, she sets you back on your heels like a green colt."

"I have to admit to some surprise as well, and I am used to her quirks." Phillipe picked up his glass and drained it.

"And you?" Bella asked. "Why are you not sending me dark looks and grumbling to yourself? It is what you would have done had I gotten involved in such a thing during the war."

"Hah! You are right. I used to be like a walking conscience. Perhaps I am drunk as well."

"Perhaps you finally realize what is important," Bella said. "Not what people think of you." She rose slowly and came to put her arms about his waist and embrace him, letting him lean on her and breathe into her hair.

"And what is important, my little soldier?"

"Staying alive. That is all that matters. Saving face means nothing if you cannot keep those dear to you and yourself alive."

"I suppose you would kill twenty men to keep Jamie safe."

"If I had to, but he was not the only one I was worried about. I was picturing you bleeding to death on the road. I had to resolve the situation quickly so that I could find you."

Phillipe chuckled. "Have I ever mentioned how much I admire you? I know I have told you of my love, but this is different. I am in awe of you."

"Phillipe, I am afraid," Bella said as she walked with him toward the stairs.

"Because they were not after money or jewels," he guessed.

"Someone must have told them we were coming to London."

"Yes," Phillipe said. "After all our lecturing to you, we led you straight into a trap."

"But who would have known we would be coming this way?" she whispered in the dark hallway.

"Anyone who knew we left Dorney Park this morning and who knew her grace's habits, anyone she had written to in town, anyone Hal or Carlos might have talked to—not more than two or three hundred people."

"Phillipe, what are we going to do? I cannot endure Jamie being in danger forever."

"You have endured it all during the war."

"I knew the war would end. But this danger will never resolve itself."

"Bella, I do not know what to say, how to advise you. I do know you can learn to live with such fears. Lady Edith has."

"So I may become like Lady Edith, controlling and . . ."

"She is only like that because she feels so powerless. You are not powerless. You know a thousand things she does not, and between us we should be able to protect Jamie, whether he is Duke of Dorney or plain James Armitage."

"Yes, of course we can. I just lost my head for a moment."

~ 15 ~

*T*he next morning Bella laced her tea with cream and two spoonfuls of honey. It was almost like food when properly made. They had frequently to drink it bitter in Spain or without milk. That goat Phillipe had forcibly purchased had, besides feeding Jamie, supplied them with sweet milk for their tea. She could not imagine why she was thinking of such a triviality as she looked out onto Portman Square, where Jamie played with his dog as a small regiment of footmen looked on while Janet tossed the ball for Lobo to fetch.

It could have turned out quite otherwise had she not been willing to kill to protect her child. It was disquieting, knowing she had ended two lives without knowing what those men were like. She had hated the times she had been pushed to kill a soldier. They were victims, too, and if they had let her alone she would never have harmed them, but these highwaymen had given her an uneasy feeling. And one of them was still at large. They must not forget that. Perhaps Mr. Wren would be able to extract some useful information from the wounded highwayman. She drained her cup and was thinking about having another when Phillipe came in.

"You should have stayed in bed," she said. "You look feverish."

"I do much better when I am up and about. I thought we would go for a ride this morning."

She stared at him in disbelief.

"Just a short one," he said.

"Why?" she asked, knowing he did nothing by chance.

"You know why," he said with his tired smile. "To make things normal again. To scare away the night horrors. To show you that London will not eat you up. Is that all you are having for breakfast?"

She had been staring at him, his poetic rush of reassurance entrancing her, but she dropped her glance to her empty plate. "No. If you will eat with me, I will get us both some food." Bella made two plates and brought them to the table. Then she made Phillipe a cup of tea the way he liked it, heavy with cream and honey.

He took a long drink and sighed. "How did you sleep last night?"

"Better than you. I was not the one who was shot. But this time you seem to have kept the damage under control."

"I do my feeble best."

"Even in the midst of the most desperate times, you always found a way to keep me from worrying. You took control and banished my fears just by being there and smiling in that way you have."

"And I was thinking I had not made a good job of taking care of you. What is my way of smiling?"

"Apologetically, as if to say you cannot help what has happened, but you can do something."

He stared at her in amazement, as though she had just smoothed salve on some wound and stopped it from hurting by magic. Then he looked at his untouched food. "Little enough, as I recall."

She saw that half-bemused smile and remembered all the times she had seen it. Why had she focused so much on his disapproval and forgotten what was behind it, how much he cared? Her hand covered his and stilled it. "Do not belittle yourself," she said. "You made me love you more for the small things than the great ones."

"There's a facer. Is my manhood one of the small things or one—"

He stopped abruptly as she leaned over to kiss him. Phillipe found himself wishing he had two good arms for no reason other than to hold Bella. She tasted of honey and desire, and he knew he would have to contrive a way to make love to her before his need overrode his forbearance. During the war, they never stood on ceremony. A mourning period for a woman was unheard of. He should have married her as soon as she had arrived. Why had he hesitated? He had not been sure of her. He broke the kiss to look at her, to look into those clear blue eyes and try to fathom her.

The dowager had once tried to make him doubt Bella. Yet Lady Edith had backed Bella the previous evening during Hal's absurd tirade. But, then, the dowager would admire ruthlessness in a woman and probably like Bella better than ever now.

"Why are you looking at me so," Bella asked, "as though you do not know me?"

"Sometimes I feel that I have not even scratched the surface." He leaned close to continue the kiss, but his sister's voice in the hall caused Bella to draw back shyly.

Ann opened the door and whirled in, looking archly at the two of them. "Am I unwelcome? You have only to say so. I am an expert at making myself scarce."

"Of course not," Bella answered. "Phillipe is taking me for a ride. Would you like to go?"

Phillipe was cutting his ham with such difficulty that Bella leaned over and cut the meat up for him as she would have done for Jamie. He stared at her ominously but made no protest.

Ann laughed and looked down at the sprigged muslin morning frock Bella had given her.

"Say no more," Bella replied for her. "You would far rather go shopping."

"Aunt means to find those ostrich plumes for her turban and to leave cards at a few friends' houses, so they know we are back in town," Ann said. "Though I suppose . . ."

"Everyone knows we are back," Phillipe said as he dug into the ham and eggs and finished his tea.

"Do you think we should not go riding then?" Bella asked.

"Go change into your riding dress," Phillipe said. "I will have the horses saddled." He thought for a moment that she meant to resist the orders he spit out so automatically. "Alta will be bursting her stall by now, and a mare with foal does need regular exercise."

"Yes, I suppose you are right," Bella agreed.

Carlos came in and sat next to Ann, trying not to stare at her but succeeding only in paying too much attention to her bodice and making her blush.

"Going shopping today, Carlos?" Phillipe asked.

Carlos looked at him as though Phillipe might be intending some double meaning, but when he could deduce none, he said, "Yes, I thought I might."

Ann nudged Carlos.

"Phillipe," he said, "if I were wishing to—"

Ann's elbow redirected his remark.

"I mean, I fully intend to—not that I am at all worthy . . ."

Bella smiled at Phillipe.

He wiped his mouth on his napkin, torturing Carlos for another moment. "You have my blessing if you wish to ask for Ann's hand in marriage, though she may do as she likes. Neither of you need consult with either me or Lady Edith."

Ann sighed with relief.

"Thank you, Phillipe," Carlos said. "But I feel it would be dishonorable to marry Ann without warning both you and her grace." Carlos took Ann's hand in both of his and worshiped her with his dark eyes. Phillipe hoped he did not appear so lovesick when he looked at Bella.

"I can tell Aunt," Ann said.

"No, I must speak to her," Carlos said. "Only a coward would draw back from such an encounter, though I have nothing to offer."

"Do remember that I will need someone to manage my estate in Norfolk," Phillipe said as he handed his teacup to Bella, hoping for a refill.

"Oh, Phillipe," Ann said. "Do you mean it?"

"Of course, you would have to come to Dorney or London several times a year." Phillipe took the hot tea from Bella gratefully. It almost felt as though she were his wife.

"But I do not know anything about managing land in England," Carlos protested. "I used to spend summers on my uncle's estate in Catalonia. It had sheep and cattle, olive and lime groves. Nothing would be the same."

"It will not take you more than a few days to get in the way of it."

"See," Ann said. "Now there is no impediment to our engagement."

"But my career," Carlos said. "I had meant to remain in the army."

"But there is no war," Ann said.

"But there might be," Carlos returned.

Bella plucked at Phillipe's sleeve, and he nodded, realizing the two needed to talk alone. As Bella went to change, he carried his tea into the library and gave a footman instructions for saddling the horses. Later, when he heard Bella trip down the stairs, he went out into the hall to admire her.

"I had your saddle put on Alta. I would not want to overwork her with my weight until she has foaled."

Bella nodded her agreement and let him take her arm as they went out the back way to the stables. Phillipe knew he would not be able to lift her, but they had led Alta up to the mounting block, so Bella hopped on herself. He gathered Sebastian's reins in his right hand and got on from the right, making his shoulder twinge. But the horse was interested enough in his new surroundings to do no more than caper a bit. Phillipe took both reins in his left hand, signaling the horse for action, and Sebastian poised to launch himself. A harsh word from Phillipe restrained the creature to an impatient trot the few blocks to Hyde Park.

Bella gave a gasp of surprise as they went through the corner gate and saw the vast expanse of grass and trees with the Serpentine beyond. They cantered along the tree-lined north road as Bella got her bearings.

"Sorry we came?" Phillipe asked as he watched the sun dance off her nearly black ringlets. Bella's rich habit of green was so dark it could almost have passed for black, and her cap was of a military cut. There were few enough strollers out at this hour of the morning. The half dozen men they encountered riding were all military or ex-military exercising their mounts.

When they came upon Fortesque, one of Edwin's captains, he promised to send them cards to a rout his mother was throwing. He expressed his regret about Edwin's death to both of them, then moved on to speak of all those who had survived and were in London.

Major Durban was training a new colt and could not stop for long. He had been under Bella's father and promised to call that afternoon for a chat so that they did not keep the horses standing. Neither had mentioned the unfortunate incidents of the previous night, either from lack of knowledge or because they did not feel it was anything out of the ordinary. To a hardened campaigner such an encounter was a trifle.

Colonel Maitland had almost ridden past them when he reined in his horse and turned it. "Bella and Armitage, I had no idea you were in town."

"We just got back last night," Phillipe said.

"You'll be here for the peace celebrations then," the soldier concluded.

"Perhaps," Bella said. "Our plans are uncertain."

"I shall send you a card for our ball. Do not say me nay. My sister wants to meet all of my acquaintances from the Peninsula. In fact, I should like to bring her to call on you."

"That would be wonderful," Bella said.

"Will you be home this afternoon?"

"I—yes, of course."

"I see you still have old Redich from Spain," Phillipe said as he glanced over the dark bay Maitland was mounted on.

The man patted the horse's neck. "The only one left of my original string. Is that Sebastian? McFarlane's stallion?"

"Yes," Phillipe said. "He is getting a little bored with peace."

"Shame about your husband, Bella," Maitland said, his ramrod-stiff back relaxing for a moment. "I expect I should call you *your grace*."

"Please do not. I will never get used to the title. I am still just Bella."

Maitland steadied his impatient horse. "I will see you this afternoon then . . . Bella." He relaxed the reins, and the animal cantered off, changing leads when he came to a turn in the path.

"I dislike the way he looked at you," Phillipe grumbled. "And I wish you had not told him to call you Bella."

"Oh, Phillipe, do not ruin everything by being jealous."

Bella urged the mare on, and Phillipe kneed Sebastian to keep up with her.

"I simply meant he need not have pawed you with his eyes in that manner."

"He was not pawing me. He was simply glad to see us."

"Us? He did not even see me. Here I am with a fresh sling, and he never said a word."

Bella glanced at Phillipe's arm and how easily he rode in spite of it. Perhaps he was simply in pain, and that was why he seemed so irritated. "Some of them consider it prying to ask about a wound. You do not do it yourself unless you know it is a trifle."

"Well, we cannot do anything about him coming to call, but a ball?"

"It will be fine for me to attend as Ann's chaperone so long as I do not dance."

"I suppose so," Phillipe said grudgingly.

"Do you feel better now that your hackles are down?" Bella cast him her most provocative smile.

He shook his head. "Is that what I am like, a stiff-legged dog?"

"Guarding a tasty bone," Bella said to make him smile.

"Well, you are a tasty morsel to these half-pay soldiers and younger sons. They must all guess you will come into a handsome jointure."

"Maitland can care nothing for money." They had made a full circuit of the park and come to the street again, so Bella brought Alta to a walk. "He has plenty, and his own estates as well. Why do you suppose he never married?"

"I have heard that the girl he was pursuing married another."

"That is not funny, Phillipe." Bella rode off in the general direction of Portman Place, and Phillipe rode after her. He caught up with her when she stopped for traffic at the corner.

"Sorry, but I cannot help how I feel," Phillipe said.

She looked at him. "You might be a little more careful not to show it."

"I feel like I did that morning you came riding out of the fog wearing a French uniform. I was just drawing my gun to fire when I saw your hair."

Bella laughed. "I had stolen his hat, too, but I lost it. Good thing I ran into you, or the pickets might have shot me."

"I was in a damnable position. Your father refused to hear my suit, and you got captured by the French. I was out looking for you, though I had no right to be. Do you know how hard it is to protect someone you are not even allowed to speak to?" They crossed the street and started up the broad thoroughfare.

"I must admit I had not realized the considerable handicap you operated under."

"Did not, in fact, realize I was trying to take care of you. I must have been doing a poor job of it."

"No, I thought it amazing how, out of so many thousand soldiers, I kept running up against you."

"Did you really think it was coincidence?" He grinned down at her from Sebastian's greater height.

"Not after a time. That was why I was so glad to see you that morning. I thought you, of all people, would understand."

"I thought they had . . ." He raked her with his eyes.

"No. I feigned ignorance of the language and an unbelievable stupidity about what that captain wanted."

"Until you got him alone," Phillipe guessed.

"Yes, he was not much of a problem. I knocked him out with a chamber pot. The hardest part was undressing him." She turned Alta toward Portman Place.

Phillipe shook his head to rid it of this picture. "How did you get away with his horse?"

"He had left it tied near his tent. Their pickets never even challenged me."

"Were you afraid?" he asked.

"I never thought to be afraid at the time it was happening. I had to focus all my attention on escape."

"I know what you mean. Panic is fatal. Sometimes your best defense is keeping your head."

"But now I am afraid all the time, for Jamie's sake. What has happened to me?"

"A child makes a difference," he said as they turned into the alley that led to the stables. "You have so much more to lose now. I felt something of the same desperation when I fell in love with you. Before I did not think about what might happen to me, and it was all a great adventure."

He dismounted and was standing by to help her down from the mounting block. "When I knew you were at risk, I started to take the war more seriously," he said, squeezing her hand.

"Then, when Jamie was born, you had two of us to worry about." She was startled when the back door opened, as though that footman had nothing to do but watch for them.

"I would have given anything to have been able to send you back to England," Phillipe said.

"Fortunate that you could not, for I would have had to protect him alone here. We cannot let life cow us." She paused as she went through the door. "We must be careful but pretend nothing will go wrong."

"Yes," he said. "Prepare for the worst, leave nothing to chance, and always be ready for a fight."

"But that is just like being at war. Now I can be comfortable. There is no real difference."

Hoskins cleared his throat behind them. "Your grace, sir, Magistrate Wren is waiting in the library."

"Let us hear what he has to say," Bella said. She walked beside Phillipe as an equal, someone who did not want to be protected.

"You need not even be here for this interview, if you do not wish," Phillipe said before Hoskins opened the door to the library.

"But I want to know," Bella insisted. She stared around her as she entered the room, having never been in it before. The books were stored randomly in glass-walled cabinets, and it had not the warmth of the library at Dorney Park. Suddenly she realized she was thinking of Dorney as being better than here, as a home of sorts.

To her surprise Lady Edith entered the room with Hal on her heels. They looked as though they had been arguing.

Bella sat beside Phillipe and braced herself for the worst. Had she killed a couple of drunken grooms in her zeal to protect her son from all harm?

"The villain who survived the attack last night has not confessed," Wren said. "He will no doubt hang anyway, since one of them killed your coachman. Of the other two, one had a price on his head of a hundred pounds, the other fifty. They were brothers and have robbed and murdered along that stretch of highway these three years."

Bella expelled a sigh of relief. As she relaxed, she could feel Phillipe grow more tense.

"You say he did not confess. So he did not say who the fourth man is. It is imperative that we find out."

"No," Wren said. "The man has some notion to trade that information for his freedom. I cannot allow that, of course."

"Would he trade it for his life?" Bella asked. "I cannot rest until we know who the man with the bandaged hand was."

Hal looked as though his neckcloth would strangle him. Only Lady Edith remained impassive in the face of this news.

"We cannot do that either," Wren said. "This man is an accessory to murder."

Phillipe was staring at Hal, who had shoved his hand into his pocket.

Wren cleared his throat. "Your grace is entitled to the reward."

It took Bella a moment to realize he meant her. "Oh, no. I could not."

"But what are we to do with it?"

"We can give it to John Bailey's family," she said.

"Your coachman? I will see to it."

"By all means," Phillipe said.

Wren turned a page in his notebook and looked uncomfortable at his next item. "I had thought that perhaps you might have someone in your household who had let slip when you meant to come to London." He waited expectantly, then continued, "But seeing that it was these highwaymen, then I think we can count the matter an accident. Had they not stopped your coach, it would have been the next one."

Bella turned her face to Phillipe, and his head moved ever so slightly, by which she divined he did not want the near abduction known. Was he afraid it would give someone else ideas? At any rate, Bella said nothing as Wren apologized for the terrible reception in town and took his leave of the dowager.

They were still sitting thus, getting used to the idea that Bella had performed a public service and that this might lead to even more gossip, when Colonel Maitland and his sister Amelia called. They went into the morning room to receive them, and Lady Amelia wasted no time in apologizing for calling at such an unfashionable hour, while Maitland engaged Bella in conversation.

Bella could hear Lady Amelia making reference to the shooting on the heath, so she only listened to Maitland with half her attention. Perhaps they had called early so that she could confirm the rumor. Maitland chuckled uneasily at her lack of response and nodded his recognition when Carlos came in, even making a joke about him growing into his uniform.

The rest of the household could not possibly have gone shopping as planned. Ann entered the room and was introduced. Maitland became almost garrulous in her presence, which was a stretch for him. Carlos made a face at Ann, who smiled sweetly. Maitland and his sister refused to stay for luncheon but formally delivered to the dowager an invitation to the ball he proposed to hold.

Lady Edith emphasized that they were in mourning and would have to consider such an entertainment carefully. This left Lady Amelia in the position of having to denigrate her own ball, assuring her grace that it was the merest evening among friends, just soldiers' families, and there would barely be dancing. Once Amelia was properly humbled, Lady Edith accepted her invitation with a nod to Bella to say, *See, she can be managed.*

Maitland bowed himself out, eyeing Bella hungrily.

"You have a new beau, Bella," Ann accused.

"Yes," Carlos agreed. "The fellow almost licked your hand when he kissed it."

"Did he? I scarcely noticed."

Phillipe stood up abruptly and walked to the window.

"His sister is one of the nastiest gossips in town," Lady Edith confirmed.

"And she knows," Bella said. "How could I deny it? But I merely said that in the confusion two highwaymen were killed. I did not say by whom."

Phillipe shook his head. "In the confusion two highwaymen were killed? I do not think that will wash. No doubt she will ferret out the true tale by the time of this ball."

"Perhaps it will have blown over by then," Carlos said hopefully.

"Three weeks," Ann announced, looking at the invitation card.

Anything could happen in three weeks.

Hal got up and left abruptly without waiting for Carlos.

"Where is he going?" Bella asked.

"Probably to his clubs," Carlos said. "That is where he

spends all his time in town. Not very healthy for him."

"Do you go with him?" Bella asked, wondering if it were possible that Hal could be leading Carlos astray.

"Sometimes. Rather dull, though, when one is not gambling. I prefer to go to a play instead."

Ann smiled at Carlos, and Bella breathed a sigh of relief.

"My guess is that faro or E and O would seem tame," Phillipe said, "even if you were gambling, compared with what you have been doing."

"You are very perceptive, Phillipe," Carlos replied.

"So you were not with Hal last night," Bella concluded.

"No, not when I knew you were coming. I had half a mind to ride out and meet you. Now I wish I had." He looked longingly at Ann, disregarding whether the dowager noticed or not.

"Oh, no," Ann said. "You might have been shot as well."

Carlos arched an eyebrow at Phillipe, who grinned at his sister.

"But I should have realized it was not safe, that road to London, and been there to protect you."

Ann blushed. The dowager rolled her eyes, and Bella managed to keep her smile to herself as she wrestled with the image of Hal with a bandaged hand. It meant nothing, really. And she could not picture Hal doing anything so daring even if he were under the hatches from gambling. Unless he were feeling jealous of Carlos and her, even of Phillipe. Or could Hal be jealous of the child who would supplant him? Bella shivered, for if that were the case, mere abduction was not what he had in mind. She thought of all the nights during the war she had slept fully clothed because she expected an advance and the need to move at a moment's notice. It had happened once or twice. Would she spend all her life on the run like that, afraid ever to relax?

She had a sudden urge to visit Jamie and was about to excuse herself when Major Durban called. He was a handsome and affable man who had lost his left arm at Waterloo but let it make so little difference to him that no one seemed to regard it.

"How sit you on entertainments, your grace?" he said to the dowager. "I know you still mourn, all of you, for Edwin."

Bella waited for the dowager to reply, but when that lady merely nodded at her, Bella said, "Lady Edith allows that if I do not dance I might attend some events as Ann's chaperone."

"Of course, there can be no harm in that. If everyone who had suffered a loss were to go into deep mourning, there would be precious little visiting or marrying going on in the whole country. I do not know a household where there is not some connection killed at Waterloo."

"Which explains the sudden popularity of black," Phillipe said.

"No doubt," Durban said. "So will you come to dinner tomorrow night? My sister-in-law is mad to have you. And especially she extends her warmest regards to you, Lady Edith. She has not seen you in an age."

"We saw each other not three months since at the Lemlys' party."

"Well, three months is an age. Come at seven. It will be an intimate affair. Carlos, the men in the Ninety-fifth are asking about you. Would you like to come to the races with me today?"

"Races?" His dark eyes lit with excitement. "Ann, you do not mind, do you?"

Before she could answer, Durban intervened. "We go to Epsom in my curricle, so you need have no fear of him springing one of his horses."

"As though I would," Carlos scoffed.

"No, I think you should enjoy yourself," Ann said generously, but Bella knew she would rather Carlos stayed home.

After the two men had left and Ann had gone to consult with the cook, Phillipe glanced at Bella. "I was thinking about bringing Jamie down out of the playroom for lunch, then taking everyone to Astley's Amphitheater. Do you wish to go, Aunt?"

"No, I have letters to write. Mind you take some footmen with you. That is what we pay them for."

Bella knew what Phillipe was doing. By deliberately exposing them to danger, he hoped to show her that the world was not so fearsome as she supposed. But she knew that was an illusion, that no matter how much time passed safely, she would never drop her guard where Jamie was concerned.

*J*amie enjoyed watching the prancing ponies at Astley's and seemed to have a particular liking for a black one. Bella had made three or four false starts at a mention of Hal's bandaged hand, but she did not want to frighten Jamie. If she had noticed the abductor's hand, perhaps Jamie had as well. Certainly Phillipe was aware of it and had probably explained it away in his own mind. She spent the rest of the afternoon with Jamie in the playroom attached to the nursery, not doing letters or numbers but getting out all the toys and playing with him. She had never had such delights when she was a child and began to think that being a duke was not the worst that could befall him.

That evening was rather grim, with Hal and Carlos gone and Lady Edith schooling Bella in all the aristocracy she would encounter. She could not know that Bella was already in possession of most of this knowledge from the soldiers who spoke of their relatives.

The next morning she could not bear to be parted from her child, so she took him up on her saddle when she and Phillipe went riding. It was something she did all the time but occasioned as much remark in Hyde Park as though she had grown an extra head. When Phillipe suggested a pony on a lead would attract less attention, he became Jamie's hero and spent the rest of the day learning the merits of the steed Jamie hoped Phillipe would buy for him. Jamie had listened with acceptance to the excuse that Tattersall's only auctioned horses twice a week and resigned himself to wait, spending his enthusiasm by rendering his future mount in charcoal all afternoon.

Bella left him to Janet's care that evening and came down to the drawing room with her pelisse and fan.

"Hoskins?" she said as she encountered him in the hall.

"Your grace?"

"I was worried about Hal. He hurt his hand since last we saw him, and I was wondering if he had it tended by a physician. Even a small wound can go septic if not properly cleaned."

"And so I told him, your grace. A horse's mouth may be cleaner than some creature's . . ."

Hoskins averted his eyes from Lobo who came up the stairs from the kitchen and continued upward as though he knew where he was going.

"But he should have had it seen to all the same," Hoskins finished.

"A horse? He was bitten by a horse?"

"His own horse, your grace, which may account for his obdurate refusal to listen to reason."

"Has Lady Edith been apprised of this?"

"I was looking for an opportunity."

"I will take care of it. If anyone can get him to do what is wise, it is his mother." As she waited in the drawing room, Bella weighed the chances of the muffled highwayman being Hal, and the scale tipped the other way. Surely she would have remarked something in his voice if it had been. And it seemed quite reasonable that impatient Hal might be bitten by his own mount.

Phillipe walked in carrying a damp piece of paper.

"Oh, no, has Janet given him the watercolors?"

"Yes, I really think the boy has talent. I can almost make out that this is an equine."

Bella took a corner of the paper and smiled. "He is better at turtles. Did Lobo get in?"

"Yes, I let him in, along with Robert, the footman Lobo frightens the least. Jamie will be safe enough tonight."

"What is that?" Carlos asked as he came into the room and looked over Phillipe's shoulder.

"Jamie's pony," Phillipe replied. "Tomorrow you can help me find him, if you have sobered up by then."

"Yes, what were you drinking, Carlos?" Bella asked. "You slept past noon."

"I do not even remember. How did I get home?"

"Hoskins says you collided with the front door about one o'clock."

"That I remember." Carlos rubbed his head and then shook it. "Is Ann very angry?"

"Is Ann ever angry?" Phillipe asked.

"I wish she were more like Bella," Carlos confessed.

"At least I can tell what she is thinking by how she holds her mouth and chin."

"Oh, really?"

"No offense, Arabella, but you are easy to read, and a fellow needs all the help he can get."

Ann came into the room with her sweet smile, and Carlos's black eyes searched her face. His rapt regard made her blush and look at her gold evening dress. "Is it too bold? Perhaps I should change into . . ."

"You look like an angel," Carlos whispered as he came to take her hands and kiss her knuckles.

The dowager had followed Ann into the room wielding her cane, which she had almost left off using recently. "I hope you two are not going to make cakes of yourselves tonight."

"Which two?" Carlos asked impertinently.

When they entered the withdrawing room at Durban House, they were greeted by Lord Durban, the major's elder brother, and his pretty wife, Sally. They found the family gathering ran strongly toward the military set, with red and blue coats far outnumbering the black frock coats, and even most of these were worn by ex-military men. Colonel Maitland was among these numbers and greeted them warmly. His sister, Lady Amelia, was enjoying the attentions of two officers of the guard. Since many of the men had no wives or female relations to escort, Bella's appearance was greeted with jovial welcomes and laughter, but when Ann crossed the threshold into the room on Carlos's arm, her innocent blond beauty in perfect contrast to his dark looks, the room fell into sudden silence. By the rapt gazes of the men, they might have been looking upon an angel. Bella broke the ice by introducing Ann to the first knot of men, where she would have been completely enveloped if not for Carlos's persistent hold on her arm. Bella then took the dowager around to the other side of the room to make her known to all the officers.

Phillipe watched Bella appreciatively as she worked her way around the room. She not only remembered everyone but each man's connections in England and France, his regiment, and the significance of his uniform. She explained all this to Lady Edith, who nodded like an overwhelmed monarch. Occasionally Bella threw in a harmless anecdote that brought chuckles from the men and Lady Edith. In spite of her rapid stream of explanation, Bella's progress was much swifter than Ann's, so Phillipe clapped one of the officers on the shoulder to make a path for Ann and Carlos to move on to the next group.

Lieutenant Fellows, from Edwin's company of riflemen, arrived and scrutinized Phillipe's arm. "I did not think you were in Belgium."

"He was not," Durban answered for him. "Got himself shot by a highwayman not six miles from London. Carlos told me about it."

Bella glared at Carlos, and he receded into the crowd.

"Yes, what a scare for all of you," Lady Amelia said. "But I hear that her grace acquitted herself well, killing two of the vermin with a single shot each."

This caused such a murmur that Bella felt the need to say something, even though Lady Edith was scowling at Lady Amelia. "I cannot take any credit at all since I fired one shot at point-blank range and the other man was killed when the dead man's gun discharged and hit him in the head. I should say that I was merely lucky."

This brought a raucous burst of laughter from the men that made the dowager scowl even more, so she was in no very good mood when they went in to dinner.

Of the eighteen people at the table, only six were women, so each had to pay attention to the men on either side of her and at least one across the table. For Bella this was no great feat; she had been used to such arrangements in Lisbon. And after her initial embarrassment, Ann gave a good account of herself, for she looked on all of the men with such worshipful eyes and listened so attentively to their stories that they instantly fell in love with her. Carlos was seated halfway down the table from Ann on the other side but just across from Bella. She pulled a rosebud off the epergne and tossed it across the table to get his attention, then addressed a low admonishment his way in Portuguese that drew a reluctant smile from him. He took a gulp of wine and straightaway became very affable.

Leave it to Bella to get the best out of everyone. Phillipe could see her scanning the table to make sure that all were having a good time. Lady Durban glanced at her husband with a secret smile that signaled the dinner was a success. Maitland had been lucky enough to draw a chair by Bella, with Major Durban on her other side. It occurred to Phillipe that they were both interested in her, not for her role in the war but because she was a beautiful and affable woman, moreover a woman who would not scorn a soldier's life. He felt the first gnawing of jealousy, but he pushed it aside. Bella was his now, or would be in less than a year. He could afford to be generous with her attentions for a few weeks.

And she played them against each other, joking them out of a competitive stance and getting them to talk. Unfortunately Lady Amelia introduced the story of Bella's capture by the French captain.

"Is it true that you spent the night in his tent, your grace?" Durban teased.

"The night? Certainly not. I had wounded to take care of. I was there for a few hours because I reasoned my chances of escape would be better after dark."

Lady Edith had heard nothing of this, so her black mood was deepened by Bella's recollections. Lady Amelia managed to looked truly shocked over this.

"You poor girl. Did he . . . molest you?"

"Not even remotely," Bella assured her. "He questioned me, but my understanding of French was so deplorable I could not make out his simplest question, so it took quite a while."

"But you speak French like a native," Durban said.

"Captain Marais had no way of knowing that. Has anyone heard? Was he demoted for what I did to him?"

"What, exactly, was that?" Phillipe prompted, thinking to draw at least half of the dowager's wrath on his head rather than Bella's.

"Knocked him out and tied him up with his sash," Bella replied, provoking more raucous laughter.

"But how did you escape?" Maitland asked. "I never heard this tale."

"I stole one of his uniforms and his best horse.

Though when Phillipe found me riding hell for leather toward the British lines, we let the horse go. I hope the poor man got him back."

The soldiers to a man toasted Bella roundly for her ingenuity, while Lady Amelia glared at them and the dowager fumed. Bella was both applauded and disgraced at the same time. She glanced at Phillipe with a helpless look, feeling so much as she did on those occasions during the war when Phillipe complained most bitterly about her carelessness. She sought his face, and he was neither laughing nor glaring but smiling. And when she caught his eye, his smile widened as he raised his glass to her.

Bella's eye caught a bandaged hand in the cluster of hands and glasses—or was it only a lace cuff? She could not scrutinize all their hands without leaning forward and being obvious. Perhaps later. But they spent so long over dinner, and the men subsequently over their port and cigars, that half the company had to leave before they retired to the drawing room, some of them still being on active duty. None of the men who came into the drawing room was wearing a bandage, though there were several slings in evidence and more than one man was limping. Ann drew close to Bella.

"They are all so alive, and there are so many of them," she said.

"There is no need to fear them," Bella said. "They are like boys, most of them, without the sense to take care of themselves."

"Did you—did you nurse any of these men?"

Bella scanned the dozen men in the room. "One or two. But they do not regard it, and neither do I. Would you play something for them? Or would it make you too nervous?"

"I would love to play something for them."

When Bella proposed this to Lady Durban, she had the chairs arranged so that all could hear Ann to advantage. Ann found several pieces of music she knew and played them, with Carlos faithfully turning the pages for her when she nodded. Even after she had finished, he stood doggedly by her as the officers came to thank her.

"Do I look like that?" Phillipe asked Bella.

"Sometimes," she teased, but when she saw guilt ride his brow, she softened her remark. "That is why they all think you so serious, because a smile does not sit lightly on your face, but when you are pleased . . ."

Phillipe smiled then in that secret way that said he had something to tell her.

"What is it?"

"Nothing. I think I am beginning to understand something about myself. I shall tell you later."

The ride home in the carriage was less than pleasant, with the dowager trotting out all their errors and upbraiding them each in turn. But the bulk of her wrath was reserved for Bella, who was scolded for doing expressly what the dowager had warned her against—discussing the highwaymen and then dragging out that disgusting tale about her capture.

"But I have always found that if someone is seeking to shred your character, it is far better to take over and give your side of it if you have a chance. People do not think so badly of you if you do not think badly of yourself."

"That is what comes of your army upbringing. It is not the way matters are conducted in polite society."

Phillipe cleared his throat. "In case it has escaped your notice, madam, the makeup of society has changed. It might be well if you accustomed yourself to soldiers and their rather . . . exuberant habits, since you will be seeing much of them while we are in town."

"I will not lower my standards just because there has been a war. This evening was a disaster, and I think we should forget about any other social engagements."

"Oh, and I was thinking things had gone rather well," Bella said in that innocent tone that warned Phillipe she was about to say something outrageous.

"Rather well?" Lady Edith almost shrieked. "You will be the talk of London by tomorrow morning."

"But no one was knifed or shot . . ." Bella offered humbly.

Both Phillipe and Carlos burst into laughter, covering any further comments from Lady Edith. Soon the carriage discharged them in front of the house, so it was Hoskins who innocently bore the brunt of the dowager's wrath for the length of her slow climb to her apartment.

While Phillipe was talking to Ann, Bella took a candle and went up the stairs. She passed her room and went up another flight to the nursery. She nodded to the footman sitting in the chair outside the door, who immediately stood up and bowed. "Good evening, Robert," she said. Bella cracked the door quietly so as not to wake Jamie or Janet, who slept in a small adjoining room.

Lobo raised his head and whimpered, and Bella went to caress him where he lay at the foot of Jamie's bed. The floorboard squeaked behind her, and she said, "Phillipe?"

"How did you know it was me?" he asked softly.

"You had something to tell me." She turned to him in the darkness, and he took the candle from her to set it on the table by the bed.

"If only we could go for one of our walks." He embraced her, wrapping his arms around her and cradling her head against him. He removed the comb from her hair and ran his fingers through it as the dark mane came undone and curled down her back.

Bella sighed and held him, luxuriating in his warmth, his strength, and his maleness. "London does not lend itself to such casual behavior. Was your aunt right? Have I disgraced myself?"

"I have no idea. London was never as it is now, full of war heroes. I should think if they approve of you, no one will gainsay them for now."

"But later I may be ostracized?" she asked hopefully as she looked up at him, searching his face in the faint light from the candle.

"I know that is what you think you want, never to have to come to London, just to stay at your farm, but you must think of Jamie."

"I came to the most awful realization over this attempted abduction."

"And what is that?"

"I was always able to protect him. Phillipe, I kept him safe through an entire war. But I now know that I cannot do it alone. He is too vulnerable, and I am not always with him. The worst of it is that I do not know who the enemy is."

"That is why I am here."

She clung to him and sought his eyes again. His mouth moved down to hers, and she snaked her arms around his neck, running her hands through his hair. "My Phillipe, I thought never to have you. That loving you was an impossible dream."

"I thought never to get you to myself. I had to fight the French and then the entire British army as well for a crumb of your attention."

"But there has never been anyone but you. No matter what I did, I thought only of you."

"No matter where I was, what I was doing, you were in my thoughts."

"Your jealous thoughts?" she chided with a smile.

He kissed her savagely and she opened her mouth to him, dueling hungrily with his tongue as she tried to outdo him. He tasted of sweet port and fragrant smoke, the tang of it bringing back the strange, exotic memories of Spain. Would those days and nights be forever with her as vividly as they were now, and did she want them to be? Or did she wish them to fade and be replaced by the green English summers and the calm of peace? It hardly mattered so long as she had Phillipe.

He paused to look at her breathlessly. "I more than love you. All those things I so disapproved of before, I find myself quite proud of them now that you are no longer in danger."

"It works both ways. I could not keep you safe either. And you were always riding off on some suicide mission in your red coat as though you were invisible. Did you have no thought for your own safety?"

"Like you I have trusted to luck far too much. I feel I have used it all up, and now we must stay together to be safe."

"What can possibly part us?"

She moaned as Phillipe's hands slid down her back to ride along the curves of her hips and legs.

Lobo whined, and Jamie sat up in bed. Phillipe released her with a low chuckle.

"Phillipe? Mother?"

Bella sat on the end of the bed. "We did not mean to wake you. I just wanted to make sure you are all right."

"I have Lobo with me. Robert is staying, too. And Janet is here."

"I know. But I missed you." Bella hugged him. And Phillipe pulled the covers up to tuck him in again.

"Ready to go seek your pony tomorrow?"

"Yes, I will bring my drawings. I have them all ready."

"Good lad. Go back to sleep."

Phillipe took up the candle and escorted Bella to her room one floor down. "I wish I could come in."

"My maid will be waiting up or sleeping in a chair. No matter how much I assure Sarah I can undress myself, she insists." Bella hesitated, hoping Phillipe would suggest another location. "What about your room?"

"Old Timms will be there. Since you dismissed him from Jamie's service, he has attached himself to me as my valet without my request or permission. He must be eighty if he is a day and deaf as a post."

"Then I must say good night to you and hope for a short stay in London. Perhaps if I am disgraced the dowager will let us go back to Dorney as soon as the will is resolved. Or perhaps she will change her mind and disown us."

"Not a chance. The more she loves a person, the more she criticizes."

"Then I have risen immensely in her estimation."

❦ 17 ❦

*T*he next morning Bella had slit and read the entire
pile of invitations by her plate as she had her tea and
had begun to compose in her mind some of the regrets
she would send, thinking about all the soldiers she would
like to see again and the families she would like to meet.
Phillipe and Ann came into the room, laughing.

"Phillipe says those soldiers are all in love with me,
Bella, and I say they are only trifling."

"Of course they are in love with you, but only for a
day or two. Soldiers are very inconstant fellows."

She caught a mock menacing glare from Phillipe.

"Oh, really?" he asked.

"Most of them, anyway. Until you meet *the one*, and
you will know it. You will meet just one who will scowl
at you and make you feel guilty every time you laugh at
another man's joke or so much as speak to someone in
a uniform."

They heard the rumble of feet on the stairs, and

Carlos came into the room, looking guiltily from Ann to Phillipe.

"I think I have already met him," Ann said.

"Met who?" Carlos asked, his voice low and vibrant.

"The man I am in love with."

Carlos hesitated at the sideboard and swallowed, looking for all the world as though he had been gut-shot.

"You, silly," Ann said to break the suspense.

He dropped his head to his hand. "I wish you would not do that to me. Last night was agonizing enough." He poured himself black tea and sat beside Ann, regarding her with a whipped-dog expression.

Ann smiled at him, and Bella knew what she was feeling: a surge of joy at being so vital to a man's existence. She hoped that Ann would be kinder to Carlos than she had been to Phillipe.

A strident voice from the hallway announced the descent of the dowager. She stomped into the breakfast parlor, stabbing the floor with her cane, and sat in her place. And it was only nine o'clock. According to Phillipe, breakfasting with the family was a new start of Lady Edith's.

"Would you like some chocolate, your grace?" Hoskins asked.

"Get out," she said economically. "Ann will serve me."

Ann rolled her eyes at Hoskins, who shrugged and left. The girl went to the sideboard and laced a cup of chocolate with cream, placing it at the dowager's right hand, then stood back, apparently to see what she would demand next.

"Sit down, Ann," Phillipe said gently. "Aunt is never hungry this early in the morning and will not eat

anything until she is in a better mood." His aunt glared
at him as he got up to examine the array of food himself. He had dispensed with the sling and was able to
bring back plates of food for both him and Bella. Carlos likewise served Ann, so that she had nothing to do
but slit the invitation cards by her plate. The dowager
looked at her diminutive pile of envelopes and glanced
covetously at the stack of cards Bella had sorted in
front of her before she sliced into her mail as though
she were killing each and every letter.

"And just what do you mean to do this morning?"
she demanded.

Since this was broadcast to the table, Phillipe answered, "Jamie and I go to Tatt's today to look for his
pony. Carlos will accompany us?"

"I would be honored, and you may need me, else you
could come back with five or six ponies. I know how
persuasive the child can be."

The dowager's penetrating gaze next fell on Bella.

"I must sit down in the library and send regrets on all
these invitations. After last night's debacle, we should
stay only to settle our legal tangle, then hie us back to
Dorney Park and hope the talk eventually dies down."

Ann gaped as the dowager stared intently at Bella's
circumspect black muslin dress and neat braid. It was
obvious this had not been the answer Lady Edith was
expecting, which was exactly what Bella had intended.

"Certainly not!" the old woman said with such a
snap of finality that Bella put down her knife and fork
and regarded her with feigned puzzlement.

"But, your grace," she said innocently, "my character
must be irretrievable after the two stories which are

even now circulating through town. We can only hope that by my absenting myself, the gossip will subside."

"I know these people, and running from a fight will never do anything but lead to more rumors. We will sit down, you, me, and Ann, decide which of these events most merit our attentions, and then answer them together."

"I concede to your superior knowledge of such matters. Certainly I would be pleased to be guided by you in this," Bella said formally, ignoring the smirk on Phillipe's face.

After one more suspicious glance at Bella, the dowager cleared her throat and gave a lengthy request for a breakfast that would choke a horse.

As Ann was preparing this, Hal came in, without his bandage. Bella tried to see his hand and noticed the yellowish bruise and broken skin where the horse had gotten him. It was healing normally, she thought, and in no danger of infection, so she said nothing about it. Hal had not been at the dinner last night, so she could only conclude that to see a bandaged hand was quite a normal event, and she should not assume every man who had met with a slight accident was the highwayman who had tried to abduct her son. Jamie was well protected now, at any rate, and they would probably hear no more about the matter.

Bella and Ann had nearly finished writing their replies, and Ann had drawn up a calendar of events for the next few weeks that the dowager approved, though she said she would no doubt be dead with fatigue by the end of it. A carriage arrived in front of the house, and Bella strode to the window to see if Jamie had gotten his pony. "Oh, no!"

"What is it?" the dowager asked. "Do not keep me in suspense."

"It is that tiresome Mr. Thackery and his sister. Do we have to receive them?"

"Of course we do, since they are staying here."

"But I fired him," Bella moaned. "And he tried to beat Lobo. After the things I said to him, I am surprised he would even come here."

"Are you telling me I cannot have the Thackerys as guests?" Lady Edith asked. "They are particular friends of mine."

"So long as he keeps his distance from me, Jamie, and Lobo, I do not care where he stays," Bella said. "But it is a strain to think of enough insults to keep him at arm's length."

"I would not have thought that would be a problem for you," the dowager said.

Thackery was ushered in with his sister. He greeted all of them warmly, completely forgetting every argument he had had with Bella.

"You are looking as beautiful as ever," he said, holding her hand in his moist grasp longer than Bella liked.

"I am surprised to see you here, Mr. Thackery."

To Ann he was somewhat more subdued.

"Where is Carlos?" Miranda asked. "He promised to show me the shops on Oxford Street."

Ann hardly knew what to say to her. "He is engaged this morning, and this afternoon he is taking *me* shopping."

"Oh, good. There is so much I need to buy," Miranda countered, assuming she would be welcome on the expedition.

Carlos strode into the room then, declaring that they had found Wellie.

Bella covered his sudden look of dismay at seeing Miranda by saying, "Oh, no. Tell me he has not named the pony after Lord Wellington."

"That is the equine's formal name, but Phillipe suggested Wellie as an everyday name."

"If you all will excuse me, I must go see this paragon."

Bella made her escape to the stable yard, and once she had become acquainted with the black pony Jamie vowed was exactly the one he had wanted, she declared they must try him in the park. Bella sneaked up the back stairs to make her way to her bedroom so that she could change into her riding habit. Fortunately her extensive experience with covert operations might aid her in avoiding Thackery during his stay. She felt a little guilty about abandoning Carlos to Miranda's unwelcome attentions, but he should have been more direct at repressing her.

The lead line was dispensed with as soon as they got into the confines of the park, for Bella could see it embarrassed the boy. Sebastian snorted his contempt of the diminutive steed, but Phillipe held the war horse to a circumspect trot as Wellie carried Jamie quite gamely at a steady, willing pace between Phillipe's mount and Bella's.

"Do you remember how to steer?" Bella asked. "We are going to turn to the right at the next trail."

"Yes, Mother."

"And press him a little with your right heel," Phillipe reminded.

They were so caught up in teaching Jamie together that Bella failed to see a sporting carriage bearing down on them from the other direction.

"Jamie, fall in behind the mare," Phillipe warned, putting Sebastian out toward the middle of the path just in case the inconsiderate driver should fail to check his team.

Bella urged her mare forward and Jamie reined his pony back enough to get behind her just as the tulip whisked by. Sebastian bared his teeth at the near horse, causing it to shy into its teammate and the phaeton's wheels to slip off the packed road. The driver was jostled and too busy managing both whip and reins to do more than mutter at Phillipe.

"Well done, Jamie," Phillipe said. "I think after this we will ride in the mornings. There is less traffic."

"Did you see that the Thackerys have arrived?" Bella asked.

"Yes, I saw their baggage."

"Why is your aunt kind to them, Phillipe? According to Ann, Thackery is a bit of a wastrel."

Bella smiled as Jamie urged his pony a little in advance of them so that he could pick the path they would try next. Or perhaps he was just distracted by them talking over his head.

"His father has been the vicar at Dorney for decades. I am sure everyone expects Thackery to get the parish after the father retires."

"But who would decide that? Surely not Lady Edith."

"No, the decision is mine," Phillipe said, keeping a watchful eye on Jamie.

"I suppose I should not say so, but I do not like the fellow." Bella glanced at Phillipe.

"Neither do I, and I cannot quite put my finger on why. I had ascribed it to jealousy—"

Bella cut him off with a laugh. "He is the most dense man I have ever encountered. I no more tell him something than he goes on planning as though my opinions, indeed my orders, mean nothing to him. He even proposed marriage to me."

"Shall I not give him the living at Dorney?" Phillipe asked, wrestling a little with Sebastian, who was getting tired of trotting.

"No, that would keep him constantly underfoot, but, self-interest aside, there must be far more worthy candidates for the post, true men of God rather than wastrels."

"I am sure there are, but we must do something with Thackery."

"Send him on some business. Surely we have some interests abroad that he could tend to."

"Banish him?" Phillipe asked with a grin.

"And his sister if you can. She is a troublemaker."

"I shall see what I can do. Look at Jamie. He is doing well. Shall we buy him a cavalry commission? He seems to have a knack for riding."

"I hope that by the time he is grown, he can do all his riding for pleasure. But you must let him become a man first."

"Is that what never happened with Hal?" Phillipe asked. "Was he overprotected?"

"Who is to say? Certainly Edwin was a man and a competent commander, but that was his nature."

"Nothing will go wrong with Jamie's upbringing,"

Phillipe said as he smiled at the boy, who got his pony to break into a canter.

That evening Phillipe shepherded the family to the carriage at least an hour after he would have liked. Dinner had seemed interminable, but not because of her grace. Thackery had been full of stories about town for his sister, which he told everyone at length, though the rest had no interest and had given up feigning it by the end of the second course.

Even though Miranda had just arrived in London, knew almost no one, and had no right to expect to be included in anything, she was disappointed that she was not invited to any of the entertainments the ladies planned to attend. But Thackery had said he would take her to the theater that night, though she broadly hinted she would rather go with Carlos.

Carlos was invited to the Fortesque rout along with Bella and the others and was adamant about going to this rather than the theater with the Thackerys. The rout party, when their carriage finally delivered them to the doorstep, ablaze with lamplight, was a bit of a crush, with not nearly enough chairs to accommodate everyone.

But then the orchestra struck up some dance tunes. Again the red of military coats screamed at the pale yellows and pinks of the ladies' gowns. Phillipe looked proudly at his sister as she drew the admiring stare of every man she encountered. Bella must have advised Ann to wear a light blue silk as the least offensive foil for red. Of course, Bella's customary black, which she wore almost like a uniform, made her a striking figure.

She held her knot of curls this night with a large Spanish comb. That, along with her lace fan, gave her an
exotic grace. Phillipe kept Bella within sight as much
as possible, though so many men he knew distracted
him with stories or greetings that he frequently had to
seek her out. Ann's steps were being dogged by Carlos,
so he had no fear for her safety even in this crush. Hal
had come reluctantly and remained at heel to his
mother until she was ensconced in a corner of the
room with a few of her cronies. Then he disappeared,
Phillipe supposed, into the card room.

Ann was included in the country dance that was
forming, not partnered by Carlos but within his protec-
tive gaze. This cleared the edges of the room enough
for Phillipe to realize that Bella was not there. He
made his way though the series of rooms looking for
her with an uneasy feeling.

"Are you sure you would not like to dance?" Fellows
asked her for the third time.

"No. I thank you for the lemonade." Bella was trying
not to look at the bandage on his hand. She was focusing on his voice but could not match it in her memory
to the highwayman.

"I saw what Lady Amelia was trying to do to you at
Durban's dinner. She is a witch."

Fellows looked angry on Bella's behalf, his dark
brows furrowed over his intent gray eyes. He had always been a most serious soldier and one of unques-
tionable courage. It was idiotic to suspect him of so
foul a crime as abduction.

"Did we come out of it badly?" Bella asked, taking a

sip from her glass as she watched him. His hair was un-fashionably long, but his green rifleman's uniform was impeccable.

"No, you accounted yourself well. I assure you every man in the room admires you more than ever. I have a special regard for you." His eyes raked hungrily over her bodice.

He raised his glass to take a drink, and Bella steeled herself not to bolt from the room, for she knew what was coming next. She was not afraid of him, but hated having to turn men down. Why did they all want to marry her?

"I hardly know you," Bella said, burying her face in the glass of lemonade.

"But I know you. I have seen you drive a team of wounded back and set to treating them as though it were your job rather than that of those incompetent surgeons' assistants."

"Perhaps if they were better trained. Things had improved by the end of the war with Doctor McGregor and his field hospitals."

"But then we forgot everything we had learned in the Peninsula at Waterloo." Fellows's voice dropped to an ominous whisper. "There was a deplorable waste of life there."

"I know," Bella said. "I was there."

"Yes, I remember helping you turn over the piles of dead to look for your husband—"

He stopped when he realized she had her eyes shut. She managed to hold back any trace of tears, managed to block out the visions of the battlefield. Edwin's tears were all shed now. When she opened her eyes again, he was looking apologetic, and she swallowed hard, more in sympathy with him than angry at his lapse.

"I am sorry. I did not mean to distress you. I only wanted you to know how much I admire, how much I want . . ."

"I did no more than any other woman would have done," Bella said calmly.

"Once you knew he could not be helped, you carried water to the others, tirelessly, until they— Forgive me."

"Clean water was not easy to find, and there were so many of them. I felt inadequate to the task for the first time during that long and bitter war."

Fellows shook his head in assent. "After all you have done, it cannot be easy for you to be under the dowager's thumb. She has a viperish reputation."

"So I have noticed. But I am making my peace with her." Bella scanned the moving throng for Phillipe, Ann, or Carlos, any rescue from this conversation.

"But if you were to marry, you could be free of her," Fellows suggested.

"Phillipe has the guardianship of Jamie," Bella said by way of evasion.

"I did not know that. What are you saying?"

Fellows thrust one leg in front of the other and leaned his bandaged hand on the hilt of his saber, cutting a fine figure by any standard but her own.

"I am tied to the family by my son."

"So, if you did marry, you could not take him with you."

"I plan not to think of marriage for a while."

Fellows thought for a moment. "If you took him,

could they stop you?" He smiled at his simple soldier's solution to the problem.

"What are you saying? Kidnap my own child?"

"There are countries where we could lose ourselves, where you could have anything you wanted—"

"No, you must not say these things." Bella backed away from him and his ardent expression.

Phillipe appeared behind Fellows. "Bella, Lady Edith is asking for you," he said calmly, even though Bella knew he had heard what Fellows was proposing.

"I will go to her then. Excuse me, sir."

Phillipe's gaze followed Bella as she made her way into the next room. Fellows downed his wine and turned to face Phillipe. "Bella is wasted as a widow."

"I am sure we all agree with you, but if she has decided to observe a mourning period for Edwin, it would behoove all of us to respect that."

"Ah, I see. You are in the running, too. I suppose I have no chance with her, then."

"This discussion should not be taking place," Phillipe said stiffly.

"I do not come to her a pauper. I have an independence from my father's business. I do not think she will object to a living made in trade rather than on the backs of serfs."

"Radical ideas, Lieutenant Fellows. And Bella is quite open-minded, but not touching on her son. That is the sum of her concern for now and a good many years to come."

"You cannot just dismiss me like this." Fellows took a belligerent stance in front of him.

"I was not aware that I had."

"If you are holding Bella prisoner with your power and money, then kindly remember that she has a friend in me, and one who does not care if she comes away with no more than the clothes on her back." Fellows clapped his glass down on the table and turned as though he were hurrying off with an important dispatch.

"What is the matter with that fellow?" Hal asked.

"A little lovesick, is all," Phillipe said tiredly as he tried to rub the headache away from his forehead.

"Half the fellows in the room are after Bella, and the rest are worshiping at Ann's feet," Hal said, looking around him as he poured wine into a glass. "It is positively disgusting."

"You might make yourself useful by watching over one or the other of them."

"Not me. I am having a run of luck. I just came out for something to drink."

"Even Edwin would have lent a hand when I needed help," Phillipe said.

"What do you mean, *even* Edwin?"

"Nothing."

"Something went wrong between you two. I could tell by your letters. What was it?"

"War does things to you."

"Yet he left you in charge."

"Yes, I was surprised by that myself."

Hal finished his wine and set the glass down. "Very well, who do you want me to watch?"

Bella did not know if Lady Edith wanting to see her was fiction or not, but she went to the dowager just in case. There was an older woman sitting with her.

"Bella, I want to introduce to you Lady Woodly," the dowager said. "She had been wanting to meet you."

"Woodly? Did I meet your son in Spain?" Bella asked kindly. "How is he?"

The woman smiled sadly. "He told me of your care of him, spoke so kindly of you that I felt I wanted to meet you for myself."

Bella felt herself tearing up. "Spoke?" she choked out in the past tense.

"Yes, Grey did not make it. Forgive me for springing the news on you like this. I thought you had heard."

Bella licked her lips. "There were so many of them that I suppose I will be in for more shocks than this." Bella steadied herself against the dowager's chair.

"Perhaps you should sit down," Lady Edith said, her voice low as it had been when Phillipe was shot.

Lady Woodly leaned toward her. "I meant only to thank you for all you did for him. He made it home, which was his dearest wish. It was inevitable that some men would be lost."

"Indeed," Bella said. "Of all the sides in the war, I felt I was on the only one that fought a truly losing battle. I begrudged every single casualty."

"And yet you persisted," Lady Woodly observed kindly.

"I had no other occupation. I could never have turned my back on them. I am glad to know you got to talk with him."

Lady Woodly excused herself and left them. Bella did sit then.

"Are you all right, Bella? Do you wish to go?"

"No, I am fine." She cleared her throat. "Depend

upon it, I shall now meet some poor fellow whom I gave up for dead and who miraculously survived my attentions. Then I will be all right again."

"How do you bear it?" Lady Edith asked.

"Bear what?" Bella pulled her gaze away from the red coats, the empty sleeves and walking sticks.

"Being flung from joy to despair so often in an evening and . . . having such a very big family?"

" 'Tis true. Once I know them, I cannot let go. But the advantage of a big family is that they are there to support you when one of them falls."

"If you all stick together."

"Yes, of course." Bella ran her knuckle under each eyelid to make sure there were no tears escaping. "Is Carlos being good?"

"Sorely tried but bearing up. Ah, here comes Phillipe."

Phillipe was still scowling vacantly. "Was Fellows bothering you, Bella?"

"No . . . well, no more than usual."

"What is that supposed to mean?" he asked, his blond hair raking his brow in the most maddening way.

"I greatly feared he was going to propose marriage to me again. He was certainly suggesting an elopement."

"And has he proposed marriage to you before?" Phillipe demanded.

"Oh, not above three or four times. He was one of my more moderate suitors in the Peninsula. Do not worry about Fellows. I can handle him."

Lady Edith looked at her as though she were insane. "Do you mean to tell me that men were in the habit of proposing to you without speaking to your father?"

"Oh, yes, no one stood on ceremony, except Phillipe, and you see where that landed us."

Lady Edith directed her glare at Phillipe. "Being the man you are, I suppose you did speak to her father."

Phillipe nodded. "And when he refused my suit, I could not tell Bella how I felt about her."

"Young idiot," the dowager said under her breath. "And you would have accepted Phillipe?" She turned to regard Bella.

"If he had asked me." Bella looked down at her hands as she fiddled with her fan.

"But I did finally cast honor and all my good intentions to the wind," Phillipe said, breaking the uneasy silence between them.

Another country dance started up, and Bella looked at him, knowing there were unshed tears shining in her eyes.

"Yes, that night on the Coa River," she whispered.

"And what happened on the Coa River?" the dowager demanded, looking from one to the other of them.

To Bella's surprise, Phillipe blushed, not her.

Lady Edith glanced between them again. "Oh—yes, I see."

Carlos strode up to them abruptly. "I have had enough and am leaving now, on foot." His normally tidy hair had been disarranged, probably by his own impatient hands, and his white teeth flashed into a grimace. "Do not look for me at home tonight." He was gone then in half a dozen quick strides that drew the gazes of all the ladies in the room.

"I had better see what Ann has done," Phillipe said.

"I am coming with you." Bella took his arm as they

circled the ballroom until they identified Ann taking part in the dance with due circumspection. Hal was watching her from the side of the room.

"Dancing with Maitland," Phillipe observed.

"He is too old for her," Bella said. "But why would that send Carlos off in a rage?"

"I do not know, but I must admit to some fellow feeling," he confessed.

"Then let us leave London as soon as our errand is accomplished," Bella countered.

A soldier bumped into them and tried to detain them, but Phillipe pulled Bella past him toward the hallway. "We are never alone, and we must talk." Phillipe led her down the hallway, opening doors and surprising more than one couple. The library seemed vacant. He pulled her inside, and she sat on a chair by the desk.

"I have had word from our solicitors that they can meet with us next week. They have been in possession of your marriage papers and Jamie's baptismal certificate long enough to have authenticated them."

"Yes, of course. Will we leave then?"

"So eager to get shut of the place?" Phillipe asked, sitting on the edge of the desk. "You used to be quite gay in Lisbon."

"That was just show. Those poor devils never knew if that day would be their last. How could I not laugh with them and dance for them?"

"So, you did not really feel gay. I have often wondered."

"I felt like a wound spring all the time, as though I dare not sleep or even sit down." She jumped up and began to pace the room. "It is difficult not to feel that way again now that I see them all . . . not all of them."

"You were closer to those men, and I was always off on a mission." His eyes followed her as she walked to the window and back, pulling her lace fan through her fingers. "It was wrong to throw you in with them again."

"How could you know what it would be like for me?" She paused in front of him. "I did not realize it myself until tonight."

He stood and embraced her in a hug that said less of love and more of comfort than she had ever known from him.

"I should have guessed. You have been through a terrible experience."

"Yes, but it is over now. I needed to see them again, Phillipe. To know that so many have mended is good for me. It means that my efforts were not wasted."

"You brought me back to life," he said into her hair. "Was that wasted?"

"You did not thank me for it at the time," she reminded him.

"You belonged to someone else. I was just your patient."

"You were never *just* anything. You were the only thing I ever cared about. And now we have Jamie."

"We are luckier than most to have come away from the war with all our limbs and a child into the bargain."

"I do not believe in luck, not really," Bella said.

"Then you should not have wandered away with Fellows," he admonished.

"I wanted to know—he had a bandage on his hand."

"What of it? There must be half a dozen— Oh." He let go of her to regard her. "The highwayman. Does that seem at all likely?"

"I do not think so. He did not even know that you are Jamie's guardian. As you said, it is common enough to have a wounded hand. Hal himself had a bandaged hand for a day or two."

"I know. Right after we came to town."

"His horse bit him," Bella said.

Phillipe stared at her. "How did you know that?"

"I asked Hoskins. What does it matter?" Bella sat at the desk and leaned her head on her hand.

"I know he seems a careless fool to you, but Hal would never . . ."

"Phillipe, I did not say he had. I only said . . ."

"You must have considered the possibility, if you asked Hoskins about it." Phillipe's voice had taken on that hard edge she hated.

"I could lie to you and say I was only worried about Hal, but, yes, I did ask to find out how long he had been injured."

"And could Hal be our highwayman?" Phillipe demanded angrily.

"Phillipe!" she pleaded.

"You are a fool if you think he would raise his hand against the child just for a title."

"I never said that!" Bella replied hotly, abandoning the chair to pace to the window again. "But he does gamble, and you hold the purse-strings now. If he thought he could get some money easily . . ."

"My God! You really think he did it?"

"No, I—I do not know what to think, except that I

want to leave here." Bella wrung her hands together. "Why are you so angry with me?"

"Hal is my cousin, just as Edwin was." Phillipe leaned on the desk with his arms crossed. "I know him as well as I did Edwin, or thought I knew Edwin."

"What—what do you mean?"

Phillipe came to her and took her face between his hands. "Do you realize I would do anything for you, murder, sell my immortal soul, anything?"

"Phillipe, you are raving. I have never asked anything of you."

"But do you not see? If I, the master of control, would perform any act to get you, how much more tempting would you be to another man?"

"Who are we talking of?" Bella stepped back from him. "Fellows or Hal?"

"Edwin," he said darkly.

"Edwin? But he is dead."

"He was right there at your elbow when you found out I was dead, was he not?"

"It was Edwin who told me." Bella found her fan and grasped it, pulling back the horrid memory of that day again against her will, shivering as she heard those fatal words: *Phillipe is dead. We could not save him.*

"Did he ask you right then to marry him, or did he give you an hour or two to think it over?"

Bella stared at Phillipe in disbelief. "I do not understand you. That you could be jealous of other men I excuse, but Edwin is dead."

"When I was riding for the British lines with that troop of lancers on my heels, the company of riflemen that was assigned to Edwin's brigade started firing at the lancers."

"But they could not protect you. The French lancers were out of range," Bella supplied.

"I was within range. I was hit in the front of the shoulder. You've seen the scar."

Bella stared at him, an icy chill creeping up from her feet to set her lips to trembling. "Yes, it is in the front. But that means . . ."

"That means the bullet came from our side," Phillipe finished.

"No, Phillipe! I will not believe it. An accident, surely. But not Edwin."

"You defend Edwin without any proof of his innocence, yet you are ready to believe his brother an abductor of children on the strength of a bandage."

Phillipe stared at her as the import sank in.

"You trapped me," she accused. "Why?"

The door opened, and Hal poked his head in. "I thought I heard you two in here. If you want to argue, you might pick a less conspicuous place."

"You are right, Hal," Bella said. "We have been very stupid. Is your mother ready to leave?"

"Yes. Ann is in a strange mood, almost a rage."

"What?" Bella asked distractedly. "You must be mistaken. Ann has no temper."

"Nevertheless, she is standing outside waiting for the carriage. Could you go to her, Phillipe?" Hal asked. "Before she throttles one of the footmen."

Phillipe pushed past Bella, and she stared after his broad shoulders as he dutifully went to take care of his sister. She had thought they had come so far since that first day on the dock when the horse had almost fallen on her. Now she felt he was a stranger to her again. But how could he possibly suspect Edwin? Edwin, who had cried when he had to tell her Phillipe was dead. Edwin, who had cared about him like a brother. There was no malice there, no jealousy. More a case of hero worship. Edwin had admired Phillipe immensely, though Phillipe was older by only a year. Edwin had tried to be like Phillipe in every way he could, even to risking his neck on Sebastian. Phillipe might be a wise man in many ways, but he was wrong about Edwin wanting him dead.

Bella and Phillipe were both silent as Ann ranted about the jealous nature of Carlos on the way home in the carriage and how she was glad she had found out what he was really like before it was too late.

Only Lady Edith had any words of comfort for her, patting her hand and embracing her when the inevitable floods of tears came. Bella had tried to warn Ann that other men and women could put a strain on a relationship. Even she and Phillipe still argued. But for them the specter of jealousy was overshadowed by more elemental issues—survival.

If she was to leave nothing to chance, how could she not have considered the possibility of Hal as the abductor? He had stayed in London while they were preparing for the trip, and they had sent him notice of when they would arrive by dispatching their personal servants ahead of them. He could have made the contacts, hired the men to help him. He could have found out exactly when they got to Hatfield and when they were likely to arrive in London if he had just one servant in his employ. The news might even have been carried to him in innocence.

She shook her head. Just because something was possible did not mean it was likely. She had to keep imagination out of this and stick to the facts. But this notion that Edwin had tried to kill Phillipe . . . that was absurd. Of that she was certain.

⮿18⮾

*T*he next morning Bella was halfway to the park, with Greenley and another groom riding escort on either side of Jamie's pony and Lobo scouting the path ahead. Phillipe cantered up to them on Alta and rode around the grooms to draw abreast of Bella and Sebastian.

"Why did you not wait for me?" he demanded. "And why are you riding that horse?"

"I did not know your mind. I was not about to ride your mare without permission," she whispered coldly. "In fact, I think I do not know you at all."

"I was angry last night with your insinuation that Hal might harm Jamie," he said in a low voice.

"I do not believe that of Hal any more than you do. But to accuse Edwin of shooting you when he cannot defend himself . . . I tell you, Phillipe, he cared more about you than he ever cared for me. The only reason he married me was because of his regard for you."

"And he never made love to you," Phillipe said almost to himself. "How did he explain that omission?"

She looked at his face, and he was staring at her in such a way that she could not tell what he was thinking. "You do not believe me, do you?"

"Of course I do."

"What else do you not believe?" Bella continued.

"I said I believe you," Phillipe insisted.

"Do you believe that Jamie is your son?" she whispered.

"It does not matter to me whether he is or not."

"Then it certainly does not matter to me if we ever marry or not." Bella turned Sebastian in a circle and came back to ride beside Jamie. The grooms dropped back and Phillipe took up his position on the other side of the pony. Bella could see him there, out of the corner of her eye, but she would not look at him, would never forgive him for his lack of trust. He had only pretended to trust her because he wanted her. In that way he was like all the others. But he did not really believe her. Perhaps it would be better to deny Jamie's inheritance and carry him back to the farm, but then he would have no father and he would have lost his grandmother and all his other relations.

She tried to go over in her mind what had happened, why they had fought, and how the argument had escalated. She heard Phillipe give Jamie a gentle hint about neck reining and watched her son turn his pony rather skillfully for such a young child. Phillipe would make a good father, but as a husband? Would it be one battle after another? She began to wonder if her love for him could survive marriage.

It took Phillipe another half an hour of freezing silence from Bella to figure out where he had gone wrong. By then they were back in the courtyard at the town house, and Jamie was supervising the unsaddling and walking of his pony. Phillipe realized now that he should have said, *Of course I believe Jamie is my son*, rather than taking the superior position of loving the child no matter whose son he was. Instead, he had spoken the truth, and that was why he was in hot water.

Bella had taken Jamie's hand to lead him back to the house when Thackery happened to emerge from the back door with Hal. Lobo growled and made for Thackery. Had Bella not gotten hold of his collar, he might have had a piece of the man's pant leg. Phillipe shook his head.

He had made a right mess of things, and all over Hal. He thought about Hal hiring ruffians, throwing a muffler about his face, and riding off to hold up a coach. He shook his head and laughed. Hal would never be put to so much bother if he needed money. He would just come to Phillipe as he usually did. Then Phillipe remembered what he had told Hal the last time he had run into debt, that he would not rescue him again, that Hal would have to get out of it himself. He shook his head. Surely Hal would know he had not meant that. Nothing was ever simple.

He had not paid much attention to Bella's description of the highwayman, and here she had been scrutinizing anyone wearing a bandage, as though they might run into the highwayman in society. More likely he was in the labyrinth of Lambeth or some other London stew where they would never see him again.

Fellows had been wearing a bandage, but that meant nothing either. Though Phillipe would prefer to suspect Fellows.

He had discussed the abduction attempt at length with both Ann and Lady Edith, not to mention the servants, but no one had shed any more light on the missing man than Bella had. The one person he had not talked to was Jamie, but Phillipe was hesitant to bring up such a terrifying experience again, not when the child was so happy. Perhaps it was best left forgotten.

Bella tripped upstairs with Jamie and Lobo, wondering if she should let the dog bite Thackery again to try to get rid of him. After having chocolate and scones with Jamie and Janet in the nursery, Bella went to the morning room, where Ann was holding court. She counted no fewer than three uniforms and two suits. Half of these gentlemen eagerly transferred their attentions to her, and she considered them harmless enough, except for Norton. He was a decent officer but rather loose where women were concerned. She would have to warn Ann about him.

When the callers had all left, Ann turned to Bella. "I suppose you are on Carlos's side."

"Side?" Bella asked. "This is not a war. What happened between you and Carlos last night?" Bella seated herself on the sofa by Ann.

"I was trying to be good. I know better than to dance with anyone more than twice. But Carlos kept insisting, and I knew it was just to keep the other men from having as many dances."

"Did you explain to Carlos what is customary here in London? Things were a little looser in Lisbon."

"You mean he did not know that an extra dance would have caused talk?"

"Probably not. Was that it?" Bella asked, realizing that she had argued with Phillipe over something as trivial as a few words and the manner in which they were spoken.

"Then he accused me of flirting, and I was only being pleasant. How could I be rude or cruel to those men, when they are all so . . ."

"So eager to please," Bella supplied. "Yes, they are like puppies, all over you with such enthusiasm you hate to speak a harsh word to them. But how do you feel about Carlos?"

Ann stared bleakly in front of her.

"Ann, Ann, look at me."

"I love him," she said, her eyes reddening ominously.

"Put aside whatever foolishness happened last night and think of how you can make up with him."

"But he does not want me now. He said so." She burst into tears and threw herself onto Bella's lap.

Phillipe picked this inauspicious moment to enter the room, and Bella could see from his hesitation that he was tempted to retreat. Instead he came in and closed the door softly behind him. Ann sat up and attempted to dry her eyes.

"You must think me a complete idiot to be making a fool of myself over a bunch of men I have just met, but I am not used to being admired," Ann said, and sniffed valiantly.

"What do you mean?" Phillipe asked, sitting beside her. "Everyone thinks you are beautiful."

"You do not count. Nor does Thackery. I do not come in the way of a lot of compliments, but I did not think they were turning my head. I was not becoming *loose*."

"I am sure you were observing every propriety." Bella handed her another handkerchief. "And I wish that I could say jealousy is a measure of devotion, but it is not."

Phillipe rolled his eyes at this. "Just what is it a measure of?" he asked.

"Control," Bella said in a punishing way. "A man who truly loves a woman trusts her and does not fly into a rage if another man dances with her or even flirts with her."

"Just what is he supposed to do?" Phillipe asked. "Sit by and watch her being stolen away?"

Ann glanced at Phillipe and then back at Bella.

"If the woman is inconstant, she would not have made him a good wife anyway," Bella said brutally. "Carlos has fallen in love with you, Ann. I wish there had been time for that love to deepen into trust before we dropped you into a nest of red uniforms."

"Perhaps if I had seen that you had a proper come-out, you would not be so unused to attention," Philip said regretfully.

"Attention must always be flattering, but it does not mean anything beyond what I let it mean," Ann replied. "If any of those soldiers passed the line of what I consider proper, I would let him know it."

Phillipe stared at his sister, thinking back to her walks about Dorney Park with Carlos, and wondered if she would have been so careful to restrain Carlos. "But you are so inexperienced."

"But men are so simple to see through," Ann replied. "I find I always know what is in their minds and can counter it so that they are not offended."

"Yes, it is an instinct," Bella agreed.

"But what should I do about Carlos?" Ann asked. "I can tell when he is becoming jealous, but I cannot prevent it."

"Wait to see if he comes back to you," Bella said. "Then you will know the strength of his love."

"Yes, you are right. If he does not come back, then his love would never have stood the test of time." Ann rose and left the room.

Phillipe sat looking at the closed door for a moment, then turned hesitantly to Bella. "Is she right? Do you always know what I am thinking?"

"No, hardly ever," Bella said with a nervous smile. "She is talking about boys. Men, you in particular, are a great deal more complex."

"Complex? That is a cold word." Phillipe stood up and folded his arms as though he were trying to decide what to do about a military problem. "But I could say the same of you."

"And you have never trusted me," Bella said.

He took a step toward her, his hands held out to her. Her mouth turned down, and her eyes were haunted by regret. "I would do anything for you," he said desperately.

"And you have always come back, even from the dead." She rose as though to leave him.

"Should I not get points for persistence, at least?" he asked.

She gasped and laughed a little as the tears welled in her eyes. He took two strides and embraced her, sighing as she melted into his arms. "What are we doing to each other?" he asked, kissing her neck and holding her so tightly he was afraid he would hurt her.

"I think almost losing Jamie affected my reason. I feel as though I can trust no one but you. When you turned on me, it was as though I had lost my last ally and would have to confront the enemy alone."

"And we do not even know who that enemy is," he said bitterly.

She looked up at him. "Please, let us not stay in this place a moment longer than we have to."

"I always thought you such a tower of strength. I can count on the fingers of one hand the times I have seen you cry."

"That is a ruse. To be cold under fire is a necessity. No one cares if you break down in your tent. Tell me you will never abandon me no matter how obsessed I become." She studied his face hungrily, taking in his regret.

"Tell me you will forgive me no matter how often I make a fool of myself." He tilted her head up and kissed her, swaying as she rested in his arms.

"I love you, Phillipe," she said breathlessly. "There is nothing you can do that will change that. I wish we did not have to go out tonight."

"I wish we could find a place where we could be alone." His hands moved down her back, hungry for the touch of her.

He was about to pursue the kiss when the tap of feet across the foyer announced the approach of Lady Edith.

Bella chuckled at his sigh of exasperation.

* * *

Phillipe had promised to ride Sebastian in a review of troops that afternoon, just the horse guards and a few units who could make a good showing. Nothing like the peace celebrations of the previous year, of course, but there was to be a short speech and a wreath laying in Hyde Park.

Even though he was still listed on the roll as being on sick leave, Phillipe had every right to wear his uniform, and he looked handsome in it. The red coat sat on his shoulders with more authority somehow than the black one he wore most of the time. And something about those white net pantaloons heated Bella from the inside out. She insisted on being there with Jamie, so Carlos appointed himself her guardian. And Hal was pressed into driving Lady Edith and Ann in the carriage. The Thackerys had another engagement, adding to Bella's enjoyment of the expedition. She would be seeing many of the soldiers she knew once more, even though she had to keep a close eye on Jamie and his pony.

But Carlos dismounted and got a tight hold on Wellie's reins before the bugler and the drums started. What would they have done during the war without their drummers beating out the march or the halt? They beat so loud they made your insides rattle. Sometimes the drummers had known more about what was happening than the officers.

The whole parade passed by them in a matter of minutes, but they would have to wait a while for Phillipe to return, so Bella thought they might as well take a ride around the park. She turned to convey this to Jamie, but he was gone. Ann had gotten down from the carriage to talk to Carlos, and he must have dropped the pony's reins.

Bella tried not to panic, but her backing Alta out of the line of observers and trotting the horse swiftly around the crowd got Carlos's attention, and when Lady Edith realized the boy was missing, that got everyone's attention.

Hal stood up in the carriage to see if he could spot the pony anywhere, but Bella did not wait for assistance. When it became clear Jamie was not in the crowd, she galloped after the retreating parade. She knew her son, and if he were to go anywhere, it would be with the soldiers, assuming he went of his own volition. As she cantered Alta toward the retreating backs of the troops, she realized she was holding her breath and that she must breathe and think if she were to find Jamie in this crowd. She could not assume he had been kidnapped just because one attempt had been made.

She saw Rufus cantering along the other side of the park. Carlos would find him if he had strayed in that direction. She caught up to the last of the soldiers who formed up along the tree-lined avenue. Jamie was nowhere in sight. And some official was finishing his speech. She was making her way around the crowd when a rifle salute was fired. Alta pricked her ears forward, listening for more battle signs. If only they had brought Lobo, he would be with Jamie.

Bella was about to turn and ride back toward the carriage, still running over in her mind all the places he could be, still mentally seeking her son, when Sebastian pushed through the retreating observers with

Wellie at his side. Jamie was waving proudly to his mother.

Bella groaned and stilled her hands on the reins, letting Alta crop grass until Phillipe and Jamie got to her. She wanted to scream, not that she had mislaid her son but that she had let it frighten her so. Whatever she did, she did not want Jamie to know how worried she had been.

"Did you lose something?" Phillipe asked.

"My sanity. Jamie, you have frightened your grandmother by riding off like that. Now you must go back and apologize."

"But I was in the parade," the boy said, as though that made up for everything.

Carlos caught sight of them, and Bella motioned for him to go to the carriage. "At least she will know you are safe," Bella said.

"Which will give her time to get angry," Phillipe replied.

But when they got to the carriage, Lady Edith was standing on the grass, looking flushed and concerned but not angry.

Jamie rode right up to her. "I was in the parade."

"But you worried us," she said as she picked him off the pony and hugged him.

Bella looked at Phillipe, and he shrugged. "She would have beaten me," he said.

"We can only conclude that grandchildren can get away with murder," Bella replied.

Carlos had dismounted and was holding both his horse and the pony. "I am sorry I lost track of him, Bella," Carlos said. "This was my fault."

"No, it was mine. He is my responsibility. I should have realized there was a danger of him wanting to join in."

"He did not just fall in at the rear," Phillipe said with a wry smile. "He rode his pony along the side, until he got to where I was, then matched Wellie's jog to Sebastian's walk. Sebastian was not amused."

Bella found herself laughing in spite of the emergency. "At least we know that every time he disappears does not mean a catastrophe."

"Just as I was saying," Phillipe agreed. "We must get used to life being normal again."

They had to miss the fireworks display that evening in Hyde Park to go to Lady Warren's dinner. As it turned out, Lady Warren was an old friend of Lady Edith's, so she had managed to wrangle invitations for Thackery and his sister. They had to be endured in the evening, as well, like burrs under Bella's saddle blanket. The Dorney party was invited to dinner with a select few, with more guests arriving later for the dancing. The spectacle Miranda made of herself left a foul taste in Bella's mouth. Miranda, always possessive, was throwing herself at Carlos again and making Ann fume. And the boy did not seem to have the wit to realize it.

Hal had not been home when they left for the Warrens', and no one seemed to know where he was. Lady Edith threatened vile retribution when he turned up. He had made the table uneven at dinner, but when they went into the ballroom for dancing, they all realized his absence would not be felt during the rest of the evening. Lady Edith was shocked to realize that her dear friend's home was hosting a decidedly military set.

Not only Ann but Bella, too, was so surrounded by admirers that it was difficult for either woman to keep her head and pay attention to where Carlos or Phillipe was.

When she finally picked him out of the crowd, Bella discovered that Phillipe was fending off his own set of admirers, and Bella forced herself to feel pleased that other women found him attractive. It was that brooding face, no doubt. When she thought about it, she was proud of him, his courage and endurance. He had never spoken much of his trek across Spain to get to her after escaping the French garrison, but she knew it must have been horrendous. He had covered more than a hundred miles in the worst weather. Would he have done as much for any other woman? She thought not, and she wondered why. It was not that he felt sorry for her. What was his attraction to her, then? Perhaps only that she was unusual for having traveled with the army at such a young age. How lowering to think he might have fallen in love with her because she was a singularity.

"I asked if this dance had been claimed." Maitland looked distinguished, as always.

"Oh, sorry, I was not attending," Bella said. "I do not dance."

"That does you credit. One has to wade through all those lieutenants and captains to get to you."

"Young officers have their uses."

"Remind me what that is sometime. I have been thinking about the war and the fact that I have spent nearly all my adult life on a horse. Were it not for my sister, my estates would have been sadly neglected."

"She must be a . . ." Bella hesitated as she saw Lady Amelia speaking behind her fan to another middle-aged woman and realized she was probably the subject of their gossip. "She must be a comfort to you," Bella said coldly.

"I think it is unfair that I have kept her at Greythorn all these years doing the work that should have fallen to my wife. Small wonder she is so resistant to my thoughts of marrying now."

By that, Bella assumed Lady Amelia had turned a thumbs-down when Maitland suggested Bella as his life's partner. Well, the woman did have her uses.

"Wife?" Bella asked critically. "I thought you were going to say your agent or manager."

"Someone must watch the agent when I am away."

Maitland's gaze drilled into her, but she had no trouble looking him in the eye. "So you mean to continue your military career. Does this not seem a good moment to retire from that life?"

"I have given it some thought. With the right inducement, I might consider selling out, though a commission is worth little these days."

He took one of her hands and held it between his two large hands, roughened from constant riding. But Bella's hand was neither helpless nor soft, and she withdrew it immediately. "I would have thought you have pushed your luck to the hilt and done your duty more so than most soldiers. You deserve to remove to your estate and enjoy an *old age* of comfort."

"But you mistake. I am still a young man, but five and forty."

"Indeed? My father was but three and forty when he died in Spain. You are lucky to have survived the war in good enough health to enjoy your *retirement*."

By now he was scowling at her, and she was congratulating herself on having dodged another unwanted proposal.

"I had always considered you to be a mature woman for your age. What is your age, by the way?"

"Three and twenty." She whipped out her fan and plied it. "Young for a duchess, or so I am told."

"When you marry again . . ."

"*If* I marry again. I am not at all inclined to do so."

"And why not?" he said in some surprise.

"I have things much as I want them. I see no particular advantage to giving up my independence. Do you?"

"Another woman might see many."

"A woman who has not knocked about the world. I know what it is to be free and I like it."

"I see that I am much mistaken in . . . that is, I had no idea you held such views."

"I am so glad we have gotten better acquainted then," Bella said as she left him.

She saw Phillipe across the room and monitored his face for jealousy, but it held only puzzlement, so she went to him.

"What the devil did you say to Maitland?" he asked, handing her a glass of champagne. "He was scowling at you worse than ever I did."

"I was giving him a disgust of me," Bella said with a subdued smile.

"Oh, no. Bella, you have not done anything scandalous, have you?"

"No, just talked a lot of rot about wanting my freedom."

Phillipe stared at her. "But I thought you did want to be free."

"It is a state of mind," she said, brushing his arm as she took a drink from her glass. "I am as free as I wish to be."

"I wish you had not vowed to give up dancing," he whispered so close to her ear that she could feel his breath blowing on it. A flush crept along her limbs and pounded in her most intimate parts, causing her to sway a little beside him.

"We can dance if we find a private place. Or is it too dangerous to leave Carlos in Miranda's clutches?"

"Poor boy. Let us hope she does not hook him. Ann seems to be keeping her head."

"And her composure, so far," Bella agreed, "though it must be difficult. Before we try to steal away to a private room, do you wish to see what you can do to draw Miranda's fire? I need to speak to Carlos."

"You throw me into the fray, a helpless . . ."

"Go and do your duty. It will not be your most dangerous mission."

"Nor the safest either," he judged. "I think she has fangs."

Bella observed the look of surprise on Miranda's face when Phillipe, who had never said more than good morning to her, asked her to dance with him. Bella noted for future reference that he could dance—and not badly, either—as she made her way to Carlos. He was leaning against a post watching Ann without seeming to, as good a job of reconnaissance as ever Bella had seen.

"How goes it with you?"

Carlos swung his troubled gaze upon her, looking suddenly so adult that she almost regretted him growing up.

"What do you think I should do, Bella? Stay in the army?"

"I think you should discuss it with Ann."

"Ann? She has been glaring at me all evening. Now Miranda has thrown herself at me like a camp follower, offering to go to the ends of the earth with me if I do stay in the army," he said bitterly.

"Ah, she realized you and Ann were reconciling."

"Yes, why does she try to make trouble like that? Damned uncomfortable to feel as though someone is manipulating you."

"But if you see through it, perhaps Ann will as well," Bella observed.

His gaze traveled to Ann, and she glanced away from her dancing partner to trade one shy look with him.

"If I do not marry Ann, what will become of her?" Carlos asked worriedly. "Will she marry one of these laughing young men? And be poor for the rest of her life, or worse, stay with the dowager, a lady-in-waiting forever?"

Bella pressed his arm to get his attention. "What should happen to her is that she should reconcile with you when you go to her, and you should decide jointly how to spend the rest of your lives together. Watching the parade today stirred up your memories of the army, but only the good ones. Are you forgetting how miserable we often were?"

"No, I do not forget, and I do not want that kind of life for Ann."

"She loves you," Bella said urgently. "I would be no friend if I did not tell you that."

Carlos looked bewildered. "What frightens me is that she might follow the drum if I decided to stay in the army." Carlos slid his gaze around to look at Ann, who was not having a good time but trying not to show it. "Since I seem to have shed Miranda for the moment, perhaps I will try to talk to Ann again, and not in the middle of a parade," he said, pushing himself away from the column.

"Do you care about her?"

He opened his mouth, then shook his head. "There are no English words to tell how much I love her."

"Then tell her in Portuguese or Spanish, even in French, but do tell her. If you go to her tonight, she will never refuse you."

"I must make a chance to talk to her tonight." Carlos bent his gaze upon Ann and marched off in her direction.

When the dance ended, Bella managed to be at the right place when Phillipe walked off the floor.

"I feel so used," Phillipe said.

"What do you mean?" Bella laughed at his bemused expression.

"That were I a more incautious man, she would have pried out of me all the details of the wills of both Edwin and his father."

"How could she ask such things without appearing a harpy?"

"It amazed me, too, and gave me a headache. Have you had enough?"

"Yes, quite enough. Try to stay out of trouble while I tell Lady Edith you are taking me home."

When she returned to him a few minutes later, he

said, "I had not realized how hard it would be for you to come to London and rub up against the army again." He took her arm and led her toward the cloakroom.

They had gained the lower hall when the noise of furniture being moved about reached their ears. Phillipe strode to the half-open door and pushed his way in past several drunken officers. Carlos was in the cleared area about to face off with a Lieutenant Lefton from Moreland's brigade. "Halt," Phillipe ordered, but the command came too late to prevent the initial exchange of blows that left neither man bloody.

Bella saw Ann cringing along the edge of the room and went to rescue her. "We must get you away from here."

"But I cannot leave Carlos. He is defending my honor."

"You reputation will not be helped by his defense of it. What happened?" Bella almost shouted over the calls and cheers of the rowdy men as Carlos and Lefton closed again and traded blows that made even Bella wince when fist fell upon flesh. The encounter produced a nosebleed from Lefton. Carlos gave him a moment to mop this up.

Since several of the half-dozen men present had already bet on the fight, Phillipe had been persuaded to let the two continue. Bella decided Carlos looked very dashing in his shirtsleeves with his fists up and his black hair falling over his brow, even though there was blood running from a cut above his eye.

"Carlos! Look out!" Ann shouted as Lefton charged Carlos unawares and caught him a blow to the ribs.

Bella looked toward Phillipe, who was complaining to Lefton's friends about such a low blow.

"What did Lefton do anyway?"

"He said he wanted to show me something, and before I realized it we were down the stairs and he had pulled me in here."

"To show you what?"

"Well, he kissed me. That's when Carlos burst in."

Bella pulled Ann out of the way when the fight descended into a wrestling match, and the two men landed on the floor in front of them.

"But how did all these other men get here?" Bella shouted.

"That must have been because I screamed."

"That would do it." Bella pulled her back a little more as the two bloody combatants tried to stand. Carlos was more successful than Lefton in that he actually made it to his feet. Phillipe stepped in and declared Carlos the winner as he grabbed the boy's coat and saber and braced him up under one arm to pull him from the room. One officer waved a glass of brandy in front of Lefton to try to revive him.

Bella did pull Ann out of the room then. By tomorrow morning she might have to choose Carlos or else an army officer. Any titled gentlemen who might have been interested in her would be put off by the gossip this would create. But in her opinion she could do far worse than marry Carlos. At least he was courageous.

Bella got their wraps and they followed the men out into the cool night air, walking along the street until they came to their carriage. They got Carlos into the carriage, but he was still mumbling about damned encroaching officers while Ann pulled out her handkerchief to dab at the cut over his eye.

When they got back to the house, Bella got a basin of water and retreated from the morning room, leaving Ann to doctor Carlos's wounds. Other than supplying Carlos with a glass of brandy, Phillipe also let the two thrash out their affairs over the basin of bloody water.

"I am going to check on Jamie," she said.

"I shall come with you. Do you think his wounds will win her?"

"It worked with me, so long as they are not too severe."

"How severe would they have to be to be unattractive?" Philipe asked as he walked up the two flights of stairs with her, still carrying the brandy decanter.

"Oh, life-threatening. But when you are wounded, you are very seldom in the mood to feel loving."

"In other words, don't get myself killed again."

"Do not joke about that," Bella said, turning to him on the landing. "When I thought you were dead, I was empty, like a shell. Knowing I carried your child was the only thing that kept me alive. When you came back, I was overjoyed . . . and in despair. But the sadness was all for me, so I could bear it."

"I was a fool." He brought her hand up and kissed the back of it. "I had no idea you loved me that much. I thought . . . you can imagine what I thought."

"I could hardly face you when you returned."

"I pretended it did not matter to me," he said heavily.

"Not very successfully." She squeezed his hand. "I pretended, too."

"You were better at it than I was. You fooled me."

"Did that make it easier or harder?" she asked, continuing their climb.

"It was bearable, thinking you did not love me."

She let out a sigh. "Then I did the right thing."

"What if Edwin were still alive?" he asked.

She hesitated but spoke the truth. Edwin had been betrayed enough. "We would not be together. Now our lives enjoined will be another joy born of despair."

They greeted Robert, then pushed the door open to have Lobo growl at them. He whimpered, explaining his mistake. Jamie was fast asleep after his adventuresome day. After watching the child for a few minutes, Phillipe embraced Bella from behind. "Send your maid away. I would like to undress you tonight."

"But what if your aunt and the Thackerys come home?"

"I sent the carriage back for them, but there is no possibility that they will arrive here within the next hour." He bent his head and kissed her neck.

"Good, for that uniform of yours has driven me into a fit of desire not to be satisfied by mere kisses."

Bella went to her room, sent her maid to bed, and locked the dressing-room door while Phillipe must have been getting old Timms off to bed. He tapped on her door once, and she let him in like a conspirator. Once he was inside, she locked the door as he set the brandy decanter on the table. She untied and threw off her pelisse.

"Somewhat better accommodations than we are used to," he remarked as he removed his jacket and turned to face her.

"Yes. It has a bed, for one thing. I need help with this dress," she said, turning her back to him.

Phillipe undid the satin buttons at the back of her dress as though they were an old married couple. He also undid the clasp on her pearls and slowly dragged the string around her neck and across her breasts, prompting a sigh of expectation from her.

His hand stole slowly around her shoulder into her low-cut bodice, grazing her nipples and bringing her to full awareness. She arched her back and leaned her head against his shoulder, knowing that speaking of control would be laughable at the moment. She had no control where Phillipe was concerned.

He pushed her dress down slowly, along with her chemise, exposing first one breast and then the other, his hands playing over them and her stomach, then down to untie the string on her drawers and let those drop as well. His hand sought her soft mound and pulled a groan from her.

He scooped her up and carried her to the bed, laying her down as gently as he had that night at the farm. She pulled the comb from her hair and shook her mane loose about her shoulders, then propped herself on her elbows to watch him undress impatiently, struggling with the buttons of his dress breeches. By the time he was done, he was panting, and her gaze was locked on his engorged manhood. He removed her shoes and stockings for her, running his supple fingers teasingly along her calves, then taking the liberty of skimming her thighs with his light touch.

Each contact with his cool fingers raised gooseflesh on her skin and sent her pulses hammering. She could feel the throbbing between her legs and wondered how long Phillipe meant to torment her. He had been fast that first time in Spain, but they'd had the French at their gates. The night in the stable had taken longer, engaged more of her body and mind, almost as though he had been saving himself for her.

By now the bed seemed to rock with her heartbeat, and she reached pleading arms to him. His hand slipped to her mound as his lips found hers. Their hungry kiss, the meeting of their tongues, occupied all her concentration, yet those fingers at work so subtly, parting, caressing, sliding, then retreating, they were like a subversive enemy at the back door. She felt a release of liquid from her as though she were begging him to enter.

This must have been what he was waiting for. He disengaged his mouth to kneel over her. She snaked her legs around him, and he slid inside her as though they had been made for each other. She gasped, her jaw trembling, afraid to move lest she end this exquisite torture. He throbbed and made her groan. The slightest movement from him sent a ripple of excitement through her.

"I can feel your heart beating," he said.

"More than my heart. All of me is throbbing."

He had to slide partway out to kiss her mouth, but this only increased the pleasure of her anticipation. He released her mouth and slipped slowly to his fullest extent inside her. She arched against him, unable to stop herself, and hooked her ankles together behind his hips.

"Why are you torturing me?" she asked breathlessly.

"You torture me all the time," he countered.

"This is different," she said in amazement. "You do

it on purpose, and you have so much control of yourself."

"That is . . ." He kissed her lips, tugging on the bottom one as he let go. "The one thing . . ." His talented tongue aroused one breast, before moving to the other. "Of which I have . . ." He thrust into her so suddenly she gasped. "More than enough—control."

He slid out again, pulling back against her legs and frightening her with the prospect that he might stop.

He kissed her longingly with more tenderness than passion in his lips. Then he began stroking in and out, causing that wonderful surge and pull that tipped her mind back and forth between desire and regret.

A cannon burst thudded in the night sky, and she gasped, tightening her internal muscles and making him groan.

"Not an attack, Bella. Just the fireworks from Hyde Park."

He resumed his concentrated thrusting as though he had no other purpose in life than to make it last as long as possible. He ignored her gasps and sighs, holding his own breath so long he thought his lungs would burst. There was a roaring in his ears as his thrusts became more rapid, and he was aware of Bella gripping his arms and writhing under him as the fireworks lit and broke the night sky outside the window. Then liquid fire surged out of him, and he gasped as control was wrenched from him. He found himself lying on top of her, hot flesh pressed to hot flesh as he panted out words of love.

When he came to full awareness, Bella was still sighing. He was breathing as though he had been sprinting across a battlefield under enemy fire.

"I love you," he said. "No matter what stupid thing I may do, remember always that I love you."

Faintly he heard Lobo whining in Jamie's room, but the dog quit, so he relaxed in Bella's arms and went to sleep.

❧19❧

*S*he dreamed of battles and fire, of desperate expeditions without enough food or water, of riding through the night without being able to see. But this must have been before Jamie was born, for he was not with her. Part of her knew she was in a dream, that she was safe in a house in London, but the part of her that wanted to pace the house like a caged wild dog needed to escape into the nightmare of war to satisfy herself. So many wounded. They were everywhere. And she was no longer in Spain, where there was some rhyme or reason to the battles. She was back at Waterloo, looking for Edwin, knowing almost assuredly that he was dead, but looking for him all the same under every pile of wounded they came to.

They finally found him, and it came back to her again, that black despair of having lost such an innocent to such a hellish war. In many ways, Edwin had seemed more like a son to her than a husband. To find him cold as stone froze her heart. She cried as Rourke and Greenley loaded him onto a horse with Fellows looking on.

They had carried him back to Brussels for a church burial. The bells tolled his passing, tolled nearly the whole day, over the constant moans of the wounded that lay on every doorstep in the city and inside many of the houses as well.

And where was Phillipe? She reminded herself that he had no part in this particular nightmare. He was safe in England. Better that he never knew what a mess was made at Waterloo after all his careful work. Better he never knew about Edwin or any other hurtful thing. If there was any good to come out of the war, let it be Phillipe and Jamie. But where was Jamie?

The boom of the cannon drowned out the bells, but that was the wrong order. Why would there be cannon fire now, after the battle? And she could actually smell smoke.

It was the smoke that awoke her. She sat up with a start. Phillipe was gone from her bed, and someone was pounding on the door. She threw on a wrapper and ran to see who it was. Janet in tears rushed in and panted out, "Jamie, is Jamie with you?"

"He is not in his bed?"

"No, he must have gone to check on his pony. There was a fire in the stable. They have put it out. When I came back upstairs, he was gone."

"Run to the stables while I dress," Bella said. "To be sure, he is out there somewhere with the grooms."

"But, your grace—"

"Just go," Bella commanded as she threw on her

clothes, pulling her oldest walking dress over her head. She pulled on her riding boots and tied her loose hair back with a scrap of black ribbon before she ran to her son's bedroom. Phillipe was there bending over Lobo.

Bella felt a chill creep over her entire body as though she would turn to ice and shatter on the spot. Finally she made her feet move to the bed. "Is he dead?"

"I am not sure. Sometimes I think I feel a pulse or a breath, then it is gone again. Bella, this was no accident."

Bella knelt on the bed and laid her ear against the dog's side. She thought she heard a heartbeat. Her hand on Lobo's head came away bloody. He had been bludgeoned. "Oh, God! They must have stolen Jamie away while we were—"

Phillipe hugged her and pressed her mouth against his shoulder as the household appeared in the doorway, all except Hal.

When he let her go, she was trembling but coherent. "How did they get into the house?" she asked.

"I do not know," Phillipe said, "but someone has a lot to answer for."

"Yes, me. I should have kept him by my side after that first attempt. I should never have . . ." She swallowed the words as she saw Lady Edith approaching the bed.

"Let me distract you," Phillipe supplied.

"Oh, God, Phillipe, we cannot afford to be arguing," Bella said as she knelt on the covers and stroked the dog. "I need you now, calm and competent, not angry like I am. What are we going to do?"

"Wait for them to contact us. There was no point in taking him if they do not have a way to ask us for money."

"Wait?" Lady Edith croaked.

"What if they already did ask?" Bella persisted. "What if they left a note somewhere?"

"I already have them searching the place from cellar to attic for Jamie," Phillipe replied as he conducted his aunt to a chair. "If there is a letter, they will find it."

Greenley ran up the stairs with his face flushed to hand Bella a twisted piece of paper. "It was in his pony's manger," the groom reported.

Bella took the paper and handed it to Carlos. "I cannot."

"They want twenty thousand in gold coin," Carlos said. "By tonight." He held the paper out to Phillipe.

"That is doable, at any rate," Phillipe replied, taking the note and scanning it.

"What will that much gold weigh?" Carlos asked.

"More than a man can carry on a horse, so we will need a gig, and so will they," Phillipe concluded.

"When?" Bella asked with dry lips. "When will I have him back?"

"We are to leave the money at ten tonight in the alley by Covent Garden Theater. I am to leave the satchel in the dustbin, and he will leave a letter with the location of Jamie."

"I am coming with you," Carlos said.

"They say I am to go alone," Phillipe reminded him.

"They will never see me, and I will follow in case anything should go amiss."

"In that uniform?" Phillipe motioned to the hastily

thrown on red coat. "You glow like a beacon." Phillipe finally noticed Ann, Miranda, and the huddle of servants behind her. "Carlos, where is Hal? And where is Thackery?"

"I do not know."

Miranda dipped her gaze. "George did not come home last night with your aunt and me." ·

"I am sorry, Bella." Phillipe held her again, but she felt numb, as though she had no feelings. It was like the war all over again.

"What if they do not tell us where to find him?" Bella asked, keeping her eyes lowered and feeling the cold steal through her flesh to catch her inside, as though she had been shot.

"Why would they not?" Phillipe asked. "I must get to our banker before he leaves his house. Ann, see to Aunt Edith. Carlos, take care of Bella. I will come back for you as soon as I have the money."

Bella did her best for Lobo and then went to wait in the morning room with the rest of them. Taking care of Bella had meant not letting her leave the house. Carlos sat with Ann on a sofa, talking quietly until Phillipe returned with the money.

The day stretched on interminably. Miranda had gone out. Bella had eaten almost nothing, Lady Edith even less. Ann wept from time to time, relieving the monotony of Bella's pacing from one window to another in the drawing room.

Phillipe and Carlos had left at eight that evening, Phillipe driving his curricle. Carlos had borrowed one of Phillipe's black suits and meant to ride Rufus, a dark bay, so as to be inconspicuous. It was his aim to follow whoever picked up the satchel in case they did not leave the location of Jamie.

"Will you please sit down, Bella," the dowager said. "You will wear yourself out."

"I cannot do *nothing*," she said.

"There is nothing to be done. Phillipe and Carlos will not rest until they have gotten Jamie back. But Hal should be here helping."

This did cause Bella to sit. What if Hal were indeed responsible for this act? How could she ever tell this woman about her son? She tried to look at it from Hal's point of view. If not for Jamie, Hal would be the next duke. Yet she could not imagine Hal harming her child.

And where was Thackery? To be sure, they had arranged to meet at some club last night, were now at a boxing match or a horse race, and would return at any moment, unaware of the current dilemma.

"Where is Hal?" Ann finally asked.

"This is not the first time he has stayed out all night," the dowager said. "Though he might be lying dead in a gutter somewhere for all I know. He never cares how much he worries me."

"Perhaps," Bella said slowly, "perhaps we should send some servants to his clubs to inquire after him."

"No, he is not a little boy. If he is going to worry me, he at least will not have the satisfaction of knowing I care."

Bella closed her eyes and took herself back to that night on the London Road. There had been something familiar about the muffled highwayman, other than the bandage, but she could not put her finger on it. If

only they had some clue about him, some idea where . . .
She jumped up and paced to the window.

"What is it?" Lady Edith demanded. "I have been
watching you, and you have thought of something."

"The wounded highwayman. Wren said he questioned him but could get nothing from him."

"What of it?" the dowager asked.

"He must be in one jail or another in the city. We
could question him ourselves if we could find him. Perhaps we could bribe him."

"Mr. Wren," Ann said. "Where does he live? He will
know what has become of the man."

"Well, how should I know?" Lady Edith said.

Bella yanked the bellpull vigorously, and Hoskins
appeared so suddenly that she thought he must have
been waiting outside the door.

"Good, Hoskins, where does the magistrate live? You
know, Mr. Wren."

"But I do not think Captain Armitage wants to send
for the magistrate."

"Neither do I. I want to go visit him. Have my horse
saddled."

"Your horse?" Lady Edith was on her feet. "It is dark.
You cannot go riding off by yourself as though this
were the outback of Portugal."

"Of course, you are right. I was not thinking. Have a
team hitched to a carriage."

"I am coming too," the dowager said. "At least it will
be something to do."

Ann got up. "I should go with you."

"No," Bella said. "We need you to stay here and help
with Jamie if they find him."

"What do you mean, 'if'?" Ann asked with trembling lips.

Bella stilled her heart for the hundredth time that day and forced an artificial calm upon herself. "When Phillipe and Carlos find him, they will need you. Explain where we have gone. Explain it as a foolish start." Bella started for the stairs to get her cloak. "Explain it as little as possible."

A half-hour later they were rolling along Oxford Street toward the city with Mr. Wren stuffed into one corner of the carriage.

"I assure you, your grace, that if the fellow had any useful information, I would have gotten it out of him. He would never hang just to protect his accomplice. Truly, he does not know the man's name and could not give any more of a description than you did."

"They must have met somewhere," Bella said. "That is where I will begin looking."

"Please, Mr. Wren, if it will ease Bella's anxiety, let her talk to this fellow."

"Very well. He has not been sent up for trial yet, so he is still at the jail on Giltspur Street. It is not far, but it is not the sort of place her grace is used to."

"I assure you I am used to conditions a good deal worse," Bella said.

When they rolled under the archway into the courtyard and the gate clanged shut behind them, Bella would have left the dowager in the carriage, but she insisted on coming in. So her two sturdy footmen each gave her an arm as she made her way over the slippery cobbles. The jailer agreed to Mr. Wren's strange request when prompted by a gold coin from Bella and led them through a maze of corridors with a smoking lantern before asking a guard to open a particular door. The straw in the corners of the room smelled of rat droppings, and Bella realized she had been boasting when she said she had been used to worse things. Still, there was no stench of death. The door was forcibly pushed open by the jailer scraping muck off the sill. The stench of urine and feces assailed them, but with Jamie at stake Bella hardly noticed.

"Her grace, the Duchess of Dorney," Mr. Wren announced. "Get up there, fellow," he said to the ragged man on the cot.

A raspy laugh emerged from the pile of clothes that moved by the wall, and Bella saw the fellow with a filthy bandage about his arm. Her first impulse normally would have been to change the dressing, but she could show no weakness here. She took a few steps into the cell, her boots grating on the filthy floor. Her foot hit something, and a bone rolled out of the way, but Bella never took her gaze off the man.

"You are one of the highwaymen who attempted to hold us up on the heath last week," she accused. Though it was July, she could see her breath in the chill air of the cell, as though winter were locked away here to add to the misery.

"I admit nothing."

"Your compatriot has managed to execute your original plan and even now is collecting twenty thousand pounds in gold." She let this sink in before she continued. "But I have no confidence that he will return my son to me."

"What do you want from me? A medal?"

"A place. Where you met the fourth man. Or where you planned to take the child once you had him. You must have had a place in mind."

"Why should I tell ye?" He moved into the feeble light of the lantern, the grime on his face looking like powder flash on a dead man.

"If you do, I will swear that you are not the one who shot the coachman."

"But you cannot," Wren interrupted.

"So, I'll not hang but rot in prison the rest of me life. Not good enough." His feet came off the rotten cot and he sat gripping the edge of it.

Bella schooled herself not to flinch as she looked at him. "I will take care of your family if you give me their direction," Bella offered.

"If I had a family, would I have fallen to this? Ye don't tempt me." He shuffled to his feet, looking around him.

"If you tell me something useful, if you help me to save my son's life, I will hire the best lawyers to intercede for you."

"Five years in any prison in the land will be a life sentence. Ye can whistle for yer son."

Bella spun on her heel. "Mr. Wren, will you leave us for a moment?"

"I do not think that is wise, your grace. No, I shall not do it."

"I can take care of myself," she said. "I will call you if I need you."

Wren stared at her a moment and said, "Very well, one minute."

The door slammed, and Bella approached the man, drawing Edwin's pistol out of the pocket of her cloak but holding the gun inside the folds of her gown. She could see the dowager waiting patiently by the wall and hoped that she would not frighten the old woman to death. "I will perjure myself and swear that you are not one of them, that you had tried to help us but were mistaken for an outlaw."

"Nay, lady. Ye get me out of here and I will tell ye what ye wants to know."

"So there is something to know," Bella said with satisfaction.

"And I will tell it for nothing less than my freedom."

"You really should have accepted one of my other offers," Bella said. She leveled the pistol at his head as though she were going to dispatch a rat.

"Wait! Ye cannot shoot me!" He staggered, bracing himself against the wall.

"You watched me shoot down two of your fellows to protect my son. You know I will do it. Where have they taken Jamie?"

"I'll not tell, and ye cannot make me."

"Then I will grant your request for freedom. I will free you of all earthly cares." Bella noisily pulled the hammer to half-cock.

"Ye cannot! 'Tis not legal to execute me."

"I do not care if I hang for it," she said, sighting along the barrel of the gun.

The dowager stepped forward and said in a biting voice, "I will tell them you sprang at her. She will never hang. One sentence saves your life and perhaps gets you out of here."

"How do I know I can trust ye?"

Bella was out of persuasion, out of threats even. She did not know what to do.

"This is useless," the dowager said coldly. "Shoot him, Bella."

Bella leveled the pistol again.

"Wait! Wait! We was to take him to my digs at the corner of Bark Lane at Fuller. I've a room upstairs."

"Very well," Bella said. "If you are telling the truth, I will do what I can for you." She lowered the pistol and turned to go.

"What if he is lying, Bella?" the dowager asked.

"I will come back and finish him." When she pounded the butt of the pistol against the door, the man shrank and cringed against the wall.

"Will you come with us, Mr. Wren?" Bella asked. "We may have need of you."

"Yes, of course, but the jailer has brought a matter to my attention . . ."

"Nothing interests me at this moment but getting to Bark Lane."

"Mister Armitage is incarcerated here, waiting for a friend to post bail."

"Hal?" the dowager asked. "Hal is here?"

"How long has he been here?" Bella demanded.

"A night and a day. He was taken up for starting a brawl and had no money for the fine or jailer's fees."

"Well, I will pay his fine," Bella said with some relief. "Trot him out, and let us be on our way."

Hal looked rather abashed when he walked down the corridor toward them, his suit grimy and his face unshaven. "Thackery was trying to raise my bail. How did you find me, Mother?"

"I have my ways. Go outside and get into the carriage."

As Bella walked beside the dowager to the waiting carriage, the old woman asked, "Would you have shot him?"

"The God's truth is, your grace, I do not know."

Bella began to shiver so badly that the dowager took the pistol from her grasp.

"I would have if it were my son," the old woman said.

Bella glanced sideways at her and smiled slightly. "Pray that the man was not lying."

When they got into the carriage, Lady Edith handed the pistol to Hal and briefed him on what had happened. Hal was in a state of outrage that someone had made off with Jamie from their very house.

The ramshackle dwelling on the appointed corner looked abandoned with half its windows broken out and a padlock holding the door shut. While the two footmen put their shoulders to the door, Hal casually picked up a barrel stave that was lying in the gutter and bashed in the only remaining window. Bella wadded her cloak over the broken glass on the sill and, with Hal's help, hopped up and then slipped inside.

The single ground-floor room was empty except for a table, a chair, and some dirty crockery. Bella pounded up the stairs to the single bedroom and gasped, "Jamie!"

"Bella," the dowager called. "Is he all right?"

Bella felt his face and neck. "He is so cold, Hal," she said, fighting tears.

Hal laid a hand on the child's nightshirt. "But still alive." He took off his coat and bundled the still body into it, then carried the boy down the stairs.

"Is he? Is he?" the dowager gasped.

"Still alive, but we must get him warmed up," Bella said. "They must have drugged him."

Bella wrapped Jamie in her cloak in the carriage and held him, trying not to cry as the dowager chafed his small hands. She should have slept in his room, and this would not have happened. She should not have been making love to Phillipe when she knew there was a danger to her son.

An hour later Jamie was warm and tucked up in his own bed with a recuperating Lobo dozing at his feet. He had stirred and his eyelids had fluttered once or twice, so Bella was hopeful that he would recover from the laudanum they had dosed him with. A doctor was on the way.

Ann reported that the dog had awakened, staggered, and then made for the door. He had to be restrained on a leash until Bella returned with Jamie.

She and Lady Edith now sat in two chairs on either side of the bed. Now that there was nothing left to do, Bella found that she could not stop shaking.

"I just thought of something." Bella looked across at the dowager. "What will poor Phillipe and Carlos think when they get to the house in Bark Lane and find it empty?"

"Bella, if all had gone as planned, they would have arrived at that house long before we did."

"Then something has gone amiss," she guessed as

she looked pathetically at Hal, who was sitting on the windowsill, still in his filthy clothes.

"I will go," Hal agreed. "Covent Garden, did you say?"

"Be careful," Bella and the dowager said in unison.

The sound of horses in the courtyard drew Bella to the window. "It is them, I think. We must let them know."

She and Ann raced down the stairs, just as Phillipe helped Carlos through the back door with a shoulder under his arm.

"What has happened?" Ann squeaked. "Carlos, my love. Bring him into the drawing room."

"I am sorry, Bella." Phillipe turned an anguished face toward her as Hoskins and a footman helped Carlos. "We failed," he said as he staggered toward her. "God help us. We do not know where Jamie is."

~20~

"*I*t is all right," Bella said as she folded him in her arms. "Jamie is home. He is going to survive."

"But how?" Phillipe asked numbly.

"Let us tend to Carlos first," she said as she walked arm in arm with him to the drawing room. "What happened?"

"Rufus dumped him. It is a long story."

Carlos was sitting uncomfortably in a chair, holding his left arm away from his body. "Hoskins," Bella said, "we will need hot water and bandages, and I suppose—make sure the doctor sees Carlos after Jamie."

"No," Carlos said. "You set my arm, Bella. You know how."

Hoskins appeared with a tray of brandy and tea without being told, and he stayed to help remove Carlos's coat and shirt.

As Bella began to work on Carlos's arm with Ann's help, Phillipe told them what had happened.

"We were there an hour early but did not put the money in place until ten o'clock," Phillipe said. He took a drink from his glass. "Not ten minutes later a gig came through the alley and picked up the satchel, strapping it onto the back. I could not see the man well enough to know him. The theater let out then. He must have counted on that crowd to keep us from following him. But he did not count on being robbed himself. I was checking the dust bin and Carlos was just starting after the gig when a footpad ran up behind the carriage and slit the valise. Gold coins poured out all over the cobbles."

"There was a riot," Carlos said. "Had I been on Sebastian, he would have shouldered through the crowd, but Rufus bolted and reared."

"Carlos almost got trampled by the crowd, not the horse. I meant to give chase in the gig, but the man fired into the crowd. And I lost the carriage in the throng. I thought—" Phillipe rubbed his hand over his eyes. "I thought I had lost Jamie, for the letter was blank. I had no way to find him."

Bella felt a chill run through her. "Then they had meant to kill him."

"We do not know that," Carlos said with a grunt as she tied off the splint that would keep his arm straight."

"What about your leg?" Bella asked.

"Just bruises," Carlos said. "At least Rufus did not fall on me."

"I should like to get my hands on those highwaymen," Hal said.

"Hal, could you help Ann and Lady Edith get Carlos up to bed?" Phillipe asked.

When the other four had left with Hoskins lighting their way, Bella poured Phillipe two more fingers of brandy and handed the glass to him. "There is blood all over your side, and it does not belong to Carlos. How badly are you hit?"

"A scratch, no more. Luckily the ball passed between my arm and side."

"Slicing both, I see," Bella said as she pulled his coat aside. "It figures that if someone fires into a crowd, he will hit you."

"I did not know how much more Aunt could take tonight."

"More than me, it appears. I find I have much fortitude where men are concerned but cannot brook the thought of harm to Jamie. He is so helpless." She squeaked into tears with the last sentence, and Phillipe jumped up to hold her.

"Do not worry about me. Just go sit with Jamie."

"I shall be fine in a moment. Well enough to stitch you up again, at any rate."

"You are a handy woman to have about. Hal came back," Phillipe stated.

"It is not what you are thinking," Bella said as she eased his coat off. "He has been locked up in jail all this time. Too proud to ask any of us for help. And all his supposed friends, including Thackery, have let him down."

"Thank God. I had almost convinced myself he was involved."

"Phillipe, I cannot do it, steal Hal's fortune," Bella said as she peeled off his shirt and began to wash his ribs.

"I shall speak to him tomorrow. Now tell me how you got Jamie back."

"Actually, Hal was a vast help to us," Bella said as she sniffed and threaded her needle. Focusing on the emergency that was past made it possible to tend Phillipe's wounds, even though she knew she hurt him. Several times, he stopped her and more than once stared at her and shook his head.

Phillipe jerked awake but did not move for a moment, trying to assess the damages. He could not for the life of him remember where he had been shot. So much of him hurt, he could not be sure. But he was not in Spain. He had stopped having those dreams. He was in the London house, and Jamie was safe. That he remembered. Carlos had a broken arm . . . his ribs had been raked by a ball. That did not seem so bad. He opened his eyes finally, hoping for a glimpse of Bella.

Instead he saw old Timms staring at him. The old man was reluctant to let him have any clothes, but when the valet realized Phillipe meant to dress himself in a ramshackle fashion, he assisted him into his pants, boots, and shirt. He then insisted on a sling and merely draped the coat over Phillipe's right arm. He also made a few acid remarks about the suit of clothes that Carlos had ruined the night before.

Phillipe made his way to the nursery and discovered Bella just removing Jamie's breakfast tray and Hal, of all people, drawing pictures of horses for the boy. Lobo occupied his usual position at the foot of the bed and had obviously broken his fast with leftover roast beef.

"How is Jamie today?" Phillipe asked, sitting on the bed and feeling the boy's head.

"Sleepy," the boy said. "But I cannot ride Wellie in the rain, anyway. Look what Hal made."

"That looks just like Wellie," Phillipe said.

"Hal is going to ride with us next time we go to the park." Jamie yawned.

"I shall look forward to it." Phillipe pulled the blanket up around his son and felt such a vast relief that the child was alive. It could so easily have been otherwise. Jamie fell asleep almost instantly.

"Phillipe," Bella whispered, "I have not talked to Hal yet."

Phillipe looked across at his nephew and saw, not a petulant boy, but a young man with an amused expression on his face. "Hal, I have something to discuss with you if you have a moment."

"Certainly. In here." Hal led the way into the deserted playroom. "What a game little lad," Hal said as he sat at the table and tinkered with one of the model ships he had built as a boy. "The man must have dumped a dose of laudanum down Jamie while he was still asleep, then kept him muffled until he lost consciousness. I do not think I would be acting so normal had I been knocked out and tossed into a cold room for the better part of a night and a day."

Phillipe cringed. "But you were, more or less," he said, pulling a stool up to the table. "Hal, why did you not send me word?"

Hal looked up at him and grinned. "That would have been easy. I wanted to get out of it myself. But all my supposed friends either never got my messages or did not feel inclined to help me, which vastly changes my opinion of them, including Thackery. He finally showed up this morning with some cock-and-bull story about passing out in the park."

"You sound very sober."

"For the first time in years. All they wanted was my money, and when that was gone they had no use for me."

"Hal, there is something I have to tell you about Jamie."

"He is your son, is he not?" Hal asked as he retied the fore topmast stay on the tiny sail.

"How on earth did you guess?"

"I am not stupid. Well, not entirely so. I see you and Bella looking at each other. You seem like a family already when you go out riding together."

"Edwin's death left her trapped, but Bella never meant to pursue any advantages from the title. Your mother's insistence on seeing Jamie put her in the suds. But Bella says she cannot steal from you, no matter what kind of scandal it causes. She means to tell the lawyers the truth."

"What?" Hal dropped the model. "She cannot do that."

"You mean . . . you cannot possibly mean you do not wish to be duke."

"That is exactly what I mean! I feel bad foisting the burden onto young Jamie, especially in light of someone trying to abduct him, but we shall be more careful of his safety in future."

"We are talking about the title, Dorney Park . . . and a good bit of money, as I recall."

"I shall have Mother's fortune eventually, probably

sooner than I wish. And I have enough ready to waste for now."

"But as the Duke of Dorney you could marry anyone you wished, your pick of the young beauties."

"What it means is that I would never be sure my wife had accepted me for my title or my money. But that I could be sure it was not because she loved me. I have seen what you and Bella have. And Carlos and Ann positively reek of hearts and roses."

"So, you wish to hold out for love?" Phillipe asked.

"Perhaps." Hal took up the ship again.

"Some women may still pursue you," Phillipe warned.

"Only the most speculative, or perhaps someday a woman who really cares for me. I think I shall wait it out."

"Once this decision is made, what if you decide to change your mind?"

"Mother would have my head if I ever breathed a word of what I know. She says she knows everything, but she does not, not really."

"I meant that if you ever have a change of heart you might send me to prison for my part in the conspiracy."

"Oh, I should think I would be regarded merely as a troublesome relative in that case. After all, Edwin acknowledged Jamie, and I am sure Mother means to do so."

Phillipe shook his head.

"I have given it a lot of thought," Hal said. "Would I rather be the one buried in paperwork, with hundreds of dependents petitioning me, or the doting uncle who shows up for the hunting season and haunts the town house? I like the role of uncle better."

"So you want Jamie to be duke," Phillipe concluded.

"Yes. Did you think you could wriggle out of this so easily? And you will be the one stuck with all the work."

Bella sat watching Jamie sleep for a while before she got up from the bed and took her book to the window where there was more light.

A quiet knock at the door pulled her attention away from the work. She went to the door to keep the caller from disturbing her son.

"Thackery? What is it?" Bella came into the hall and pulled the door closed behind her.

"Just wanted to know how Jamie does."

"He is still recovering from the laudanum he was dosed with. We will be returning to Dorney Park as soon as he is well enough. So it might be well for you and your sister to go home now. We will hardly be entertaining after this."

"I could not leave you in such straits."

"Please do. Please leave us. Friday we see the lawyers. We may be leaving as early as Saturday."

"If there is anything I can do . . . sit with the boy and read to him . . . you will let me know."

"Of course," Bella said, wondering if he would take the hint and leave. Bella began to open the door.

He restrained her with a hand on her shoulder. "This cannot have been easy for you. I have found out a little of what happened, and I have to tell you how much I admire your courage."

"Thank you, Mr. Thackery."

"Do you still go to Colonel Maitland's ball on Saturday?"

"I doubt it."

"That is a pity. Miranda and I have been invited."

"I cannot be thinking of balls now."

"I just wanted to assure you that I would escort you . . ."

"You. But why? If I were going, I would go with the family."

"After all you have been through, I thought you might need my support."

Bella stared at him and was about to refute this, but she saw no reason to air her feelings in front of someone she disliked. Besides, ten-to-one he would argue with her about them. "I am sure I do not need any escort if I wish to go to the ball. So you had better see to your sister." She did close the door on him then. After all their arguments, the damned fellow was persistent enough and stupid enough to think he could get in her good graces again. It just showed that it did not pay to be polite to some people.

When Bella left Jamie in Janet's care to run downstairs for a quick luncheon, she was hailed in the hallway by Phillipe and led into the library. There sat a small man in a brown suit, along with Mr. Wren. Phillipe guided her to a chair.

"Bella, I want you to meet Mr. Mayer. He will be guarding Jamie the rest of the time we are in town."

Bella stared at Phillipe. "I will be sleeping in Jamie's room. But why have you hired someone from outside to guard him?"

Mr. Wren cleared his throat. "Mr. Mayer is from Bow Street and comes highly recommended. You understand that as magistrate, I can arrest and gather evidence for prosecution. But if it comes to actual investigation or a task such as guarding something, I have no staff. You are on your own."

"Yes, I understand," Bella said numbly. "But I would have thought we have enough footmen . . ."

"Here is what I have found so far." Mayer flipped open a tiny notebook that she would have thought too small to write anything in. "When the fire was set in the stables, it was meant to smoke and cause a general alarm, drawing all the house staff out back to fight the fire. During that time, one of your neighbors across the square saw a man in blue livery come out the front door carrying a bundle and get into a gig."

"Jamie?" Bella asked.

Mayer continued. "I have interviewed all the footmen except for the one who left before I could talk to him. I will mount a search for him."

"So the man was in the house all the time?" Bella felt her lips start to tremble, and Phillipe came behind her chair to lay a comforting hand on her shoulder. "We truly did not know who the enemy was. Which is the missing footman?"

"Paul Luten," Mayer replied.

"Paul? I find that hard to believe," Bella said.

"His references are forgeries," Phillipe said gently.

"But does that mean he was capable of this? And did anyone remember him injuring his hand?"

"You must trust me, your grace," Mayer said. "I shall keep the lad safe until you depart for your country place."

"I shall take all the help I can get. But I will still sleep in Jamie's room."

"No one will try to dissuade you from that," Phillipe assured her.

That Friday Bella had brought Jamie with them to the solicitors' office, not because of any request on their part to produce him but because she could not bear to be parted from him for more than a few minutes at a time. Indeed, the team of three lawyers seemed very surprised to see Jamie, and each scrutinized him as though mere looks would be enough to prove his birthright.

Bella had accepted Hal's abdication with difficulty but thought that perhaps she knew better than Phillipe why Hal did not wish to expose her son as illegitimate. If Hal meant to help her keep her promise to Edwin, then she should do so even if it meant a lifetime of worry and close care of Jamie.

"The proofs of marriage and birth are uncontested and therefore accepted," Moreton, the oldest solicitor, said. "The guardianship of James is left to Phillipe Armitage until the boy is one and twenty. Of the properties, Dorney Park, of course, will be held in trust by Phillipe Armitage for James. Phillipe is left the estate in Norfolk, and Hallowell the hunting box in Leicester—"

"Oh, that was decent of Edwin," Hal said. "I had forgotten about that place."

"Hallowell is also to have any of the duke's racing horses, hunters, or carriage horses he wishes to take."

"Well, that is handsome of him."

"Since the state of investments was so uncertain during the war, rather than trust the income of his mother and wife to the vicissitudes of the market, Edwin gave Phillipe power of attorney to buy and sell as he chose. The investments and their income are to be divided six ways equally among James, Hallowell, Phillipe, Lady Edith, her grace, and Ann Armitage."

There was a moment of silence when everyone stared at Phillipe, and he looked sheepishly back at them.

"Ah, well. That was when the market dived," Hal said. "Did you salvage anything, Phillipe?"

"I did not sell, if that is what you mean."

"You didn't?" Hal asked in surprise.

The lawyer cleared his throat. "Mr. Armitage in fact emptied all accounts and bought heavily into stocks. I have to admit we advised against his trying to shore up the economy in a fashion so wasteful to the estate's resources."

"But prices shot back up again," Hal said, staring at Phillipe. "When exactly did you dump all this money into them?"

"When they were at rock bottom."

"But then . . . but then you gambled every pound the estate had on a dead horse. . . ." Hal was left speechless with admiration.

The lawyer consulted his sheaf of papers. "The total income is somewhere in the neighborhood of a hundred thousand pounds a year."

Hal whistled.

"We will begin the probate of both wills. It will be some few months before the papers are all ready to be put in your hands."

As the family walked to the carriage, Hal was still shaking his head. "This is awful, a disaster."

Phillipe clapped him on the shoulder. "That you will be a somewhat wealthy doting uncle now? Not such a disaster."

"But I do not want any responsibility," Hal protested. "Mother, what should I do?"

"I am sure those three nodcocks will be willing to advise you."

"As though I trust them," Hal said. "They could make a balls of my share, and I would not be able to stop them."

"Hal! Your language!" The dowager held her hands over Jamie's ears. "If you dislike those three as advisers, I am sure Phillipe or I will be able to help, but the responsibility is yours. If you waste it, there will be no more fortune to worry about."

"What is wrong, Uncle Hal?" Jamie asked.

"Oh, not much, I suppose," said Hal, "but I will still be pursued by all the women in town."

"We can ride away from them," Jamie suggested as Hal lifted him into the carriage. "Women cannot run fast, except for Mother."

Phillipe laughed. "Jamie has a point, Hal. Simply do not let them catch you."

The rest of them got in. Bella stared at Hal as the team moved forward. "But is it not better to be pursued than to pursue?"

"No man likes to be a quarry," Hal said. "Does a woman?"

"Tell him the truth, Bella," Phillipe said.

"Hard to answer," Bella replied. "Perhaps we are used to being pursued. It never bothered me in Spain, because those men had nothing. I could joke them out of being serious. It is not so pleasant when you are pursued by someone you cannot like."

"And your kindness prevents you from giving him his marching orders," Hal concluded.

"Thackery," Phillipe spit out. "Is he being a nuisance again?"

"He simply will not take no for an answer," Bella said.

If possible, Hal got an even more harassed look on his face. "Do not tell anyone about this turn in affairs, I beg of you."

"Are you afraid your friends will importune you?" Phillipe asked.

"The ones who could not be bothered to bail me out? I shall have a ready answer for them. But that is not my greatest fear."

"Miranda," Bella guessed.

Hal rolled his eyes and nodded.

~ 21 ~

*C*arlos had not spent more than a day in bed, and only that much time because it gave him a chance to talk to Ann in private. If the servants thought it was not the thing for her to be closeted with him in his bedroom, then they would have had to criticize the duchess, who assigned her the task of keeping him in a reclining position until they saw if he meant to come down with a fever.

He had been up and about the next day with the sudden urge to explore the fairly extensive library in the town house, where he spent a deal of time showing Ann maps of Spain and telling her all about the country. Perhaps even teaching her those words of Portuguese or Spanish in which he was able to express his love for her.

On the day of the Maitlands' ball, the family breakfast held a note of finality. Miranda and Thackery did not even appear, but that was not unusual. Bella and Phillipe had nearly finished eating by the time Lady

Edith looked around the table and declared, "We will leave for Dorney Park tomorrow morning. See that you all get back from Maitlands' at a decent hour. I've already told the Thackerys they have to be out tomorrow, that we are closing up the house."

She then looked suggestively at Carlos, who cleared his throat and said, "I wish I had brought this up before yesterday."

"Why?" the dowager prompted.

"Because now you will declare me a fortune hunter. But that will not deter me from marrying Ann. I have—we have decided that I will leave the army and manage Phillipe's estate."

"And about time too," Lady Edith said with a sigh of relief. "I was afraid that money Ann came into might put you off. Glad to see you have some sense, both of you."

"But I bring nothing to the marriage but my devotion, my . . ."

"Let us not get maudlin now," Lady Edith said as she cracked her soft-boiled egg. "I expect grandchildren from you. That should keep you busy enough."

Phillipe burst out laughing and Bella suspected Carlos was blushing under his dark skin. Certainly Ann was, but she also looked pleased.

"What is so funny?" Lady Edith asked. "I find I like grandchildren a great deal more than children. If only someone could find a way to eliminate that difficult intervening step."

This caught Hal with a sip of tea in his mouth, and he nearly choked when he started to laugh.

"As to the wedding, I leave you to plan that, Ann." She turned to her son. "I see some minion in the law offices must have leaked the news of your sudden stroke of good fortune. Your pile of invitations may topple over and injure you, Hal, if you are not careful."

The others laughed as Hal scooped up the entire bundle and cast them into the fireplace to be used for tinder next time they had a chilly morning.

Bella pointed at the letters. "One of your friends might have written you."

"I have no friends in London but those who are in this room." He got himself more tea and some food, then seated himself at the table. "And if there are any tailors' bills in there, they should apply to my man of business."

"You do not have . . ." Phillipe started to say.

"I engaged one yesterday. Staple. Hoskins recommended him. Is he sound?"

"Yes," Phillipe said, setting down his cup. "You could not have put your affairs in better hands. But no celebration? No wild fling?"

"I am not a boy anymore," Hal announced.

"Apparently not," Bella said. She looked around the table at all of them, a family, though a rather tattered one. "I wish we could leave today, that we did not have to stay for this ball tonight. I find that I have grown very tired of London."

"We accepted and we should go," Lady Edith said. "It will be a chance to say good-bye to all your friends."

Bella was about to argue that the dowager did not approve of their army friends but decided against it. "They would understand that Jamie needs me."

Phillipe took her hand. "I will stay home too."

"But none of the rest of us knows Maitland all that

well," Lady Edith said. "Perhaps we should all stay home."

"We have the runner guarding the hall now," Phillipe said. "Perhaps we can steal away for an hour or two after Jamie goes to sleep."

"You cannot be with him round the clock, Bella," Lady Edith said. "And you must trust someone sometime."

"Yes, you are right," Bella conceded, taking another drink of her sweet warm tea. "I will go, but I will not enjoy myself."

"That's the spirit, Bella," the old woman said. "And I shall mark this in my journal. Bella has agreed with me."

"It can hardly be the first time," Bella protested, thinking back over the previous weeks. She remembered she had told Phillipe that she would think she had won her war when her enemy was her ally. Magically that had happened, and she was not sure how.

"Very nearly," the dowager said.

Lady Edith stirred her chocolate, with the hint of a smile on her lips that reminded Bella of the painting hanging at the head of the stairs of the young Lady Edith.

"I have decided that your early marriage could be as productive as the one between Ann and Carlos. I might find myself a great-aunt twice over within the year."

Phillipe laughed at the whoops from Carlos and Hal. "Very likely, Aunt, very likely."

Ann blushed prettily, but Bella did not. She merely looked confidently at Phillipe. She was relieved that Lady Edith expected her and Phillipe to present her with a child in a year, for they may already have made a start on one.

Though feeling better, Jamie had been reluctant to let Bella out of his sight for more than the length of a meal. What he had really wanted to do was ride his pony with them, but Phillipe pointed out that Wellie needed to rest before he made the trek to Dorney Park. So Jamie was content to stay in the nursery and play with all the toys Janet found to entertain him. Bella and Phillipe spent most of the day there playing with him, and Bella kept thinking, *This is what our life will be like. What house we are in does not matter.*

During their last visit of the day, dressed in evening clothes, they promised Jamie he and Lobo would get to ride back to the lake in the carriage with his grandmother the next day. The child went to sleep with a quiet mind.

"What is it, Bella?" Phillipe asked as they entered Maitland's house that night.

She looked up at the grand, columned exterior, thinking it was a stiff, cold-looking place in spite of the lamps lit everywhere. She felt chilled under her cloak, even though the evening was a warm one. "I do not know. I simply have the most uneasy feeling about this ball."

Bella's tension increased as the women gave up their wraps in the downstairs hall and got into the line that wound up the elegant stairway. "I should like to go home," she said, feeling for some reason on the point of tears.

"This is the first time you have been parted from

Jamie since he was abducted. We will only stay a little while if you like. But we would not want Maitland to think we are cutting him. We can leave as soon as we make a circuit of the room."

They had just reached the top of the stairs when Lady Edith said, "Bella, look. The Thackerys are in the receiving line ahead of us. What nerve! So that is why they hired their own carriage. So they could beat us here." The dowager sailed through the receiving line and into the ballroom with the vigor of a woman half her age to begin spreading news of the engagement between Ann and Carlos.

Bella thought she should warn Maitland, especially when he squeezed Ann's hand and said he would like to speak with her later. Lady Amelia glared at both Bella and Ann as she greeted them.

The din in the room was a mixture of high-pitched women's buzzing and the lower, droning voices of the men, with an occasional boyish laugh rising above the rest. The smell was a mélange of perfumes mixed with melted wax and sweat. Bella was used to much worse, but tonight the combination assaulted her senses. As soon as the music began, the general level of noise died down. Bella could pick out individual soldiers from the mass as they took partners for a country dance.

The evening was enlivened by Bella getting to witness Miranda's approach to Hal, with an apology for her lovesick behavior. "I am over Carlos. I do not know how I could have found him attractive. He is so very dark, you know."

"But not at all stupid," Hal added.

"I much more admire Englishmen, especially one I have known from the cradle."

"One who would have no excuse for falling prey to your machinations," Hal said.

"My what?"

"Cut line, Miranda. You have just learned I am to get a share of Edwin's fortune. Now you are trying your wiles on me, and it will not work. I know you too well."

Miranda turned on her heel and left him.

"Not very subtle," Bella said, unfurling her fan and wafting some air toward Hal's rather heated countenance, "but effective."

"I shall have to step lively after this." He drained his glass of champagne and set it on a side table. "I am a mark for half a dozen of Mother's bosom friends, each with an eligible daughter."

"Can you like none of them?" Bella teased.

"I do not intend to marry until I have found a woman like you or Ann. That should take me a dozen years at least."

"I . . . I am flattered, I think." Bella snapped her fan shut.

"I just hope we do not have to fight another war over it," Hal confided as he drifted off to the card room, skillfully evading a matron who was after him to dance with her daughter. The movement of dancers to the floor aided him in his escape.

Phillipe came up to Bella, laughing, and handed her a glass of champagne "I have never seen Hal so . . ."

"Agile?" she suggested as she took a drink. It seemed to settle her nerves.

"Perhaps that is not the best word," he replied.

"You would rather he did sidestep a loveless marriage, would you not? Do you remember how you accused me of agility?"

"God, Bella, you should have slapped my face. How did I ever come to hurt you like that?"

"You were still hurting yourself." She leaned against him.

"And you simply stopped talking, withdrew from the field, and saved your resources to fight another day. Are you feeling unwell? You look quite pale."

"I will be fine. Let us never be like that when we are married," she said. "Not on speaking terms. It is far worse than a blistering argument."

"I agree. But I think you might warn me when I am being particularly stupid."

"I shall let you know. Have you seen Ann with Maitland? I wonder if I should have warned the poor fellow. Now that I think of it, he may have meant to propose to her. He called several days this week, but neither you nor Ann was at home. I was so absorbed with Jamie, perhaps I did not convey his urgency."

"I had rather he heard the news from Ann than from me. There is nothing so uncomfortable as having a fellow twice your age applying to you for someone's hand."

"Have you had a lot of offers for Ann?" Bella snapped her fan open and plied it vigorously, for the champagne was having its effect.

"I was speaking of you, though why they think they need my permission is beyond me."

"Oh, really? Just how many proposals did you turn down for me?"

"The odd dozen or so. But you would not have liked any of them half as well as me."

"I never know just when you are teasing, Phillipe."

"Will you be safe alone for a few minutes? I want to steal a dance with my sister."

"You can talk to Ann anytime," Bella said, reluctant to let him leave her side. She felt safe with Phillipe there.

"But I do not want there to be talk about her dancing every dance with Carlos."

"But they are going to be married. Oh, very well, do your duty. I will try not to get engaged in your absence. I know. I will see if Lady Edith wants something to drink." Bella finished her champagne and began to make her way around the room which seemed to spin of its own accord. She ignored it and sought the safety of the dowager's companionship.

Ann had finished her dance with Maitland and must have fobbed off his suggestion for a private conversation. Bella could see Maitland's face turn white when his sister whispered the news to him, her wicked lips twisting into a grim smile as she drove the verbal knife home. Poor man. He was far too military, expecting everyone to fall into line with his plans as though they had to take orders from him and could not think for themselves. Perhaps he was right; civilian life would not be the thing for him.

Bella was still making her way toward Lady Edith when Fellows barred her path so that she could not squeeze past him with a brief greeting.

"I have watched you riding with your little boy. He is a game lad."

He smiled affably, his dark brows concentrating in the effort to hear her mumbled reply. She began to suspect he was a little deaf from all the rifle shooting he did. Since that accounted for his loud voice, Bella would never have snubbed him.

"He would have to be to keep up with me," she repeated, putting her fan to work again. A fluttering fan made most men so nervous they let her go immediately.

"I like children. I would raise him as my own son if you would marry me."

"But I told you I do not wish to marry you."

"I suppose circumstance will trap you into marrying Captain Armitage." He nodded in Phillipe's direction. Phillipe and Ann were laughing at each other's mistakes on the dance floor.

"What makes you say that?" Bella asked, the fan stilled now.

"All of London knows you are trapped by the trust set up by his cousin. If you marry, you must abandon your child and live without fortune. I promise that you would never be far from the boy and that I will take care of you."

"You have been misinformed. I have my own money and no intention of giving up my son."

"I have loved you for years. You refused my offer after your father died, though it seemed to pain you to do so."

Bella cast her eyes down, looking for the words, but a rejection would never seem palatable no matter how it was phrased. "I . . . I could have liked you quite well had I not been in love with someone else."

"So, that is why you accepted Major Armitage. It was not his rank or title. I did not think so."

Bella shook her head helplessly and turned away from him. "I cannot talk about it."

"Now that he is dead, he has left you in a damnable position," Fellows said at her shoulder. "I offer you freedom."

With a shock Bella realized the word now stood as a threat to her. "But I do not want to be free."

Even as she said it, Bella realized it was true. The encumbrances of family and home, even several homes, were something she now wanted. Not to have to sleep in her clothes and mount up in the middle of the night to escape a military advance. To be able to go to bed with a man and know neither your lovemaking nor your sleep would be interrupted. To be able to have children and know they would always have enough to eat. This wonderful trap was what she wanted.

"Are you telling me you will marry Armitage?" Fellows persisted.

"Yes."

Bella pushed past him, but before she could gain the dowager's side, Thackery thrust himself in front of her. She began to wish she were on a horse so that she could jump over such unwanted obstacles.

"I leave London tomorrow, and I wanted to speak to you one last time."

"Must you?" Bella asked.

His face registered confusion, then changed back to that oily smile. "You do not mean you would leave without saying good-bye."

As the music stopped, Bella saw Maitland hold his hand up as though he were about to lead a charge on the battlefield. "May I have your attention? I should like to announce my engagement to Miss Miranda Thackery."

A confused smattering of applause and some cheers

from the drunker junior officers covered Bella's surprised gasp.

Thackery, who had been looking speculatively toward his sister, said, "We could make it a double wedding. I would be a good husband to you."

"Do you not understand the word *no?*" Bella pushed past him, but he grabbed her bare arm.

"But you must marry someone, and I live so close. Lady Edith would approve the match even if Captain Armitage takes some time to get used to the idea."

"You must be the most dense man on earth. Phillipe would never be reconciled to the match because he is going to marry me himself."

"Why, you—you knew this before?" he demanded, his voice harsh, his face a mask of anger.

"You are hurting my arm," Bella complained.

He looked at his hand as though it belonged to someone else and willed it to open, releasing her but leaving red marks that would be bruises by the next day. His face had gone cold and inscrutable, as though he had died and all the blood were draining away. Bella stared at him in horrified fascination. She had seen men die often enough, but she had never witnessed such a transformation. She began to edge away from him, uncertain what he might do next even in the presence of hundreds of witnesses.

"I was trying to keep it to myself, but if it is the only thing that will discourage you, then I do not mind that it is public knowledge."

Thackery's face reanimated with a murderous look; he turned on his heel and strode away from her. She must find Phillipe and warn him.

Lady Edith had moved by now and had already been supplied with a glass of punch, so Bella sat down on a chair in the corner of the room to regain her composure. Her head was beginning to pound from the noise, the smells, and some inward sense of impending doom. She stood up just in time to see Fellows walk up to Phillipe and wordlessly cant his head in the direction of the hallway. What now? All she wanted to do was go home to be with Jamie, and now it looked as though they would be treated to yet another scene. Why had she ever come?

Phillipe led Fellows into what looked like an office. He was not expecting it to be a pleasant interview, but by the black look the man cast at him he knew Fellows was already angry, and that lit the fires of his own impatience. He hated his position, men applying to him for Bella's hand when he planned to marry her himself. But there was no way to tell them that without seeming a complete ogre.

"You know the matter at hand," Fellows growled.

"I can make a guess. You want to marry Bella."

"I am not asking you. I am telling you that I intend to marry her and remove her and her son from your despotic rule."

"Does Bella know about this?" Phillipe crossed his arms and winced as he abraded both of his most recent wounds.

"We have talked."

"And unless I miss my guess, she has refused you."

"Because of the hold you have on her son."

"Ah, there is the rub. Though she has a handsome

settlement from the estate and may marry as she chooses, she cannot take Jamie with her."

"The boy needs a father figure. I realize his life must be protected at all costs."

"You were always astute. But I will be the one to protect Jamie."

Fellows frowned and adjusted his thinking. "That is neither here nor there. My interest is Bella."

"She will never leave her child."

"I will be a better example to him than a grasping cousin who hopes to trap Bella into marriage by chaining her to Dorney for the rest of her days."

"That is a lie!" Phillipe shouted.

"Deny that you do not want her," Fellows taunted.

"Of course I want her. What man would not? But I have the discipline to discharge my duties without—"

"You could think of a way to release her. A tidy little trap you have set for her. How clever of you to persuade Major Armitage to leave his affairs in your charge. Clever also to be on another continent when he met his end."

Phillipe snorted his disdain. "Oh, yes, exceedingly clever of me to get my leg shot up. Let me tell you, taking care of my dead cousin's affairs has been a far worse charge than serving under Wellington."

Fellows took a martial stance and rested his left hand on his saber hilt. "I can see why, with half the army sniffing after her, but such a woman needs a certain kind of man to tame her, to cherish her."

"And you think you are that man?" Phillipe scoffed.

"I am, and I have."

Phillipe stared at him, his heart thudding against his

ribs, making the bullet crease burn. He swallowed. "What are you saying?"

"I have lain with her already. I have made her mine in all but name. You must release her."

Phillipe lunged at Fellows and carried him to the wall, his hands about his throat. "I think that lie gives me grounds to kill you."

"I can prove it," Fellows said in a choked voice, gripping Phillipe's arms with both hands.

"Impossible!" Phillipe growled.

"She has a scar from the war, a small cut under her right breast."

Phillipe's restraint crumbled quickly, like a stone wall coming down after being battered for days with cannon fire. His grip on Fellows tightened, and he heard him choking. "I can think of a dozen ways you could have come to know that," Phillipe said through gritted teeth.

Bella whirled through the door and slammed it after her. "What the devil are you two playing at? You can be heard shouting by half the people in the ballroom."

Phillipe unclenched his fingers slowly, taking a shuddering breath and a step back. "You will still meet me for that."

"So you are going to shoot at each other at twenty paces and perhaps both die over something as bothersome as me? I had thought the end to the war would bring men to their senses, but you all still behave like stupid boys."

"Armitage accused me of coveting your money," Fellows rasped when he could talk at all.

"Of course, you must both needs die over that," Bella ranted. "I may as well tell you, Phillipe and I plan to be married immediately."

"So he *has* coerced you," Fellows said, feeling his tender throat.

"No, I have always wanted to marry Phillipe."

Fellows looked from one to the other of them. "He is the one you were in love with? Then why did you marry Major Armitage and not me?"

Phillipe gave an impatient groan and turned his back on the man, staring out the dark window but picturing Edwin firing at him.

"I thought Phillipe was dead, and . . ."

"So," Fellows said, "it was the title and the money after all."

"No, that was not it," Bella said.

Phillipe turned to look at her, beautiful in spite of her desperation, desirable even as she sought to keep two idiots from shooting at each other.

"You have that now, the title and the money," Fellows growled. "If you are not interested in me, why did you approach me at Lord Fortesque's rout party?"

"Your hand was bandaged," Bella said, staring at his right hand. "My son was nearly abducted by a man wearing a bandage on his right hand."

"You—you suspected me?" Fellows worked his right hand inside his left, staring at Bella as though he could not quite believe her.

"I must confess, I did."

"How could you think such a thing of me?"

"Remember, I am a mother made in the crucible of

war. I trust no one when it comes to my son. I would do anything . . ."

Fellows stared at her for a moment, then began removing the bandage. "It is an old wound. Too ugly to show to women . . . most women. I keep it covered so as not to shock anyone."

Bella breathed a sigh of relief. "It is an old scar. I am sorry."

"Satisfied?" Fellows asked bitterly.

"Yes," Bella answered. "Phillipe, are you satisfied?"

Phillipe stared at them. "No, I am not satisfied." He lost coherence for a moment then. He could not tell Bella why he had to silence this man, to keep him from spreading lies about her. "He accused me of wanting Edwin dead, when, if the truth be known, the shoe was on the other foot," Phillipe growled.

"No," Bella said. "Why do you come back to that? I told you that was not true."

Fellows stared at Phillipe as though he had run mad.

"Edwin stole you from me," Phillipe accused. "Do you deny that?"

"Edwin was in despair at your death," Bella said.

"That is the God's truth," Fellows agreed, rewinding his bandage. "I never saw a man take on so."

Phillipe glared at Fellows, trying to think of a way to bring the quarrel to a head, to have an excuse to kill Fellows.

"Edwin saw it happen," Bella said. "He saw you fall too far from our lines. Your horse went down with you, and the lancers were stabbing you. Edwin was distraught because he could not get to you."

"The French were trying to drag me out of range without getting shot themselves."

Fellows stared at him in disbelief. "The French wanted you alive?"

"I was quite a prize for them. They knew I was one of Wellington's cartographers. And they were in awe of me for another reason."

"What was that?" Fellows asked.

"The bullet that knocked me off my horse came from our lines."

Bella stared at him. "It was not Edwin," she said. "I told you that before."

"They wondered what sort of man could be so hated that he would be executed in such a way. I gave them to know that someone wanted my woman. *That* they understood."

"Impossible," Fellows said. "No, you are wrong."

Phillipe curled his lip at the soldier. "How would you know?"

"As I recall," Bella said, "Lieutenant Fellows was also present with his troop of riflemen. He can tell you that it was not Edwin."

"You were there?" Phillipe asked. "Did you covet Bella even then?"

Fellows gaped at Phillipe and Bella. "You must be mad to think that I would assassinate a soldier over a woman."

Bella looked from one to the other of them, feeling sick and angry that she could not keep them from fighting.

"What sort of devil do you think me?" Fellows demanded.

Phillipe's eyes narrowed. "Either way, it was convenient for Edwin to think me dead."

"He believed it enough to make me believe it," Bella said. "But he was in despair. Someone may have betrayed you, but it was not him."

"It was not me," Fellows insisted, and swallowed hard. " 'Tis true," he said. "You were shot by one of our men, but . . ."

It took some moments for this news to sink in. Phillipe slowly turned his head to look at Fellows in amazement, wondering what the man would say next. *Not Edwin*, he kept thinking. *Please, God, let it not have been Edwin.*

"Think about it. The major's pistol would never have carried that far. Only a rifleman could have hit you at that range."

"You?" Phillipe asked, no longer caring much what the answer was.

"It was the green recruit. He came to me blubbering later that he thought he had hit you by mistake. When we thought you dead, I told him to shut his trap about it."

"It was an accident?" Phillipe said as though to himself.

"So, you finally have your answer," Bella said, trembling. "I hope you are satisfied."

Phillipe turned to her, but he saw only the back of her as she spun and left the room, giving the door a decided slam.

Fellows blew out a tired breath. "Later, when you came back, he wanted to tell you but I stopped him, said it was enough that you were alive. What sort of man would think that about his own cousin?"

"A very stupid one. I owe you . . . and Edwin an apology."

"Not to mention Bella," Fellows said. "As mad as you made her, I may have a chance with her yet." He walked toward the door but turned and looked at Phillipe. "Unless you still want to shoot me."

There was a dead silence for a while as Phillipe discovered in the ruins of his heart that he could not hate Fellows enough to kill him when he loved Bella so much. "Who else have you told about that scar?"

"Captain Armitage, half the army knows about that scar. I was there when it happened. She came onto the battlefield looking for the major and carrying as many canteens of water as her horse would bear. She covered the ground more slowly for giving succor to all the wounded, but she knew her husband was dead by then. A French dragoon must have thought she was a looter and cut at her with his dagger. She laughed it off and gave him his drink of water. He was singularly apologetic."

"I must go to her," Phillipe said almost to himself.

"Please convey my apologies for what I have done."

Fellows was gone then, but still Phillipe did not move. He finally had his answer. It had not been Edwin. He regretted now all those hard stares, all that jealousy. He had let his physical need for Bella, his obsession with her, get in the way of reason. He should have remembered how much Edwin admired him and had more faith in his cousin. He should have had more faith in Bella, even then, when he did not know her all that well. He must find her and apologize, not just for this latest idiocy, but for the past as well.

Bella felt that terrible anxiety to ride off, as though there were a battle to be fought. She could not imagine what was causing her to be so jumpy, except that she had just had another stupid argument with Phillipe and she was away from Jamie for the first time since the abduction. In spite of the runner guarding his door, in spite of a staff of servants committed to waiting on him hand and foot, she still felt uneasy.

Perhaps it was because they had never discovered who had designs on her son. It was someone who knew what the family meant to do, someone who had no trouble getting into the house. Her maid, she supposed, would know that, or any of the servants. And any of them might gossip.

She stopped abruptly. What if it were more than one of them? They were all paid well, and they all seemed devoted, but there was a lot of money at stake. What if it were a conspiracy? She remembered how they had all been against her at Dorney Park and felt a sudden doubt of them, all of them. An agonizing chill swept her security from her and made her feel as vulnerable as though she were trekking across an icy mountain naked.

"Here, you," she said to a footman. "Tell Lady Edith that I am tired and have taken the carriage and gone home. I will send it back for them."

She retrieved her cloak and started down the line of waiting vehicles, recognizing their team without difficulty. The new driver pulled the equipage out of line and set off for Portland Place. Perhaps she was being foolish. Well, she was tired, tired of this whole damned city. She wanted to go home, wherever that was.

When she thought of home, she did not fasten on the farm, or Dorney Park, or the Quesada house in Lisbon. She thought of Phillipe and Jamie.

When she got into the town house, her hand shook on the candle so that she handed it to a footman to light her way to the nursery. Mayer was sitting outside the door just where they had left him. He stood up and saluted her as he opened the door for her. Lobo barked and Jamie woke when she entered, and then she felt foolish. He was perfectly fine. She dismissed the footman and sat on the bed to read to him for a while. They were talking about the lake at Dorney Park when a sudden thud in the hall snapped her to attention. Lobo started to growl and raise his hackles. She leaped up and locked the door, then huddled Jamie and the dog through the connecting door into the playroom. She knew she should cry out for help, but what if more than one footman were involved?

The splintering of wood from the other room was her signal. She cracked the door into the hall and saw a man in the blue livery of a footman push in past the splintered panel. She hustled Jamie out, not letting him see the unconscious runner and hoping that the man had not been killed. Lobo ran after her, and she picked Jamie up and ran down the back stairs, flight after flight, until she was standing outside. She turned and fled toward the stable with Jamie under her cloak.

Once inside, she secreted Jamie in a corner as she saddled Alta.

"Mother, we cannot ride at night."

"This is a special night, Jamie. I am going to take you up on Alta with me."

"But what about my pony?"

"We shall send for Wellie later."

"I want to ride him now," Jamie said as he peeked through the railing at her.

"Your grace!" Greenley said, peering at her by the light of a lantern.

"Greenley, do not scare me like that."

"But what are you doing?"

"We have to get away. I do not know how many of the servants are in on it, but the man who tried to take Jamie this time was wearing a footman's livery."

"This is not possible," Greenley protested. "Let me get the other two grooms, and we will go after this man."

"No! Just help me, please. I must get Jamie away just for tonight, just until Phillipe can figure it out. Half the staff, the ones most likely to be faithful, have already left to be at Dorney ahead of us. I do not trust any of the rest of them but you."

Greenley watched her desperately positioning the saddle on the mare and said, "Very well, but I will come with you."

They left London, not at a wild gallop but at a sedate trot, for that was the most Wellie could manage tethered to Greenley's saddle, and they had to go slowly since Lobo was still recovering. Bella thought the wise thing to do would be to put up at an inn and send word to Phillipe, but the appearance of a woman in evening dress on horseback carrying a child wrapped in a horse blanket might give rise to the suspicion that she was the abductor, so she held to her plan to go to Dorney. After all, it was only thirty miles.

She would have liked to retreat to the farm, but it was much farther, and she knew Hoskins was at Dorney by now. She knew she could trust him, so it seemed safe enough to go there instead.

"If you are afraid, we can go to my mother's cottage," Greenley offered.

"Perfect. She will not regard how we are dressed?"

"She is half-blind. She will not even notice."

Phillipe stood numbly in the ballroom, watching Carlos bear up as the object of envy of every young officer of their acquaintance. There was also the picture of Ann, beaming and blushing, taking the jokes of the young men in her stride now. Not to mention his aunt filling Maitland's sister in on the seamier side of Miranda. The woman looked as though she were going to burst. Maitland would have a lively household, if the marriage came off at all.

He was amazed that, after everything they had been through, he had acted so stupidly. Even under Fellows's severe provocation, he should have shown more control, but at least Edwin had been vindicated.

When he could finally get a word with his aunt, she told him Bella had taken the carriage home. He said he would take a hackney and go back to the house as well, but when he found none, he began to walk the seven or eight squares to Portland Place to clear his head. Groveling to Bella was something he was getting used to, but he wanted to have all his words in order before he started. He should have believed her when she said Edwin was devoted to him.

He arrived at a house in chaos. Janet, the nursery maid, was weeping and Phillipe could get no straight answers out of Mayer, who was nursing a bruised head. He just kept saying one of the footmen had hit him. No one had even seen Bella. And Jamie was missing again. Phillipe took a lightning survey of the destruction in the nursery and ran to the stables. He started saddling Sebastian as he shouted for Greenley. Another groom came and announced that Greenley was gone when he should have been on duty.

Phillipe looked around him at the empty stalls. Alta was gone, along with Wellie and the hack Greenley rode. Suddenly, he knew that they had escaped. But why would they leave a house full of servants to . . . but perhaps Bella did not trust any of them except Greenley.

He mounted and shouted to the sleepy groom. "Tell her grace that I have gone after Jamie and Bella. Tell her not to worry." Then he cantered out of the yard and set himself on the road that would take him to the farm.

They need not run so far to be safe, of course, but, knowing Bella, she would not leave anything to chance. He galloped and trotted Sebastian by turn, not wanting to kill him but well aware that the horse gloried in just such an expedition, a chance to run until he was truly tired.

At times Phillipe almost fell asleep on the horse's back. He deliberately drew the animal to a walk for ten minutes each hour. There was a half moon somewhere above the clouds, so they had enough light to make out the road. He had only to remember all the turns.

Phillipe thought they must be almost to the farm and was looking for the lane when Sebastian turned left without consulting him, and the road spun up to meet his head. The next thing he knew, someone was pouring brandy into his mouth. He choked and sputtered on the fiery liquid, then glared about him in the candlelight.

"Bella?" Phillipe asked.

"Nay, 'tis Rourke."

"How did you find me?"

"Sebastian woke me, trumpeting for his mares. I might have thought he made the trip alone, but the saddle brought me down to look for Carlos's body. I did not think you would ever be thrown by Sebastian."

"So, I am at the farm? How long have I been out, and where are Bella and Jamie?"

"Not here. You mean you have mislaid them?"

"She left London around midnight, by my guess. What time is it now?"

"Full morning."

"Then she must have made for Dorney instead." Phillipe sat up, ignoring the swimming in his head. "Is Sebastian rested?"

"Aye, but you're never going to get back on that horse in your condition. We can take you to Dorney in the gig."

"But I must know." Phillipe stood and staggered. His head was thumping royally now, but at least it was clear.

"Would ye look at yerself? I always said ye was insane,

galloping all over Spain in a red coat, drawing maps and setting yerself up as a target fer the French snipers."

Phillipe walked shakily to the cracked mirror over the washbasin, regarding with disfavor the marks on his shoulder and arm reddening toward black and blue. "Has Bella sent any word from Dorney Park? If that was her destination, she should had gotten there by now."

"No, she has not, and why would she if she thinks the likes of ye are in London? If ye have let anything happen to her and that child . . ."

"That is why I must go. Where are my clothes?"

"Shredded when you landed on the road. I'll find you something to wear while you wash up and Maria cooks you food."

Phillipe had to admit he felt slightly better for having slept, shaved, and gotten one of Maria's breakfasts inside him. He had stared at the shirt and red uniform Rourke had produced for him to wear.

"Ye should not turn your nose at Major Edwin's hand-me-downs. Beggars cannot be choosers."

"I suppose not."

The hack Rourke rode was no match even for a tired Sebastian, so their arrival at Dorney Park was delayed until late afternoon.

Even so, they would not have found Bella and Jamie if Phillipe had not spotted Wellie grazing in a small field along the carriage way leading to the main house. When he looked closer, Alta and Greenley's hack were there too. He looked again at the small cottage and realized this was where Greenley's old mother lived.

When knocking produced no result, he opened the

door and walked through the single downstairs room toward the garden. Rourke followed him. There was Bella sitting on a bench under a tree in a worn dress of indeterminate age. Jamie was swinging on an old swing, his bare legs sticking out from under his night shirt, and Lobo was napping in the grass. The dog sat up and gave a delighted bark at sight of him.

"Phillipe!" Bella shouted, and ran to him, hugging him to her as though she had not expected to see him ever again. "You look awful. Have you been riding all night?"

"No," Rourke said. "Lying unconscious part of the time."

"Never mind that." Phillipe hugged her back, just glad that she did not hate him. "Are you and Jamie all right?"

"Yes, Phillipe, it is one of the footmen. I saw his livery just before we fled. And if there are more than one involved . . . I could not risk staying."

"Bella, they cannot all be involved," he said, but was reluctant to condemn her hasty retreat. He had not been there to protect her when she had needed him, and for that he blamed himself.

"Shall I be taking the horses up to the stable?" Rourke asked.

"Yes. Thanks for coming," Phillip replied, finally letting go of Bella to pick up Jamie, who had run to him.

"I was afraid," Bella said. "I felt half insane with fear. Oh, Phillipe, I have never felt like that before."

He put one arm around her as he walked with them back to the bench. "It will be all right now. We will find out who it is."

"I felt so alone," Bella said. "I know I could have done a thousand other things, go back to Maitlands', go to an inn. I really think I should have gone to Magistrate Wren, but I was not thinking very clearly. Must have been the champagne."

Phillipe sat tiredly on the bench and held Jamie on his lap. "Or my stupid suspicions about Edwin. Are you all alone here, Bella?"

"Mrs. Greenley has gone to do the marketing and I sent Greenley up to steal a horse before first light so that he could ride back to town and let them know we are all right. Phillipe, is Mr. Mayer dead?"

He looked at her with regret and longing. "No, he is just embarrassed that he was knocked out by the footman who brought his dinner."

"And who was that?"

"No one. The cook had not thought to send him dinner. I left before they sorted it out."

"Oh, Phillipe, we still do not know."

He touched her face and discovered to his surprise that she was crying, now that it was all over. "Not yet, and if only I had not been quarreling with Fellows, I might have caught the man by now."

Lobo brought a stick to try to get some attention for himself, and Jamie got down to run and play with him.

"At least you now know that Edwin was faithful to you."

Phillipe hugged her to him. "I should have told you about Edwin. Did you never wonder why he did not make love to you?"

"I told him I was pregnant." Bella looked down, hiding something, perhaps her embarrassment at not being able to entrance Edwin.

"That was not the only reason."

"I do not want to hurt you, Phillipe," she said, and he wondered what she was talking about.

Phillipe swallowed hard. "It suited Edwin to marry someone who did not want his love because he did not care for women. But a wife and child would put down any lingering taint of scandal in England. That was why he wanted to marry you so desperately. He needed you."

"You knew!" Bella gasped.

"Yes, he needed you. But not desperately enough to kill me to get you. I was wrong about him, as I have been wrong about so many things."

"Edwin told me about himself," Bella said, looking Phillipe in the eyes now. "He knew I was in love with you, and he said I would be safe from the rest of them if I married him. He was a very tightly controlled man. It was not just that he could not love a woman. He did not let himself love anyone."

"So, he did play the hero. I am sorry I doubted him."

"We must never tell Lady Edith."

Phillipe thought for a moment. "I half suspect she knows."

"And I think Hal suspects," Bella added.

"But you are right," Phillipe said. "We shall never speak of it. Let us go home now?"

"Wherever home is, let us go there." Bella called to Jamie, and Phillipe took the boy in his aching arms, glad to take up such a burden. Lobo followed them up the drive carrying his stick.

While Bella went to the house to look for clothes for her and Jamie, Phillipe stopped at the stable to see how Sebastian was. He was hanging on the stall door watching Rourke brush the white horse when he became conscious of a horse blowing hard and the presence of a hired gig in the courtyard.

"Is one of them sick?" Phillipe asked as he went down the row of stalls until he came to a job horse, standing with its head drooping as it heaved, between sips of water from a young groom's hand. "Mister Thackery drove him too hard. I think he's ruptured its windpipe."

Phillipe stared at him and then at the miserable horse. "Thackery? What the devil is he doing here?" And why was he so desperate to get here? The lethargy drained from his body like water from a goatskin as he spun and ran unsteadily toward the house. Why would Thackery come back here unless he was after Bella . . . or Jamie?

Bella was not in the drawing room or the library. He checked her bedroom and Jamie's. Finally, as the last rays of the sun knifed through the third-story windows, he burst into the schoolroom.

Jamie huddled by Bella's leg in his little shirt and breeches. Bella was wearing her work clothes, the buff skirt and shirt from Peninsular days, and Thackery was holding a pistol on them. A branch of candelabra had been lit and was sitting on the work table. Phillipe could see Bella trembling from where he stood, and Jamie's eyes were wide with terror.

Thackery swung the pistol toward Phillipe, and Bella took that chance to hide Jamie behind her as she edged toward the window.

"So, it was you all along," Phillipe said, sliding into the room. "Just because you were so stupid, it never occurred to us you could be plotting."

"I would have married her. It did not have to be this way. It's really all her fault."

Thackery shifted his gaze to Bella, and she cringed.

"I offered to marry her again last night. Then she tells me she always planned to have you." Thackery's head snapped around to stare at Phillipe, his red-rimmed eyes glittering insanely. His lips moved, changed from a surprised gape to a determined, savage grin. "Bad choice," Thackery enunciated as he cocked the gun and pointed it at Phillipe.

Bella rushed him, knocking his arm up in the air as the gun went off, exploding a splinter of wood from the doorframe as powder smoke filled the air. Thackery knocked her aside with the butt of the gun and repelled Phillipe's lunge with a savage kick to the stomach. From the floor Phillipe saw the branch of candles topple and hit the worn carpet only a foot or two from Bella.

Jamie ran to his mother and tried to wake her, then tried to tramp on the flames. Phillipe shouted to Jamie to run for help until Thackery's fist connected with his jaw, then his ribs. He instinctively knew where Phillipe was already hurt and pummeled those areas most.

Bella woke up and dragged herself to the window as flames knifed across the tinder-dry carpet and up the wall hangings. She put herself between Jamie and the fire as she managed to force the window open and look out into the yard. A carriage was pulling in, and Carlos leaped out along with Hal.

They started shouting, but she had no breath to shout back. Thackery was going to kill Phillipe, and she could not stop it because she had to save Jamie. She looked around for a rope or something, but there was nothing. The window cords were too rotten, and the fire had now cut her off from the desperate battle on the other side of the room. She felt the slate shingles where they ran down beside the dormer, and they were dry.

"Jamie, take off your shoes. We are going to climb onto the roof. I shall go first," she said as she shed her slippers. The roof was steep, but she found she could get a purchase with her bare feet, enough to reach Jamie and pull him around to sit in the valley between the dormer and roof.

Once the choice was made, she knew it had been the right one, but that would never make it less bitter—your future husband or your child. You had to choose your child. She started crying, knowing how useless that was at this point. Flames were beginning to shoot out the window, so there was no going back. She could only hope Phillipe could escape Thackery and get out by the door.

They began to crawl up over the attic space where they still had a ceiling between them and the fire. She could not hear Phillipe and Thackery fighting anymore for the noise of the fire and the shouting in the yard from Lady Edith and Ann.

A *ladder*, she thought. *Someone find a ladder*. She hugged Jamie to her.

"Mama, where is Phillipe? I'm afraid."

"He will come for us. He always does." She wiped her sleeve across her eyes. But she was not sure even Phillipe could best a madman. She was not sure she would ever see him again.

Time was running out, Phillipe thought. He could not waste any more time on Thackery, or he would not be able to help Bella and Jamie. He managed to reach the knife in his boot, but when he swung Thackery leaped through the flames. Phillipe saw him make for the same window Bella had used. Now he must move fast.

Coughing from the smoke, he flung open the closet that held the steps to the attic and raced up with no light. He found a barrel and rolled it beside the chimney, then used his knife to break through the rotten purlins to which the slates were nailed.

He put his head and shoulders through the hole he had made and shouted, "Bella, can you get this far?"

"Jamie, slide along the peak," Bella said, hope reviving in her heart at Phillipe's dear voice.

Jamie obeyed and looked back at her. "Mother, we are riding the house."

"I know. Grab Phillipe's hand."

Phillipe got hold of Jamie and lifted him down through the hole into the attic, which was beginning to fill with smoke. He turned to reach for Bella and heard her curse. Thackery had crossed the roof, the sleeves of his coat smoking, half his face burned, and he was pulling on Bella's foot. Phillipe grabbed her hand in a desperate tug of war. She slid off the peak and kicked at Thackery with her free foot, but he hung on to her as he slid down the roof, pulling a mass of shingles with him and stretching Bella out between them.

Phillipe heard her gasp in pain and bit his own lip to think he was hurting her. He was gripping Bella's hand with only one of his hands, but he could not reach his knife. He used the other arm to heave himself farther out the hole and managed to get a grip on Bella's shirt.

He hooked one knee over a purlin and lay flat down the slope of the roof while the desperate tug-of-war continued.

Thackery thrashed, and his weight tore Bella out of Phillipe's hands. He watched her slide toward the edge of the roof and heard Thackery scream as he went over. Bella miraculously clung to the shingles that remained near the edge and began to crawl back toward Phillipe, her braid undone and a bruise reddening on her cheek where Thackery had hit her.

"My Phillipe!" she cried desperately, her lips trembling as she reached for him. Bella was almost within his grasp when another landslide of slate shingles carried her to the edge. He could see one of her hands and then nothing.

"Bella!" he screamed. But there was no sound, no scream even. How like her not to cry out. He righted himself and slid back through the hole, gasping for air.

"Where is Mother?" Jamie asked, coughing.

Phillipe grabbed his son and ran down the steps. A dozen men, Rourke included, had nearly beaten the flames out on the floor and walls, but the fire had taken hold in the bookshelves, so they were dumping these into the yard.

Phillipe ran into the hall and down two more flights, thinking he would have to leave Jamie with someone, that he could never let his child see . . . when he ran into Bella on her way up.

"You are alive!" he wailed, hugging her to himself and Jamie.

"Yes, are you both all right?" she asked, the tears streaming down her face.

"Except for this heart attack I am having," Phillipe said as he sat on the steps. "I saw you slide off the edge. Do you know what that did to me?" He put Jamie down finally between them and wiped a sleeve across his eyes.

Hal and Carlos came into the hall carrying the hangings from the drawing room. Lady Edith and Ann were close behind.

"It did not do much for me either," Bella said, regarding the scrapes on her hands, "but fortunately Hal and Carlos had seen us and had the inspiration to hold those wall hangings out like a blanket. So I had an easy ride."

"We all helped," Ann said proudly.

"Come, Jamie," the dowager said. "I will take care of you now."

"We rode on the roof, Grandmother," Jamie said as he went to her, remembering to hold the handrail.

"Yes, I saw you, and if anyone can lay claim to a heart seizure it is me. You are never to do that again, do you understand?"

"Yes, Grandmother. That man made me afraid, and he hit Mother."

"Never mind now, dear. Let us go to the kitchen and see what we can find to feed you."

Rourke tramped down the steps. "Well, it's out, but what a mess."

Bella stood up, and Phillipe with her, not willing to let go of her yet. She was still shaking in his arms.

"Sorry, your grace," Rourke said to Lady Edith.

"Ah, well, we needed a new roof anyway." She took Jamie's hand and led him downstairs.

"I think we should all go to the kitchen," Bella said.

"I shall make us a cauldron of tea with milk and sugar."

"It will be like old times," Rourke said.

The bathwater was tepid, not quite heated enough to keep Phillipe in the tub for long, but he did not want to delay, not with Bella temptingly wrapped in a bath sheet and drying her long hair. It was Bella who had insisted on a bath, and the dowager had humored her, setting the servants to heating water and filling a tub in her ruined apartment. Lady Edith had hinted that Bella could have the duchess's suite, but Bella had insisted she liked the old part of the house, smoking ruin or not. Phillipe scrubbed at the soot on his face and hands, then dunked his head to rinse his hair.

When he came up for air, Bella had shed the sheet and was combing the tangles out of her long hair with her back to him. A flash of memory from Spain came to him. She had been years younger, but she was just as trim and firm as ever. Perhaps her breasts were . . .

She glanced toward him with a mischievous smile. "What are you thinking?"

"About a mountain stream and a stolen moment. I told myself I went to guard your privacy, but I knew in my heart I had gone to look at you."

"Carlos was on guard to prevent anyone from spying on me."

"Then why did he not stop me?"

"Because I told him not to."

Enlightenment dawned on him and he began to laugh. "You meant to have me, even then."

"And it has been a hard struggle." She sat on the bed and watched as he stepped from the bath and sho himself like a great dog, then lay down on the comforter. She took the sheet and dried him, patting his wounded shoulder and ribs gently and inspecting the new bruises from his fall off Sebastian. "You look as though you have been through a war. Are you sure you are up to this?"

Phillipe laughed harshly. "I feel as though I have fought two wars, nay, three if we count mad Thackery. Did he die instantly?"

"Yes. Her grace means to tell his father that he was trying to save Jamie. Are you all right with that, Phillipe?"

"Yes, I can afford to be generous now that I have both of you. He cupped her face in his hand, careful to avoid the bruise. "We could sleep in my room in the main part of the house."

"I think that is why Lady Edith put Jamie to sleep on her daybed. She knew we needed each other. And I rather like sleeping in a ruin." Bella looked at the water that had seeped down the walls from the floor above and at least one gaping hole in the ceiling.

"Yes, that ruined village on the Coa River." He pulled her to him and sighed as her hot flesh kissed his still cool stomach muscles. "That is where it all started."

"It started long before that. It started the first time I saw you scowling at me at Talavera." Bella wriggled against him and ran her right hand along his shoulders and then his back to rest it on his hip. Phillipe felt his arousal start like hot brandy being poured into him. He felt drunk with relief and joy, drunk with expectation.

had taken all the worst hurdles that a man and could confront early in their relationship. ng had already stood the test of time, and en wed yet.

He ran his fingers through a hank of her hair and pulled it around over her aroused breast, admiring the way the dark curl lay on her white flesh.

Her left hand crept around to his manhood to stroke it teasingly. When he groaned, she laughed at him. He rolled toward her, pinning her under his legs and kissing her mercilessly. She opened her mouth and tasted him, drank of his kisses as she writhed under him.

"My Phillipe!" she whispered.

"I am yours, have ever been yours, no matter what you thought."

"That is always how I thought of you. So odd I have never been jealous of any other woman, and you are jealous of nearly every other man."

"I am no great prize. You, on the other hand . . ."

"I am tired of being pursued for what I am worth, for what I can do, even for what I am."

"Then do not evade me," he said as he knelt over her.

She parted her legs and twisted them around his waist. He lowered himself enough to tease her with his manhood.

"You are without a doubt the most maddening creature," she said of his slow entrance.

"But reliable," he pointed out. "You said it yourself. I always come for you."

Bella laughed, and he entered her as she was still gasping, causing an almost instant trill of sighs from her.

"My, you have been deprived."

"I think it would be nice to be settled in one place, to have one bedroom . . ."

Phillipe started his thrusts slowly, withdrawing and entering, advancing and retreating in a maddening series of motions that had Bella gasping for breath as she clung to his back.

As he rested, he suckled at her breasts, wracking her with even more pleasure until she arched her back, begging for more. This time he was merciless in his assault, setting up a rhythmic tattoo that reminded her of the drummer boys beating out the march.

"My *Phillipe!*" she cried as her release came again and his with it. His breath was heavy in her ear, and she felt his forehead to make sure he was not turning feverish on her. He laughed at her touch and pulled a sheet over them, encircling her with his strong arms as though he would never let go.

"Phillipe, you are different somehow. You are more relaxed, not quite so desperate."

"Tell me the truth, Bella. What is my worst flaw?" he asked.

"You have none," she said worshipfully as she cuddled against his chest.

"Be honest." He ran a finger along one breast, watching for its quick response.

"Your jealousy, then. It turns you from a reasonable man into a savage in an instant. But it is also endearing at the same time." She ran her hands along his back, feeling the supple muscles and kneading them in her excitement.

"I have finally gotten over my jealousy of you."

"That I do not like to hear. I rather enjoy those dark looks you direct toward other men. It keeps them in line."

"No, I will always be jealous of other men, but I realize that I was jealous of you."

"Of me?" She pulled back to look at him. "You are not making any sense, Phillipe."

"You were in the war first, for one thing, courageously caring for the wounded. You survived so much on your own . . ."

She watched him toying with a lock of her hair. "Not to mention the news of your death. That was worse than any of the rest."

"And you took over when Edwin died. You managed to take care of Jamie without me."

"But you were not always there," Bella said with a pout. "Sometimes I had to think for myself."

"You always seemed so much more in control than me. I could help you, but I could not rescue you. And I could not do it again tonight. I almost died when I saw your hand slip over the edge. If it had been only me, I would have dived after you. But I had Jamie to think of." He ran his thumb along her injured cheek to wipe away her tears.

"I had the same choice to make on the roof. I could not help you, but I had to try to save our son. I want never to have to make that choice again."

"The three of us will never be parted again," he said. Phillipe kissed her longingly, then pressed her against him so that she could hear his heart beating steadily and surely in his chest.

Bella was amazed to discover that she now loved Phillipe even more than before, that her love was not something she had to share between her son and her husband but rather encompassed them and grew with every day they spent together. She realized now that Phillipe might sometimes make her unhappy, might sometimes make her angry to the point where they would argue, that he would occasionally do something so stupid as to defy logic, but that she would forgive him without his asking forgiveness.

Together they had survived the worst that could happen to two people. Surely their love would see them through anything that life could throw at them after this.

Breathtaking romance from

BARBARA MILLER

Dearest Max

Sonnet Books
Published by Pocket Books